Pr...
THE WARDED MAN

"I enjoyed *The Warded Man* immensely. There is much to admire in Peter Brett's writing, and his concept is brilliant. Action and suspense all the way; he made me care about his characters and want to know what's going to happen next."
—TERRY BROOKS

"Peter Brett's tremendously readable first novel, *The Warded Man,* is set in a harsh and feudal world in which demons rule the night. No one is free until a hero rises who is willing to defy the demons, but at a terrible price. *The Warded Man* works not only as a great adventure novel, but as a reflection on the nature of heroism."
—CHARLAINE HARRIS

"[An] impressive debut about old-fashioned heroism."
—*The Kansas City Star*

"Brett ably blends fantasy and horror in this arresting first novel, the first in a planned series. An imaginative and exciting tale, recommended where there is interest in epic fantasy."
—*Library Journal* (starred review)

"Brett's fantasy debut is a highly readable adventure with a unique setting and three strong protagonists. Brett includes plenty of exciting battles, terrifying monsters, and heart-wrenching moments to make the focus of his story—the development of flawed, ordinary children into legends—believable. Consider the series this begins worth tracking."
—*Booklist*

"Brett's debut builds slowly and grimly on a classic high-fantasy framework of black-and-white morality and bloodshed. Brett's gritty tale will appeal to those who tire of sympathetic villains and long for old-school orc massacres."
—*Publishers Weekly*

"A strong debut. Its highly inventive plot will captivate the imagination immediately. A page turner with a satisfying climax, it promises much more to come in future books."
—*Romantic Times BOOKreviews Magazine*

"An assured and promising first novel from author Peter V. Brett. The world he has created is vivid and intriguing . . . definitely worth a read."
—SF Site

"The plot development from the harsh banality of small village life, to the complex immensity of city dwelling, and then to the world outside most humans' knowledge, is very well done. The book's biggest strength, though, is the characterization. . . . A great page turner which . . . soon becomes an irresistible read. The characters evolve into people you care about and the world is pleasantly engaging. . . . I was pleased, though a little surprised, to place this in my top five Fantasy reads for 2008."

—sffworld.com

"Captivating and well written, quickly drawing readers in. *The Warded Man* is a must-read for anyone looking for a new fantasy world to explore."

—*School Library Journal*

"Brett provides complex characters and plenty of action."

—SFRevu

"Overall with superb characterization, suspenseful action and accomplished writing, *The Warded Man* is a very assured debut that will make its way onto many Best of 2008 lists. Highly, highly recommended."

—Fantasy Book Critic

"It's rare these days that I can't put a book down without my fingers itching to pick it up again, and rarer still for it to be a debut book from a first-time author. But Peter V. Brett's *The Warded Man* comes up trumps. Brett has the knack of making you care about his characters and want to know what happens to them. And better yet, to make you hungrily look forward to the next book, *The Desert Spear*."
—*The Dominion Post*
(Wellington, New Zealand)

"An absolute masterpiece . . . For me, the novel was literally 'unputdownable,' and certainly deserves to be the next Big Thing in dark fantasy."
—*HorrorScope* (Woodvale, Australia)

"Very likeable . . . a very accomplished debut fantasy, without doubt exciting and with exceptionally well-rendered characters—the fate of whom the reader cares very much about. How the fight against demonkind will develop, I cannot guess, but I will most certainly be visiting Peter V. Brett's misty and murky world to find out. Recommended."

—SFRevu (U.K.)

"Makes you genuinely excited by the idea of reading more . . . will leave you impatient for the next installment."

—*SFX* (U.K.)

"Like many fantasy epics before it, this debut from Peter V. Brett bursts onto shelves with much anticipation and plenty of buzz. On opening this promised gem of literature, I was surprised to find that this time the hype is largely justified. . . . *The Warded Man* is a real treat, with Brett displaying a bucket-load of talent in making the familiar so gripping."

—Total Sci-Fi Online

"Brett is a spectacular writer. I cannot recommend *The Warded Man* highly enough. It is thoroughly entertaining, having the right mix of suspense, action and introspection. It never bogs down for any of its length, as Brett paces the story masterfully. The world itself and the concept of the wards make the story unique among epic fantasies. The tale ends on a note of expectation, making me eager to read the second book, *The Desert Spear,* to find out what happens. *The Warded Man* is truly unputdownable. Make sure you have plenty of time for reading it, because you will not want to leave its pages for anything."

—Grasping for the Wind

THE
WARDED
MAN

BY PETER V. BRETT

The Warded Man
The Great Bazaar
The Desert Spear
Brayan's Gold
The Daylight War
The Skull Throne

THE
WARDED
MAN

PETER V. BRETT

BALLANTINE BOOKS • NEW YORK

2010 Del Rey Mass Market Edition

ISBN 978-0-345-51870-5

20 19 18 17

To Otzi,
the original Warded Man

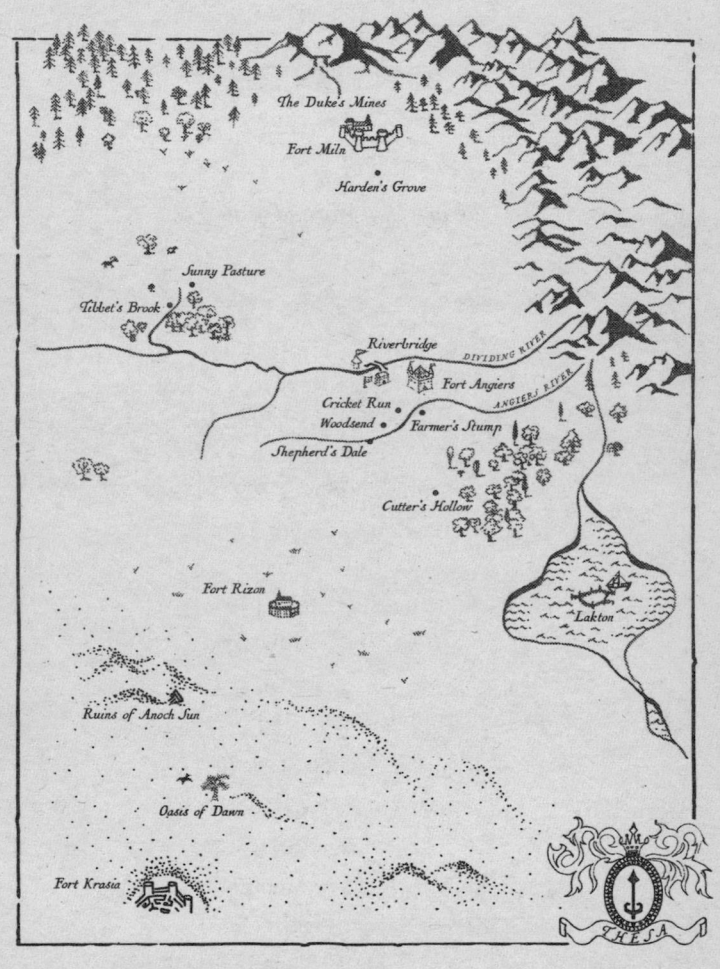

CONTENTS

ACKNOWLEDGMENTS

Special thanks to all the people who test-read this book: Dani, Myke, Amelia, Neil, Matt, Joshua, Steve, Mom, Dad, Trisha, Netta, and Cobie. Your advice and encouragement made it possible for me to turn a hobby into something more. And to my editors, Liz and Emma, who took a chance on a new author and challenged me to exceed even my own high standards. I could never have done it without you.

SECTION I

TIBBET'S BROOK

318–319 AR

(After Return)

CHAPTER I

AFTERMATH
319 AR

THE GREAT HORN SOUNDED.

Arlen paused in his work, looking up at the lavender wash of the dawn sky. Mist still clung to the air, bringing with it a damp, acrid taste that was all too familiar. A quiet dread built in his gut as he waited in the morning stillness, hoping that it had been his imagination. He was eleven years old.

There was a pause, and then the horn blew twice in rapid succession. One long and two short meant south and east. The Cluster by the Woods. His father had friends among the cutters. Behind Arlen, the door to the house opened, and he knew his mother would be there, covering her mouth with both hands.

Arlen returned to his work, not needing to be told to hurry. Some chores could wait a day, but the stock still needed to be fed and the cows milked. He left the animals in the barns and opened the hay stores, slopped the pigs, and ran to fetch a wooden milk bucket. His mother was already squatting beneath the first of the cows. He snatched the spare stool and they found cadence in their work, the sound of milk striking wood drumming a funeral march.

As they moved to the next pair down the line, Arlen saw his father begin hitching their strongest horse, a five-year-old chestnut-colored mare named Missy, to the cart. His face was grim as he worked.

What would they find this time?

Before long, they were in the cart, trundling toward the small cluster of houses by the woods. It was dangerous there, over an hour's run to the nearest warded structure, but the lumber was needed. Arlen's mother, wrapped in her worn shawl, held him tightly as they rode.

"I'm a big boy, Mam," Arlen complained. "I don't need you to hold me like a baby. I'm not scared." It wasn't entirely true, but it would not do for the other children to see him clinging to his mother as they rode in. They made mock of him enough as it was.

"*I'm* scared," his mother said. "What if it's me who needs to be held?"

Feeling suddenly proud, Arlen pulled close to his mother again as they traveled down the road. She could never fool him, but she always knew what to say just the same.

A pillar of greasy smoke told them more than they wanted to know long before they reached their destination. They were burning the dead. And starting the fires this early, without waiting for others to arrive and pray, meant there were a great many. Too many to pray over each one, if the work was to be complete before dusk.

It was more than five miles from Arlen's father's farm to the Cluster by the Woods. By the time they arrived, the few remaining cabin fires had been put out, though in truth there was little left to burn. Fifteen houses, all reduced to rubble and ash.

"The woodpiles, too," Arlen's father said, spitting over the side of the cart. He gestured with his chin toward the blackened ruin that remained of a season's cutting. Arlen grimaced at the thought of how the rickety fence that penned the animals would have to last another year, and immediately felt guilty. It was only wood, after all.

The town Speaker approached their cart as it pulled up. Selia, whom Arlen's mother sometimes called Selia the Barren, was a hard woman, tall and thin, with skin like tough leather. Her long gray hair was pulled into a tight bun, and she wore her shawl like a badge of office. She brooked no nonsense, as Arlen had learned more than once at the end of her stick, but today he was comforted by her presence. Like Arlen's father, something about Selia made him feel safe. Though she had never had children of her own, Selia acted as a parent to everyone in Tibbet's Brook. Few could match her wisdom, and fewer still her stubbornness. When you were on Selia's good side, it felt like the safest place in the world.

"It's good that you've come, Jeph," Selia told Arlen's father.

"Silvy and young Arlen, too," she said, nodding to them. "We need every hand we can get. Even the boy can help."

Arlen's father grunted, stepping down from the cart. "I brought my tools," he said. "Just tell me where we can throw in."

Arlen collected the precious tools from the back of their cart. Metal was scarce in the Brook, and his father was proud of his two shovels, his pick, and his saw. They would all see heavy use this day.

"How many lost?" Jeph asked, though he didn't really seem to want to know.

"Twenty-seven," Selia said. Silvy choked and covered her mouth, tears welling in her eyes. Jeph spat again.

"Any survivors?" he asked.

"A few," Selia said. "Manie"—she pointed with her stick at a boy who stood staring at the funeral pyre—"ran all the way to my house in the dark."

Silvy gasped. No one had ever run so far and lived. "The wards on Brine Cutter's house held for most of the night," Selia went on. "He and his family watched everything. A few others fled the corelings and succored there, until the fires spread and their roof caught. They waited in the burning house until the beams started to crack, and then took their chances outside in the minutes before dawn. The corelings killed Brine's wife Meena and their son Poul, but the others made it. The burns will heal and the children will be all right in time, but the others . . ."

She didn't need to finish the sentence. Survivors of a demon attack had a way of dying soon after. Not all, or even most, but enough. Some of them took their own lives, and others simply stared blankly, refusing to eat or drink until they wasted away. It was said you did not truly survive an attack until a year and a day had passed.

"There are still a dozen unaccounted for," Selia said, but with little hope in her voice.

"We'll dig them out," Jeph agreed grimly, looking at the collapsed houses, many still smoldering. The cutters built their homes mostly out of stone to protect against fire, but even stone would burn if the wards failed and enough flame demons gathered in one place.

Jeph joined the other men and a few of the stronger women in clearing the rubble and carting the dead to the pyre. The bodies had to be burned, of course. No one would want to be buried in the same ground the demons rose out of each night. Tender Harral, the sleeves of his robe rolled up to bare his thick arms, lifted each into the fire himself, muttering prayers and drawing wards in the air as the flames took them.

Silvy joined the other women in gathering the younger children and tending to the wounded under the watchful eye of the Brook's Herb Gatherer, Coline Trigg. But no herbs could ease the pain of the survivors. Brine Cutter, also called Brine Broadshoulders, was a great bear of a man with a booming laugh who used to throw Arlen into the air when they came to trade for wood. Now Brine sat in the ashes beside his ruined house, slowly knocking his head against the blackened wall. He muttered to himself and clutched his arms tightly, as if cold.

Arlen and the other children were put to work carrying water and sorting through the woodpiles for salvageable lumber. There were still a few warm months left to the year, but there would not be time to cut enough wood to last the winter. They would be burning dung again this year, and the house would reek.

Again Arlen weathered a wave of guilt. He was not in the pyre, nor banging his head in shock, having lost everything. There were worse fates than a house smelling of dung.

More and more villagers arrived as the morning wore on. Bringing their families and whatever provisions they could spare, they came from Fishing Hole and Town Square; they came from the Boggin's Hill, and Soggy Marsh. Some even came all the way from Southwatch. And one by one, Selia greeted them with the grim news and put them to work.

With more than a hundred hands, the men doubled their efforts, half of them continuing to dig as the others descended upon the only salvageable structure left in the Cluster: Brine Cutter's house. Selia led Brine away, somehow supporting the giant man as he stumbled, while the men cleared the rubble and began hauling new stones. A few took out warding kits and began to paint fresh wards while children made thatch. The house would be restored by nightfall.

Arlen was partnered with Cobie Fisher in hauling wood. The children had amassed a sizable pile, though it was only a fraction of what had been lost. Cobie was a tall, thickly built boy with dark curls and hairy arms. He was popular among the other children, but it was popularity built at others' expense. Few children cared to weather his insults, and fewer still his beatings.

Cobie had tortured Arlen for years, and the other children had gone along. Jeph's farm was the northernmost in the Brook, far from where the children tended to gather in Town Square, and Arlen spent most of his free time wandering the Brook by himself. Sacrificing him to Cobie's wrath seemed a fair trade to most children.

Whenever Arlen went fishing, or passed by Fishing Hole on the way to Town Square, Cobie and his friends seemed to hear about it, and were waiting in the same spot on his way home. Sometimes they just called him names, or pushed him, but other times he came home bloody and bruised, and his mother shouted at him for fighting.

Finally, Arlen had enough. He left a stout stick hidden in that spot, and the next time Cobie and his friends pounced, Arlen pretended to run, only to produce the weapon as if from thin air and come back swinging.

Cobie was the first one struck, a hard blow that left him crying in the dirt with blood running from his ear. Willum received a broken finger, and Gart walked with a limp for over a week. It had done nothing to improve Arlen's popularity among the other children, and Arlen's father had caned him, but the other boys never bothered him again. Even now, Cobie gave him a wide berth and flinched if Arlen made a sudden move, even though he was bigger by far.

"Survivors!" Bil Baker called suddenly, standing by a collapsed house at the edge of the Cluster. "I can hear them trapped in the root cellar!"

Immediately, everyone dropped what they were doing and rushed over. Clearing the rubble would take too long, so the men began to dig, bending their backs with silent fervor. Soon after, they broke through the side of the cellar, and began hauling out the survivors. They were filthy and terrified, but all were very much alive. Three women, six children, and one man.

"Uncle Cholie!" Arlen cried, and his mother was there in an instant, cradling her brother, who stumbled drunkenly. Arlen ran to them, ducking under his other arm to steady him.

"Cholie, what are you doing here?" Silvy asked. Cholie seldom left his workshop in Town Square. Arlen's mother had told the tale a thousand times of how she and her brother had run the farrier's shop together before Jeph began breaking his horses' shoes on purpose for a reason to come court.

"Came to court Ana Cutter," Cholie mumbled. He pulled at his hair, having already torn whole clumps free. "We'd just opened the bolt-hole when they came through the wards . . ." His knees buckled, pulling Arlen and Silvy down with his weight. Kneeling in the dirt, he wept.

Arlen looked at the other survivors. Ana Cutter wasn't among them. His throat tightened as the children passed. He knew every one of them; their families, what their houses were like inside and out, their animals' names. They met his eyes for a second as they went by, and in that moment, he lived the attack through their eyes. He saw himself shoved into a cramped hole in the ground while those unable to fit turned to face the corelings and the fire. Suddenly he started gasping, unable to stop until Jeph slapped him on the back and brought him to his senses.

They were finishing a cold midday meal when a horn sounded on the far side of the Brook.

"Not two in one day?" Silvy gasped, covering her mouth.

"Bah," Selia grunted. "At midday? Use your head, girl!"

"Then what . . . ?"

Selia ignored her, rising to fetch a horn blower to signal back. Keven Marsh had his horn ready, as the folks from Soggy Marsh always did. It was easy to get separated in the marshes, and no one wanted to be wandering lost when the swamp demons rose. Keven's cheeks inflated like a frog's chin as he blew a series of notes.

"Messenger horn," Coran Marsh advised Silvy. A graybeard, he was Speaker for Soggy Marsh and Keven's father. "They prob'ly saw the smoke. Keven's telling 'em what's happened and where everyone is."

"A Messenger in spring?" Arlen asked. "I thought they come in the fall after harvest. We only finished planting this past moon!"

"Messenger never came last fall," Coran said, spitting foamy brown juice from the root he was chewing through the gap of his missing teeth. "We been worried sumpin' happened. Thought we might not have a Messenger bring salt till next fall. Or maybe that the corelings got the Free Cities and we's cut off."

"The corelings could never get the Free Cities," Arlen said.

"Arlen, shush your mouth!" Silvy hissed. "He's your elder!"

"Let the boy speak," Coran said. "Ever bin to a free city, boy?" he asked Arlen.

"No," Arlen admitted.

"Ever know anyone who had?"

"No," Arlen said again.

"So what makes you such an expert?" Coran asked. "Ent no one been to one 'cept the Messengers. They're the only ones what brave the night to go so far. Who's to say the Free Cities ent just places like the Brook? If the corelings can get us, they can get them, too."

"Old Hog is from the Free Cities," Arlen said. Rusco Hog was the richest man in the Brook. He ran the general store, which was the crux of all commerce in Tibbet's Brook.

"Ay," Coran said, "an' old Hog told me years ago that one trip was enough for him. He meant to go back after a few years, but said it wasn't worth the risk. So you ask him if the Free Cities are any safer than anywhere else."

Arlen didn't want to believe it. There had to be safe places in the world. But again the image of himself being thrown into the cellar flashed across his mind, and he knew that nowhere was truly safe at night.

The Messenger arrived an hour later. He was a tall man in his early thirties, with cropped brown hair and a short, thick beard. Draped about his broad shoulders was a shirt of metal links, and he wore a long dark cloak with thick leather breeches and boots. His mare was a sleek brown courser. Strapped to the horse's saddle was a harness holding a number of different spears. His face was grim as he approached, but his shoulders were high and proud. He scanned the crowd and spotted the Speaker easily as she stood giving orders. He turned his horse toward her.

Riding a few paces behind on a heavily laden cart pulled by a pair of dark brown mollies was the Jongleur. His clothes were a brightly colored patchwork, and he had a lute resting on the bench next to him. His hair was a color Arlen had never seen before, like a pale carrot, and his skin was so fair it seemed the sun had never touched it. His shoulders slumped, and he looked thoroughly exhausted.

There was always a Jongleur with the annual Messenger. To the children, and some of the adults, the Jongleur was the more important of the two. For as long as Arlen could remember, it had been the same man, gray-haired but spry and full of cheer.

This new one was younger, and he seemed sullen. Children ran to him immediately, and the young Jongleur perked up, the frustration melting from his face so quickly Arlen began to doubt it was ever there. In an instant, the Jongleur was off the cart and spinning his colored balls into the air as the children cheered.

Others, Arlen among them, forgot their work, drifting toward the newcomers. Selia whirled on them, having none of it. "The day is no longer because the Messenger's come!" she barked. "Back to your work!"

There were grumbles, but everyone went back to work. "Not you, Arlen," Selia said. "Come here." Arlen pulled his eyes from the Jongleur and went to her as the Messenger arrived.

"Selia Barren?" the Messenger asked.

"Just Selia will do," Selia replied primly. The Messenger's eyes widened, and he blushed, the tops of his pale cheeks turning a deep red above his beard. He leapt down from his horse and bowed low.

"Apologies," he said. "I did not think. Graig, your usual Messenger, told me that's what you were called."

"It's pleasing to know what Graig thinks of me after all these years," Selia said, sounding not at all pleased.

"Thought," the Messenger corrected. "He's dead, ma'am."

"Dead?" Selia asked, looking suddenly sad. "Was it . . . ?"

The Messenger shook his head. "It was a chill took him, not corelings. I'm Ragen, your Messenger this year, as a favor to his widow. The guild will select a new Messenger for you starting next fall."

"A year and a half again before the next Messenger?" Selia asked, sounding like she was readying a scolding. "We barely made it through this past winter without the fall salt," she said. "I know you take it for granted in Miln, but half our meat and fish spoiled for lack of proper curing. And what of our letters?"

"Sorry, ma'am," Ragen said. "Your towns are well off the common roads, and paying a Messenger to commit for a month and more of travel each year is costly. The Messengers' Guild is shorthanded, what with Graig catching that chill." He chuckled and shook his head, but noticed Selia's visage darken in response.

"No offense meant, ma'am," Ragen said. "He was my friend as well. It's just . . . it's not many of us Messengers get to go with a roof above, a bed below, and a young wife at our side. The night usually gets us before that, you see?"

"I do," Selia said. "Do *you* have a wife, Ragen?" she asked.

"Ay," the Messenger said, "though to her pleasure and my pain, I see my mare more than my bride." He laughed, confusing Arlen, who didn't think having a wife not miss you was funny.

Selia didn't seem to notice. "What if you couldn't see her at all?" she asked. "What if all you had were letters once a year to connect you to her? How would you feel to hear your letters would be delayed half a year? There are some in this town with kin in the Free Cities. Left with one Messenger or another, some as much as two generations gone. Those people ent going to come home, Ragen. Letters are all we have of them, and they of us."

"I am in full agreement with you, ma'am," Ragen said, "but the decision is not mine to make. The duke . . ."

"But you will speak to the duke upon your return, yes?" Selia asked.

"I will," he said.

"Shall I write the message down for you?" Selia asked.

Ragen smiled. "I think I can remember it, ma'am."

"See that you do."

Ragen bowed again, still lower. "Apologies, for coming to call on such a dark day," he said, his eyes flicking to the funeral pyre.

"We cannot tell the rain when to come, nor the wind, nor the cold," Selia said. "Not the corelings, either. So life must go on despite these things."

"Life goes on," Ragen agreed, "but if there's anything I or my Jongleur can do to help; I've a strong back and I've treated coreling wounds many times."

"Your Jongleur is helping already," Selia said, nodding toward the young man as he sang and did his tricks, "distracting the young ones while their kin do their work. As for you, I've much to do over the next few days, if we're to recover from this loss. I won't have time to hand the mail and read to those who haven't learned their letters."

"I can read to those who can't, ma'am," Ragen said, "but I don't know your town well enough to distribute."

"No need," Selia said, pulling Arlen forward. "Arlen here will take you to the general store in Town Square. Give the letters and packages to Rusco Hog when you deliver the salt. Most everyone will come running now that the salt's in, and Rusco's one of the few in town with letters and numbers. The old crook will complain and try to insist on payment, but you tell him that in time of trouble, the whole town must throw in. You tell him to give out the letters and read to those who can't, or I'll not lift a finger the next time the town wants to throw a rope around his neck."

Ragen looked closely at Selia, perhaps trying to tell if she was joking, but her stony face gave no indication. He bowed again.

"Hurry along, then," Selia said. "Lift your feet and you'll both be back as everyone is readying to leave here for the night. If you and your Jongleur don't want to pay Rusco for a room, any here will be glad to offer their homes." She shooed the two of them away and turned back to scold those pausing their work to stare at the newcomers.

"Is she always so . . . forceful?" Ragen asked Arlen as they walked over to where the Jongleur was mumming for the youngest children. The rest had been pulled back to work.

Arlen snorted. "You should hear her talk to the graybeards. You're lucky to get away with your skin after calling her 'Barren.'"

"Graig said that's what everyone called her," Ragen said.

"They do," Arlen agreed, "just not to her face, unless they're looking to take a coreling by the horns. Everyone hops when Selia speaks."

Ragen chuckled. "And her an old Daughter, at that," he mused. "Where I come from, only Mothers expect everyone to jump at their command like that."

"What difference does that make?" Arlen asked.

Ragen shrugged. "Don't know, I suppose," he conceded. "That's just how things are in Miln. People make the world go, and Mothers make people, so they lead the dance."

"It's not like that here," Arlen said.

"It never is, in the small towns," Ragen said. "Not enough people to spare. But the Free Cities are different. Apart from Miln, none of the others give their women much voice at all."

"That sounds just as dumb," Arlen muttered.

"It is," Ragen agreed.

The Messenger stopped, and handed Arlen the reins to his

courser. "Wait here a minute," he said, and headed over to the Jongleur. The two men moved aside to talk, and Arlen saw the Jongleur's face change again, becoming angry, then petulant, and finally resigned as he tried to argue with Ragen, whose face remained stony throughout.

Never taking his glare off the Jongleur, the Messenger beckoned with a hand to Arlen, who brought the horse over to them. ". . . don't care how tired you are," Ragen was saying, his voice a harsh whisper, "these people have grisly work to do, and if you need to dance and juggle all afternoon to keep their kids occupied while they do it, then you'd damn well better! Now put your face back on and get to it!" He grabbed the reins from Arlen and thrust them at the man.

Arlen got a good look at the young Jongleur's face, full of indignation and fear, before the Jongleur took notice of him. The second he saw he was being watched, the man's face rippled, and a moment later he was the bright, cheerful fellow who danced for children.

Ragen took Arlen to the cart and the two climbed on. Ragen snapped the reins, and they turned back up the dirt path that led to the main road.

"What were you arguing about?" Arlen asked as the cart bounced along.

The Messenger looked at him a moment, then shrugged. "It's Keerin's first time so far out of the city," he said. "He was brave enough when there was a group of us and he had a covered wagon to sleep in, but when we left the rest of our caravan behind in Angiers, he didn't do near as well. He's got day-jitters from the corelings, and it's made him poor company."

"You can't tell," Arlen said, looking back at the cartwheeling man.

"Jongleurs have their mummers' tricks," Ragen said. "They can pretend so hard to be something they're not that they actually convince themselves of it for a time. Keerin pretended to be brave. The guild tested him for travel and he passed, but you never really know how people will hold up after two weeks on the open road until they do it for real."

"How *do* you stay out on the roads at night?" Arlen asked. "Da says drawing wards in the dirt's asking for trouble."

"Your da is right," Ragen said. "Look in that compartment by your feet."

Arlen did, and produced a large bag of soft leather. Inside was a knotted rope, strung with lacquered wooden plates bigger than his hand. His eyes widened when he saw wards carved and painted into the wood.

Immediately, Arlen knew what it was: a portable warding circle, large enough to surround the cart and more besides. "I've never seen anything like it," Arlen said.

"They're not easy to make," the Messenger said. "Most Messengers spend their whole apprenticeship mastering the art. No wind or rain is going to smudge those wards. But even then, they're not the same as having warded walls and a door.

"Ever see a coreling face-to-face, boy?" he asked, turning and looking at Arlen hard. "Watched it take a swipe at you with nowhere to run and nothing to protect you except magic you can't see?" He shook his head. "Maybe I'm being too hard on Keerin. He handled his test all right. Screamed a bit, but that's to be expected. Night after night is another matter. Takes its toll on some men, always worried that a stray leaf will land on a ward, and then . . ." He hissed suddenly and swiped a clawed hand at Arlen, laughing when the boy jumped.

Arlen ran his thumb over each smooth, lacquered ward, feeling their strength. There was one of the little plates for every foot of rope, much as there would be in any warding. He counted more than forty of them. "Can't wind demons fly into a circle this big?" he asked. "Da puts posts up to keep them from landing in the fields."

The man looked over at him, a little surprised. "Your da's probably wasting his time," he said. "Wind demons are strong fliers, but they need running space or something to climb and leap from in order to take off. Not much of either in a cornfield, so they'd be reluctant to land, unless they saw something too tempting to resist, like some little boy sleeping in the field on a dare." He looked at Arlen in that same way Jeph did, when warning Arlen that the corelings were serious business. As if he didn't know.

"Wind demons also need to turn in wide arcs," Ragen continued, "and most of them have a wingspan larger than that circle. It's possible that one could get in, but I've never seen it happen. If it does, though . . ." He gestured to the long, thick spear he kept next to him.

"You can kill a coreling with a spear?" Arlen asked.

"Probably not," Ragen replied, "but I've heard that you can stun them by pinning them against your wards." He chuckled. "I hope I never have to find out."

Arlen looked at him, wide-eyed.

Ragen looked back at him, his face suddenly serious. "Messaging's dangerous work, boy," he said.

Arlen stared at him a long time. "It would be worth it, to see the Free Cities," he said at last. "Tell me true, what's Fort Miln like?"

"It's the richest and most beautiful city in the world," Ragen replied, lifting his mail sleeve to reveal a tattoo on his forearm of a city nestled between two mountains. "The Duke's Mines run rich with salt, metal, and coal. Its walls and rooftops are so well warded, it's rare for the house wards to even be tested. When the sun shines on its walls, it puts the mountains themselves to shame."

"Never seen a mountain," Arlen said, marveling as he traced the tattoo with a finger. "My da says they're just big hills."

"You see that hill?" Ragen asked, pointing north of the road.

Arlen nodded. "Boggin's Hill. You can see the whole Brook from up there."

Ragen nodded. "You know what a 'hundred' means, Arlen?" he asked.

Arlen nodded again. "Ten pairs of hands."

"Well, even a small mountain is bigger than a hundred of your Boggin's Hills piled atop each other, and the mountains of Miln are not small."

Arlen's eyes widened as he tried to contemplate such a height. "They must touch the sky," he said.

"Some are above it," Ragen bragged. "Atop them, you can look down at the clouds."

"I want to see that one day," Arlen said.

"You could join the Messengers' Guild, when you're old enough," Ragen said.

Arlen shook his head. "Da says the people that leave are deserters," he said. "He spits when he says it."

"Your da doesn't know what he's talking about," Ragen said. "Spitting doesn't make things so. Without Messengers, even the Free Cities would crumble."

"I thought the Free Cities were safe?" Arlen asked.

"Nowhere is safe, Arlen. Not truly. Miln has more people and can absorb the deaths more easily than a place like Tibbet's Brook, but the corelings still take a toll each year."

"How many people are in Miln?" Arlen asked. "We have nine hundreds in Tibbet's Brook, and Sunny Pasture up the ways is supposed to be almost as big."

"We have over thirty thousands in Miln," Ragen said proudly.

Arlen looked at him, confused.

"A thousand is ten hundreds," the Messenger supplied.

Arlen thought a moment, then shook his head. "There ent that many people in the world," he said.

"There are and more," Ragen said. "There's a wide world out there, for those willing to brave the dark."

Arlen didn't answer, and they rode in silence for a time.

It took about an hour and a half for the trundling cart to reach Town Square. The center of the Brook, Town Square held a few dozen warded wooden houses for those whose trade did not have them working in the fields or rice paddies, fishing, or cutting wood. It was here one came to find the tailor and the baker, the farrier, the cooper, and the rest.

At the center lay the square where people would gather, and the biggest building in the Brook, the general store. It had a large open front room that housed tables and the bar, an even larger storeroom in back, and a cellar below, filled with most everything of value in the Brook.

The kitchen was run by Hog's daughters, Dasy and Catrin. Two credits could buy a meal to leave you stuffed, but Silvy called old Hog a cheat, since two credits could buy enough raw grain for a week. Still, plenty of unmarried men paid the price, and not all for the food. Dasy was homely and Catrin fat, but Uncle Cholie said the men who married them would be set for life.

Everyone in the Brook brought Hog their goods, be it corn or meat or fur, pottery or cloth, furniture or tools. Hog took the items, counted them up, and gave the customers credits to buy other things at the store.

Things always seemed to cost a lot more than Hog paid for them, though. Arlen knew enough numbers to see that. There were some famous arguments when people came to sell, but Hog set the prices, and usually got his way. Just about everyone hated Hog, but they needed him all the same, and were more likely to brush his coat and open his doors than spit when he passed.

Everyone else in the Brook worked throughout the sun, and barely saw all their needs met, but Hog and his daughters always had fleshy cheeks, rounded bellies, and clean new clothes. Arlen had to wrap himself in a rug whenever his mother took his overalls to wash.

Ragen and Arlen tied off the mules in front of the store and went inside. The bar was empty. Usually the air inside the taproom was thick with bacon fat, but there was no smell of cooking from the kitchen today.

Arlen rushed ahead of the Messenger to the bar. Rusco had a small bronze bell there, brought with him when he came from the Free Cities. Arlen loved that bell. He slapped his hand down on it and grinned at the clear sound.

There was a thump in the back, and Rusco came through the curtains behind the bar. He was a big man, still strong and straight-backed at sixty, but a soft gut hung around his middle, and his iron-gray hair was creeping back from his lined forehead. He wore light trousers and leather shoes with a clean white cotton shirt, the sleeves rolled halfway up his thick forearms. His white apron was spotless, as always.

"Arlen Bales," he said with a patient smile, seeing the boy. "Did you come just to play with the bell, or do you have some business?"

"The business is mine," Ragen said, stepping forward. "You Rusco Hog?"

"Just Rusco will do," the man said. "The townies slapped the 'Hog' on, though not to my face. Can't stand to see a man prosper."

"That's twice," Ragen mused.

"Say again?" Rusco said.

"Twice that Graig's journey log has led me astray," Ragen said. "I called Selia 'Barren' to her face this morning."

"Ha!" Rusco laughed. "Did you now? Well, that's worth a drink on the house, if anything is. What did you say your name was?"

"Ragen," the Messenger said, dropping his heavy satchel and taking a seat at the bar. Rusco tapped a keg, and plucked a slatted wooden mug off a hook.

The ale was thick and honey-colored, and foamed to a white

head atop the mug. Rusco filled one for Ragen and another for himself. Then he glanced at Arlen, and filled a smaller cup. "Take that to a table and let your elders talk at the bar," he said. "And if you know what's good for you, you won't tell your mum I gave it to you."

Arlen beamed, and ran off with his prize before Rusco had a chance to reconsider. He had snuck a taste of ale from his father's mug at festivals, but had never had a cup of his own.

"I was starting to worry no one was coming ever again," he heard Rusco tell Ragen.

"Graig took a chill just before he was to leave last fall," Ragen said, drinking deeply. "His Herb Gatherer told him to put the trip off until he got better, but then winter set in, and he got worse and worse. In the end, he asked me to take his route until the guild could find another. I had to take a caravan of salt to Angiers anyway, so I added an extra cart and swung this way before heading back north."

Rusco took his mug and filled it again. "To Graig," he said, "a fine Messenger, and a dangerous haggler." Ragen nodded and the two men clapped mugs and drank.

"Another?" Rusco asked, when Ragen slammed his mug back down on the bar.

"Graig wrote in his log that you were a dangerous haggler, too," Ragen said, "and that you'd try to get me drunk first."

Rusco chuckled, and refilled the mug. "After the haggling, I'll have no need to serve these on the house," he said, handing it to Ragen with a fresh head.

"You will if you want your mail to reach Miln," Ragen said with a grin, accepting the mug.

"I can see you're going to be as tough as Graig ever was," Rusco grumbled, filling his own mug. "There," he said, when it foamed over, "we can both haggle drunk." They laughed, and clashed mugs again.

"What news of the Free Cities?" Rusco asked. "The Krasians still determined to destroy themselves?"

Ragen shrugged. "By all accounts. I stopped going to Krasia a few years ago, when I married. Too far, and too dangerous."

"So the fact that they cover their women in blankets has nothing to do with it?" Rusco asked.

Ragen laughed. "Doesn't help," he said, "but it's mostly how they think all Northerners, even Messengers, are cowards for not spending our nights trying to get ourselves cored."

"Maybe they'd be less inclined to fight if they looked at their women more," Rusco mused. "How about Angiers and Miln? The dukes still bickering?"

"As always," Ragen said. "Euchor needs Angiers' wood to fuel his refineries, and grain to feed his people. Rhinebeck needs Miln's metal and salt. They have to trade to survive, but instead of making it easy on themselves, they spend all their time trying to cheat each other, especially when a shipment is lost to corelings on the road. Last summer, demons hit a caravan of steel and salt. They killed the drivers, but left most of the cargo intact. Rhinebeck retrieved it, and refused to pay, claiming salvage rights."

"Duke Euchor must have been furious," Rusco said.

"Livid," Ragen agreed. "I was the one that brought him the news. He went red in the face, and swore Angiers wouldn't see another ounce of salt until Rhinebeck paid."

"Did Rhinebeck pay?" Rusco asked, leaning in eagerly.

Ragen shook his head. "They did their best to starve each other for a few months, and then the Merchants' Guild paid, just to get their shipments out before the winter came and they rotted in storage. Rhinebeck is angry at them now, for giving in to Euchor, but his face was saved and the shipments were moving again, which is all that mattered to anyone other than those two dogs."

"Wise to watch what you call the dukes," Rusco warned, "even this far out."

"Who's going to tell them?" Ragen asked. "You? The boy?" He gestured at Arlen. Both men laughed.

"And now I have to bring Euchor news of Riverbridge, which will make things worse," Ragen said.

"The town on the border of Miln," Rusco said, "barely a day out from Angiers. I have contacts there."

"Not anymore, you don't," Ragen said pointedly, and the men were quiet for a time.

"Enough bad news," Ragen said, hauling his satchel onto the bar. Rusco considered it dubiously.

"That doesn't look like salt," he said, "and I doubt I have that much mail."

"You have six letters, and an even dozen packages," Ragen

said, handing Rusco a sheaf of folded paper. "It's all listed here, along with all the other letters in the satchel and packages on the cart to be distributed. I gave Selia a copy of the list," he warned.

"What do I want with that list, or your mailbag?" Rusco asked.

"The Speaker is occupied, and won't be able to distribute the mail and read to those that can't. She volunteered you."

"And how am I to be compensated for spending my business hours reading to the townies?" Rusco asked.

"The satisfaction of a good deed to your neighbors?" Ragen asked.

Rusco snorted. "I didn't come to Tibbet's Brook to make friends," he said. "I'm a businessman, and I do a lot for this town."

"Do you?" Ragen asked.

"Damn right," Rusco said. "Before I came to this town, all they did was *barter*." He made the word a curse, and spat on the floor. "They collected the fruits of their labor and gathered in the square every Seventhday, arguing over how many beans were worth an ear of corn, or how much rice you had to give the cooper to make you a barrel to put your rice in. And if you didn't get what you needed on Seventhday, you had to wait until the next week, or go door to door. Now everyone can come here, any day, any time from sunup to sundown, and trade for credits to get whatever else they need."

"The town savior," Ragen said wryly. "And you asking nothing in return."

"Nothing but a tidy profit," Rusco said with a grin.

"And how often do the villagers try to string you up for a cheat?" Ragen asked.

Rusco's eyes narrowed. "Too often, considering half of them can't count past their fingers, and the other half can only add their toes to that," he said.

"Selia said the next time it happens, you're on your own"—Ragen's friendly voice had suddenly gone hard—"unless you do your part. There's plenty on the far side of town suffering worse than having to read the mail."

Rusco frowned, but he took the list and carried the heavy bag into his storeroom.

"How bad is it, really?" he asked when he returned.

"Bad," Ragen said. "Twenty-seven so far, and a few still unaccounted for."

"Creator," Rusco swore, drawing a ward in the air in front of him. "I had thought a family, at worst."

"If only," Ragen said.

They were both silent for a moment, as was decent, then looked up at each other as one.

"You have this year's salt?" Rusco asked.

"You have the duke's rice?" Ragen replied.

"Been holding it all winter, you being so late," Rusco said.

Ragen's eyes narrowed.

"Oh, it's still good!" Rusco said, his hands coming up suddenly, as if pleading. "I've kept it sealed and dry, and there are no vermin in my cellar!"

"I'll need to be sure, you understand," Ragen said.

"Of course, of course," Rusco said. "Arlen, fetch that lamp!" he ordered, pointing the boy toward the corner of the bar.

Arlen scurried over to the lantern, picking up the striker. He lit the wick and lowered the glass reverently. He had never been trusted to hold glass before. It was colder than he imagined, but quickly grew warm as the flame licked it.

"Carry it down to the cellar for us," Rusco ordered. Arlen tried to contain his excitement. He had always wanted to see behind the bar. They said if everyone in the Brook put all their possessions in one pile, it would not rival the wonders of Hog's cellar.

He watched as Rusco pulled a ring on his floor, opening a wide trap. Arlen came forward quickly, worried old Hog would change his mind. He went down the creaking steps, holding the lantern high to illuminate the way. As he did, the light touched on stacks of crates and barrels from floor to ceiling, running in even rows stretching back past the edges of the light. The floor was wooden to prevent corelings from rising directly into the cellar from the Core, but there were still wards carved into the racks along the walls. Old Hog was careful with his treasures.

The storekeeper led the way through the aisles to the sealed barrels in the back. "They look unspoiled," Ragen said, inspecting the wood. He considered a moment, then chose at random. "That one," he said, pointing to a barrel.

Rusco grunted and hauled out the barrel in question. Some people called his work easy, but his arms were as hard and thick as any that swung an axe or scythe. He broke the seal and popped the top off the barrel, scooping rice into a shallow pan for Ragen to inspect.

"Good Marsh rice," he told the Messenger, "and not a weevil to be seen, nor sign of rot. This will fetch a high price in Miln, especially after so long." Ragen grunted and nodded, so the cask was resealed and they returned upstairs.

They argued for some time over how many barrels of rice the heavy sacks of salt on the cart were worth. In the end, neither of them seemed happy, but they shook hands on the deal.

Rusco called his daughters, and they all went out to the cart to begin unloading the salt. Arlen tried lifting a bag, but it was far too heavy, and he staggered and fell, dropping it.

"Be careful!" Dasy scolded, slapping the back of his head.

"If you can't lift, then get the door!" Catrin barked. She herself had one sack over her shoulder and another tucked under her meaty arm. Arlen scrambled to his feet and rushed to hold the portal for her.

"Fetch Ferd Miller and tell him we'll pay five . . . make it four credits for every sack he grinds," Rusco told Arlen. Most everyone in the Brook worked for Hog, one way or another, but the Squarefolk most of all. "Five if he packs it in barrels with rice to keep it dry."

"Ferd is off in the Cluster," Arlen said. "Most everyone is."

Rusco grunted, but did not reply. Soon enough the cart was empty, save for a few boxes and sacks that did not contain salt. Rusco's daughters eyed those hungrily, but said nothing.

"We'll carry the rice up from the cellar tonight and keep it in the back room until you're ready to head back to Miln," Rusco said, when the last sack was hauled inside.

"Thank you," Ragen said.

"The duke's business is done, then?" Rusco asked with a grin, his eyes flicking knowingly to the remaining items on the cart.

"The duke's business, yes," Ragen said, grinning in return. Arlen hoped they would give him another ale while they haggled. It made him feel light-headed, like he had caught a chill, but without the coughing and sneezing and aches. He liked the feeling, and wanted to try it again.

He helped carry the remaining items into the taproom, and Catrin brought out a platter of sandwiches thick with meat. Arlen was given a second cup of ale to wash it down, and old

Hog told him he could have two credits in the book for his work. "I won't tell your parents," Hog said, "but if you spend it on ale and they catch you, you'll be working off the grief your mum gives me." Arlen nodded eagerly. He'd never had credits of his own to spend at the store.

After lunch, Rusco and Ragen went over to the bar and opened up the other items the Messenger had brought. Arlen's eyes flared as each treasure was presented. There were bolts of cloth finer than anything he had ever seen; metal tools and pins, ceramics, and exotic spices. There were even a few cups made of bright, sparkling glass.

Hog seemed less impressed. "Graig had a better haul last year," he said. "I'll give you . . . a hundred credits for the lot." Arlen's jaw dropped. A hundred credits! Ragen could own half the Brook for that.

Ragen didn't care for the offer, though. His eyes went hard again, and he slammed his hand down on the table. Dasy and Catrin looked up from their cleaning at the sound.

"To the Core with your credit!" he growled. "I'm not one of your bumpkins, and unless you want the guild to know you for a cheat, you'll not mistake me for one again."

"No hard feelings!" Rusco laughed, patting the air in that placating way he had. "Had to try . . . you understand. They still like gold up there in Miln?" he asked with a sly smile.

"Same as everywhere," Ragen said. He was still frowning, but the anger had drained from his voice.

"Not out here," Rusco said. He went back behind the curtain, and they could hear him rummaging around, raising his voice to still be heard. "Out here, if you can't eat something, or wear it, paint a ward with it, or use it to till your field, it's not worth much of anything." He returned a moment later with a large cloth sack he deposited on the counter with a clink.

"People here have forgotten that gold moves the world," he went on, reaching into the bag and pulling out two heavy yellow coins, which he waved in Ragen's face. "The miller's kids were using these as game pieces! Game pieces! I told them I'd trade the gold for a carved wood game set I had in the back; they thought I was doing them a favor! Ferd even came by the next day to thank me!" He laughed a deep belly laugh. Arlen felt like he should be offended by that laugh, but he wasn't quite sure why. He had played the Millers' game many times, and it seemed worth more than two metal disks, however shiny they might be.

"I brought a lot more than two suns' worth," Ragen said, nodding at the coins and then looking toward the bag.

Rusco smiled. "Not to worry," he said, untying the bag fully. As the cloth flattened on the counter, more bright coins spilled out, along with chains and rings and ropes of glittering stones. It was all very pretty, Arlen supposed, but he was surprised at how Ragen's eyes bulged and took on a covetous glitter.

Again they haggled, Ragen holding the stones up to the light and biting the coins, while Rusco fingered the cloth and tasted the spices. It was a blur to Arlen, whose head was spinning from the ale. Mug after mug came to the men from Catrin at the bar, but they showed no signs of being as affected as Arlen.

"Two hundred and twenty gold suns, two silver moons, the rope chain, and the three silver rings," Rusco said at last. "And not a copper light more."

"No wonder you work out in a backwater," Ragen said. "They must have run you out of the city for a cheat."

"Insults won't make you any richer," Hog said, confident he had the upper hand.

"No riches for me this time," Ragen said. "After my traveling costs, every last light will go to Graig's widow."

"Ah, Jenya," Rusco said wistfully. "She used to pen for some of those in Miln with no letters, my idiot nephew among them. What will become of her?"

Ragen shook his head. "The guild paid no death-price to her, because Graig died at home," he said. "And since she isn't a Mother, a lot of jobs will be denied her."

"I'm sorry to hear that," Rusco said.

"Graig left her some money," Ragen said, "though he never had much, and the guild will still pay her to pen. With the money from this trip, she should have enough to get by for a time. She's young, though, and it will run out eventually unless she remarries or finds better work."

"And then?" Rusco asked.

Ragen shrugged. "It'll be hard for her to find a new husband, having already married and failed to bear children, but she won't become a Beggar. My guild brothers and I have sworn that. One of us will take her in as a Servant before that happens."

Rusco shook his head. "Still, to fall from Merchant class to Servant . . ." He reached into the much lighter bag and produced a ring with a clear, sparkling stone set into it. "See that she gets this," he said, holding the ring out.

As Ragen reached for it, though, Rusco pulled it back suddenly. "I'll have a message back from her, you understand," he said. "I know how she shapes her letters." Ragen looked at him a moment, and he quickly added, "No insult meant."

Ragen smiled. "Your generosity outweighs your insult," he said, taking the ring. "This will keep her belly full for months."

"Yes, well," Rusco said gruffly, scooping up the remains of the bag, "don't let any of the townies hear, or I'll lose my reputation as a cheat."

"Your secret is safe with me," Ragen said with a laugh.

"You could earn her a bit more, perhaps," Rusco said.

"Oh?"

"The letters we have were meant to go to Miln six months ago. You stick around a few days while we pen and collect more, and maybe help pen a few, and I'll compensate you. No more gold," he clarified, "but surely Jenya could do with a cask of rice, or some cured fish or meal."

"Indeed she could," Ragen said.

"I can find work for your Jongleur, too," Rusco added. "He'll see more custom here in the Square than by hopping from farm to farm."

"Agreed," Ragen said. "Keerin will need gold, though."

Rusco gave him a wry look, and Ragen laughed. "Had to try . . . you understand!" he said. "Silver, then."

Rusco nodded. "I'll charge a moon for every performance, and for every moon, I'll keep one star and he the other three."

"I thought you said the townies had no money," Ragen noted.

"Most don't," Rusco said. "I'll sell the moons to them . . . say at the cost of five credits."

"So Rusco Hog skims from both sides of the deal?" Ragen asked.

Hog smiled.

Arlen was excited during the ride back. Old Hog had promised to let him see the Jongleur for free if he spread the word that Keerin would be entertaining in the Square at high sun the next day for five credits or a silver Milnese moon. He wouldn't have much time; his parents would be readying to leave just as he and Ragen returned, but he was sure he could spread the word before they pulled him onto the cart.

"Tell me about the Free Cities," Arlen begged as they rode. "How many have you seen?"

"Five," Ragen said, "Miln, Angiers, Lakton, Rizon, and Krasia. There may be others beyond the mountains or the desert, but none that I know have seen them."

"What are they like?" Arlen asked.

"Fort Angiers, the forest stronghold, lies south of Miln, across the Dividing River," Ragen said. "Angiers supplies wood for the other cities. Farther south lies the great lake, and on its surface stands Lakton."

"Is a lake like a pond?" Arlen asked.

"A lake is to a pond what a mountain is to a hill," Ragen said, giving Arlen a moment to digest the thought. "Out on the water, the Laktonians are safe from flame, rock, and wood demons. Their wardnet is proof against wind demons, and no people can ward against water demons better. They're fisherfolk, and thousands in the southern cities depend on their catch for food.

"West of Lakton is Fort Rizon, which is not technically a fort, since you could practically step over its wall, but it shields the largest farmlands you've ever seen. Without Rizon, the other Free Cities would starve."

"And Krasia?" Arlen asked.

"I only visited Fort Krasia once," Ragen said. "The Krasians aren't welcoming to outsiders, and you need to cross weeks of desert to get there."

"Desert?"

"Sand," Ragen explained. "Nothing but sand for miles in every direction. No food nor water but what you carry, and nothing to shade you from the scorching sun."

"And people live there?" Arlen asked.

"Oh, yes," Ragen said. "The Krasians used to be even more numerous than the Milnese, but they're dying off."

"Why?" Arlen asked.

"Because they fight the corelings," Ragen said.

Arlen's eyes widened. "You can fight corelings?" he asked.

"You can fight anything, Arlen," Ragen said. "The problem with fighting corelings is that more often than not, you lose. The

Krasians kill their share, but the corelings give better than they get. There are fewer Krasians every year."

"My da says corelings eat your soul when they get you," Arlen said.

"Bah!" Ragen spat over the side of the cart. "Superstitious nonsense."

They had turned a bend not far from the Cluster when Arlen noticed something dangling from the tree ahead of them. "What's that?" he asked, pointing.

"Night," Ragen swore, and cracked the reins, sending the mollies into a gallop. Arlen was thrown back in his seat, and took a moment to right himself. When he did, he looked at the tree, which was coming up fast.

"Uncle Cholie!" he cried, seeing the man kicking as he clawed at the rope around his neck.

"Help! Help!" Arlen screamed. He leapt from the moving cart, hitting the ground hard, but he bounced to his feet, darting toward Cholie. He got up under the man, but one of Cholie's thrashing feet kicked him in the mouth, knocking him down. He tasted blood, but strangely there was no pain. He came up again, grabbing Cholie's legs and trying to lift him up to loosen the rope, but he was too short, and Cholie too heavy besides, and the man continued to gag and jerk.

"Help him!" Arlen cried to Ragen. "He's choking! Somebody help!"

He looked up to see Ragen pull a spear from the back of the cart. The Messenger drew back and threw with hardly a moment to aim, but his aim was true, severing the rope and collapsing poor Cholie onto Arlen. They both fell into the dirt.

Ragen was there in an instant, pulling the rope from Cholie's throat. It didn't seem to make much difference, the man still gagged and clawed at his throat. His eyes bulged so far it looked as if they would pop right out of his head, and his face was so red it looked purple. Arlen screamed as he gave a tremendous thrash, and then lay still.

Ragen beat Cholie's chest and breathed huge gulps of air into him, but it had no effect. Eventually, the Messenger gave up, slumping in the dirt and cursing.

Arlen was no stranger to death. That specter was a frequent visitor to Tibbet's Brook. But it was one thing to die from the corelings or from a chill. This was different.

"Why?" he asked Ragen. "Why would he fight so hard to survive last night, only to kill himself now?"

"Did he fight?" Ragen asked. "Did any of them really fight? Or did they run and hide?"

"I don't . . ." Arlen began.

"Hiding isn't always enough, Arlen," Ragen said. "Sometimes, hiding kills something inside of you, so that even if you survive the demons, you don't really."

"What else could he have done?" Arlen asked. "You can't fight a demon."

"I'd sooner fight a bear in its own cave," Ragen said, "but it can be done."

"But you said the Krasians were dying because of it," Arlen protested.

"They are," Ragen said. "But they follow their hearts. I know it sounds like madness, Arlen, but deep down, men *want* to fight, like they did in tales of old. They want to protect their women and children as men should. But they can't, because the great wards are lost, so they knot themselves like caged hares, hiding terrified through the night. But sometimes, especially when you see loved ones die, the tension breaks you and you just snap."

He put a hand on Arlen's shoulder. "I'm sorry you had to see this, boy," he said. "I know it doesn't make a lot of sense right now . . ."

"No," Arlen said, "it does."

And it was true, Arlen realized. He understood the need to fight. He had not expected to win when he attacked Cobie and his friends that day. If anything, he had expected to be beaten worse than ever. But in that instant when he grabbed the stick, he hadn't cared. He only knew he was tired of just taking their abuse, and wanted it to end, one way or another.

It was comforting to know he wasn't alone.

Arlen looked at his uncle, lying in the dirt, his eyes wide with fear. He knelt and reached out, brushing his eyes closed with his fingertips. Cholie had nothing to fear any longer.

"Have you ever killed a coreling?" he asked the Messenger.

"No," Ragen said, shaking his head. "But I've fought a few. Got the scars to prove it. But I was always more interested in getting away, or keeping them away from someone else, than I was in killing any."

Arlen thought about that as they wrapped Cholie in a tarp and put him in the back of the wagon, hurrying back to the Cluster. Jeph and Silvy had already packed the cart and were waiting impatiently to leave, but the sight of the body diffused their anger at Arlen's late return.

Silvy wailed and threw herself on her brother, but there was no time to waste, if they were to make it back to the farm by nightfall. Jeph had to hold her back as Tender Harral painted a ward on the tarp and led a prayer as he tossed Cholie into the pyre.

The survivors who weren't staying in Brine Cutter's house were divided up and taken home with the others. Jeph and Silvy had offered succor to two women. Norine Cutter was over fifty summers old. Her husband had died some years back, and she had lost her daughter and grandson in the attack. Marea Bales was old, too; almost forty. Her husband had been left outside when the others drew lots for the cellar. Like Silvy, both slumped in the back of Jeph's cart, staring at their knees. Arlen waved good-bye to Ragen as his father cracked the whip.

The Cluster by the Woods was drawing out of sight when Arlen realized he hadn't told anyone to come see the Jongleur.

CHAPTER 2

IF IT WAS YOU
319 AR

THEY HAD JUST ENOUGH TIME to stow the cart and check the wards before the corelings came. Silvy had little energy for cooking, so they ate a cold meal of bread, cheese, and sausage, chewing with little enthusiasm. The demons came soon after sunset to test the wards, and every time the magic flared to throw them back, Norine cried out. Marea never touched her food. She sat on her pallet with her arms wrapped tightly around her legs, rocking back and forth and whimpering whenever the magic flared. Silvy cleared the plates, but she never returned from the kitchen, and Arlen could hear her crying.

Arlen tried to go to her, but Jeph caught his arm. "Come talk with me, Arlen," he said.

They went into the small room that housed Arlen's pallet, his collection of smooth rocks from the brook, and all his feathers and bones. Jeph selected one of these, a brightly colored feather about ten inches long, and fingered it as he spoke, not looking Arlen in the eye.

Arlen knew the signs. When his father wouldn't look at him, it meant he was uncomfortable with whatever he wanted to talk about.

"What you saw on the road with the Messenger . . ." Jeph began.

"Ragen explained it to me," Arlen said. "Uncle Cholie was dead already, he just didn't know it right away. Sometimes people live through an attack, but die anyway."

Jeph frowned. "Not how I would have put it," he said. "But true enough, I suppose. Cholie . . ."

"Was a coward," Arlen finished.

Jeph looked at him in surprise. "What makes you say that?" he asked.

"He hid in the cellar because he was scared to die, and then killed himself because he was scared to live," Arlen said. "Better if he had just picked up an axe and died fighting."

"I don't want to hear that kind of talk," Jeph said. "You can't fight demons, Arlen. No one can. There's nothing to be gained by getting yourself killed."

Arlen shook his head. "They're like bullies," he said. "They attack us because we're too scared to fight back. I hit Cobie and the others with that stick, and they didn't bother me again."

"Cobie ent a rock demon," Jeph said. "No stick is going to scare those off."

"There's got to be a way," Arlen said. "People used to do it. All the old stories say so."

"The stories say there were magic wards to fight with," Jeph said. "The fighting wards are lost."

"Ragen says they still fight demons in some places. He says it can be done."

"I'm going to have a talk with that Messenger," Jeph grumbled. "He shouldn't be filling your head with such thoughts."

"Why not?" Arlen said. "Maybe more people would have survived last night, if all the men had gotten axes and spears . . ."

"They would be just as dead," Jeph finished. "There's other ways to protect yourself and your family, Arlen. Wisdom. Prudence. Humility. It's not brave to fight a battle you can't win.

"Who would care for the women and the children if all the men got themselves cored trying to kill what can't be killed?" he went on. "Who would chop the wood and build the homes? Who would hunt and herd and plant and slaughter? Who would seed the women with children? If all the men die, the corelings win."

"The corelings are already winning," Arlen muttered. "You keep saying the town gets smaller each year. Bullies keep coming when you don't fight back."

He looked up at his father. "Don't you feel it? Don't you want to fight sometimes?"

"Of course I do, Arlen," Jeph said. "But not for no reason. When it matters, when it *really* matters, all men are willing to fight. Animals run when they can, and fight when they must, and people are no different. But that spirit should only come out when needed.

"But if it was you out there with the corelings," he said, "or your mam, I swear I would fight like mad before I let them get near you. Do you understand the difference?"

Arlen nodded. "I think so."

"Good man," Jeph said, squeezing his shoulder.

Arlen's dreams that night were filled with images of hills that touched the sky, and ponds so big you could put a whole town on the surface. He saw yellow sand stretching as far as his eyes could see, and a walled fortress hidden in the trees.

But he saw it all between a pair of legs that swayed lazily before his eyes. He looked up, and saw his own face turning purple in the noose.

He woke with a start, his pallet damp with sweat. It was still dark, but there was a faint lightening on the horizon, where the indigo sky held a touch of red. He lit a candle stub and pulled on his overalls, stumbling out to the common room. He found a crust to chew on as he took out the egg basket and milk jugs, putting them by the door.

"You're up early," said a voice behind him. He turned, startled, to find Norine staring at him. Marea was still on her pallet, though she tossed in her sleep.

"The days don't get any longer while you sleep," Arlen said.

Norine nodded. "So my husband used to say," she agreed. " 'Baleses and Cutters can't work by candlelight, like the Squares,' he'd say."

"I have a lot to do," Arlen said, peeking through the shutter to see how long he had before he could cross the wards. "The Jongleur is supposed to perform at high sun."

"Of course," Norine agreed. "When I was your age, the Jongleur was the most important thing in the world to me, too. I'll help you with your chores."

"You don't have to do that," Arlen said. "Da says you should rest."

Norine shook her head. "Rest just makes me think of things best left unthought," she said. "If I'm to stay with you, I should earn my keep. After chopping wood in the Cluster, how hard could it be to slop pigs and plant corn?"

Arlen shrugged, and handed her the egg basket.

With Norine's help, the chores went by fast. She was a quick learner, and no stranger to hard work and heavy lifting. By the time the smell of eggs and bacon wafted from the house, the animals were all fed, the eggs collected, and the cows milked.

"Stop squirming on the bench," Silvy told Arlen as they ate.

"Young Arlen can't wait to go see the Jongleur," Norine advised.

"Maybe tomorrow," Jeph said, and Arlen's face fell.

"What!" Arlen cried. "But . . ."

"No buts," Jeph said. "A lot of work went undone yesterday, and I promised Selia I'd drop by the Cluster in the afternoon to help out."

Arlen pushed his plate away and stomped into his room.

"Let the boy go," Norine said when he was gone. "Marea and I will help out here." Marea looked up at the sound of her name, but went back to playing with her food a moment later.

"Arlen had a hard day, yesterday," Silvy said. She bit her lip. "We all did. Let the Jongleur put a smile on his face. Surely there's nothing that can't wait."

Jeph nodded after a moment. "Arlen!" he called. When the boy showed his sullen face, he asked, "How much is old Hog charging to see the Jongleur?"

"Nothing," Arlen said quickly, not wanting to give his father reason to refuse. "On account of how I helped carry stuff from the Messenger's cart." It wasn't exactly true, and there was a good chance Hog would be angry that he forgot to tell people, but maybe if he spread word on the walk over, he could bring enough people for his two credits at the store to get him in.

"Old Hog always acts generous right after the Messenger comes," Norine said.

"Ought to, after how he's been fleecing us all winter," Silvy replied.

"All right, Arlen, you can go," Jeph said. "Meet me in the Cluster afterwards."

The walk to Town Square took about two hours if you followed the path. Nothing more than a wagon track of hard-packed dirt that Jeph and a few other locals kept clear, it went well out of the way to the bridge at the shallowest part of the brook. Nimble and quick, Arlen could cut the trip in half by skipping across the slick rocks jutting from the water.

Today, he needed the extra time more than ever, so he could make stops along the way. He raced along the muddy bank at breakneck speed, dodging treacherous roots and scrub with the sure-footed confidence of one who had followed the trail countless times.

He popped back out of the woods as he passed the farmhouses on the way, but there was no one to be found. Everyone was either out in the fields or back at the Cluster helping out.

It was getting close to high sun when he reached Fishing Hole. A few of the Fishers had their boats out on the small pond, but Arlen didn't see much point in shouting to them. Otherwise, the Hole was deserted, too.

He was feeling glum by the time he got to Town Square. Hog might have seemed nicer than usual yesterday, but Arlen had seen what he was like when someone cost him profit. There was no way he was going to let Arlen see the Jongleur for just two credits. He'd be lucky if the storekeep didn't take a switch to him.

But when he reached the square, he found over three hundred people gathered from all over the Brook. There were Fishers and Marshes and Boggins and Bales. Not to mention the town locals, Squares, Tailors, Millers, Bakers, and all. None had come from Southwatch, of course. Folk there shunned Jongleurs.

"Arlen, my boy!" Hog called, seeing him approach. "I've saved you a spot up front, and you'll go home tonight with a sack of salt! Well done!"

Arlen looked at him curiously, until he saw Ragen, standing next to Hog. The Messenger winked at him.

"Thank you," Arlen said, when Hog went off to mark another arrival in his ledger. Dasy and Catrin were selling food and ale for the show.

"People deserve a show," Ragen said with a shrug. "But not without clearing it with your Tender, it seems." He pointed to Keerin, who was deep in conversation with Tender Harral.

"Don't be selling any of that Plague nonsense to my flock!" Harral said, poking Keerin hard in the chest. He was twice the Jongleur's weight, and none of it fat.

"Nonsense?" Keerin asked, paling. "In Miln, the Tenders will string up any Jongleur that doesn't tell of the Plague!"

"I don't care what they do in the Free Cities," Harral said. "These're good people, and they have it hard enough without you telling 'em their suffering's because they ent pious enough!"

"What . . . ?" Arlen began, but Keerin broke off, heading to the center of the square.

"Best find a seat quick," Ragen advised.

As Hog promised, Arlen got a seat right in front, in the area usually left for the younger children. The others looked on enviously, and Arlen felt very special. It was rare for anyone to envy him.

The Jongleur was tall, like all Milnese, dressed in a patchwork of bright colors that looked like they were stolen from the dyer's scrap bin. He had a wispy goatee, the same carrot color as his hair, but the mustache never quite met the beard, and the whole thing looked like it might wash off with a good scrubbing. Everyone, especially the women, talked in wonder about his bright hair and green eyes.

As people continued to file in, Keerin paced back and forth, juggling his colored wooden balls and telling jokes, warming to the crowd. When Hog gave the signal, he took his lute and began to play, singing in a strong, high voice. People clapped along to the songs they didn't know, but whenever he played one that was sung in the Brook, the whole crowd sang along, drowning out the Jongleur and not seeming to care. Arlen didn't mind; he was singing just as loud as the others.

After the music came acrobatics, and magic tricks. Along the way, Keerin made a few jests about husbands that had the women shrieking with laughter while the men frowned, and a few about wives that had the men slapping their thighs as the women glared.

Finally, the Jongleur paused and held up his hands for silence. There was a murmur from the crowd, and parents nudged their youngest children forward, wanting them to hear. Little Jessi Boggin, who was only five, climbed right into Arlen's lap for a better view. Arlen had given her family a few pups from one of Jeph's dogs a few weeks ago, and now she clung to him whenever he was near. He held her as Keerin began the Tale of the Return, his high voice dropping into a deep, booming call that carried far into the crowd.

"The world was not always as you see it," the Jongleur told the children. "Oh, no. There was a time when humanity lived in balance with the demons. Those early years are called the Age of Ignorance. Does anyone know why?" He looked around the children in front, and several raised their hands.

"Because there wasn't any wards?" a girl asked, when Keerin pointed to her.

"That's right!" the Jongleur said, turning a somersault that brought squeals of glee from the children. "The Age of Ignorance was a scary time for us, but there weren't as many demons then, and they couldn't kill *every*one. Much like today, humans built what they could during the day, and the demons would tear it down each night.

"As we struggled to survive," Keerin went on, "we adapted, learning how to hide food and animals from the demons, and how to avoid them." He looked around as if in terror, then ran behind one child, cringing. "We lived in holes in the ground, so they couldn't find us."

"Like bunnies?" Jessi asked, laughing.

"Just so!" Keerin called, putting a twitching finger up behind each ear and hopping about, wriggling his nose.

"We lived any way we could," he went on, "until we discovered writing. From there, it wasn't long before we had learned that some writing could hold the corelings back. What writing is that?" he asked, cupping an ear.

"Wards!" everyone cried in unison.

"Correct!" the Jongleur congratulated with a flip. "With wards, we could protect ourselves from the corelings, and we practiced them, getting better and better. More and more wards were discovered, until someone learned one that did more than hold the demons back. It hurt them." The children gasped, and Arlen, even though he had heard almost this same performance every year for as long as he could remember, found himself sucking in his breath. What he wouldn't give to know such a ward!

"The demons did not take well to this advancement," Keerin said with a grin. "They were used to us running and hiding, and when we turned and fought, they fought back. Hard. Thus began the First Demon War, and the second age, the Age of the Deliverer.

"The Deliverer was a man called upon by the Creator to lead our armies, and with him to lead us, we were winning!" He thrust his fist into the air and the children cheered. It was infectious, and Arlen tickled Jessi with glee.

"As our magics and tactics improved," Keerin said, "humans began to live longer, and our numbers swelled. Our armies grew larger, even as the number of demons dwindled. There was hope that the corelings would be vanquished once and for all."

The Jongleur paused then, and his face took on a serious expression. "Then," he said, "without warning, the demons stopped coming. Never in the history of the world had a night passed without the corelings. Now night after night went by with no sign of them, and we were baffled." He scratched his head in mock confusion. "Many believed that the demon losses in the war had been too great, and that they had given up the fight, cowering with fright in the Core." He huddled away from the children, hissing like a cat and shaking as if with fear. Some of the children got into the act, growling at him menacingly.

"The Deliverer," Keerin said, "who had seen the demons fight fearlessly every night, doubted this, but as months passed without sign of the creatures, his armies began to fragment.

"Humanity rejoiced in their victory over the corelings for years," Keerin went on. He picked up his lute and played a lively tune, dancing about. "But as the years passed without the common foe, the brotherhood of men grew strained, and then faded. For the first time, we fought against one another." The Jongleur's voice turned ominous. "As war sparked, the Deliverer was called upon by all sides to lead, but he shouted, 'I'll not fight 'gainst men while a single demon remains in the Core!' He turned his back, and left the lands as armies marched and all the land fell into chaos.

"From these great wars arose powerful nations," he said, turning the tune into something uplifting, "and mankind spread far and wide, covering the entire world. The Age of the Deliverer came to a close, and the Age of Science began.

"The Age of Science," the Jongleur said, "was our greatest time, but nestled in that greatness was our biggest mistake. Can any here tell me what it was?" The older children knew, but Keerin signaled them to hold back and let the young ones answer.

"Because we forgot magic," Gim Cutter said, wiping his nose with the back of his hand.

"Right you are!" Keerin said, snapping his fingers. "We learned a great deal about how the world worked, about medicine and machines, but we forgot magic, and worse, we forgot the corelings. After three thousand years, no one believed they had ever even existed.

"Which is why," he said grimly, "we were unprepared when they came back.

"The demons had multiplied over the centuries, as the world forgot them. Then, three hundred years ago, they rose from the Core one night in massive numbers to take it back.

"Whole cities were destroyed that first night, as the corelings celebrated their return. Men fought back, but even the great weapons of the Age of Science were poor defense against the demons. The Age of Science came to a close, and the Age of Destruction took hold.

"The Second Demon War had begun."

In his mind's eye, Arlen saw that night, saw the cities burning as people fled in terror, only to be savaged by the waiting corelings. He saw men sacrifice themselves to buy time for their families to flee, saw women take claws meant for their children. Most of all, he saw the corelings dance, cavorting in savage glee as blood ran from their teeth and talons.

Keerin moved forward even as the children drew back in fear. "The war lasted for years, with people slaughtered at every turn. Without the Deliverer to lead them, they were no match for the corelings. Overnight, the great nations fell, and the accumulated knowledge of the Age of Science burned as flame demons frolicked.

"Scholars desperately searched the wreckages of libraries for answers. The old science was no help, but they found salvation at last in stories once considered fantasy and superstition. Men began to draw clumsy symbols in the dirt, preventing the corelings from approaching. The ancient wards held power still, but the shaking hands that drew them often made mistakes, and they were paid for dearly.

"Those that survived gathered people to them, protecting them through the long nights. Those men became the first Warders, who protect us to this very day." The Jongleur pointed to the crowd. "So the next time you see a Warder, thank him, because you owe him your life."

That was a variation on the story Arlen had never heard. Warders? In Tibbet's Brook, everyone learned warding as soon as they were old enough to draw with a stick. Many had poor aptitude for it, but Arlen couldn't imagine anyone not taking the time to learn the basic forbiddings against flame, rock, swamp, water, wind, and wood demons.

"So now we stay safe within our wards," Keerin said, "letting the demons have their pleasures outside. Messengers," he gestured to Ragen, "the bravest of all men, travel from city to city for us, bringing news and escorting men and goods."

He walked about, his eyes hard as he met the frightened looks of the children. "But we are strong," he said. "Aren't we?"

The children nodded, but their eyes were still wide with fear.

"What?" he asked, putting a hand to his ear.

"Yes!" the crowd cried.

"When the Deliverer comes again, will we be ready?" he asked. "Will the demons learn to fear us once more?"

"Yes!" the crowd roared.

"They can't hear you!" the Jongleur shouted.

"Yes!" the people screamed, punching fists in the air; Arlen most of all. Jessi imitated him, punching the air and shrieking as if she were a demon herself. The Jongleur bowed and, when the crowd quieted, lifted his lute and led them into another song.

As promised, Arlen left Town Square with a sack of salt. Enough to last weeks, even with Norine and Marea to feed. It was still unmilled, but Arlen knew his parents would be happy to pound the salt themselves, rather than pay Hog extra for the service. Most would, really, but old Hog never gave them a choice, milling the salt as soon as it came and tacking on the extra cost.

Arlen had a spring in his step as he walked down the road toward the Cluster. It wasn't until he passed the tree that Cholie had hung from that Arlen's spirits fell. He thought again about what Ragen had said about fighting corelings, and what his father had said about prudence.

He thought his father probably had the right of it: Hide when you can and fight when you must. Even Ragen seemed to agree with that philosophy. But Arlen couldn't shake the feeling that hiding hurt people too, in ways they couldn't see.

He met his father in the Cluster and earned a clap on the back when he showed his prize. He spent the rest of the afternoon running to and fro, helping rebuild. Already, another house was repaired and would be warded by nightfall. In a few more weeks, the Cluster would be fully rebuilt, and that was in everyone's interest, if they wanted enough wood to last the winter.

"I promised Selia I'd throw in here for the next few days," Jeph said as they packed the cart that afternoon. "You'll be the man of the farm while I'm gone. You'll have to check the ward-posts and weed the fields. I saw you show Norine your chores this morning. She can handle the yard, and Marea can help your mother inside."

"All right," Arlen said. Weeding the fields and checking the posts was hard work, but the trust made him proud.

"I'm counting on you, Arlen," Jeph said.

"I won't let you down," Arlen promised.

The next few days passed with little event. Silvy still cried at times, but there was work to do, and she never once complained of the additional mouths to feed. Norine took to caring for the animals naturally, and even Marea began to come out of her shell a bit, helping with the sweeping and cooking, working the loom after supper. Soon she was taking turns with Norine in the yard. Both women seemed determined to do their share, though their faces, too, grew pained and wistful whenever there was a lull in the work.

Arlen's hands blistered from pulling weeds, and his back and shoulders ached at the end of each day, but he didn't complain. The only one of his new responsibilities he enjoyed was work-ing on the wardposts. Arlen had always loved warding, master-ing the basic defensive symbols before most children began learning at all, and more complex wardnets soon after. Jeph didn't even check his work anymore. Arlen's hand was steadier than his father's. Warding wasn't the same as attacking a demon with a spear, but it was fighting in its own way.

Jeph arrived at dusk each day, and Silvy had water from the well waiting for him to wash off. Arlen helped Norine and Marea lock up the animals, and then they had supper.

On the fifth day, a wind kicked up in the late afternoon that sent dust whorls dancing in the yard, and had the barn door banging. Arlen could smell rain coming, and the darkening sky confirmed it. He hoped Jeph saw the signs, too, and came back early, or stayed on in the Cluster. Dark clouds meant an early dusk, and early dusk sometimes meant corelings before full sunset.

Arlen abandoned the fields and began to help the women herd the spooked animals back into the barn. Silvy was out as well, battening down the cellar doors and making sure the wardposts around the day pens were lashed tight. There was little time to spare when Jeph's cart came into sight. The sky was darkening quickly, and already there was no direct sun. Corelings could rise at any moment.

"No time to unhitch the cart," Jeph called, cracking the whip to drive Missy faster toward the barn. "We'll do it in the morning. Everyone in the house, now!" Silvy and the other women complied, heading inside.

"We can do it if we hurry," Arlen yelled over the roar of the wind as he ran after his father. Missy would be in foul spirits for days if she spent the night harnessed.

Jeph shook his head. "It's too dark already! A night hitched won't kill her."

"Lock me in the barn, then," Arlen said. "I'll unhitch her and wait out the storm with the animals."

"Do as you're told, Arlen!" Jeph shouted. He leapt from the cart and grabbed the boy by the arm, half dragging him out of the barn.

The two of them pulled the doors shut and threw the bar as lightning split the sky. The wards painted on the barn doors were illuminated for a moment, a reminder of what was to come. The air was pregnant with the promise of rain.

They ran for the house, scanning the way before them for the mist that would herald the rising. For the moment, the way was clear. Marea held the door open, and they darted inside, just as the first fat drops of rain stirred the dust of the yard.

Marea was pulling the door closed when a howl sounded from the yard. Everyone froze.

"The dog!" Marea cried, covering her mouth. "I left him tied to the fence!"

"Leave him," Jeph said. "Close the door."

"What?" Arlen cried, incredulous. He whirled to face his father.

"The way is still clear!" Marea cried, and darted out of the house.

"Marea, no!" Silvy cried, running out after her.

Arlen, too, ran for the door, but not before Jeph grabbed the shoulder straps of his overalls and yanked him backward. "Stay inside!" he ordered, moving to the door.

Arlen stumbled back a moment, then ran forward again. Jeph

and Norine were out on the porch, but stayed within the line of the outer wards. By the time Arlen reached the porch, the dog was running past him into the house, the rope still trailing from its neck.

Out in the yard, wind howled, turning the drops of rain into stinging insects. He saw Marea and his mother running back toward the house just as the demons began to rise. As always, flame demons came first, their misty forms seeping from the ground. The smallest of corelings, they crouched on all fours as they coalesced, barely eighteen inches tall at the shoulder. Their eyes, nostrils, and mouths glowed with a smoky light.

"Run, Silvy!" Jeph screamed. "Run!"

It seemed that they would make it, but then Marea stumbled and went down. Silvy turned to help her, and in that moment the first coreling solidified. Arlen moved to run to his mother, but Norine's hand clamped hard on his arm, holding him fast.

"Don't be stupid," the woman hissed.

"Get up!" Silvy demanded, yanking Marea's arm.

"My ankle!" Marea cried. "I can't! Go on without me!"

"Like night I will!" Silvy growled. "Jeph!" she called. "Help us!"

By then, corelings were forming all over the yard. Jeph stood frozen as they took note of the women and shrieked with pleasure, darting toward them.

"Let *go!*" Arlen growled, stomping hard on Norine's foot. She howled, and Arlen yanked his arm free. He grabbed the nearest weapon he could find, a wooden milk bucket, and ran out into the yard.

"Arlen, *no!*" Jeph cried, but Arlen was done listening to him.

A flame demon, no bigger than a large cat, leapt atop Silvy's back, and she screamed as talons raked deep lines in her flesh, leaving the back of her dress a bloody tatter. From its perch, the coreling spat fire into Marea's face. The woman shrieked as her skin melted and her hair ignited.

Arlen was there an instant later, swinging the bucket with all his strength. It broke apart as it struck, but the demon was knocked from his mother's back. She stumbled, but Arlen was there to support her. More flame demons closed in on them, even as wind demons began to stretch their wings, and, a dozen yards off, a rock demon began to take form.

Silvy groaned, but she got to her feet. Arlen pulled her away from Marea and her agonized wails, but the way back to the house was blocked by flame demons. The rock demon caught sight of them, too, and charged. A few wind demons, preparing to take off, got in the massive beast's way, and its talons swept them aside as easily as a scythe cut through cornstalks. They tumbled broken through the air, and flame demons set on them, tearing them to pieces.

It was only a moment's distraction, but Arlen took it, pulling his mother away from the house. The barn was blocked as well, but the path to the day pen was still clear, if they could keep ahead of the corelings. Silvy was screaming, out of fear or pain Arlen didn't know, but she stumbled along, keeping pace even in her wide skirts.

As he broke into a run, so too did the flame demons half surrounding them. The rain began to fall harder, and the wind howled. Lightning split the sky, illuminating their pursuers and the day pen, so close, yet still too far.

The dust of the yard was slick with the growing wet, but fear granted them agility, and they kept their feet under them. The rock demon's footfalls were as loud as the thunder as it charged, growing ever closer, making the ground shake with its stride.

Arlen skidded to a stop at the pens and fumbled with the latch. The flame demons caught up in that split second, coming in range to use their deadliest weapon. They spat flame, and Arlen and his mother were struck. The blast was weakened by distance, but still he felt his clothes ignite, and smelled burning hair. A flare of pain washed over him, but he ignored it, finally getting the gate to the pen open. He had started to take his mother inside when another flame demon leapt on her, claws digging deep into her chest. With a yank, Arlen pulled her into the pen. As they crossed the wards, Silvy passed through easily, but magic flared and the coreling was thrown back. Its claws, hooked deep in her, came free in a spray of blood and flesh.

Their clothes were still burning. Wrapping Silvy in his arms, Arlen threw them both to the ground, taking the brunt of the impact himself, and then rolled them into the mud, extinguishing the flames.

There was no chance to close the gate. The demons ringed the pen now, pounding at the wardnet, sending flares of magic skittering along the web of wards. But the gate didn't really matter.

Nor did the fence. So long as the wardposts were intact, they were safe from the corelings.

But not from the weather. The rain became a cold pour, whipping at them in cutting sheets. Silvy could not rise again after the fall. Blood and mud caked her, and Arlen didn't know if she could survive her wounds and the rain together.

He stumbled over to the slop trough and kicked it over, sloshing the unfinished remnants of the pigs' dinner to rot in the mud. Arlen could see the rock demon pounding at the wardnet, but the magic held, and the demon could not pass. Between the flashes of lightning and the spurts of demon flame, he caught sight of Marea, buried under a swarm of flame demons, each tearing off a piece and dancing away to feast.

The rock demon gave up a moment later, stomping over and grabbing Marea by the leg in a massive talon the way a cruel man might grab a cat. Flame demons scattered as the rock demon swung the woman into the air. She let out a hoarse gasp, and Arlen was horrified to discover she was still alive. He screamed, and considered trying to dart from the wardnet and get to her. But then the demon brought her crashing down to the ground with a sickening crunch.

Arlen turned away before the creature could begin to eat, his tears washed away by the pouring rain. Dragging the trough to Silvy, he tore the lining from her skirt and let it soak in the rain. He brushed the mud from her cuts as best he could, and wadded more lining into them. It was hardly clean, but cleaner than pig mud.

She was shivering, so he lay against her for warmth, and pulled the stinking trough over them as a shield from the downpour, and the sight of the leering demons.

There was one more flash of lightning as he lowered the wood. The last thing he saw was his father, still standing frozen on the porch.

If it was you out there . . . or your mam . . . Arlen remembered him saying. But for all his promises, it seemed that nothing could make Jeph Bales fight.

The night passed with interminable slowness; there was no hope of sleep. Raindrops drummed a steady beat on the trough, spattering them with the remains of the slop that clung to the inside. The mud they lay in was cold, and stank of pig droppings.

Silvy shivered in her delirium, and Arlen clutched her tightly, willing what little heat he had into her. His own hands and feet were numb.

Despair crept over him, and he wept into his mother's shoulder. But she groaned and patted his hand, and that simple, instinctive gesture pulled him free of the terror and disillusionment and pain.

He had fought a demon, and lived. He stood in a yard full of them, and survived. Corelings might be immortal, but they could be outmaneuvered. They could be outsped.

And as the rock demon had shown when it swept the other coreling out of the way, they could be hurt.

But what difference did it make in a world where men like Jeph wouldn't stand up to the corelings, not even for their own families? What hope did any of them have?

He stared at the blackness around him for hours, but in his mind's eye all he saw was his father's face, staring at them from the safety of the wards.

The rain tapered off before dawn. Arlen used the break in the weather as a chance to lift the trough, but he immediately regretted it as the collected heat the wood had stored was lost. He pulled it down again, but stole peeks until the sky began to brighten.

Most of the corelings had faded away by the time it was light enough to see, but a few stragglers remained as the sky went from indigo to lavender. He lifted the trough and clambered to his feet, trying vainly to brush off the slime and muck that clung to him.

His arm was stiff, and stung when he flexed it. He looked down and saw that the skin was bright red where the firespit had struck. *The night in the mud did one good thing,* he thought, knowing his and his mother's burns would have been far worse had they not been packed in the cold muck all night.

As the last flame demons in the yard began to turn insubstantial, Arlen strode from the pen, heading for the barn.

"Arlen, no!" a cry came from the porch. Arlen looked up, and saw Jeph there, wrapped in a blanket, keeping watch from the safety of the porch wards. "It's not full dawn yet! Wait!"

Arlen ignored him, walking to the barn and opening the doors. Missy looked thoroughly unhappy, still hitched to the cart, but she would make it to Town Square.

A hand grabbed his arm as he led the horse out. "Are you trying to get yourself killed?" Jeph demanded. "You mind me, boy!"

Arlen tore his arm away, refusing to look his father in the eye. "Mam needs to see Coline Trigg," he said.

"She's alive?" Jeph asked incredulously, his head snapping over to where the woman lay in the mud.

"No thanks to you," Arlen said. "I'm taking her to Town Square."

"*We're* taking her," Jeph corrected, rushing over to lift his wife and carry her to the cart. Leaving Norine to tend the animals and seek out poor Marea's remains, they headed off down the road to town.

Silvy was bathed in sweat, and while her burns seemed no worse than Arlen's, the deep lines the flame demons' talons had dug still oozed blood, the flesh an ugly swollen red.

"Arlen, I . . ." Jeph began as they rode, reaching a shaking hand toward his son. Arlen drew back, looking away, and Jeph recoiled as if burned.

Arlen knew his father was ashamed. It was just as Ragen had said. Maybe Jeph even hated himself, as Cholie had. Still, Arlen could find no sympathy. His mother had paid the price for Jeph's cowardice.

They rode the rest of the way in silence.

Coline Trigg's two-story house, in Town Square, was one of the largest in the Brook, and filled with beds. In addition to her family upstairs, Coline always had at least one person in the sickbeds on the ground floor.

Coline was a short woman with a large nose and no chin. She was not yet thirty, but six children had made her thick around the middle. Her clothes always smelled of burnt weeds, and her cures usually involved some type of foul-tasting tea. The people of Tibbet's Brook made fun of that tea, but every one of them drank it gratefully when they took a chill.

The Herb Gatherer took one look at Silvy and had Arlen and his father bring her right inside. She asked no questions, which was just as well, as neither Arlen nor Jeph knew what they would say if she did. As she cut at each wound, squeezing out a sickly brown pus, the air filled with a rotten stench. She cleaned the drained wounds with water and ground herbs, then sewed them shut. Jeph turned green, and brought his hand to his mouth suddenly.

"Out of here with that!" Coline barked, sending Jeph from the room with a pointed finger. As Jeph scurried out of the house, she looked to Arlen.

"You, too?" she demanded. Arlen shook his head. Coline stared at him a moment, then nodded in approval. "You're braver than your father," she said. "Fetch the mortar and pestle. I'm going to teach you to make a balm for burns."

Never taking her eyes from her work, Coline talked Arlen through the countless jars and pouches in her pharmacy, directing him to each ingredient and explaining how to mix them. She kept to her grisly work as Arlen applied the balm to his mother's burns.

Finally, when Silvy's wounds were all tended, she turned to inspect Arlen. He protested at first, but the balm did its work, and only as the coolness spread along his arms did he realize how much his burns had stung.

"Will she be all right?" Arlen asked, looking at his mother. She seemed to be breathing normally, but the flesh around her wounds was an ugly color, and that stench of rot was still thick in the air.

"I don't know," Coline said. She wasn't one to honey her words. "I've never seen anyone with wounds so severe. Usually, if the corelings get that close . . ."

"They kill you," Jeph said from the doorway. "They would have killed Silvy, too, if not for Arlen." He stepped into the room, his eyes down. "Arlen taught me something last night, Coline," Jeph said. "He taught me fear is our enemy, more than the corelings ever were."

Jeph put his hands on his son's shoulders and looked into his eyes. "I won't fail you again," he promised. Arlen nodded and looked away. He wanted to believe it was so, but his thoughts kept returning to the sight of his father on the porch, frozen with terror.

Jeph went over to Silvy, gripping her clammy hand in his own. She was still sweating, and thrashed in her drugged sleep now and then.

"Will she die?" Jeph asked.

The Herb Gatherer blew out a long breath. "I'm a fair hand at setting bones," she said, "and delivering children. I can chase a fever away and ward a chill. I can even cleanse a demon wound, if it's still fresh." She shook her head. "But this is demon fever.

I've given her herbs to dull the pain and help her sleep, but you'll need a better Gatherer than I to brew a cure."

"Who else is there?" Jeph asked. "You're all the Brook has."

"The woman who taught me," Coline said, "Old Mey Friman. She lives on the outskirts of Sunny Pasture, two days from here. If anyone can cure it, she can, but you'd best hurry. The fever will spread quickly, and if you take too long, even Old Mey won't be able to help you."

"How do we find her?" Jeph demanded.

"You can't really get lost," Coline said. "There's only the one road. Just don't turn at the fork where it goes through the woods, unless you want to spend weeks on the road to Miln. That Messenger left for the Pasture a few hours ago, but he had some stops in the Brook first. If you hurry, you might catch him. Messengers carry their own wards with them. If you find him, you'll be able to keep moving right until dusk instead of stopping for succor. The Messenger could cut your trip in twain."

"We'll find him," Jeph said, "whatever it takes." His voice took on a determined edge, and Arlen began to hope.

A strange sense of longing pulled at Arlen as he watched Tibbet's Brook recede into the distance from the back of the cart. For the first time, he was going to be more than a day's travel from home. He was going to see another town! A week ago, an adventure like that was his greatest dream. But now all he dreamed was that things could go back to the way they were.

Back when the farm was safe.

Back when his mother was well.

Back when he didn't know his father was a coward.

Coline had promised to send one of her boys up to the farm to let Norine know they would likely be gone a week or more, and to help tend the animals and check the wards while they were away. The neighbors would throw in, but Norine's loss was too raw for her to face the nights alone.

The Herb Gatherer had also given them a crude map, carefully rolled and slipped into a protective hide tube. Paper was a rarity in the Brook, and not given away lightly. Arlen was fascinated by the map, and studied it for hours, even though he couldn't read the few words labeling the places. Neither Arlen nor his father had letters.

The map marked the way to Sunny Pasture, and what lay

along the road, but the distances were vague. There were farms marked along the way where they could beg succor, but there was no way to tell how far apart they were.

His mother slept fitfully, sodden with sweat. Sometimes she spoke or cried out, but her words made little sense. Arlen daubed her with wet cloth and made her drink the sharp tea as the Herb Gatherer had instructed him, but it seemed to do little good.

Late in the afternoon, they approached the house of Harl Tanner, a farmer who lived on the outskirts of the Brook. Harl's farm was only a couple of hours past the Cluster by the Woods, but by the time Arlen and his father had gotten under way, it was midafternoon.

Arlen remembered seeing Harl and his three daughters at the summer solstice festival each year, though they had been absent since the corelings had taken Harl's wife, two summers past. Harl had become a recluse, and his daughters with him. Even the tragedy in the Cluster had not brought them out.

Three-quarters of the Tanner fields were blackened and scorched; only those closest to the house were warded and sown. A gaunt milking cow chewed cud in the muddy yard, and ribs showed clearly on the goat tied up by the chicken coop.

The Tanners' home was a single story of piled stones, held together with packed mud and clay. The larger stones were painted with faded wards. Arlen thought them clumsy, but they had lasted thus far, it seemed. The roof was uneven, with short, squat wardposts poking up through the rotting thatch. One side of the house connected to the small barn, its windows boarded and its door half off the hinges. Across the yard was the big barn, looking even worse. The wards might hold, but it looked ready to collapse on its own.

"I've never seen Harl's place before," Jeph said.

"Me neither," Arlen lied. Few people apart from Messengers had reason to head up the road past the Cluster by the Woods, and those who lived up that way were sources of great speculation in Town Square. Arlen had snuck off to see Crazy Man Tanner's farm more than once. It was the farthest he had ever been from home. Getting back before dusk had meant hours of running as fast as he could.

One time, a few months before, he almost didn't make it. He had been trying to catch a glimpse of Harl's eldest daughter,

Ilain. The other boys said she had the biggest bubbies in the Brook, and he wanted to see for himself. He waited one day, and saw her come running out of the house, crying. She was beautiful in her sadness, and Arlen had wanted to go comfort her, even though she was eight summers older than him. He hadn't been so bold, but he'd watched her longer than was wise, and almost paid a heavy price for it when the sun began to set.

A mangy dog began barking as they approached the farm, and a young girl came out onto the porch, watching them with sad eyes.

"We might have to succor here," Jeph said.

"It's still hours till dark," Arlen said, shaking his head. "If we don't catch Ragen by then, the map says there's another farm up by where the road forks to the Free Cities."

Jeph peered over Arlen's shoulder at the map. "That's a long way," he said.

"Mam can't wait," Arlen said. "We won't make it all the way today, but every hour is an hour closer to her cure."

Jeph looked back at Silvy, bathed in sweat, then up at the sun, and nodded. They waved at the girl on the porch, but did not stop.

They covered a great distance in the next few hours, but found no sign of the Messenger or another farm. Jeph looked up at the orange sky.

"It will be full dark in less than two hours," he said. "We have to turn back. If we hurry, we can make it back to Harl's in time."

"The farm could be right around that next bend," Arlen argued. "We'll find it."

"We don't know that," Jeph said, spitting over the side of the cart. "The map ent clear. We turn back while we still can, and no arguing."

Arlen's eyes widened in disbelief. "We'll lose half a day that way, not to mention the night. Mam might die in that time!" he cried.

Jeph looked back at his wife, sweating in her bundled blankets, breathing in short fits. Sadly, he looked around at the lengthening shadows, and suppressed a shiver. "If we're caught out after dark," he replied quietly, "we'll all die."

Arlen was shaking his head before his father finished, refusing to accept it. "We could . . ." he floundered. "We could draw wards in the dirt," he said at last. "All around the cart."

"And if a breeze comes along and mars them?" his father asked. "What then?"

"The farm could be just over the next hill!" Arlen insisted.

"Or it could be twenty more miles down the road," his father shot back, "or burned down a year ago. Who knows what's happened since that map was drawn?"

"Are you saying Mam ent worth the risk?" Arlen accused.

"Don't you tell me what she's worth!" his father screamed, nearly bowling the boy over. "I've loved her all my life! I know better than you! But I'm not going to risk all three of us! She can last the night. She *has* to!"

With that, he pulled hard on the reins, stopping the cart and turning it about. He cracked the leather hard into Missy's flanks, and sent her leaping back down the road. The animal, frightened by the coming dark, responded with a frantic pace.

Arlen turned back toward Silvy, swallowing bitter anger. He watched his mother bounce around as the wheels ran over stones and dips, not reacting at all to the bumpy ride. Whatever his father thought, Arlen knew her chances had just been cut in half.

The sun was nearly set when they reached the lonely farmhouse. Jeph and Missy seemed to share a panicked terror, and they screamed their haste as one. Arlen had leapt into the back of the cart to try and keep his mother from being thrown about by the widely jolting ride. He held her tight, taking many of the bruises and bashes for her.

But not all; he could feel Coline's careful stitches giving, the wounds oozing open again. If the demon fever didn't claim her, there was a good chance the ride would.

Jeph ran the cart right up to the porch, shouting, "Harl! We seek succor!"

The door opened almost immediately, even before they could get out of the cart. A man in worn overalls came out, a long pitchfork in hand. Harl was thin and tough, like dried meat. He was followed by Ilain, the sturdy young woman holding a stout metal-headed shovel. The last time Arlen saw her, she had been crying and terrified, but there was no terror in her eyes now. She ignored the crawling shadows as she approached the cart.

Harl nodded as Jeph lifted Silvy out of the cart. "Get her inside," he ordered, and Jeph hurried to comply, letting a deep breath out as he crossed the wards.

"Open the big barn door!" he told Ilain. "That cart won't fit in the little'un." Ilain gathered her skirts and ran. He turned to Arlen. "Drive the cart to the barn, boy! Quick!"

Arlen did as he was told. "No time to unhitch her," the farmer said. "She'll have to do." It was the second night in a row. Arlen wondered if Missy would ever get unhitched.

Harl and Ilain quickly shut the barn door and checked the wards. "What are you waiting for?" the man roared at Arlen. "Run for the house! They'll be here in a moment!"

He had barely spoken the words when the demons began to rise. He and Arlen sprinted for the house as spindly, clawed arms and horned heads seemed to grow right out of the ground.

They dodged left and right around the rising death, adrenaline and fear giving them agility and speed. The first corelings to solidify, a group of lissome flame demons, gave chase, gaining on them. As Arlen and Ilain ran on, Harl turned and hurled his pitchfork into their midst.

The weapon struck the lead demon full in the chest, knocking it into its fellows, but even the skin of a tiny flame demon was too knobbed and tough for a pitchfork to pierce. The creature picked up the tool in its claws and spat a gout of flame upon it, setting the wooden haft alight, then tossed it aside.

But though the coreling hadn't been hurt, the throw delayed them. The demons rushed forward, but as Harl leapt onto the porch, they came to an abrupt halt, slamming into a line of wards that stopped them as surely as if they had run into a brick wall. As the magic flared brightly and hurled them back into the yard, Harl rushed into the house. He slammed and bolted the door, throwing his back against the portal.

"Creator be praised," he said weakly, panting and pale.

The air inside Harl's farmhouse was thick and hot, stinking of must and waste. The buggy reeds on the floor absorbed some of the water that made it past the thatch, but they were far from fresh. Two dogs and several cats shared the home, forcing everyone to step carefully. A stone pot hung in the fireplace, adding to the mix the sour scent of a stew perpetually cooking, added to as it diminished. A patchwork curtain in one corner gave a touch of privacy for the chamber pot.

Arlen did his best to redo Silvy's bandages, and then Ilain and her sister Beni put her in their room, while Harl's youngest,

Renna, set another two cracked wooden bowls at the table for Arlen and his father.

There were only three rooms, one shared by the girls, another for Harl, and the common room where they cooked and ate and worked. A ragged curtain divided the room, partitioning off the area for cooking and eating. A warded door in the common room led to the small barn.

"Renna, take Arlen and check the wards while the men talk and Beni and I get supper ready," Ilain said.

Renna nodded, taking Arlen's hand and pulling him along. She was almost ten, close to Arlen's age of eleven, and pretty beneath the smudges of dirt on her face. She wore a plain shift, worn and carefully mended, and her brown hair was tied back with a ragged strip of cloth, though many locks had freed themselves to fall about her round face.

"This one's scuffed," the girl commented, pointing to a ward on one of the sills. "One of the cats must have stepped on it." Taking a stick of charcoal from the kit, she carefully traced the line where it had been broken.

"That's no good," Arlen said. "The lines ent smooth anymore. That weakens the ward. You should draw it over."

"I'm not allowed to draw a fresh one," Renna whispered. "I'm supposed to tell Father or Ilain if there's one I can't fix."

"I can do it," Arlen said, taking the stick. He carefully wiped clean the old ward and drew a new one, his arm moving with quick confidence. Stepping back as he finished, he looked around the window, and then swiftly replaced several others as well.

While he worked, Harl caught sight of them and started to rise nervously, but a motion and a few confident words from Jeph brought him back to his seat.

Arlen took a moment to admire his work. "Even a rock demon won't get through that," he said proudly. He turned, and found Renna staring at him. "What?" he asked.

"You're taller than I remember," the girl said, looking down and smiling shyly.

"Well, it's been a couple of years," Arlen replied, not knowing what else to say. When they finished their sweep, Harl called his daughter over. He and Renna spoke softly to one another, and Arlen caught her looking at him once or twice, but he couldn't hear what was said.

Dinner was a tough stew of parsnip and corn with a meat Arlen couldn't identify, but it was filling enough. While they ate, they told their tale.

"Wish you'da come to us first," Harl said when they finished. "We been t'Old Mey Friman plenty times. Closer'n going all the way to Town Square t'see Trigg. If it took you two hours of cracking the whip t'get back to us, you'da reached Mack Pasture's farm soon, you pressed on. Old Mey, she's only an hour-so past that. She never did cotton to living in town. You'd really whipped that mare, you mighta made it tonight."

Arlen slammed down his spoon. All eyes at the table turned to him, but he didn't even notice, so focused was he on his father.

Jeph could not weather that glare for long. He hung his head. "There was no way to know," he said miserably.

Ilain touched his shoulder. "Don't blame yourself for being cautious," she said. She looked at Arlen, reprimand in her eyes. "You'll understand when you're older," she told him.

Arlen rose sharply and stomped away from the table. He went through the curtain and curled up by a window, watching the demons through a broken slat in the shutters. Again and again they tried and failed to pierce the wards, but Arlen didn't feel protected by the magic. He felt imprisoned by it.

"Take Arlen into the barn and play," Harl ordered his younger daughters after the rest had finished eating. "Ilain will take the bowls. Let'cher elders talk."

Beni and Renna rose as one, bouncing out of the curtain. Arlen was in no mood to play, but the girls didn't let him speak, yanking him to his feet and out the door into the barn.

Beni lit a cracked lantern, casting the barn in a dull glow. Harl had two old cows, four goats, a pig with eight sucklings, and six chickens. All were gaunt and bony; underfed. Even the pig's ribs showed. The stock seemed barely enough to feed Harl and the girls.

The barn itself was no better. Half the shutters were broken, and the hay on the floor was rotted. The goats had eaten through the wall of their stall, and were pulling the cow's hay. Mud, slop, and feces had churned into a single muck in the pig stall.

Renna dragged Arlen to each stall in turn. "Da doesn't like us naming the animals," she confessed, "so we do it secret. This one's Hoofy." She pointed to a cow. "Her milk tastes sour, but Da says it's fine. Next to her is Grouchy. She kicks, but only if you milk too hard, or not soon enough. The goats are . . ."

"Arlen doesn't care about the animals," Beni scolded her sister. She grabbed his arm and pulled him away. Beni was taller than her sister, and older, but Arlen thought Renna was prettier. They climbed into the hayloft, plopping down on the clean hay.

"Let's play succor," Beni said. She pulled a tiny leather pouch from her pocket, rolling four wooden dice onto the floor of the loft. The dice were painted with symbols: flame, rock, water, wind, wood, and ward. There were many ways to play, but most rules agreed you needed to throw three wards before rolling four of any other kind.

They played at the dice for a while. Renna and Beni had their own rules, many of which Arlen suspected were made up to let them win.

"Two wards three times in a row counts as three wards," Beni announced, after throwing just that. "We win." Arlen disagreed, but he didn't see much point in arguing.

"Since we won, you have to do what we say," Beni declared.

"Do not," Arlen said.

"Do too!" Beni insisted. Again, Arlen felt as if arguing would get him nowhere.

"What would I have to do?" he asked suspiciously.

"Make him play kissy!" Renna clapped.

Beni swatted her sister on the head. "I know, dumbs!"

"What's kissy?" Arlen asked, afraid he already knew the answer.

"Oh, you'll see," Beni said, and both girls laughed. "It's a grown-up game. Da plays it with Ilain sometimes. You practice being married."

"What, like saying your promises?" Arlen asked, wary.

"No, dumbs, like this," Beni said. She put her arms around Arlen's shoulders, and pressed her mouth to his.

Arlen had never kissed a girl before. She opened her mouth to him, and so he did the same. Their teeth clicked, and both of them recoiled. "Ow!" Arlen said.

"You do it too hard, Beni," Renna complained. "It's my turn."

Indeed, Renna's kiss was much softer. Arlen found it rather pleasant. Like being near the fire when it was cold.

"There," Renna said, when their lips parted. "That's how you do it."

"We have to share the bed tonight," Beni said. "We can practice later."

"I'm sorry you had to give up your bed on account of my mam," Arlen said.

"It's okay," Renna said. "We used to have to share a bed every night, until Mam died. But now Ilain sleeps with Da."

"Why?" Arlen asked.

"We're not supposed to talk about it," Beni hissed at Renna.

Renna ignored her, but she kept her voice low. "Ilain says that now that Mam's gone, Da told her it's her duty to keep him happy the way a wife is supposed to."

"Like cooking and sewing and stuff?" Arlen asked.

"No, it's a game like kissy," Beni said. "But you need a boy to play it." She tugged on his overalls. "If you show us your thingie, we'll teach you."

"I am not showing you my thingie!" Arlen said, backing away.

"Why not?" Renna asked. "Beni showed Lucik Boggin, and now he wants to play all the time."

"Da and Lucik's father said we're promised," Beni bragged. "So that makes it okay. Since you're going to be promised to Renna, you should show her yours." Renna bit her finger and looked away, but she watched Arlen out of the corner of her eye.

"That's not true!" Arlen said. "I'm not promised to anyone!"

"What do you think the elders are talking about inside, dumbs?" Beni asked.

"Are not!" Arlen said.

"Go see!" Beni challenged.

Arlen looked at both girls, then climbed down the ladder, slipping into the house as quietly as he could. He could hear voices from behind the curtain, and crept closer.

"I wanted Lucik right away," Harl was saying, "but Fernan wants him makin' mash for another season. Without an extra back around the farm, it's hard keepin' our bellies full, 'specially since them chickens quit layin' and one of the milk cows soured."

"We'll take Renna on our way back from Mey," Jeph said.

"Gonna tell him they's promised?" Harl asked. Arlen's breath caught.

"No reason not to," Jeph said.

Harl grunted. "Reckon you should wait till t'morrer," he said. "While yur alone on the road. Sometime boys cause a scene when they's first told. It kin hurt a girl's feelin's."

"You're probably right," Jeph said. Arlen wanted to scream.

"Know I am," Harl said. "Trust a man with daughters; they'll get upset over any old thing, ent that right, Lainie?" There was a smack, and Ilain yelped. "But still," Harl went on, "you kin do them no hurt that a few hours of cryin' won't solve."

There was a long silence, and Arlen started to edge back toward the barn door.

"I'm off t'bed," Harl grunted. Arlen froze. "See'n how Silvy's in yur bed tonight, Lainie," he went on, "you c'n sleep with me after you scrape the bowls and round up the girls."

Arlen ducked behind a workbench and stayed there as Harl went to the privy to relieve himself and then went into his room, closing the door. Arlen was about to creep back to the barn when Ilain spoke.

"I want to go, too," she blurted, just after the door closed.

"What?" Jeph asked.

Arlen could see their feet under the curtain from where he crouched. Ilain came around the table to sit next to his father.

"Take me with you," Ilain repeated. "Please. Beni will be fine once Lucik comes. I need to get away."

"Why?" Jeph asked. "Surely you have enough food for three."

"It's not that," Ilain said. "It doesn't matter why. I can tell Da I'll be out in the fields when you come for Renna. I'll run down the road, and meet you there. By the time Da realizes where I've gone, there'll be a night between us. He'll never follow."

"I wouldn't be too sure of that," Jeph said.

"Your farm is as far from here as there is," Ilain pleaded. Arlen saw her put her hand on Jeph's knee. "I can work," she promised. "I'll earn my keep."

"I can't just steal you away from Harl," Jeph said. "I've no quarrel with him, and I'm not about to start one."

Ilain spat. "The old wretch would have you think I'm sharing his bed because of Silvy," she said quietly. "Truer is he raises his hand to me if I don't join him every night after Renna and Beni are off to bed."

Jeph was silent a long time. "I see," he said at last. He made a fist, and started to rise.

"Don't, please," Ilain said. "You don't know what he's like. He'll kill you."

"I should just stand by?" Jeph asked. Arlen didn't understand what the fuss was. So what if Ilain slept in Harl's room?

Arlen saw Ilain move closer to his father. "You'll need some-one to take care of Silvy," she whispered. "And if she should pass"—she leaned in further, and her hand went to Jeph's lap the way Beni had tried to do to Arlen—"I could be your wife. I would fill your farm with children," she promised. Jeph groaned.

Arlen felt nauseous and hot in the face. He gulped, tasting bile in his mouth. He wanted to scream their plan to Harl. The man had faced a coreling for his daughter, something Jeph would never do. He imagined Harl would punch his father. The image was not displeasing.

Jeph hesitated, then pushed Ilain away. "No," he said. "We'll get Silvy to the Herb Gatherer tomorrow, and she'll be fine."

"Then take me anyway," Ilain begged, falling to her knees.

"I'll . . . think about it," his father replied. Just then, Beni and Renna burst in from the barn. Arlen rose quickly, pretending he had just entered with them as Ilain hurriedly stood. He felt the moment to confront them slip past.

After putting the girls to bed and producing a pair of grimy blankets for Arlen and Jeph in the main room, Ilain drew a deep breath and went into her father's room. Not long after, Arlen heard Harl grunting quietly, and the occasional muffled yelp from Ilain. Pretending not to hear it, he glanced over at Jeph, seeing him biting his fist.

Arlen was up before the sun the next morning, while the rest of the house slept. Moments before sunrise, he opened the door, staring at the remaining corelings impatiently as they hissed and clawed the air at him from the far side of the wards. As the last demon in the yard went misty, he left the house and went to the big barn, watering Missy and Harl's other horses. The mare was in foul temper, and nipped at him. "Just one more day," Arlen told her as he put her feed bag on.

His father was still snoring as he went back into the house and knocked on the doorframe of the room shared by Renna and Beni. Beni pulled the curtain aside, and immediately Arlen noted the worried looks on the sisters' faces.

"She won't wake up," Renna, who was kneeling by Arlen's mother, choked. "I knew you wanted to leave as soon as the sun rose, but when I shook her . . ." She gestured toward the bed, her eyes wet. "She's so pale."

Arlen rushed to his mother's side, taking her hand. Her fingers were cold and clammy, but her forehead burned to the touch. Her breathing came in short gasps, and the rotting stink of demon sickness was thick about her. Her bandages were soaked with brownish yellow ooze.

"Da!" Arlen cried. A moment later, Jeph appeared with Ilain and Harl close behind.

"We don't have any time to waste," Jeph said.

"Take one'a my horses t'go with yours," Harl said. "Switch 'em when they tire. Push hard, and you should reach Mey by afternoon."

"We're in your debt," Jeph said, but Harl waved the thought away.

"Hurry, now," he said. "Ilain will pack you something to eat on the road."

Renna caught Arlen's arm as he turned to go. "We's promised now," she whispered. "I'll wait on the porch every dusk till you're back." She kissed him on the cheek. Her lips were soft, and the feel of them lingered long after she pulled away.

The cart bumped and jerked as they raced along the rough dirt road, pausing only once to rotate the horses. Arlen looked at the food Ilain had packed as if it were poison. Jeph ate it hungrily.

As Arlen picked at the grainy bread and hard, pungent cheese, he started to think that maybe it was all a misunderstanding. Maybe he hadn't overheard what he thought he had. Maybe Jeph hadn't hesitated in pushing Ilain away.

It was a tempting illusion, but Jeph shattered it a moment later. "What do you think of Harl's younger daughter?" he asked. "You spent some time with her." Arlen felt as if his father had just punched him in the stomach.

"Renna?" Arlen asked, playing innocent. "She's okay, I guess. Why?"

"I spoke to Harl," his father said. "She's going to come live with us when we go back to the farm."

"Why?" Arlen asked.

"To look after your mam, help around the farm, and . . . other reasons."

"What other reasons?" Arlen pressed.

"Harl and I want to see if you two will get along," Jeph said.

"What if we don't?" Arlen asked. "What if I don't want some

girl following me around all day asking me to play kissy with her?"

"One day," Jeph said, "you might not mind playing kissy so much."

"So let her come then," Arlen said, shrugging his shoulders and pretending not to know what his father was getting at. "Why is Harl so eager to be rid of her?"

"You've seen the state of their farm; they can barely feed themselves," Jeph said. "Harl loves his daughters very much, and he wants the best for them. And what's best is marrying them while they're still young, so he can have sons to help him out and grandchildren before he dies. Ilain is already older than most girls who marry. Lucik Boggin is going to come out to help on Harl's farm starting in the fall. They're hoping he and Beni will get along."

"I suppose Lucik didn't have any choice, either," Arlen grumbled.

"He's happy to go, and lucky at that!" Arlen's father snapped, losing his patience. "You're going to have to learn some hard lessons about life, Arlen. There are a lot more boys than girls in the Brook, and we can't just fritter our lives away. Every year, we lose more to dotage and sickness and corelings. If we don't keep children coming, Tibbet's Brook will fade away just like a hundred other villages! We *can't* let that happen!"

Arlen, seeing his normally placid father seething, wisely said nothing.

An hour later, Silvy started screaming. They turned to find her trying to stand up right there in the cart, clutching at her chest, her breath coming in loud, horrid gasps. Arlen leapt into the back of the cart, and she gripped him with surprisingly strong hands, coughing thick phlegm onto his shirt. Her bulging, bloodshot eyes stared wildly into his, but there was no recognition in them. Arlen screamed as she thrashed about, holding her as steadily as he could.

Jeph stopped the cart and together they forced her to lie back down. She thrashed about, screaming in hoarse gasps. And then, like Cholie, she gave a final wrack, and lay still.

Jeph looked at his wife, and then threw his head back and screamed. Arlen nearly bit through his lip trying to hold back his tears, but in the end he failed. They wept together over the woman.

When their sobs eased, Arlen looked around, his eyes lifeless. He tried to focus, but the world seemed blurry, as if it wasn't real.

"What do we do now?" he asked finally.

"We turn around," his father said, and the words cut Arlen like a knife. "We take her home and burn her. We try to go on. There's still the farm and the animals to care for, and even with Renna and Norine to help us, there's going to be some hard times ahead."

"Renna?" Arlen asked incredulously. "We're still taking her with us? Even now?"

"Life goes on, Arlen," his father said. "You're almost a man, and a man needs a wife."

"Did you arrange one for both of us?" Arlen blurted.

"What?" Jeph asked.

"I heard you and Ilain last night!" Arlen screamed. "You've got another wife all ready! What do you care about Mam? You've already got someone else to take care of your thingie! At least, until she gets killed too, because you're too scared to help her!"

Arlen's father hit him; a hard slap across the face that cracked the morning air. His anger faded instantly, and he reached out to his son. "Arlen, I'm sorry . . . !" he choked, but the boy pulled away and jumped off the cart.

"Arlen!" Jeph cried, but the boy ignored him, running as hard as he could for the woods off to the side of the road.

CHAPTER 3

A NIGHT ALONE

319 AR

ARLEN RAN THROUGH THE WOODS as fast as he could, making sharp, sudden turns, picking his direction at random. He wanted to be sure his father couldn't track him, but as Jeph's calls faded, he realized his father wasn't following at all.

Why should he bother? he thought. *He knows I have to come back before nightfall. Where else could I go?*

Anywhere. The answer came unbidden, but he knew in his heart that it was true.

He couldn't go back to the farm and pretend everything was all right. He couldn't watch Ilain claim his mother's bed. Even pretty Renna, who kissed so softly, would only be a reminder of what he had lost, and why.

But where could he go? His father was right about one thing. He couldn't run forever. He would have to find succor before dark, or the coming night would be his last.

Going back to Tibbet's Brook was not an option. Whoever he sought succor from would drag him home by the ear the next day, and he'd be switched for the stunt with nothing to show.

Sunny Pasture, then. Unless Hog was paying them to carry something, almost no one from Tibbet's Brook ever went there, unless they were Messengers.

Coline had said Ragen was heading to Sunny Pasture before returning to the Free Cities. Arlen liked Ragen, the only elder he'd ever met who didn't talk down to him. The Messenger and Keerin were a day and more ahead of him, and mounted, but if he hurried, perhaps he could catch them in time and beg passage to the Free Cities.

He still had Coline's map, strung around his neck. It showed the road to Sunny Pasture, and the farms along the way. Even deep in the woods, he was pretty sure which way was north.

At midday he found the road, or rather the road found him, cutting straight across the woods ahead of him. He must have lost his sense of direction in the trees.

He walked on for a few hours, but he saw no sign of a farm, or the old Herb Gatherer's home. Looking at the sun, his worry increased. If he was walking north, the sun should be off to his left, but it wasn't. It was right in front of him.

He stopped and looked at the map, and his fears were confirmed. He wasn't on the road to Sunny Pasture, he was on the road to the Free Cities. Worse, after the road split off from the path to Sunny Pasture, it went right off the edge of the map.

The idea of backtracking was daunting, especially with no way to know if he could make it to succor in time. He took a step back the way he had come.

No, he decided. *Going back is Da's way. Whatever happens, I'm going forward.*

Arlen started walking again, leaving both Tibbet's Brook and Sunny Pasture behind. Each step was lighter and easier than the one before.

He walked for hours more, eventually leaving the trees behind and entering grassland: wide, lush fields untouched by plow or grazing. He crested a hilltop, breathing deeply of the fresh, untainted air. There was a large boulder jutting from the ground, and Arlen scrambled atop it, looking out at a wide world that had always been beyond his reach. There was no sign of habitation, no place to seek succor. He was afraid of the coming night, but it was a distant feeling, like knowing you would grow old and die one day.

As the afternoon turned to evening, Arlen began looking for places to make his stand. A copse of trees held promise; there was little grass beneath them, and he could draw wards in the dirt, but a wood demon might climb one of the trees, and drop into his warding ring from above.

There was a small, stony hillock free of grass, but when Arlen stood atop it, the wind was strong, and he feared it might mar the wards, rendering them useless.

Finally, Arlen came to a place where flame demons had set a recent blaze. New buds had yet to pierce the ash, and a scuff of his foot found hard dirt beneath. He cleared the ash from a wide area and began his warding circle. He had little time, so he kept it small, not wanting his haste to make him careless.

Using a sharp stick, Arlen drew the sigils in the dirt, gently blowing away loose scrapings. He worked for over an hour, ward by ward, stepping back frequently to assure himself that they were aligned properly. His hands, as always, moved with confidence and alacrity.

When he finished, Arlen had a circle six feet in diameter. He checked the wards three times, finding no error. He put the stick in his pocket and sat at the circle's center, watching the shadows lengthen and the sun dip low, setting the sky awash with color.

Perhaps he would die tonight. Perhaps not. Arlen told himself it did not matter. But as the light waned, so too did his nerve. He felt his heart pounding, and every instinct told him to leap to his feet and run. But there was nowhere to run *to*. He was miles away from the nearest place of succor. He shivered, though it was not cold.

This was a bad idea, a tiny voice whispered in his mind. He snarled at it, but the brave front did little to loosen his knotting muscles as the last rays of the sun winked out, and he was bathed in darkness.

Here they come, that frightened voice in his head warned, as the wisps of mist began to rise from the ground.

The mist coalesced slowly, demon bodies gaining substance as they slipped from the ground. Arlen rose with them, clenching his small fists. As always, the flame demons came first, scampering about in delight, trailing flickering fire as they went. These were followed by the wind demons, which immediately ran and spread their leathery wings, leaping into the air. Last came the rock demons, laboriously hauling their heavy frames from the Core.

And then the corelings saw Arlen and howled with delight, charging the helpless boy.

A swooping wind demon struck first, raking its hooked wing claws to tear out Arlen's throat. Arlen screamed, but sparks flew as the talons struck his wards, deflecting the attack. Momentum carried the demon on, and its body slammed into the shield only to be hurled back in a shimmering burst of energy. The creature howled as it struck the ground, but it pulled itself upright, twitching as energy danced across its scales.

Next came the nimble flame demons, the largest no bigger

than a dog. They skittered forward, shrieking, and began clawing at the shield. Arlen flinched each time the wards flared, but the magic held. When they saw that Arlen had woven an effective net, they spat fire at him.

Arlen was wise to the trick, of course. He had been warding since he was old enough to hold a stick of charcoal, and he knew the wards against firespit. The flames were turned as effectively as the claws. He didn't even feel the heat.

Corelings gathered to the spectacle, and each flash of light as the wards activated showed Arlen more and more of them: a fell horde, eager to flay the flesh from his bones.

More wind demons swooped in, and were thrown back by the wards. The flame demons, too, began to hurl themselves at him in frustration, accepting the stinging burn of the magic in hope of powering their way through. Again and again they were thrown back. Arlen ceased to flinch. He began to scream curses at them, shoving his terror aside.

His defiance only enraged the demons further. Unused to being taunted by their prey, they doubled their efforts to penetrate the wards as Arlen shook his fists and made rude gestures he had seen the adults in Tibbet's Brook make to Hog's back sometimes.

This was what he feared? This was what humanity lived in terror of? These pathetic, frustrated beasts? Ridiculous. He spat, and the spit sizzled on a flame demon's scales, trebling its fury.

There was a hush from the howling creatures then. In the flickering light of the flame demons, he saw the coreling host part, clearing a path for a rock demon that stomped toward him, its footsteps like an earthquake.

All his life, Arlen had watched corelings from afar, from behind windows and doors. Before the terrifying events of the last few days, he had never been outside in the air with a fully formed demon, and had certainly never stood his ground. He knew their size could vary, but he had never appreciated just how much.

The rock demon was fifteen feet tall.

The rock demon was enormous.

Arlen craned his head upward as the monster approached. Even at a distance, it was a towering, hulking mass of sinew and sharp edges. Its thick black carapace was knobbed with bony protrusions, and its spiked tail slid back and forth, balancing its massive shoulders. It stood hunched on two clawed feet that dug great grooves in the dirt with every thunderous step. Its long, gnarled arms ended in talons the size of butchering knives, and its drooling maw split wide to reveal row after row of bladelike teeth. A black tongue slipped out, tasting Arlen's fear.

One of the flame demons failed to move from its path quickly enough, and the rock demon swiped at it in an offhand manner, its talons tearing great gashes as the blow launched the smaller coreling through the air.

Terrified, Arlen took a step back, and then another, as the giant coreling approached. It was only at the last moment that he came to his senses and stopped before he retreated right out of the protective circle.

Remembering the circle gave fleeting comfort. Arlen doubted his wards were strong enough for this test. He doubted *any* wards were.

The demon regarded him for a long moment, savoring his terror. Rock demons seldom hurried, though when they chose to, they could move with astonishing speed.

As the demon struck, Arlen's nerve broke. He screamed and fell to the ground, curling up in a tight ball, covering his head with his arms.

The resulting explosion was deafening. Even through his covered eyes, Arlen saw the bright flash of magic, as if night had become day. He heard the demon's shriek of frustration, and peeked out as the coreling whirled, smashing its heavy, horned tail against the wards.

Again the magic flared, and again the creature was thwarted.

Arlen forced himself to let go the breath he had been holding. He watched as the demon struck his wards again and again, screaming in rage. A warm dampness clung to his thighs.

Ashamed of himself, of his cowardice, Arlen came to his feet and met the demon's eyes. He screamed, a primal cry from deep within him that rejected everything the coreling was and everything it represented.

He picked up a stone and threw it at the demon. "Go back to the Core where you belong!" he cried. "Go back and die!"

The demon barely seemed to feel the stone bounce off its armor, but its rage multiplied as it tore at the wards, unable to get through. Arlen called the demon every foul and pathetic thing in his somewhat limited vocabulary, clawing at the ground for anything he could throw.

When he ran out of stones, he began jumping up and down, waving his arms, screaming his defiance.

Then he slipped, and stepped on a ward.

Time seemed to freeze in the long, silent moment shared by Arlen and the giant demon, the enormity of what had just happened slowly dawning on them. When they moved, they moved as one, Arlen whipping out his etching stick and diving for the ward even as the demon swiped a massive, clawed hand at him.

His mind racing, Arlen assessed the damage in an instant; a single line of the sigil marred. Even as he repaired the ward with a slash of the tool, he knew he was too late. The claws had begun to cut into his flesh.

But then the magic took effect once more, and the demon was hurled back, screaming in agony. Arlen, too, screamed in pain, rolling over and pulling the claws from his back; hurling them away before he could realize what had happened.

He saw it then, lying in the circle, twitching and smoking.

The demon's arm.

Arlen looked at the severed limb in shock, turning to see the demon roaring and thrashing about, savaging any demon foolish enough to come within reach. Savaging with one arm.

He looked at the arm, its end neatly severed and cauterized, oozing a foul smoke. With more bravery than he felt, Arlen picked the massive thing up and tried to hurl it from the circle, but the wards made a two-way barrier. The stuff of corelings could no more pass out than in. The arm bounced off the wards and landed back at Arlen's feet.

Then the pain set in. Arlen touched the wounds along his back, and his hands came away wet with blood. Sickened, his strength ebbing, he fell to his knees, weeping for the pain, weeping for fear of moving and scuffing another ward, and weeping, most of all, for his mam. He understood now the pain she had felt that night.

Arlen spent the rest of the night cowering in fright. He could hear the demons circling, waiting, hoping for an error that would allow them acccss. Even if sleep had been possible, he would not have dared attempt it, lest a shift in his slumber grant the corelings their wish.

Dawn seemed to take years to come. Arlen looked up at the

sky often that night, but each time he saw only the giant, crippled rock demon, clutching its caked and ichorous wound as it stalked the circle, hatred in its eyes.

After an eternity, a hint of red tinged the horizon, followed by orange, yellow, and then a glorious white. The other corelings slipped back down to the Core before the yellow touched the sky, but the giant waited until the last, its rows of teeth bared as it hissed at him.

But even the one-armed rock demon's hatred was no match for its fear of the sun. As the last shadows scurried away, its massive horned head sank beneath the ground. Arlen straightened and stepped from the circle, wincing in pain. His back was on fire. The wounds had stopped bleeding in the night, but he felt them tear open once more as he stretched.

The thought led his eyes back to the clawed forearm lying next to him. It was like a tree trunk, covered in hard, cold plates. Arlen picked the heavy thing up and held it before him.

Got a trophy, at least, he thought, making an effort to be brave even though the sight of his blood on the black talons sent a shudder through him.

Just then, a ray of light reached him, the sun finally more above the horizon than below. The demon's limb began to sizzle and smoke, popping like a wet log thrown on a fire. In a moment, it burst into flame, and Arlen dropped it in fright. He watched, fascinated, as it flared brighter and brighter, the sun's light bearing down upon it until there was naught left but a thin, charred remain. He stepped over and gingerly nudged it with his toe, collapsing it into dust.

Arlen found a branch to use as a walking stick as he trudged on. He understood how lucky he was. And how stupid. Wards in the dirt were untrustworthy. Even Ragen said that. What would he have done if the wind had marred them, as his father threatened?

Creator, what if it had rained?

How many nights could he survive? Arlen had no idea what lay over the next hill, no reason to think that there was anyone between here and the Free Cities, which, by all accounts, were weeks away.

He felt tears welling in his eyes. Brutally, he wiped them off, growling in defiance. Giving in to fear was his father's solution to problems, and Arlen already knew it didn't work.

"I'm not afraid," he told himself. "I'm not."

Arlen pressed on, knowing the lie for what it was.

Around midday, he came to a rocky stream. The water was cold and clear, and he bent to drink. The move sent lances of pain through his back.

He had done nothing for the wounds. It wasn't as if he could stitch them closed as Coline might. He thought of his mother, and how when he came home with cuts or scrapes the first thing she did was wash them out.

He stripped off his shirt, finding the back torn and soaked through with blood, now crusted and hard. He dunked the shirt and watched as dirt and blood washed downstream. He laid his clothes out on the rocks to dry, and lowered himself into the cold water.

The chill made him wince, but it soon numbed the pain in his back. He scrubbed as best he could, gently washing out the stinging wounds until he could stand it no more. Shivering, he climbed from the stream and lay on the rocks by his clothes.

He awoke some time later with a start. Cursing, he saw that the sun had moved far across the sky, and that the day was nearly done. He could travel a little farther, but he knew the risk would be a foolish one. Better to spend the extra time on his defenses.

Not far from the stream was a wide area of moist soil, and the sod pulled free easily, clearing him a space. He tamped down the loose dirt, smoothed it, and set to warding. He drew a wider circle this time, and then, after checking it thrice, drew another concentric ring within the first for added safety. The moist dirt would resist the wind, and the sky showed no threat of rain.

Satisfied, Arlen dug a pit and gathered dry twigs, building a small fire. He sat in the center of the inner circle as the sun dipped, trying to ignore his hunger. He doused the fire as the red sky grew lavender, then purple, breathing deeply to steady his pounding heart. At last, the light vanished and the corelings rose.

Arlen held his breath, waiting. Finally, a flame demon caught his scent, and raced at him with a shriek. In that moment, the terror of the previous night came rushing back to him, and Arlen felt his blood go cold.

The corelings were oblivious to his wards until they were upon them. With the first flare of magic, Arlen breathed his relief. The demons clawed at the barrier, but they could not pass.

A wind demon, flying up high where the wards were weak, passed the first ring, but it smashed into the second as it swooped down at him, landing hard in the space between. Arlen struggled to maintain his calm as it lurched to its feet.

It was bipedal, with a long, thin body, and spindly limbs that ended in six-inch hooked claws. The undersides of its arms and the outsides of its legs were webbed with a thin, leathery membrane, supported by flexible bones jutting from the creature's sides. The demon was barely taller than an adult man, but its spread wings spanned twice its height, making it seem huge in the sky. A curving horn grew from its head, bent back and webbed like its limbs to form a ridge down its back. Its long snout held rows of inch-long teeth, yellow in the moonlight.

The coreling moved clumsily on land, despite its graceful mastery of the air. Up close, the wind demons were not nearly as impressive as their cousins. Wood and rock demons had impenetrable armor and otherworldly strength to power their thick claws. Flame demons were faster than any man, and spat fire that could set anything alight. Wind demons . . . Arlen thought Ragen could puncture one of those thin wings with a hard stab of his spear, crippling it.

Night, he thought, *I'm pretty sure I could do it myself.*

But he didn't have a spear, and impressive or not, the coreling could still kill him, if his inner wards did not hold. He tensed as it drew close.

It swiped the hooked talon at the end of its wing at him, and Arlen winced, but magic sparked along the wardnet, and it was thwarted.

After a few more futile strikes, the coreling attempted to get airborne again. It ran and spread its wings to catch the wind, but it struck the outer wards before it could gain sufficient momentum. The magic threw it back into the mud.

Arlen laughed in spite of himself as the coreling tried to pick itself up from the dirt. Its huge wings might make it a terror in the sky, but on the ground they dragged and threw it off balance. It had no hands to push up with, and its spindly arms bowed under its weight. It thrashed desperately for a moment before it was able to rise.

Trapped, it tried again and again to take off, but the space between the circles was not great enough, and it was foiled each time. The flame demons sensed their cousin's distress, and shrieked with glee, hopping around the circle to follow the creature and taunt its misfortune.

Arlen felt a swell of pride. He made mistakes the night before, but he would not make them again. He began to hope that he might live to see the Free Cities after all.

The flame demons soon tired of mocking the wind demon, and moved off in search of easier prey, flushing small animals from hiding with gouts of fire. One small, frightened hare leapt into Arlen's outer ring, the demon in pursuit stopped by the wards. The wind demon snatched clumsily at it, but the hare dodged it easily, running through the circle and out the far side, only to find corelings there as well. It turned and darted back in, again running too far.

Arlen wished there were a way he could communicate with the poor creature, to let it know it was safe in the inner ring, but he could only watch as it darted in and out of the wards.

Then the unthinkable happened. The hare, scampering back into the circle, scratched out a ward. With a howl, flame demons poured through the gap after the animal. The lone wind demon escaped, leaping into the air and winging away.

Arlen cursed the hare, and cursed all the more when it darted right for him. If it damaged the inner wards, they were both doomed.

With a farmboy's quickness, Arlen reached from the circle and snatched up the hare by its ears. It thrashed wildly, willing to tear itself apart to escape, but Arlen had handled hares in his father's fields often enough. He swung it into his arms, cradling it on its back, hindquarters up above its head. In a moment, the hare was staring up at him blankly, its struggles ceased.

He was tempted to throw the creature to the demons. It would be safer than risking it getting free and scuffing another ward. *And why not?* he wondered. *If I'd found it in the light, I'd've eaten it myself.*

Still, he found he could not do it. The demons had taken too much from the world, from him. He swore then that he would give them nothing willingly, not now, not ever.

Not even this.

As the night wore on, Arlen held the terrified creature firmly, cooing at it and stroking its soft fur. All around, the demons howled, but Arlen blocked them out, focusing on the animal.

The meditation worked for a time, until a roar brought him

back. He looked up to find the massive, one-armed rock demon towering over him, its drool sizzling as it struck the wards. The creature's wound had healed into a knobby stump at the end of its elbow. Its rage seemed even greater than the night before.

The coreling hammered at the barrier, ignoring the stinging flare of the magic. With deafening blows, the rock demon struck again and again, attempting to power through and take its vengeance. Arlen clutched the hare tightly, his eyes wide as he watched. He knew that the wards would not weaken from repeated blows, but it did little to stop the fear that the demon was determined enough to manage it anyway.

When the morning light banished the demons for another day, Arlen finally let go of the hare, and it bounded away immediately. His stomach growled as he watched it go, but after what they had shared, he could not bring himself to look at the creature as food.

Rising, Arlen stumbled and almost fell as a wave of nausea took him. The cuts along his back were lances of fire. He reached back to touch the tender, swollen skin, and his hand came away wet with the stinking brown ooze that Coline had drained from Silvy's wounds. The cuts burned, and he felt flushed. He bathed in the cold pool again, but the chill water did little to ease his inner heat.

Arlen knew then he was going to die. Old Mey Friman, if she existed at all, was over two days away. If he truly had demon fever, though, it didn't matter. He wouldn't last two days.

Still, Arlen could not bring himself to give in. He stumbled on down the road, following the wagon ruts toward wherever they came from.

If he was to die, let it be closer to the Free Cities than the prison behind.

CHAPTER 4

LEESHA
319 AR

LEESHA SPENT THE NIGHT IN TEARS.

That, in and of itself, was nothing out of the ordinary, but it wasn't her mother that had her weeping this night. It was the screams. Someone's wards had failed; it was impossible to tell whose, but cries of terror and agony echoed in the dark, and smoke billowed into the sky. The whole village glowed with a hazy orange light as smoke refracted coreling fire.

The people of Cutter's Hollow couldn't search for survivors. They dared not even fight the fire. They could do nothing save pray to the Creator that embers did not carry on the wind and spread the flames. Houses in Cutter's Hollow were built well apart for just this reason, but a strong breeze could carry a spark a long way.

Even if the fire remained contained, the ash and smoke in the air could easily obscure more wards with their greasy stain, giving corelings the access they desperately sought.

No corelings tested the wards around Leesha's house. It was a bad sign, hinting that the demons had found easier prey in the dark.

Helpless and afraid, Leesha did the only thing she could. She cried. Cried for the dead, cried for the wounded, and cried for herself. In a village with fewer than four hundred people, there was no one whose death would not cut her.

Just shy of thirteen summers, Leesha was an exceptionally pretty girl, with long, wavy black hair and sharp eyes of pale blue. She was not yet flowered, and thus could not wed, but she was promised to Gared Cutter, the handsomest boy in the village. Gared was two summers older than her, tall and thick-muscled. The other girls squealed as he passed, but he was Leesha's, and they all knew. He would give her strong babies.

If he lived through the night.

The door to her room opened. Her mother never bothered to knock.

In face and form, Elona was much like her daughter. Still beautiful at thirty, she had long hair that hung rich and black about her proud shoulders. She also had a full, womanly figure that was the envy of all, the only thing Leesha hoped to inherit from her. Her own breasts had only just started to bud, and had a long way to go before they matched her mother's.

"That's enough of your blubbering, you worthless girl," Elona snapped, throwing Leesha a rag to dry her eyes. "Crying alone gets you nothing. Cry in front of a man, if you want your way, but wetting your pillow won't bring the dead to life." She pulled the door closed, leaving Leesha alone again in the evil orange light flickering through the slats of the shutters.

Do you feel anything at all? Leesha wondered at her.

Her mother was right that tears would not bring back the dead, but she was wrong that it was good for nothing. Crying had always been Leesha's escape when things were hard. Other girls might think Leesha's life was perfect, but only because none of them saw the face Elona showed her only child when they were alone. It was no secret Elona had wanted sons, and Leesha and her father both endured her scorn for failing to oblige.

But she angrily dried her eyes all the same. She couldn't wait until she flowered and Gared took her away. The villagers would build them a house for their wedding boon, and Gared would carry her across the wards and make a woman of her while they all cheered outside. She would have her own children, and treat them nothing like her mother treated her.

Leesha was dressed when her mother banged on her door. She had not slept at all.

"I want you out the door when the dawn bell rings," Elona said. "And I'll not hear a murmur about you being tired! I won't have our family seen lagging to help."

Leesha knew her mother well enough to know that "seen" was the operative word. Elona didn't care about helping anyone but herself.

Leesha's father, Erny, was waiting by the door under Elona's stern gaze. He was not a large man, and to call him wiry would have implied a strength that wasn't there. He was no stronger of will than of body, a timid man whose voice never rose. Erny was Elona's elder by a dozen years; his thin brown hair had deserted the top of his head, and he wore thin-rimmed glasses he had bought from a Messenger years ago, the only man in town with the like.

He was, in short, not the man Elona wanted him to be, but there was great demand in the Free Cities for the fine paper he made, and she liked his money well enough.

Unlike her mother, Leesha really wanted to help her neighbors. She was out and running toward the fire the moment the corelings fled, even before the bell.

"Leesha! Stay with us!" Elona cried, but Leesha ignored her. The smoke was thick and choking, but she raised her apron to cover her mouth, and did not slow.

A few townsfolk were already gathered by the time she reached the source. Three houses had burned to the ground, and two more still blazed, threatening to set their neighbors alight. Leesha shrieked when she saw that one of the houses was Gared's.

Smitt, who owned the inn and general store in town, was on the scene, barking orders. Smitt had been town Speaker as long as Leesha could remember. He was never eager to give orders, preferring to let people solve their own problems, but everyone agreed he was good at it.

". . . never pull water from the well fast enough," Smitt was saying as Leesha approached. "We'll have to form a bucket line to the stream and wet the other houses, or the whole village will be ashes by nightfall!"

Gared and Steave came running up just then, harried and sooty, but otherwise healthy. Gared, just fifteen, was bigger than most grown men in the village. Steave, his father, was a giant, towering over everyone. Leesha felt a knot in her stomach unclench at the sight of them.

But before she could run to Gared, Smitt pointed to him. "Gared, pull the bucket cart to the stream!" He looked over the others. "Leesha!" he said. "Follow him and start filling!"

Leesha ran for all she was worth, but even pulling the heavy cart, Gared beat her to the small stream flowing from the River

Angiers, miles to the north. The moment he pulled up short, she fell into his arms. She had thought seeing him alive would dispel the horrible images in her head, but it only intensified them. She didn't know what she would do if she lost Gared.

"I feared you dead," she moaned, sobbing into his chest.

"I'm safe," he whispered, hugging her tightly. "I'm safe."

Quickly, the two began unloading the cart, filling buckets to start the line as others arrived. Soon, more than a hundred villagers were in a neat row stretching from the stream to the blaze, passing up full buckets and handing back empty ones. Gared was called back to the fire with the cart, his strong arms needed to throw water.

It wasn't long before the cart returned, this time pulled by Tender Michel and laden with wounded. The sight brought mixed feelings. Seeing fellow villagers, friends all, burned and savaged cut her deeply, but a breach that left survivors was rare, and each one was a gift she thanked the Creator for.

The Holy Man and his acolyte, Child Jona, laid the injured out by the stream. Michel left the young man to comfort them while he brought the cart back for more.

Leesha turned from the sight, focusing on filling buckets. Her feet went numb in the cold water and her arms grew leaden, but she lost herself in the work until a whisper got her attention.

"Hag Bruna is coming," someone said, and Leesha's head snapped up. Sure enough, the ancient Herb Gatherer was coming down the path, led by her apprentice, Darsy.

No one knew for sure how old Bruna was. It was said she was old when the village elders were young. She had delivered most of them herself. She had outlived her husband, children, and grandchildren, and had no family left in the world.

Now she was little more than a wrinkle of translucent skin stretched over sharp bone. Half blind, she could walk only at a slow shuffle, but Bruna could still shout to be heard from the far end of the village, and she swung her gnarled walking stick with surprising strength and accuracy when her ire was roused.

Leesha, like most everyone in the village, was terrified of her.

Bruna's apprentice was a homely woman of twenty summers, thick of limb and wide of face. After Bruna outlived her last apprentice, a number of young girls had been sent to her for training. After a constant stream of abuse from the old woman, all but Darsy had been driven off.

"She's ugly as a bull and just as strong," Elona once said of Darsy, cackling. "What does she have to fear from that sour hag? It's not as if Bruna will drive the suitors from her door."

Bruna knelt beside the injured, inspecting them with firm hands as Darsy unrolled a heavy cloth covered in pockets, each marked with symbols and holding a tool, vial, or pouch. Injured villagers moaned or cried out as she worked, but Bruna paid them no mind, pinching wounds and sniffing her fingers, working as much from touch and smell as sight. Without looking, Bruna's hands darted to the pockets of the cloth, mixing herbs with a mortar and pestle.

Darsy began laying a small fire, and looked up to where Leesha stood staring from the stream. "Leesha! Bring water, and be quick about it!" she barked.

As Leesha hurried to comply, Bruna pulled up, sniffing the herbs she was grinding.

"Idiot girl!" Bruna shrieked. Leesha jumped, thinking she meant her, but Bruna hurled the mortar and pestle at Darsy, hitting her hard in the shoulder and covering her in ground herbs.

Bruna fumbled through her cloth, snatching the contents of each pocket and sniffing at them like an animal.

"You put stinkweed where the hogroot should be, and mixed all the skyflower with tampweed!" The old crone lifted her gnarled staff and struck Darsy across the shoulders. "Are you trying to kill these people, or are you still too stupid to read?"

Leesha had seen her mother in such a state before, and if Elona was as frightening as a coreling, Hag Bruna was the mother of all demons. She began to edge away from the two, fearing to draw attention to herself.

"I won't take this abuse forever, you evil old hag!" Darsy screamed.

"Be off, then!" Bruna said. "I'd sooner mar every ward in this town than leave you my herb pouch when I pass! The people would be no worse off!"

Darsy laughed. "Be off?" she asked. "Who'll carry your bottles and tripods, old woman? Who'll lay your fire, fix your meals, and wipe the spit from your face when the cough takes you? Who'll cart your old bones around when chill and damp sap your strength? You need me more than I need you!"

Bruna swung her staff, and Darsy wisely scurried out of the way, tripping over Leesha, who had been doing her best to remain invisible. Both of them tumbled to the ground.

Bruna used the opportunity to swing her staff again. Leesha rolled through the dirt to avoid the blows, but Bruna's aim was true. Darsy cried out in pain, covering her head with her arms.

"Off with you!" Bruna shouted again. "I have sick to tend!"

Darsy growled and got to her feet. Leesha feared she might strike the old woman, but instead she ran off. Bruna let fly a stream of curses at Darsy's back.

Leesha held her breath and kept to her knees, inching away. Just as she thought she might escape, Bruna took notice of her.

"You, Elona's brat!" she shouted, pointing her gnarled stick at Leesha. "Finish laying the fire and set my tripod over it!"

Bruna turned back to the wounded, and Leesha had no choice but to do as she was told.

Over the next few hours, Bruna barked an endless stream of orders at the girl, cursing her slowness, as Leesha scurried to do her bidding. She fetched and boiled water, ground herbs, brewed tinctures, and mixed balms. It seemed she never got more than halfway through a task before the ancient Herb Gatherer ordered her on to the next, and she was forced to work faster and faster to comply. Fresh wounded streamed in from the fires with deep burns and broken bones from collapses. She feared half the village was aflame.

Bruna brewed teas to numb pain for some and drug others into a dreamless sleep as she cut them with sharp instruments. She worked tirelessly, stitching, poulticing, and bandaging.

It was late afternoon when Leesha realized that not only were there no more injuries to tend, but the bucket line was gone, as well. She was alone with Bruna and the wounded, the most alert of whom stared off dazedly into space thanks to Bruna's herbs.

A wave of suppressed weariness fell over her, and Leesha fell to her knees, sucking in a deep breath. Every inch of her ached, but with the pain came a powerful sense of satisfaction. There were some that might not have lived, but now would, thanks in part to her efforts.

But the real hero, she admitted to herself, was Bruna. It occurred to her that the woman had not ordered her to do anything for several minutes. She looked over, and saw Bruna collapsed on the ground, gasping.

"Help! Help!" Leesha cried. "Bruna's sick!" New strength came to her, and she flew to the woman, lifting her up into a sitting position. Hag Bruna was shockingly light, and Leesha could feel little more than bone beneath her thick shawls and wool skirts.

Bruna was twitching, and a thin trail of spit ran from her mouth, caught in the endless grooves of her wrinkled skin. Her eyes, dark behind a milky film, stared wildly at her hands, which would not stop shaking.

Leesha looked around frantically, but there was no one nearby to help. Still holding Bruna upright, she grabbed at one of the woman's spasming hands, rubbing the cramped muscles. "Oh, Bruna!" she pleaded. "What do I do? Please! I don't know how to help you! You must tell me what to do!" Helplessness cut at Leesha, and she began to cry.

Bruna's hand jerked from her grasp, and Leesha cried out, fearing a fresh set of spasms. But her ministrations had given the old Herb Gatherer the control to reach into her shawl, pulling free a pouch that she thrust Leesha's way. A series of coughs wracked her frail body, and she was torn from Leesha's arms and hit the ground, flopping like a fish with each cough. Leesha was left holding the pouch in horror.

She looked down at the cloth bag, squeezing experimentally and feeling the crunch of herbs inside. She sniffed it, catching a scent like potpourri.

She thanked the Creator. If it had all been one herb, she would have never been able to guess the dose, but she had made enough tinctures and teas for Bruna that day to understand what she had been given.

She rushed to the kettle steaming on the tripod and placed a thin cloth over a cup, layering it thick with herbs from the pouch. She poured boiling water over the herbs slowly, leaching their strength, then deftly tied the herbs up in the cloth and tossed it into the water.

She ran back to Bruna, blowing on the liquid. It would burn, but there was no time to let it cool. She lifted Bruna in one arm, pressing the cup to her spit-flecked lips.

The Herb Gatherer thrashed, spilling some of the cure, but Leesha forced her to drink, the yellow liquid running out of the sides of her mouth. She kept twitching and coughing, but the symptoms began to subside. As her heaves eased, Leesha sobbed in relief.

"Leesha!" she heard a call. She looked up from Bruna, and saw her mother racing toward her, ahead of a group of townsfolk.

"What have you done, you worthless girl?" Elona demanded. She reached Leesha before the others could draw close and hissed, "Bad enough I have a useless daughter and not a son to fight the fire, but now you've gone and killed the town crone?" She drew back her hand to smack at her daughter, but Bruna reached up and caught Elona's wrist in her skeletal grip.

"The crone lives because of her, you idiot!" Bruna croaked. Elona turned bone-white and drew back as if Bruna had become a coreling. The sight gave Leesha a rush of pleasure.

By then, the rest of the villagers had gathered around them, asking what had happened.

"My daughter saved Bruna's life!" Elona shouted, before Leesha or Bruna could speak.

Tender Michel held his warded Canon aloft so all could see the holy book as the remains of the dead were thrown on the ruin of the last burning house. The villagers stood with hats in hand, heads bowed. Jona threw incense on the blaze, flavoring the acrid stench permeating the air.

"Until the Deliverer comes to lift the Plague of demonkind, remember well that it was the sins of man that brought it down!" Michel shouted. "The adulterers and the fornicators! The liars and thieves and usurers!"

"The ones that clench their rears too tight," Elona murmured. Someone snickered.

"Those leaving this world will be judged," Michel went on, "and those who served the Creator's will shall join with him in Heaven, while those who have broken his trust, sullied by sins of indulgence or flesh, will burn in the Core for eternity!" He closed the book, and the assembled villagers bowed in silence.

"But while mourning is good and proper," Michel said, "we should not forget those of us the Creator has chosen to live. Let us break casks and drink to the dead. Let us tell the tales of them we love most, and laugh, for life is precious, and not to be wasted. We can save our tears for when we sit behind our wards tonight."

"That's our Tender," Elona muttered. "Any excuse to break open a cask."

"Now dear," Erny said, patting her hand, "he means well."

"The coward defends the drunk, of course," Elona said, pulling her hand away. "Steave rushes into burning houses, and my husband cringes with the women."

"I was in the bucket line!" Erny protested. He and Steave had been rivals for Elona, and it was said that his winning of Elona was more to do with his purse than her heart.

"Like a woman," Elona agreed, eyeing the muscular Steave across the crowd.

It was always like this. Leesha wished she could shut her ears to them. She wished the corelings had taken her mother, instead of seven good people. She wished her father would stand up to her for once; for himself, if not his daughter. She wished she would flower already, so she could go with Gared and leave them both behind.

Those too old or young to fight the flames had prepared a great meal for the village, and they laid it out as the others sat, too exhausted to move, and stared at the smoldering ashes.

But the fires were out, the wounded bandaged and healing, and there were hours before sunset. The Tender's words took the guilt from those relieved to be alive, and Smitt's strong Hollow ale did the rest. It was said that Smitt's ale could cure any woe, and there was much to cure. Soon the long tables rang with laughter at stories of those who had passed from the world.

Gared sat a few tables away with his friends Ren and Flinn, their wives, and his other friend Evin. The other boys, all woodcutters, were older than Gared by a few years, but Gared was bigger than all save Ren, and it seemed he would pass even him before his growing was done. Of the group, Evin alone was unpromised, and many girls eyed him, despite his short temper.

The older boys teased Gared relentlessly, especially about Leesha. She wasn't happy to be forced to sit with her parents, but sitting with Gared while Ren and Flinn made lewd suggestions and Evin picked fights was often worse.

After they had eaten their share, Tender Michel and Child Jona rose from the table, carrying a large platter of food to the Holy House, where Darsy looked after Bruna and the wounded. Leesha excused herself to help them. Gared spotted the move and rose to join her, but no sooner had she stood than she was swept off by Brianne, Saira, and Mairy, her closest friends.

"Is it true what happened?" Saira asked, pulling her left arm.

"Everyone's saying you knocked Darsy down and saved Hag Bruna!" Mairy said, pulling her right. Leesha looked back helplessly at Gared, and allowed herself to be led away.

"The grizzly bear can wait his turn," Brianne told her.

"Yull come second to them girls even after yur married, Gared!" Ren cried, causing his friends to roar with laughter and pound the table. The girls ignored them, spreading their skirts and sitting on the grass, away from the increasing noise, as their elders drained cask after cask.

"Gared's gonna be hearing that one awhile," Brianne laughed. "Ren bet five klats he won't get to kiss you before dusk, much less a good grope." At sixteen, she was already two years a widow, but had no shortage of suitors. She said it was because she knew a wife's tricks. She lived with her father and two older brothers, woodcutters, and was mother to them all.

"Unlike some people, I don't invite every passing boy to grope me," Leesha said, bringing a mock look of indignation from Brianne.

"I'd let Gared grope if I was promised to him," Saira said. She was fifteen, with cropped brown hair and freckles on her chipmunk cheeks. She had been promised to a boy last year, but the corelings had taken him and her father in a single night.

"I wish I was promised," Mairy complained. She was gaunt at fourteen years, with a hollow face and a prominent nose. She was full flowered, but despite the efforts of her parents, not yet promised. Elona called her scarecrow. "No man will want to put a child between those bony hips," she had sneered once, "lest the scarecrow crack in two when the babe breaks."

"It will happen soon enough," Leesha told her. She was the youngest of the group at thirteen, but the others seemed to center around her. Elona said it was because she was prettier and better moneyed, but Leesha could never believe her friends so petty.

"Did you really beat Darsy with a stick?" Mairy asked.

"It didn't happen like that," Leesha said. "Darsy made some mistake, and Bruna started hitting her with her stick. Darsy tried to back away, and walked right into me. We both fell down, and Bruna kept hitting her until she ran off."

"If she hit me with a stick, I'da hit her right back," Brianne said. "Da says Bruna's a witch, and she slaps stomachs with demons in her hut at night."

"That's disgusting nonsense!" Leesha snapped.

"Then why's she live so far from town?" Saira demanded. "And how is it she's still alive when her grandchildren are dead of old age?"

"Because she's an Herb Gatherer," Leesha said, "and you don't find herbs growing in the center of town. I helped her today, and it was amazing. I thought half the people brought to her were too hurt to live, but she saved every one."

"Did you see her cast spells on them?" Mairy asked excitedly.

"She's not a witch!" Leesha said. "She did it all with herbs and knives and thread."

"She cut people?" Mairy said in disgust.

"Witch," Brianne said. Saira nodded.

Leesha gave them all a sour look, and they quieted. "She didn't just go around cutting people," Leesha said. "She healed them. It was . . . I can't explain it. Old as she is, she never stopped working until she treated everyone. It was like she kept on by will alone. She collapsed right after she treated the last one."

"And that's when you saved her?" Mairy asked.

Leesha nodded. "She gave me the cure just before the coughing started. Really, all I did was brew it. I held her until the coughing stopped, and that's when everyone found us."

"You touched her?" Brianne made a face. "I bet she stunk of sour milk and weeds."

"Creator!" Leesha cried. "Bruna saved a dozen lives today, and all you can do is mock!"

"Goodness," Brianne quipped, "Leesha saves the hag, and suddenly her paps are too big for her corset." Leesha scowled. She was the last of her friends to bloom, and her breasts, or lack thereof, were a sore spot for her.

"You used to say the same things about her, Leesh," Saira said.

"Maybe so, but not anymore," Leesha said. "She may be a mean old woman, but she deserves better."

Just then, Child Jona came over to them. He was seventeen, but too small and slight to swing an axe or pull a saw. Jona spent most of his days penning and reading letters for those in town with no letters, which was almost everyone. Leesha, one of the few children who could read, often went to him to borrow books from Tender Michel's collection.

"I've a message from Bruna," he said to Leesha. "She wishes . . ."

His words were cut off as he was yanked backward. Jona was two years senior, but Gared spun him like a paper doll, gripping his robes and pulling him so close their noses touched.

"I told you before about talking to those what arn't promised to ya," Gared growled.

"I wasn't!" Jona protested, his feet kicking an inch off the ground. "I just . . . !"

"Gared!" Leesha barked. "You put him down this instant!"

Gared looked at Leesha, then back to Jona. His eyes flicked to his friends, then back to Leesha. He let go, and Jona crashed to the ground. He scrambled to his feet and scurried off. Brianne and Saira giggled, but Leesha silenced them with a glare before rounding on Gared.

"What in the Core is the matter with you?" Leesha demanded.

Gared looked down. "I'm sorry," he said. "It's jus' . . . well, I ent gotten to talk to ya all day, and I guess I got mad when I saw ya talking to him."

"Oh, Gared," Leesha touched his cheek, "you don't have to be jealous. There's no one for me but you."

"Really?" Gared asked.

"Will you apologize to Jona?" Leesha asked.

"Yes," Gared promised.

"Then yes, really," Leesha said. "Now go on back to the tables. I'll join you in a bit." She kissed him, and Gared broke into a wide smile and ran off.

"I suppose it's something like training a bear," Brianne mused.

"A bear that just sat in a briar patch," Saira said.

"You leave him be," Leesha said. "Gared doesn't mean any harm. He's just too strong for his own good, and a little . . ."

"Lumbering?" Brianne offered.

"Slow?" Saira supplied.

"Dim?" Mairy suggested.

Leesha swatted at them, and they all laughed.

Gared sat protectively by Leesha, he and Steave having come over to sit with Leesha's family. She longed for his arms around her, but it wasn't proper, even promised as they were, until she was of age and their engagement formalized by the Tender. Even then, chaste touching and kisses were supposed to be the limit until their wedding night.

Still, Leesha let Gared kiss her when they were alone, but she held it at that, regardless of what Brianne thought. She wanted to keep tradition, so their wedding night would be a special thing they would remember forever.

And of course, there was Klarissa, who had loved to dance and flirt. She had taught Leesha and her friends to reel and braided flowers in their hair. An exceptionally pretty girl, Klarissa had her pick of suitors.

Her son would be three now, and still no man in Cutter's Hollow would claim him as their own. It was broadly assumed that meant he was a married man, and over the months when her belly fattened, not a sermon had gone by where Tender Michel had failed to remind her that it was her sin, and that of those like her, that kept the Creator's Plague strong.

"The demons without echo the demons within," he said.

Klarissa had been well loved, but after that, the town had quickly turned. Women shunned her, whispering behind her passage, and men refused to meet her eyes while their wives were about, making lewd comments when they were not.

Klarissa had left with a Messenger bound for Fort Rizon soon after the boy was weaned, and never returned. Leesha missed her.

"I wonder what Bruna wanted when she sent Jona," Leesha said.

"I hate that little runt," Gared growled. "Every time he looks at you, I can see him imagining you as his wife."

"What do you care," Leesha asked, "if imagination is all it is?"

"I won't share you, even in other men's dreams," Gared said, putting his giant hand over hers under the table. Leesha sighed and leaned in to him. Bruna could wait.

Just then, Smitt stood, legs shaky with ale, and banged his stein on the table. "Everyone! Your attention, please!" His wife, Stefny, helped him stand up on the bench, propping him when he wobbled. The crowd quieted, and Smitt cleared his throat. He might dislike giving orders, but he liked giving speeches well enough.

"It's the worst times that bring out the best in us," he began. "But it's them times that show the Creator our mettle. Show that we've mended our ways and are worthy for him to send the Deliverer and end the Plague. Show that the evil of the night cannot take our sense of family.

"Because that's what Cutter's Hollow is," Smitt went on. "A

family. Oh, we bicker and fight and play favorites, but when the corelings come, we see those ties of family like the strings of a loom, tying us all together. Whatever our differences, no one is left to them.

"Four houses lost their wards in the night," Smitt told the crowd, "putting a score at the corelings' absent mercy. But due to heroism out in the naked night, only seven were taken.

"Niklas!" Smitt shouted, pointing at the sandy-haired man sitting across from him. "Ran into a burning house to pull his mother out!

"Jow!" He pointed to another man, who jumped at the sound. "Not two days ago, he and Dav were before me, arguing all the way to blows. But last night, Jow hit a wood demon, a *wood demon,* with his axe to hold it off while Dav and his family ran across his wards!"

Smitt hopped up on the table, passion lending agility to his drunken body. He walked its length, calling people by name, and telling of their deeds in the night. "Heroes were found in the day, as well," he went on. "Gared and Steave!" he cried, pointing. "Left their own house to burn to douse those that had a better chance! Because of them and others, only eight houses burned, when by rights it should have been the whole town!"

Smitt turned, and suddenly he was looking right at Leesha. His hand raised, and the finger he pointed to her struck her like a fist. "Leesha!" he called. "Thirteen years old, and she saved Gatherer Bruna's life!

"In every person in Cutter's Hollow beats the heart of a hero!" Smitt said, sweeping his hand over all. "The corelings test us, and tragedy tempers us, but like Milnese steel, Cutter's Hollow will not break!"

The crowd roared in approval. Those who had lost loved ones cried the loudest, their cheeks wet with tears.

Smitt stood in the center of the din, soaking in its strength. After a time, he patted his hands, and the villagers quieted.

"Tender Michel," he said, gesturing to the man, "has opened the Holy House to the wounded, and Stefny and Darsy have volunteered to spend the night there tending them. Michel also offers the Creator's wards to all others who have nowhere else to go."

Smitt raised a fist. "But hard pews are not where heroes should lay their heads! Not when they're among family. My tavern can hold ten comfortably, and more if need be. Who else among us will share their wards and their beds to heroes?"

Everyone shouted again, this time louder, and Smitt broke into a wide smile. He patted his hands again. "The Creator smiles on you all," he said, "but the hour grows late. I'll assign . . ."

Elona stood up. She too had drunk a few mugs, and her words slurred. "Erny and I will take in Gared and Steave," she said, causing Erny to look sharply at her. "We've plenty of room, and with Gared and Leesha promised, they're practically family already."

"That's very generous of you, Elona," Smitt said, unable to hide his surprise. Rarely did Elona show generosity, and even then, there was usually a hidden price.

"Are you sure that's proper?" Stefny asked loudly, causing everyone to turn eyes to her. When she wasn't working in her husband's tavern, Stefny was volunteering at the Holy House, or studying the Canon. She hated Elona—a mark in her favor in Leesha's mind—but she had also been the first to turn on Klarissa when her state became clear.

"Two promised children living under one roof?" Stefny asked, but her eyes flicked to Steave, not Gared. "Who knows what improprieties might occur? Perhaps it would be best for you to take in others, and let Gared and Steave stay at the tavern."

Elona's eyes narrowed. "I think three parents enough to chaperone two children, Stefny," she said icily. She turned to Gared, squeezing his broad shoulders. "My soon-to-be son-in-law did the work of five men today," she said. "And Steave," she reached out and drunkenly poked the man's burly chest, "did the work of ten."

She spun back toward Leesha, but stumbled a bit. Steave, laughing, caught her about the waist before she fell. His hand was huge on her slender midsection. "Even my," she swallowed the word "useless," but Leesha heard it anyway, "daughter did great deeds today. I'll not have my heroes bed down in some other's home."

Stefny scowled, but the rest of the villagers took the matter as closed, and started offering up their own homes to the others in need.

Elona stumbled again, falling into Steave's lap with a laugh.

"You can sleep in Leesha's room," she told him. "It's right next to mine." She dropped her voice at that last part, but she was drunk, and everyone heard. Gared blushed, Steave laughed, and Erny hung his head. Leesha felt a stab of sympathy for her father.

"I wish the corelings had taken *her* last night," she muttered.

Her father looked up at her. "Don't ever say that," he said. "Not about anyone." He looked hard at Leesha until she nodded.

"Besides," he added sadly, "they'd probably just give her right back."

Accommodations had been made for all, and people were preparing to leave when there was a murmur, and the crowd parted. Through that gap limped Hag Bruna.

Child Jona held one of the woman's arms as she walked. Leesha leapt to her feet to take her other. "Bruna, you shouldn't be up," she admonished. "You should be resting!"

"It's your own fault, girl," Bruna snapped. "There's those sicker than I, and I need herbs from my hut to treat them. If your bodyguard"—she glared at Gared and he fell back in fright— "had let Jona bring my message, I could have sent you with a list. But now it's late, and I'll have to go with you. We can stay behind my wards for the night, and come back in the morn."

"Why me?" Leesha asked.

"Because none of the other lackwit girls in this town can read!" Bruna shrieked. "They'd mix up the labels on the bottles worse'n that cow Darsy!"

"Jona can read," Leesha said.

"I offered to go," the acolyte began, but Bruna slammed her stick down on his foot, cutting his words off in a yelp.

"Herb Gathering is women's work, girl," Bruna said. "Holy Men are just there to pray while we do it."

"I . . ." Leesha began, looking back at her parents for an escape.

"I think it's a fine idea," Elona said, finally extricating herself from Steave's lap. "Spend the night at Bruna's." She shoved Leesha forward. "My daughter is glad to help," she said with a broad smile.

"Perhaps Gared should go as well?" Steave suggested, kicking his son.

"You'll need a strong back to carry your herbs and potions back in the morning," Elona agreed, pulling Gared up.

The ancient Herb Gatherer glared at her, then at Steave, but nodded finally.

The trip to Bruna's was slow, the hag setting a shuffling crawl of a pace. They made it to the hut just before sunset.

"Check the wards, boy," Bruna told Gared. While he complied, Leesha took her inside, setting the old woman down in a cushioned chair, and laying a quilt blanket over her. Bruna was breathing hard, and Leesha feared she would start coughing again any minute. She filled the kettle and laid wood and tinder in the hearth, casting her eyes about for flint and steel.

"The box on the mantel," Bruna said, and Leesha noticed the small wooden box. She opened it, but there was no flint or steel within, only short wooden sticks with some kind of clay at the ends. She picked up two and tried rubbing them together.

"Not like that, girl!" Bruna snapped. "Have you never seen a flamestick?"

Leesha shook her head. "Da keeps some in the shop where he mixes chemics," Leesha said, "but I'm not to go in there."

The old Herb Gatherer sighed and beckoned the girl over. She took one of the sticks and braced it against her gnarled, dry thumbnail. She flicked her thumb, and the end of the stick burst into flame. Leesha's eyes bulged.

"There's more to Herb Gathering than plants, girl," Bruna said, touching the flame to a taper before the flamestick burned out. She lit a lamp, and handed the taper to Leesha. She held the lamp out, illuminating a dusty shelf filled with books in its flickering light.

"Sweet day!" Leesha exclaimed. "You have more books than Tender Michel!"

"These aren't witless stories censored by the Holy Men, girl. Herb Gatherers are keepers of a bit of the knowledge of the old world, from back before the Return, when the demons burned the great libraries."

"Science?" Leesha asked. "Was that not the hubris that brought on the Plague?"

"That's Michel talking," Bruna said. "If I'd known that boy would grow into such a pompous ass, I'd have left him between his mother's legs. It was science, as much as magic, that drove the corelings off the first time. The sagas tell of great Herb Gatherers healing mortal wounds, and mixing herbs and minerals that killed demons by the score with fire and poison."

Leesha was about to ask another question when Gared returned. Bruna waved her toward the hearth, and Leesha lit the fire and set the kettle over it. Soon the water was boiling, and Bruna reached into the many pockets of her robe, putting her special mixture of herbs in her cup, and tea in Leesha's and Gared's. Her hands were quick, but Leesha still noticed the old woman throw something extra in Gared's cup.

She poured the water, and they all sipped in an awkward silence. Gared drank his quickly, and soon began rubbing his face. A moment later, he slumped over, fast asleep.

"You put something in his tea," Leesha accused.

The old woman cackled. "Tampweed resin and skyflower pollen," she said. "Each with many uses alone, but together, a pinch can put a bull to sleep."

"But why?" Leesha asked.

Bruna smiled, but it was a frightening thing. "Call it chaperoning," she said. "Promised or no, you can't trust a boy of fifteen summers alone with a young girl at night."

"Then why let him come along?" Leesha asked.

Bruna shook her head. "I told your father not to marry that shrew, but she dangled her udders at him and left him dizzy," she sighed. "Drunk as they are, Steave and your mum are going to have at it no matter who's in the house," she said. "But that don't mean Gared ought to hear it. Boys are bad enough at his age, as is."

Leesha's eyes bulged. "My mother would never . . . !"

"Careful finishing that sentence, girl," Bruna cut her off. "The Creator abhors a liar."

Leesha deflated. She knew what Elona was like. "Gared's not like that, though," she said.

Bruna snorted. "Midwife a village and tell me that," she said.

"It wouldn't even matter if I was flowered," Leesha said. "Then Gared and I could marry, and I could do for him as a wife should."

"Eager for that, are you?" Bruna said with a wicked grin. "It's no sad affair, I'll admit. Men have more uses than swinging axes and carrying heavy things."

"What's taking so long?" Leesha asked. "Saira and Mairy

reddened their sheets in their twelfth summers, and this will be my thirteenth! What could be wrong?"

"Nothing's wrong," Bruna said. "Each girl bleeds in her own time. It may be you have a year yet, or more."

"A year!" Leesha exclaimed.

"Don't be so quick to leave childhood behind, girl," Bruna said. "You'll find you miss it when its gone. There's more to the world than laying under a man and making his babies."

"But what else could compare?" Leesha asked.

Bruna gestured to her shelf. "Choose a book," she said. "Any book. Bring it here, and I'll show you what else the world can offer."

CHAPTER 5

CROWDED HOME
319 AR

LEESHA WOKE WITH A START as Bruna's old rooster crowed to mark the dawn. She rubbed her face, feeling the imprint of the book on her cheek. Gared and Bruna were still fast asleep. The Herb Gatherer had passed out early, but despite her own fatigue, Leesha kept on reading late into the night. She had thought Herb Gathering was just setting bones and birthing babes, but there was so much more. Herb Gatherers studied the entire natural world, finding ways to combine the Creator's many gifts for the benefit of His children.

Leesha took the ribbon that held back her dark hair and laid it across the page, closing the book as reverently as she did the Canon. She rose and stretched, laying fresh wood on the fire and stirring the embers into a flame. She put the kettle on, and then went over to shake Gared.

"Wake up, lazybones," she said, keeping her voice low. Gared only groaned. Whatever Bruna had given him, it was strong. She shook harder, and he swatted at her, eyes still closed.

"Get up or there'll be no breakfast for you," Leesha laughed, kicking him.

Gared groaned again, and his eyes cracked. When Leesha drew her foot back a second time, he reached out and grabbed her leg, pulling her down on top of him with a yelp.

He rolled atop her, encircling her in his burly arms, and Leesha giggled at his kisses.

"Stop it," she said, swatting at him halfheartedly, "you'll wake Bruna."

"So what if I do?" Gared asked. "The old hag is a hundred years old and blind as a bat."

"The hag's ears are still sharp," Bruna said, cracking open one of her milky white eyes. Gared yelped and practically flew to his feet, distancing himself from Leesha and Bruna both.

"You keep your hands to yourself in my home, boy, or I'll brew a potion to keep your manhood slack for a year," Bruna said. Leesha saw the color drain from Gared's face, and bit her lip to keep from laughing. For some reason, Bruna no longer frightened her, but she loved watching the old woman intimidate everyone else.

"We understand one another?" Bruna asked.

"Yes'm," Gared said immediately.

"Good," Bruna said. "Now put those burly shoulders to work and split some wood for the firebox." Gared was out the door before she finished. Leesha laughed as the door slammed.

"Liked that, did you?" Bruna asked.

"I've never seen anyone send Gared scurrying like that," Leesha said.

"Come closer, so I can see you," Bruna said. When Leesha did, she went on, "Being village healer is more than brewing potions. A strong dose of fear is good for the biggest boy in the village. Maybe help him think twice before hurting someone."

"Gared would never hurt anyone," Leesha said.

"As you say," Bruna said, but she didn't sound at all convinced.

"Could you really have made a potion to take his manhood away?" Leesha asked.

Bruna cackled. "Not for a year," she said. "Not with one dose, anyway. But a few days, or even a week? As easily as I dosed his tea."

Leesha looked thoughtful.

"What is it, girl?" Bruna asked. "Having doubts your boy will leave you unplucked before your wedding?"

"I was thinking more on Steave," Leesha said.

Bruna nodded. "And well you should," she advised. "But have care. Your mother is wise to the trick. She came to me often when she was young, needing Gatherer's tricks to stem her flow and keep her from getting with child while she had her fun. I didn't see her for what she was, then, and I'm sad to say I taught her more than I should have."

"Mum wasn't a virgin when Da carried her across his wards?" Leesha asked in shock.

Bruna snorted. "Half the town had a roll with her before Steave drove the others away."

Leesha's jaw dropped. "Mum condemned Klarissa when she got with child," she said.

Bruna spat on the floor. "Everyone turned on that poor girl. Hypocrites, all! Smitt talks of family, but he didn't lift a finger when his wife led the town after that girl like a pack of flame demons. Half those women pointing at her and crying 'Sin!' were guilty of the same deed, they were just lucky enough to marry fast, or smart enough to take precautions."

"Precautions?" Leesha asked.

Bruna shook her head. "Elona's so eager to have a grandson she's kept you in the dark about everything, eh?" she asked. "Tell me, girl, how are babies made?"

Leesha blushed. "The man, I mean, your husband . . . He . . ."

"Out with it, girl," Bruna snapped, "I'm too old to wait for the red to leave your face."

"He spends his seed in you," Leesha said, her face reddening further.

Bruna cackled. "You can treat burns and demon wounds, but blush at how life is made?"

Leesha opened her mouth to reply, but Bruna cut her off.

"Make your boy spend his seed on your belly, and you can lie with him to your heart's content," Bruna said. "But boys can't be trusted to pull from you in time, as Klarissa learned. The smarter ones come to me for tea."

"Tea?" Leesha asked, leaning on every word.

"Pomm leaves, leached in the right dose with some other herbs, create a tea that will keep a man's seed from taking root."

"But Tender Michel says . . ." Leesha began.

"Spare me the recitation from the Canon," Bruna cut her off. "It's a book written by men, without a thought given towards the plight of women."

Leesha's mouth closed with a click.

"Your mum visited me often," Bruna went on, "asking questions, helping me around the hut, grinding herbs for me. I had thought to make her my apprentice, but all she wanted was the secret of the tea. Once I told her how it was made, she left and never returned."

"That does sound like her," Leesha said.

"Pomm tea is safe enough in small doses," Bruna said, "but

Steave is lusty, and your mother took too much. The two of them must have slapped stomachs a thousand times before your father's business began to prosper, and his purse caught her eye. By then, your mum's womb was scraped dry."

Leesha looked at her curiously.

"After she married your father, Elona tried for two years to conceive without success," Bruna said. "Steave married some young girl and got her with child overnight, which only made your mum more desperate. Finally, she came back to me, begging for help."

Leesha leaned in close, knowing her existence had hinged on whatever Bruna said next.

"Pomm tea must be taken in small doses," Bruna repeated, "and once a month it is best to stop it and allow your flow to come. Fail this, and you risk becoming barren. I warned Elona, but she was a slave to her loins, and failed to listen. For months I gave her herbs and checked her flow, giving her herbs to slip into your father's food. Finally, she conceived."

"Me," Leesha said. "She conceived me."

Bruna nodded. "I feared for you, girl. Your mum's womb was weak, and we both knew she would not have another chance. She came to me every day, asking me to check on her son."

"Son?" Leesha asked.

"I warned her it might not be a boy," Bruna said, "but Elona was stubborn. 'The Creator could not be so cruel,' she'd say, forgetting that the same Creator made the corelings."

"So all I am is some cruel joke of the Creator?" Leesha asked.

Bruna grabbed Leesha's chin in her bony fingers and pulled her in close. Leesha could see the long gray hairs, like cat's whiskers, on the crone's wrinkled lips as she spoke.

"We are what we choose to be, girl," she said. "Let others determine your worth, and you've already lost, because no one wants people worth more than themselves. Elona has no one to blame but herself for her bad choices, but she's too vain to admit it. Easier to take it out on you and poor Erny."

"I wish she'd been exposed and run out of town," Leesha said.

"You would betray your gender out of spite?" Bruna asked.

"I don't understand," Leesha said.

"There's no shame in a girl wanting a man twixt her legs, Leesha," Bruna said. "An Herb Gatherer can't judge folks for doing what nature intended they do when they are young and free. It's oath breakers I can't abide. You say your vows, girl, you'd best plan on keeping them."

Leesha nodded.

Gared returned, just then. "Darsy's come to see ya back to town," he told Bruna.

"I swear I sacked that dim-witted sow," Bruna grumbled.

"The town council met yesterday and reinstated me," Darsy said, pushing into the hut. She was not as tall as Gared, but she was not far off, and easily topped his weight. "It's your own fault. No one else would take the job."

"They can't do that!" Bruna barked.

"Oh, yes they can," Darsy said. "I don't like it any more than you, but you could pass any day now, and the town needs someone to tend the sick."

"I've outlived better than you," Bruna sneered. "I'll choose who I teach."

"Well I'm to stay until you do," Darsy said, looking at Leesha and baring her teeth.

"Then make yourself useful and put the porridge on," Bruna said. "Gared's a growing boy and needs to keep his strength up."

Darsy scowled, but she rolled her sleeves and headed for the boiling kettle nonetheless.

"Smitt and I are going to have a little chat when I get to town," Bruna grumbled.

"Is Darsy really so bad?" Leesha asked.

Bruna's watery eyes turned Gared's way. "I know you're stronger than an ox, boy, but I imagine there are still a few cords to split out back."

Gared didn't need to be told twice. He was out the door in a blink, and they heard him put the axe back to work.

"Darsy's useful enough around the hut," Bruna admitted. "She splits wood almost as fast as your boy, and makes a fair porridge. But those meaty hands are too clumsy for healing, and she has little aptitude for the Gatherer's art. She'll make a passable midwife—any fool can pull a babe from its mother—and at setting bones she's second to none, but the subtler work is beyond her. I weep at the thought of this town with her as Herb Gatherer."

"You won't make Gared much of a wife if you can't get a simple dinner together!" Elona called.

Leesha scowled. So far as she knew, her mother had never prepared a meal in her life. It had been days since she'd had a proper sleep, but Creator forbid her mother lift a hand to help.

She had spent the day tending the sick with Bruna and Darsy. She picked up the skills quickly, causing Bruna to use her as an example to Darsy. Darsy did not care for that.

Leesha knew Bruna wanted to apprentice her. The old woman didn't push, but she had made her intentions clear. But there was her father's papermaking business to think of as well. She had worked in the shop, a large connected section of their house, since she was a little girl, penning messages for villagers and making sheets. Erny told her she had a gift for it. Her bindings were prettier than his, and Leesha liked to embed her pages with flower petals, which the ladies in Lakton and Fort Rizon paid more for than their husbands did for plain sheets.

Erny's hope was to retire while Leesha ran the shop and Gared made the pulp and handled the heavy work. But paper-making had never held much interest for Leesha. She did it mostly to spend time with her father, away from the lash of her mother's tongue.

Elona might have liked the money it made, but she hated the shop, complaining of the smell of the lye in the pulping vats and the noise of the grinder. The shop was a retreat from her that Leesha and Erny took often, a place of laughter that the house proper would never be.

Steave's booming laugh made Leesha look up from the vegetables she was chopping for stew. He was in the common room, sitting in her father's chair, drinking his ale. Elona sat on the chair's arm, laughing and leaning in, her hand on his shoulder.

Leesha wished she were a flame demon, so she could spit fire on them. She had never been happy trapped in the house with Elona, but now all she could think of was Bruna's stories. Her mother didn't love her father and probably never had. She thought her daughter a cruel joke of the Creator. And she hadn't been a virgin when Erny carried her across the wards.

For some reason, that cut the deepest. Bruna said there was no sin in a woman taking pleasure in a man, but her mother's hypocrisy stung nonetheless. She had helped force Klarissa out of town to hide her own indiscretion.

"I won't be like you," Leesha swore. She would have her

wedding day as the Creator intended, and become a woman in a proper marriage bed.

Elona squealed at something Steave said, and Leesha began to sing to herself to drown them out. Her voice was rich and pure; Tender Michel was forever asking her to sing at services.

"Leesha!" her mother barked a moment later. "Quit your warbling! We can hardly hear ourselves think out here!"

"Doesn't sound like there's much thinking going on," Leesha muttered.

"What was that?" Elona demanded.

"Nothing!" Leesha called back in her most innocent voice.

They ate just after sunset, and Leesha watched proudly as Gared used the bread she had made to scrape clean his third bowl of her stew.

"She's not much of a cook, Gared," Elona apologized, "but it's filling enough if you hold your nose."

Steave, gulping ale at the time, snorted it out his nose. Gared laughed at his father, and Elona snatched the napkin from Erny's lap to dry Steave's face. Leesha looked to her father for support, but he kept his eyes on his bowl. He hadn't said a word since emerging from the shop.

It was too much for Leesha. She cleared the table and retreated to her room, but there was no sanctuary there. She had forgotten that her mother had given the room to Steave for the duration of his and Gared's indefinite stay. The giant woodcutter had tracked mud across her spotless floor, leaving his filthy boots atop her favorite book, where it lay by her bed.

She cried out and ran to the treasure, but the cover was hopelessly muddied. Her bedclothes of soft Rizonan wool were stained with Creator knew what, and stank of a foul blend of musky sweat and the expensive Angierian perfume her mother favored.

Leesha felt sick. She clutched her precious book tightly and fled to her father's shop, weeping as she tried futilely to clean the stains from her book. It was there Gared found her.

"So this is where ya run off to," he said, moving to encircle her in his burly arms.

Leesha pulled away, wiping her eyes and trying to compose herself. "I just needed a moment," she said.

Gared caught her arm. "Is this about the joke yur mum made?" he asked.

Leesha shook her head, trying to turn away again, but Gared held her fast.

"I was only laughing at my da," he said. "I loved yur stew."

"Really?" Leesha sniffed.

"Really," he promised, pulling her close and kissing her deeply. "We could feed an army of sons on cooking like that," he husked.

Leesha giggled. "I might have trouble squeezing out an army of little Gareds," she said.

He held her tighter, and put his lips to her ear. "Right now, I'm only interested in you squeezing one in," he said.

Leesha groaned, but she gently pushed him away. "We'll be wed soon enough," she said.

"Yesterday ent soon enough," Gared said, but he let her go.

Leesha lay curled up in blankets by the common room fire. Steave had her room, and Gared was on a cot in the shop. The floor was drafty and cold at night, and the wool rug was rough and hard to lie upon. She longed for her own bed, though nothing short of burning would erase the stench of Steave and her mother's sin.

She wasn't even sure why Elona bothered with the ruse. It wasn't as if she was fooling anyone. She might as well put Erny out in the common room and take Steave right to her bed.

Leesha couldn't wait until she and Gared could leave.

She lay awake, listening to the demons testing the wards and imagining running the papermaking shop with Gared, her father retired and her mother and Steave sadly passed on. Her belly was round and full, and she kept books while Gared came in flexed and sweaty from working the grinder. He kissed her as their little ones raced about the shop.

The image warmed her, but she remembered Bruna's words, and wondered if she would be missing something if she devoted her life to children and papermaking. She closed her eyes again, and imagined herself as the Herb Gatherer of Cutter's Hollow, everyone depending on her to cure their ills, deliver their babies, and heal their wounds. It was a powerful image, but one harder to fit Gared or children into. An Herb Gatherer had to visit the sick, and the image of Gared carrying her herbs and tools from place to place didn't ring true, nor did the idea of him keeping an eye on the children while she worked.

Bruna had managed it, however many decades ago, marrying, raising children, and still tending the folk, but Leesha didn't see how. She would have to ask the old woman.

She heard a click, and looked up to see Gared gingerly stepping from the shop. She pretended to be asleep until he drew near, then rolled over suddenly. "What are you doing out here?" she whispered. Gared jumped and covered his mouth to muffle a yelp. Leesha had to bite her lip to keep from laughing aloud.

"I just came to use the privy," Gared whispered, coming over and kneeling beside her.

"There's a privy in the shop," Leesha reminded him.

"Then I came for a good-night kiss," he said, leaning in with his lips puckered.

"You had three when you first went to bed," Leesha said, playfully smacking him away.

"Is it so bad to want another?" Gared asked.

"I suppose not," Leesha said, putting her arms around his shoulders.

Some time later, there was the creak of another door. Gared stiffened, looking about for a place to hide. Leesha pointed to one of the chairs. He was far too big to be covered completely, but with only the dim orange glow from the fireplace to see by, it might prove enough.

A faint light appeared a moment later, dashing that hope. Leesha barely managed to lie back down and close her eyes before it swept into the room.

Through slitted eyes, Leesha saw her mother looking into the common room. The lantern she held was mostly shuttered, and the light threw great shadows, giving Gared room enough to hide if she didn't look too closely.

They needn't have worried. After satisfying herself that Leesha was asleep, Elona opened the door to Steave's room and disappeared inside.

Leesha stared after her for a long time. That Elona was being untrue was no great revelation, but until this very moment, Leesha had allowed herself the luxury of doubting that her mother could truly be so willing to throw away her vows.

She felt Gared's hand on her shoulder. "Leesha, I'm sorry," he said, and she buried her face in his chest, weeping. He held her tightly, muffling her sobs and rocking back and forth. A demon roared somewhere off in the distance, and Leesha wanted to scream along with it. She held her tongue in the vain hope that her father was sleeping, oblivious to Elona's grunting, but the likelihood seemed remote unless she had used one of Bruna's sleeping draughts on him.

"I'll take you away from this," Gared said. "We'll waste no time in making plans, and I'll have a house for us before the ceremony if I have to cut and carry all the logs myself."

"Oh, Gared," she said, kissing him. He returned the embrace, and laid her down again. The thumping from Steave's room and the sound of the demons without all faded away into the thrum of blood in her ears.

Gared's hands roamed her body freely, and Leesha let him touch places that only a husband should. She gasped and arched her back in pleasure, and Gared took the opportunity to position himself between her legs. She felt him slip free of his breeches, and knew what he was doing. She knew she should push him away, but there was a great emptiness inside her, and Gared seemed the only person in the world who might be able to fill it.

He was about to drive forward when Leesha heard her mother cry out in pleasure, and she stiffened. Was she any better than Elona, if she gave up her vows so easily? She swore to cross the wards of her marriage house a virgin. She swore to be nothing like Elona. But here she was, throwing all that away to rut with a boy mere feet from where her mother sinned.

It's oath breakers I can't abide, she heard Bruna say again, and Leesha pressed her hands hard against Gared's chest.

"Gared, no, please," she whispered. Gared stiffened for a long moment. Finally, he rolled away from her and retied his breeches.

"I'm sorry," Leesha said weakly.

"No, I'm sorry," Gared said. He kissed her temple. "I can wait."

Leesha hugged him tightly, and Gared rose to leave. She wanted him to stay and sleep beside her, but they had stretched their luck thin as it was. If they were caught together, Elona would punish her severely, despite her own sin. Perhaps even because of it.

As the door to the shop clicked shut, Leesha lay back filled with warm thoughts of Gared. Whatever pain her mother might bring her, she could weather it so long as she had Gared.

Breakfast was an uncomfortable affair, the sounds of chewing and swallowing thunderous in the mute pall hanging over the table. It seemed there was nothing to say not better left unsaid. Leesha wordlessly cleared the table while Gared and Steave fetched their axes.

"Will you be in the shop today?" Gared asked, finally breaking the silence. Erny looked up for the first time that morning, interested in her reply.

"I promised Bruna I'd help tend the wounded again today," Leesha said, but she looked apologetically at her father as she did. Erny nodded in understanding and smiled weakly.

"And how long is that to go on for?" Elona asked.

Leesha shrugged. "Until they're better, I suppose," she said.

"You're spending too much time with that old witch," Elona said.

"At your request," Leesha reminded.

Elona scowled. "Don't get smart with me, girl."

Anger flared in Leesha, but she flashed her most winning smile as she swung her cloak around her shoulders. "Don't worry, Mother," she said, "I won't drink too much of her tea."

Steave snorted, and Elona's eyes bulged, but Leesha swept out the door before she could recover enough to reply.

Gared walked with her a ways, but soon they reached the place where the woodcutters met each morning, and Gared's friends were already waiting.

"Yur late, Gar," Evin grumbled.

"Gotta woman t'cook for him, now," Flinn said. "That'll make any man linger."

"If he even slept." Ren snorted. "My guess is he got her doing more'n cooking, an' right under her father's nose."

"Ren got that right, Gar?" Flinn asked. "Find a new place to keep yur axe last night?"

Leesha bristled and opened her mouth to retort, but Gared laid a hand on her shoulder. "Pay them no mind," he said. "They're just tryin' to make you spit."

"You could defend my honor," Leesha said. Creator knew, boys would fight for any other reason.

"Oh, I will," Gared promised. "I just don't want ya to see it. I'd rather ya keep thinking me gentle."

"You *are* gentle," Leesha said, standing on tiptoes to kiss his cheek. The boys hooted, and Leesha stuck her tongue out at them as she walked off.

"Idiot girl," Bruna muttered, when Leesha told her what she had said to Elona. "Only a fool shows their cards when the game's just getting started."

"This isn't a game, it's my life!" Leesha said.

Bruna grabbed her face, squeezing her cheeks so hard her lips puckered apart. "All the more reason to show a little sense," she growled, glaring with her milky eyes.

Leesha felt anger flare hotly within her. Who was this woman, to speak to her so? Bruna seemed to hold the entire town in scorn, grabbing, hitting, and threatening anyone she pleased. Was she any better than Elona, really? Had she had Leesha's best interests at heart when she told her all those horrible things about her mother, or was she just manipulating her to become her apprentice, like Elona's pressure to marry Gared early and bear his children? In her heart, Leesha wanted both of those things, but she was tiring of being pushed.

"Well, well, look who's back," came a voice from the door, "the young prodigy."

Leesha looked up to see Darsy standing in the doorway of the Holy House with an armful of firewood. The woman made no effort to hide her dislike for Leesha, and she could be just as intimidating as Bruna when she wished. Leesha had tried to assure her that she was not a threat, but her overtures only seemed to make things worse. Darsy was determined not to like her.

"Don't blame Leesha if she's learned more in two days than you did in your first year," Bruna said, as Darsy slammed down the wood and lifted a heavy iron poker to stoke the fire.

Leesha was sure she would never get along with Darsy so long as Bruna kept picking at the wound, but she busied herself grinding herbs for poultices. Several of those burned in the attack had skin infections that needed regular attention. Others were worse still. Bruna had been shaken awake twice in the night to tend those, but so far, her herbs and skills had not failed her.

Bruna had assumed complete control of the Holy House,

ordering Tender Michel and the rest around like Milnese servants. She kept Leesha close by, talking continuously in her phlegmy rasp, explaining the nature of the wounds, and the properties of the herbs she used to treat them. Leesha watched her cut and sew flesh, and found her stomach was strengthening to such things.

Morning faded into afternoon, and Leesha had to force Bruna to pause and eat. Others might not notice the strain in the old woman's breath or the shake of her hands, but Leesha did.

"That's it," she said finally, snatching the mortar and pestle from the Herb Gatherer's hands. Bruna looked up at her sharply.

"Go and rest," Leesha said.

"Who are you, girl, to . . ." Bruna began, reaching for her stick.

Leesha was wise to the move and faster, grabbing the stick and pointing it right at Bruna's hooked nose. "You're going to have another attack if you don't rest," she scolded. "I'm taking you outside, and no arguing! Stefny and Darsy can handle things for an hour."

"Barely," Bruna grumbled, but she allowed Leesha to help her up and lead her outside.

The sun was high in the sky, and the grass by the Holy House was lush and green, save for a few patches blackened by flame demons. Leesha spread a blanket and eased Bruna down, bringing her special tea and soft bread that would not strain the crone's few remaining teeth.

They sat in comfortable silence for a time, enjoying the warm spring day. Leesha thought she had been unfair, comparing Bruna to her mother. When was the last time she and Elona had shared a comfortable silence in the sun? Had they ever?

She heard a rasping sound, and turned to find Bruna snoring. She smiled and spread the woman's shawl over her. She stretched her legs, and spotted Saira and Mairy a short ways off, sewing out on the grass. They waved and beckoned, scooching over on their blanket to make room as Leesha came to sit.

"How goes the Herb Gathering?" Mairy asked.

"Exhausting," Leesha said. "Where's Brianne?"

The girls looked at one another and giggled. "Off in the woods with Evin," Saira said.

Leesha tsked. "That girl is going to end up like Klarissa," she said.

Saira shrugged. "Brianne says you can't scorn something you haven't tried."

"Are *you* planning to try?" Leesha asked.

"You think you've no reason not to wait," Saira said. "I thought that, too, before Jak was taken. Now I'd give anything to have had him once before he died. To have his child, even."

"I'm sorry," Leesha said.

"It's all right," Saira replied sadly. Leesha embraced her, and Mairy joined in.

"Oh, how sweet!" came a cry from behind them. "I want to hug, too!" They looked up just as Brianne crashed into them, knocking them laughing into the grass.

"You're in good spirits today," Leesha said.

"A romp in the woods'll do that," Brianne said with a wink, elbowing her in the ribs. "Besides," she sang, "Eevin told me a seecret!"

"Tell us!" the three girls cried at once.

Brianne laughed, and her eyes flicked to Leesha. "Maybe later," she said. "How's the crone's new apprentice today?"

"I'm not her apprentice, whatever Bruna may think," Leesha said. "I'm still going to run my father's shop once Gared and I marry. I'm just helping with the sick."

"Better you'n me," Brianne said. "Herb Gathering seems like hard work. You look a mess. Get enough sleep last night?"

Leesha shook her head. "The floor by the hearth isn't as comfortable as a bed," she said.

"I wouldn't mind sleeping on the floor if I had Gared for a pallet," Brianne said.

"And just what is that supposed to mean?" Leesha asked.

"Don't play dumb, Leesh," Brianne said with a hint of irritation. "We're your friends."

Leesha puffed up. "If you're insinuating . . . !"

"Come off the pedestal, Leesha," Brianne said. "I know Gared had you last night. I'd hoped you'd be honest with us about it."

Saira and Mairy gasped, and Leesha's eyes bulged, her face reddening. "He had no such thing!" she shouted. "Who told you that?"

"Evin," Brianne smiled. "Said Gared's been bragging all day."

"Then Gared's a ripping liar!" Leesha barked. "I'm not some tramp, to go around . . ."

Brianne's face darkened, and Leesha gasped and covered her mouth. "Oh, Brianne," she said. "I'm sorry! I didn't mean . . ."

"No, I think you did," Brianne said. "I think it's the only true thing you've said today."

She stood and brushed off her skirts, her usual good mood vanished. "Come on, girls," she said. "Let's go somewhere where the air's cleaner."

Saira and Mairy looked at each other, then at Leesha, but Brianne was already walking, and they rose quickly to follow. Leesha opened her mouth, but choked, not knowing what to say.

"Leesha!" she heard Bruna cry. She turned to see the old woman bracing on her cane and struggling to rise. With a pained glance at her departing friends, Leesha rushed to aid her.

Leesha was waiting as Gared and Steave came sauntering down the path toward her father's house. They joked and laughed, and their joviality gave Leesha the strength she needed. She gripped her skirts in white-knuckled fists as she strode up to them.

"Leesha!" Steave greeted with a mocking smile. "How's my soon-to-be daughter today?" He spread his arms wide, as if to sweep her into a hug.

Leesha ignored him, going right up to Gared and slapping him full in the face.

"Hey!" Gared cried.

"Oh ho!" Steave laughed. Leesha fixed him with her mother's best glare, and he put up his hands placatingly.

"I see yuv some talkin' to do," he said, "so I'll leave you to it." He looked at Gared and winked. "Pleasure has its price," he advised as he left.

Leesha whirled on Gared, swinging at him again. He caught her wrist and squeezed hard. "Leesha, stop it!" he demanded.

Leesha ignored the pain in her wrist, slamming her knee hard between his legs. Her thick skirts softened the blow, but it was enough to break his grip and drop him to the ground, clutching his crotch. Leesha kicked him, but Gared was thick with hard muscle, and his hands protected the one place vulnerable to her strength.

"Leesha, what the Core is the matter with you?" Gared gasped, but it was cut off as she kicked him in the mouth.

Gared growled, and the next time she lifted her foot, he

grabbed it and shoved hard, sending her flying backward. The breath was knocked out of her as she landed on her back, and before she could recover, Gared pounced, catching her arms and pinning her to the ground.

"Have you gone crazy?" he shouted, as she continued to thrash under him. His face was flushed purple, and his eyes were tearing.

"How could you?" Leesha shrieked. "Son of a coreling, how could you be so cruel?"

"Night, Leesha, what are you about?" Gared croaked, leaning more heavily on her.

"How could you?" she asked again. "How could you lie and tell everyone you broke me last night?"

Gared looked genuinely taken aback. "Who told you that?" he demanded, and Leesha dared to hope that the lie was not his.

"Evin told Brianne," she said.

"I'll kill that son of the Core," Gared growled, easing his weight back. "He promised to keep his mouth shut."

"So it's true?" Leesha shrieked. She brought her knee up hard, and Gared howled and rolled off her. She was up and out of his reach before he recovered enough to grasp at her again.

"Why?" she demanded. "Why would you lie like that?"

"It was just cutter talk," Gared groaned, "it dint mean anything."

Leesha had never spat in her life, but she spat at him. "Didn't mean anything?" she screamed. "You've ruined my life for something that didn't mean anything?"

Gared got up, and Leesha backed off. He held up his hands and kept his distance.

"Your life ent ruined," he said.

"Brianne knows!" Leesha shouted back. "And Saira and Mairy! The whole village will know by tomorrow!"

"Leesha . . ." Gared began.

"How many others?" she cut him off.

"What?"

"How many others did you tell, you idiot?" she screamed.

He stuck his hands in his pockets and looked down. "Just the other cutters," he said.

"Night! *All* of them?" Leesha ran at him, clawing at his face, but he caught her hands.

"Calm down!" Gared shouted. His hands, like two hams,

squeezed, and a jolt of pain ran down her arms, bringing her to her senses.

"You're hurting me," she said with all the calm she could muster.

"That's better," he said, easing the pressure without letting go. "Doubt it hurts anywhere near as much as a kick in the seed-pods."

"You deserved it," Leesha said.

"Suppose I did," Gared said. "Now can we talk civilized?"

"If you let go of me," she said.

Gared frowned, then let go quickly and skittered out of kicking range.

"Will you tell everyone you lied?" Leesha asked.

Gared shook his head. "Can't do that, Leesh. I'll look a fool."

"Better that I look a whore?" Leesha countered.

"You ent no whore, Leesh, we's promised. It's not like yur Brianne."

"Fine," Leesha said. "Maybe I'll tell a few lies myself. If your friends teased you before, what do you think they'll say if I tell them you weren't stiff enough to do the deed?"

Gared balled one of his huge fists and raised it slightly. "Ya don' wanna do that, Leesha. I'm being patient with ya, but if you go spreading lies like that, I swear . . ."

"But it's fine to lie about me?" Leesha asked.

"Won't matter once we're married," Gared said. "Everyone will forget."

"I'm not marrying you," Leesha said, and suddenly felt a huge weight shift from her.

Gared scowled. "Not like you have a choice," he said. "Even if someone would take ya now, that bookmole Jona or some-such, I will beat him down. Ent no one in Cutter's Hollow gonna take what's mine."

"Enjoy the fruits of your lie," Leesha said, turning away before he saw her tears, "because I'll give myself to the night before I let you make it a reality."

It took all of Leesha's strength to keep from breaking down in tears as she prepared supper that night. Every sound from Gared and Steave was like a knife in her heart. She had been tempted by Gared the night before. She had almost let him have his way, knowing full well what it meant. It had hurt to refuse him, but she had thought her virtue was hers to give. She had never imagined that he could take it with but a word, much less that he would.

"Just as well you've been spending so much time with Bruna," came a whisper at her ear. Leesha whirled to find Elona standing there, smirking at her.

"We wouldn't want you to have a round belly on your wedding day," Elona said.

Regretting her tea comment from that morning, Leesha opened her mouth to reply, but her mother cackled and whirled away before she could find a word.

Leesha spat in her bowl. Gared and Steave's, too. She felt hollow satisfaction as they ate.

Dinner was a horrid affair, Steave whispering in her mother's ear, and Elona snickering at his words. Gared stared at her the whole time, but Leesha refused to look at him. She kept her eyes on her bowl, stirring numbly like her father beside her.

Only Erny seemed not to have heard Gared's lie. Leesha was thankful for that, but she knew in her heart it could not last. Too many people seemed intent to destroy her with it.

She left the table as soon as she could. Gared kept his seat, but Leesha felt his eyes following her. The moment he retired into the shop, she barred him inside, feeling slightly safer.

Like so many nights before, Leesha cried herself to sleep.

Leesha rose doubting she had ever slept. Her mother had paid Steave another late-night visit, but Leesha felt only numbness as she listened to their grunts over the cacophony of the demons.

Gared, too, caused a thump deep in the night, discovering the door to the house barred. She smiled grimly as he tried the latch a few more times before finally giving up.

Erny came over to kiss the top of her head as she set the porridge on the fire. It was the first time they'd been alone together in days. She wondered what it would do to her already broken father when Gared's lie found his ears. He might have believed her once, but with his wife's betrayal still fresh, Leesha doubted he had much trust left to give.

"Healing the sick again today?" Erny asked. When Leesha nodded, he smiled and said, "That's good."

"I'm sorry I haven't had more time for the shop," Leesha said.

He took hold of her arms and leaned in close, looking her in the eyes. "People are always more important than paper, Leesha."

"Even the bad ones?" she asked.

"Even the bad ones," he confirmed. His smile was pained, but there was neither hesitation nor doubt in his answer. "Find the worst human being you can, and you'll still find something worse by looking out the window at night."

Leesha started to cry, and her father pulled her close, rocking her back and forth and stroking her hair. "I'm proud of you, Leesh," he whispered. "Papermaking was my dream. The wards won't fail if you choose another path."

She hugged him tightly, soaking his shirt with her tears. "I love you, Da," she said. "Whatever happens, never doubt that."

"I never could, sunlight," he said. "I'll always love you, as well."

She held on for a long time; her father the only friend she had left in the world.

She scooted out the door while Gared and Steave were still pulling on their boots. She hoped to avoid everyone on her way to the Holy House, but Gared's friends were waiting just outside. Their greeting was a hail of whistles and catcalls.

"Jus' came by to make sure you and yur mum ent keeping Gared and Steave abed when they oughta be working!" Ren called. Leesha turned bright red, but said nothing as she pushed past and hurried down the road. Their laughter cut at her back.

She didn't think she was imagining it; the way people stared and broke into whispers as she passed. She hurried to the security of the Holy House, but when she arrived, Stefny blocked the door, her nostrils flaring as if Leesha stunk of the lye her father used to make paper.

"What are you doing?" Leesha asked. "Let me pass. I'm here to help Bruna."

Stefny shook her head. "You'll not taint this sacred place with your sin," she sneered.

Leesha pulled herself up to her full height, taller than Stefny by inches, but she still felt like a mouse before a cat. "I have committed no sin," she said.

"Hah!" Stefny laughed. "The whole town knows what you and Gared have been up to in the night. I had hopes for you, girl, but it seems you're your mother's daughter after all."

"What's all this?" came Bruna's hoarse rasp before Leesha could reply.

Stefny turned, filled with haughty pride, and looked down at the old Herb Gatherer. "This girl is a whore, and I won't have her in the Creator's house."

"*You* won't have?" Bruna asked. "Are you the Creator now?"

"Do not blaspheme in this place, old woman," Stefny said. "His words are written for all to see." She held up the leather-bound copy of the Canon she carried everywhere. "Fornicators and adulterers keep the Plague upon us, and that sums this slut and her mother well."

"And where is your proof of her crime?" Bruna asked.

Stefny smiled. "Gared has boasted their sin to any who would listen," she said.

Bruna growled, and lashed out suddenly, striking Stefny on the head with her staff and knocking her to the ground. "You would condemn a girl with no more proof than a boy's boast?" she shrieked. "Boys' bragging isn't worth the breath that carries it, and you know it well!"

"Everyone knows her mother is the town whore," Stefny sneered. A trickle of blood ran down her temple. "Why should the pup be different from the bitch?"

Bruna thrust her staff into Stefny's shoulder, making her cry out in pain.

"Hey there!" Smitt called, rushing over. "Enough of that!"

Tender Michel was hot on his heels. "This is a Holy House, not some Angierian tavern . . ."

"Women's business is what this is, and you'll stay out of it, if you know what's good for you!" Bruna snapped, taking the wind from their sails. She looked back to Stefny. "Tell them, or shall I lay bare your sin as well?" she hissed.

"I have no sin, hag!" Stefny said.

"I've delivered every child in this village," Bruna replied, too quietly for the men to hear, "and despite the rumors, I see quite well when things are as close as a babe in my hands."

Stefny blanched, and turned to her husband and the Tender. "Stay out of this!" she called.

"The Core I will!" Smitt cried. He grabbed Bruna's staff and pulled it off of his wife. "See here, woman," he told Bruna. "Herb Gatherer or no, you can't just go around hitting whomever you please!"

"Oh, but your wife can go around condemning whomever she pleases?" Bruna snapped. She yanked her staff from his hands and clonked him on the head with it.

Smitt staggered back, rubbing his head. "All right," he said, "I tried being nice."

Usually, Smitt said that just before rolling up his sleeves and hurling someone bodily from his tavern. He wasn't a tall man, but his squat frame was powerful, and he'd had plenty of experience in dealing with drunken cutters over the years.

Bruna was no thick-muscled cutter, but she didn't appear the least bit intimidated. She stood her ground as Smitt stormed toward her.

"Fine!" she cried. "Throw me out! Mix the herbs yourself! You and Stefny heal the ones that vomit blood and catch demon fever! Deliver your own babies while you're at it! Brew your own cures! Make your own flamesticks! What do you need to put up with the hag for?"

"What, indeed?" Darsy asked. Everyone stared at her as she strode up to Smitt.

"I can mix herbs and deliver babies as well as she can," Darsy said.

"Hah!" Bruna said. Even Smitt looked at her doubtfully.

Darsy ignored her. "I say it's time for a change," she said. "I may not have a hundred years of experience like Bruna, but I won't go around bullying everyone, either."

Smitt scratched his chin, and glanced over to Bruna, who cackled.

"Go on," she dared. "I could use the rest. But don't come begging to my hut when the sow stitches what she should have cut, and cuts what she should have stitched."

"Perhaps Darsy deserves a chance," Smitt said.

"Settled, then!" Bruna said, thumping her staff on the floor. "Be sure to tell the rest of the town who to go to for their cures. I'll thank you for the peace at my hut!"

She turned to Leesha. "Come, girl, help an old crone walk home." She took Leesha's arm, and the two of them turned for the door.

As they passed Stefny, though, Bruna stopped, pointing her staff at her and whispering for only the three women to hear. "You say one more word against this girl, or suffer others to, and the whole town will know your shame."

Stefny's look of terror stayed with Leesha the whole way back to Bruna's hut.

Once they were inside, Bruna whirled on her.

"Well, girl? Is it true?" she asked.

"No!" Leesha cried. "I mean, we almost . . . but I told him to stop and he did!"

It sounded lame and implausible, and she knew it. Terror gripped her. Bruna was the only one who stood up for her. She thought she would die if the old woman thought her a liar, too.

"You . . . you can check me, if you want," she said, her cheeks coloring. She looked at the floor, and squinted back tears.

Bruna grunted, and shook her head. "I believe you, girl."

"Why?" Leesha asked, almost pleading. "Why would Gared lie like that?"

"Because boys get praise for the same things that get girls run out of town," Bruna said. "Because men are ruled by what others think of their dangling worms. Because he's a petty, hurtful little wood-brained shit with no concept of what he had."

Leesha started to cry again. She felt like she'd been crying forever. Surely a body could not hold so many tears.

Bruna opened her arms, and Leesha fell into them. "There, there, girl," she said. "Get it all out, and then we'll figure out what to do."

There was silence in Bruna's hut while Leesha made tea. It was still early in the day, but she felt utterly drained. How could she hope to live the rest of her life in Cutter's Hollow?

Fort Rizon is only a week away, she thought. *Thousands of people. No one would hear of Gared's lies there. I could find Klarissa and . . .*

And what? She knew it was just a fantasy. Even if she could find a Messenger to take her, the thought of a week and more on the open road made her blood run cold, and the Rizonans were farmers, with little use for letters or papermaking. She could find a new husband, perhaps, but the thought of tying her fate to another man gave little comfort.

She brought Bruna her tea, hoping the old woman had an answer, but the Herb Gatherer said nothing, sipping quietly as Leesha knelt beside her chair.

"What am I going to do?" she asked. "I can't hide here forever."

"You could," Bruna said. "Whatever Darsy boasts, she hasn't retained a fraction of what I've taught her, and I haven't taught her a fraction of what I know. The folk'll be back soon enough, begging my help. Stay, and a year from now the people of Cutter's Hollow won't know how they ever got along without you."

"My mother will never allow that," Leesha said. "She's still set on me marrying Gared."

Bruna nodded. "She would be. She's never forgiven herself for not bearing Steave's sons. She's determined that you correct her mistakes."

"I won't do it," Leesha said. "I'll give myself to the night before I let Gared touch me." She was shocked to realize that she meant every word.

"That's very brave of you, dearie," Bruna said, but there was disdain in her tone. "So brave to throw your life away over a boy's lie and fear of your mother."

"I am not afraid of her!" Leesha said.

"Just of telling her you won't marry the boy who destroyed your reputation?"

Leesha was quiet a long time before nodding. "You're right," she said. Bruna grunted.

Leesha stood. "I suppose I had best get it over with," she said. Bruna said nothing.

At the door, Leesha stopped, and looked back.

"Bruna?" she asked. The old woman grunted again. "What was Stefny's sin?"

Bruna sipped her tea. "Smitt has three beautiful children," she said.

"Four," Leesha corrected.

Bruna shook her head. "Stefny has four," she said. "Smitt has three."

Leesha's eyes widened. "But how could that be?" she asked. "Stefny never leaves the tavern, but to go to the Holy . . ." She gasped.

"Even Holy Men are men," Bruna said.

Leesha walked home slowly, trying to choose words, but in the end she knew that phrasing was meaningless. All that mattered was that she would not marry Gared, and her mother's reaction.

It was late in the day when she walked into the house. Gared and Steave would be back from the woods soon. She needed the confrontation over with before they arrived.

"Well, you've really made a mess of things now," her mother said acidly as she walked in. "My daughter, the town tramp."

"I'm not a tramp," Leesha said. "Gared has been spreading lies."

"Don't you dare blame him because you couldn't keep your legs closed!" Elona said.

"I didn't sleep with him," Leesha said.

"Hah!" Elona barked. "Don't take me for a fool, Leesha. I was young once, too."

"You've been 'young' every night this week," Leesha said, "and Gared is still a liar."

Elona slapped her, knocking her to the floor. "Don't you dare speak to me like that, you little whore!" she screeched.

Leesha lay still, knowing that if she moved, her mother would hit her again. Her cheek felt like it was on fire.

Seeing her daughter humbled, Elona took a deep breath, and seemed to calm. "It's no matter," she said. "I've always thought you needed a knocking from the pedestal your idiot father put you on. You'll marry Gared soon enough, and folk will tire of whispering eventually."

Leesha steeled herself. "I'm not marrying him," she said. "He's a liar, and I won't do it."

"Oh, yes you will," Elona said.

"I won't," Leesha said, the words giving her strength as she rose to her feet. "I won't say the words, and there's nothing you can do to make me."

"We'll just see about that," Elona said, snatching off her belt. It was a thick leather strap with a metal buckle that she always wore loosely around her waist. Leesha thought she wore it just to have it at hand to beat her.

She came at Leesha, who shrieked and retreated into the kitchen before realizing it was the last place she should have gone. There was only one way in or out.

She screamed as the buckle cut through her dress and into her back. Elona swung again, and Leesha threw herself at her mother in desperation. As they tumbled to the floor, she heard the door open, and Steave's voice. At the same time, there was a questioning call from the shop.

Elona made good use of the distraction, punching her daughter full in the face. She was on her feet in an instant, whipping the belt into Leesha, drawing another scream from her lips.

"What in the Core is going on?" came a cry from the doorway. Leesha looked up to see her father struggling to get into the kitchen, blocked by Steave's meaty arm.

"Get out of my way!" Erny cried.

"This is between them," Steave said with a grin.

"This is my home you're a guest in!" Erny cried. "Get out of the way!"

When Steave did not budge, Erny punched him.

Everyone froze. It wasn't clear that Steave had felt the punch at all. He broke the sudden silence with a laugh, casually shoving Erny and sending him flying into the common room.

"You ladies settle yur differences in private," Steave said with a wink, pulling the kitchen door shut as Leesha's mother rounded on her once more.

Leesha wept quietly in the back room of her father's shop, daubing gently at her cuts and bruises. Had she the proper herbs, she could have done more, but cold water and cloth were all she had.

She had fled into the shop right after her ordeal, locking the doors from the inside, and ignoring even the gentle knocks of her father. When the wounds were clean and the deepest cuts bound, Leesha curled up on the floor, shaking with pain and shame.

"You'll marry Gared the day you bleed," Elona had promised, "or we'll do this every day until you do."

Leesha knew she meant it, and knew Gared's rumor would have many people taking her mother's side and insisting they wed, ignoring Leesha's bruises as they had many times before.

I won't do it, Leesha promised herself. *I'll give myself to the night first.*

Just then, a cramp wracked her guts. Leesha groaned, and felt dampness on her thighs. Terrified, she swabbed herself with a clean cloth, praying fervently, but there, like a cruel joke of the Creator, was blood.

Leesha shrieked. She heard an answering call from the house.

There was a pounding at the door. "Leesha, are you all right?" her father called.

Leesha didn't answer, staring at the blood in horror. Was it only two days ago she had been praying for it to come? Now she looked at it as if it had come from the Core.

"Leesha, open the door this instant, or you'll have night to pay!" her mother screeched.

Leesha ignored her.

"If you don't listen to yur mother and open this door before I count to ten, Leesha, I swear I will break it down!" Steave boomed.

Fear gripped Leesha as Steave began to count. She had no doubt he could and would splinter the heavy wooden door with a single blow. She ran to the outer door, throwing it open.

It was almost dark. The sky was deep purple, and the last sliver of sun would dip below the horizon in mere minutes.

"Five!" Steave called. "Four! Three!"

Leesha sucked in her breath and ran from the house.

CHAPTER 6

THE SECRETS OF FIRE
319 AR

LEESHA LIFTED HER SKIRTS HIGH and ran for all she was worth, but it was over a mile to Bruna's hut, and she knew deep down she could never make it in time. Her family's cries rang out behind her, the sound muted by the pounding of her heart and the thud of her feet.

There was a sharp stitch in her side, and her back and thighs were on fire from Elona's belt. She stumbled, and scraped her hands catching herself. She forced herself upright, ignoring the pain and driving forward on pure will.

Halfway to the Herb Gatherer, the light faded, and the new night beckoned the demons from the Core. Dark mists began to rise, coalescing into harsh alien forms.

Leesha did not want to die. She knew that now; too late. But even if she wished to turn back, home was farther away now than Bruna's hut, and there was nothing in between. Erny had purposefully built his house away from the others, after complaints about the smell of his chemicals. She had no choice but to go on, heading toward Bruna's hut at the woods' edge, where the wood demons gathered in force.

A few corelings swiped at her as she passed, but they were still insubstantial, and found no purchase. She felt cold as their claws passed through her breast, as if she had been touched by a ghost, but there was no pain, and she did not slow.

There were no flame demons this close to the woods. Wood demons killed flame demons on sight. Firespit could set a wood demon alight, even if normal fire could not. A wind demon solidified in front of her, but Leesha dodged around it, and the creature's spindly legs were not equipped to pursue her afoot. It shrieked at her as she ran on.

She glimpsed a light ahead; the lantern that hung by Bruna's front door. She put on a last burst of speed, crying out, "Bruna! Bruna, please open your door!"

There was no reply, and the door remained shut, but the way was clear, and she dared to think she might make it.

But then an eight-foot wood demon stepped in her path.

And hope died.

The demon roared, showing rows of teeth like kitchen knives. It made Steave look puny by comparison, all thick twisted sinew covered by knobbed, barklike armor.

Leesha drew a ward in the air before her, silently praying that the Creator grant her a quick death. Tales said that demons consumed the soul as well as the body. She supposed she was about to find out.

The demon stalked toward her, closing the gap steadily, waiting to see which way she would try to run. Leesha knew she should do just that, but even had she not been paralyzed with fear, there was nowhere to run. The coreling stood between her and the only hope of succor.

There was a creak as Bruna's front door opened, spilling more light into the yard. The demon turned as the old hag shuffled into view.

"Bruna!" Leesha cried. "Stay behind the wards! There's a wood demon in the yard!"

"My eyes aren't what they used to be, dearie," Bruna replied, "but I'm not about to miss an ugly beast like that."

She took another step forward, crossing her wards. Leesha screamed as the demon roared and launched itself toward the old woman.

Bruna stood her ground as the demon charged, dropping to all fours and moving with terrifying speed. She reached into her shawl, and pulled forth a small object, touching it to the flame of the lantern by the door. Leesha saw it catch fire.

The demon was nearly upon her when Bruna drew back her arm and threw. The object burst apart, covering the wood demon in liquid fire. The blaze lit up the night, and even from yards away, Leesha felt the flash of heat on her face.

The demon screamed, its momentum lost as it fell to the

ground, rolling in the dirt in a desperate attempt to extinguish it-self. The fire clung to it tenaciously, leaving the coreling thrash-ing and howling on the ground.

"Best come inside, Leesha," Bruna advised as it burned, "lest you catch a chill."

Leesha sat wrapped in one of Bruna's shawls, staring at the steam rising off tea she had no desire to drink. The wood de-mon's cries had gone on a long time before reducing to a whim-per and fading away. She imagined the smoldering ruin in the yard, and thought she might retch.

Bruna sat nearby in her rocking chair, humming softly as she deftly worked a pair of knitting needles. Leesha could not un-derstand her calm. She felt she might never be calm again.

The old Herb Gatherer had examined her wordlessly, grunt-ing occasionally as she salved and bandaged Leesha's wounds, few of which, it was clear, had come from her flight. She had also shown Leesha how to wad and insert clean cloth to stem the flow of blood between her legs, and warned her to change it frequently.

But now Bruna sat back as if nothing out of the ordinary had happened, the clicks of her knitting and the crackle of the fire the only sounds in the room.

"What did you do to that demon?" Leesha asked, when she could stand it no longer.

"Liquid demonfire," Bruna said. "Difficult to make. Very dangerous. But it's the only thing I know that can stop a wood demon. Woodies are immune to normal flames, but liquid de-monfire burns as hot as firespit."

"I didn't know anything could kill a demon," Leesha said.

"I told you before, girl, that Herb Gatherers guard the science of the old world," Bruna said. She grunted and spat on the floor. "A scant few of us, anyway. I may be the last to know that in-fernal recipe."

"Why not share it?" Leesha said. "We could be free of the demons forever."

Bruna cackled. "Free?" she asked. "Free to burn the village to the ground, perhaps. Free to set the woods on fire. No heat known can do more than tickle a flame demon, or give a rock demon pause. No fire can burn higher than a wind demon can soar, or set a lake or pond alight to reach a water demon."

"But still," Leesha pressed, "what you did tonight shows how useful it could be. You saved my life."

Bruna nodded. "We keep the knowledge of the old world for the day it will be needed again, but that knowledge comes with a great responsibility. If the histories of the ancient wars of man tell us anything, it's that men cannot be trusted with the secrets of fire.

"That's why Herb Gatherers are always women," she went on. "Men cannot hold such power without using it. I'll sell thunder-sticks and festival crackers to Smitt, dearly, but I won't tell him how they're made."

"Darsy's a woman," Leesha said, "but you never taught her, either."

Bruna snorted. "Even if that cow was smart enough to mix the chemics without setting herself on fire, she's practically a man in her thinking. I'd no sooner teach her to brew demonfire or flame powder than I would Steave."

"They're going to come looking for me tomorrow," Leesha said.

Bruna pointed at Leesha's cooling tea. "Drink," she ordered. "We'll deal with tomorrow when it comes."

Leesha did as she was told, noting the sour taste of tampweed and the bitterness of skyflower as a wave of dizziness washed over her. Distantly, she was aware of dropping her cup.

Morning brought pain with it. Bruna put stiffroot in Leesha's tea to dull the ache of her bruises and the cramps that clutched her abdomen, but the mixture played havoc with her senses. She felt as if she were floating above the cot she lay upon, and yet her limbs felt leaden.

Erny arrived not long after dawn. He burst into tears at the sight of her, kneeling by the cot and clutching her tightly. "I thought I'd lost you," he sobbed.

Leesha reached out weakly, running her fingers through his thinning hair. "It's not your fault," she whispered.

"I should have stood up to your mother long ago," he said.

"That's undersaid," Bruna grunted from her knitting. "No man should let his wife walk over him so."

Erny nodded, having no retort. His face screwed up, and more tears appeared behind his spectacles.

There was a pounding at the door. Bruna looked at Erny, who went to open it.

"Is she here?" Leesha heard her mother's voice, and the cramps doubled. She felt too weak to fight anymore. She couldn't even find the strength to stand.

A moment later Elona appeared, Gared and Steave at her heels like a pair of hounds.

"There you are, you worthless girl!" Elona cried. "Do you know the fright you gave me, running off into the night like that? We've got half the village out looking for you! I should beat you within an inch of your life!"

"No one's beating anyone, Elona," Erny said. "If there's blame to be had, it's yours."

"Shut up, Erny," Elona said. "It's your fault she's so willful, coddling her all the time."

"I won't shut up," Erny said, coming to face his wife.

"You will if you know what's good for ya," Steave warned, balling a fist.

Erny looked at him and swallowed hard. "I'm not afraid of you," he said, but it came out as a squeak. Gared snickered.

Steave grabbed Erny by the front of his shirt, lifting him clear off the ground with one hand as he drew back his hamlike fist.

"You're going to stop acting like a fool," Elona told him, "and you," she turned to Leesha, "are coming home with us this instant."

"She's not going anywhere," Bruna said, setting down her knitting and leaning on her stick as she rose to her feet. "The only ones leaving are you three."

"Shut it, you old witch," Elona said. "I won't let you ruin my daughter's life the way you did mine."

Bruna snorted. "Did I pour pomm tea down your throat and force you to open your legs all about town?" she asked. "Your misery is your own doing. Now get out of my hut."

Elona rounded on her. "Or you'll do what?" she challenged.

Bruna gave a toothless smile and slammed her stick down on Elona's foot, bringing a scream from the younger woman's lips. She followed the blow with one to the gut, doubling Elona over and cutting her outburst short.

"Here, now!" Steave cried. Tossing poor Erny aside, he and Gared rushed the old woman.

Bruna seemed no more concerned than she had at the wood demon's charge. She reached into her shawl and brought forth a fistful of powder, blowing it into the faces of the two men.

Gared and Steave fell to the floor, clutching their faces and screaming.

"There's more where that came from, Elona," Bruna said. "I'll see you all blind before I take orders in my own home."

Elona scampered for the door on all fours, shielding her face with her arm as she went. Bruna laughed, helping Elona out the door with a powerful blow to the posterior.

"Off with you two!" she shouted at Gared and Steave. "Out, before I set you both afire!" The two men fumbled blindly, moaning in pain, their red faces awash in tears. Bruna swatted at them with her stick, guiding them out the door as she would a dog that had peed on the floor.

"Come back at your peril!" Bruna cackled wildly as they ran from her yard.

There was another knock, later in the day. Leesha was up and about by then, but still weak. "What now?" Bruna barked. "I haven't had this many visitors in one day since my paps sagged!"

She stomped over to the door, opening it to find Smitt standing there, wringing his hands nervously. Bruna's eyes narrowed as she regarded him.

"I'm retired," she said. "Fetch Darsy." She started to close the door.

"Wait, please," Smitt begged, reaching out to hold the door open. Bruna scowled, and he drew the hand back as if it had been burned.

"I'm waiting," Bruna said testily.

"It's Ande," Smitt said, referring to one of the men hurt in the attack that week. "The wound in his gut started to rot, so Darsy cut him, and now he's passing blood from both ends."

Bruna spat on Smitt's boots. "I told you this would happen," she said.

"I know," Smitt said. "You were right. I should have listened. Please come back. I'll do anything you ask."

Bruna grunted. "I won't make Ande pay for your stupidity," she said. "But I'll hold you at your word, don't you think for a second I won't!"

"Anything," Smitt promised again.

"Erny!" Bruna barked. "Fetch my herb cloth! Smitt here can carry it. You help your daughter along. We're going to town."

Leesha leaned on her father's arm as they went. She was afraid she would slow them, but even in her weakened state she could keep pace with Bruna's slow shuffle.

"I should make you carry me on your back," Bruna grumped to Smitt as they went. "My old legs aren't as fast as they once were."

"I'll carry you, if you wish," Smitt said.

"Don't be an idiot," Bruna said.

Half the village was gathered outside the Holy House. There was a general sigh of relief as Bruna appeared, and whispers at the sight of Leesha, with her torn dress and bruises.

The crone ignored everyone, shoving people out of the way with her stick and going right inside. Leesha saw Gared and Steave lying on cots with damp cloth over their eyes, and swallowed a smirk. Bruna had explained that the pepper and stinkweed she dosed them with would do no permanent damage, but she hoped Darsy had not known enough to tell them that. Elona's eyes shot daggers at her from their side.

Bruna went straight to Ande's cot. He was bathed in sweat, and stank. His skin was yellowed, and the cloth wrapped around his loins was stained with blood, urine, and feces. Bruna looked at him and spat. Darsy sat nearby. It was clear she had been crying.

"Leesha, unroll the herbs," Bruna ordered. "We have work to do."

Darsy rushed over, reaching to take the blanket from Leesha. "I can do that," she said. "You look about to collapse yourself."

Leesha pulled the blanket away and shook her head. "It's my place," she replied, untying the blanket and rolling it open to reveal the many pockets of herbs.

"Leesha is my apprentice now!" Bruna shouted for all to hear. She looked Elona in the eye as she went on. "Her promising to Gared is dissolved, and she will serve me for seven years and a day! Anyone with an ill word to say about that, or her, can heal their own sick!"

Elona opened her mouth, but Erny pointed straight at her. "Shut it!" he barked. Elona's eyes bulged, and she coughed as she swallowed her words. Erny nodded, and then moved over to Smitt. The two men went and spoke quietly in a corner.

Leesha lost track of time as she and Bruna worked. Darsy had accidentally cut into Ande's intestine while trying to excise the demon rot, poisoning him with his own filth. Bruna cursed continually as she sought to undo the damage, sending Leesha scurrying to clean instruments, fetch herbs, and mix potions. She taught as she went, explaining Darsy's errors and what she was doing to correct them, and Leesha listened attentively.

Finally, they had done all they could, and stitched the wound closed, wrapping it in clean bandages. Ande remained drugged into a deep slumber, but he seemed to be breathing easier, and his skin was closer to its normal tone.

"Will he be all right?" Smitt asked, as Leesha helped Bruna to her feet.

"No thanks to you or Darsy," Bruna snapped. "But if he stays right where he is, and does exactly as he's told, then this won't be what kills him in the end."

As they headed for the door, Bruna walked over to the cots where Gared and Steave lay. "Take those stupid bandages off your eyes, and quit your whining," she snapped.

Gared was the first to comply, squinting in the light. "I can see!" he cried.

"Of course you can see, you wood-brained idiot," Bruna said. "The town needs someone to move heavy things from place to place, and you can't do that blind." She shook her stick at him. "But you cross me again, and blindness will be the least of your worries!"

Gared went pale, and nodded.

"Good," Bruna said. "Now say true. Did you take Leesha's flower?"

Gared looked around, frightened. Finally, his eyes dropped. "No," he said. "It was a lie."

"Speak up, boy," Bruna snapped. "I'm an old woman, and my ears aren't what they used to be." Louder, so that everyone could hear, she asked, "Did you take Leesha's flower?"

"No!" Gared called, his face flushing even redder than it had from the powder. Whispers spread like fire through the crowd at that.

Steave had removed his own bandage by then, and slapped his son hard on the back of the head. "There's going to be the Core to pay when we get home," he growled.

"Not my home," Erny said. Elona looked up at him sharply, but Erny ignored her, pointing his thumb at Smitt. "There's a room for the two of you at the inn," he said.

"The cost of which you will work off," Smitt added, "and you'll be out in a month, even if all you've managed to build in that time is a lean-to."

"Ridiculous!" Elona said. "They can't work for their room and build a house in a month!"

"I think you have your own worries," Smitt said.

"What do you mean?" Elona asked.

"He means you have a decision to make," Erny said. "Either you learn to keep your marriage vows, or I have the Tender dissolve it and you join Steave and Gared in their lean-to."

"You can't be serious," Elona said.

"I've never been more," Erny replied.

"The Core with him," Steave said. "Come with me."

Elona looked at him sideways. "To live in a lean-to?" she asked. "Not likely."

"Then you'd best head home," Erny said. "It's going to take you a while to learn your way around the kitchen."

Elona scowled, and Leesha knew her father's struggle was just beginning, but her mother left as she was told, and that said much for his chances.

Erny kissed his daughter. "I'm proud of you," he said. "And I hope one day to make you proud of me, as well."

"Oh, Da," Leesha said, hugging him, "you have."

"Then you'll come home?" he asked hopefully.

Leesha looked back at Bruna, then back at him, and shook her head.

Erny nodded, and hugged her again. "I understand."

CHAPTER 7

ROJER
318 AR

ROJER FOLLOWED HIS MOTHER as she swept the inn, his little broom swishing side to side in imitation of her broad strokes. She smiled down at him, ruffling his bright red hair, and he beamed back at her. He was three years old.

"Sweep behind the firebox, Rojer," she said, and he hurried to comply, slapping the bristles into the crevice between the box and wall, sending wood dust and bits of bark flying. His mother swept the results into a neat pile.

The door swung open, and Rojer's father came in, arms full of wood. He trailed bits of bark and dirt as he crossed the room.

"Jessum!" his mother cried. "I just swept in here!"

"I help sweep!" Rojer proclaimed loudly.

"That's right," his mother agreed, "and your father's making a mess."

"You want to run out of wood in the night with the duke and his entourage upstairs?" Jessum asked.

"His Grace won't be here for a week at least," his mother replied.

"Best do the work now while the inn's quiet, Kally," Jessum said. "No telling how many courtiers the duke will bring, running us to and fro like little Riverbridge was Angiers itself."

"If you want to do something useful," Kally said, "the wards outside are starting to peel."

Jessum nodded. "I saw," he said. "The wood warped in that last cold snap."

"Master Piter was supposed to redraw them a week ago," Kally said.

"Spoke to him yesterday," Jessum said. "He's putting everyone off to work on the bridge, but he says they'll be ready before the duke comes."

"It's not the *duke* I'm worried about," Kally said. "Piter's only concern may be impressing Rhinebeck in hopes of a royal commission, but I have simpler concerns, like not having my family cored in the night."

"All right, all right," Jessum said, holding up his hands. "I'll go talk to him again."

"You'd think Piter would know better," Kally went on. "Rhinebeck ent even our duke."

"He's the only one close enough to get help to us if we need it quick," Jessum said. "Euchor doesn't care for Riverbridge, long as Messengers get through and taxes come on time."

"See the light," Kally said. "If Rhinebeck's coming, it's because he's sniffing for taxes, too. We'll be paying from both ends afore Rojer sees another summer."

"What would you have us do?" Jessum asked. "Anger the duke a day away for the sake of the one two weeks to the north?"

"I didn't say we should spit in his eye," Kally said. "I just don't see why impressing him comes before warding our own homes."

"I said I'd go," Jessum said.

"So go," Kally said. "It's past noon already. And take Rojer with you. Maybe that will remind you what's really important."

Jessum swallowed his scowl and squatted before his son. "Want to go see the bridge, Rojer?" he asked.

"Fishing?" Rojer asked. He loved to fish off the side of the bridge with his father.

Jessum laughed, sweeping Rojer into his arms. "Not today," he said. "Your mum wants us to have a word with Piter."

He sat Rojer up on his shoulders. "Now hold on tight," he said, and Rojer held on to his father's head as he ducked out the door. His cheeks were scratchy with stubble.

It wasn't far to the bridge. Riverbridge was small even for a hamlet; just a handful of houses and shops, the barracks for the men-at-arms who collected tolls, and his parents' inn. Rojer waved to the guards as they passed the tollhouse, and they waved back.

The bridge spanned the Dividing River at its narrowest point. Built in generations gone, it had two arches, spanning over three hundred feet, and was wide enough for a large cart with a horse to either side. A team of Milnese engineers maintained the ropes and supports daily. The Messenger Road—the only road—stretched as far as the eye could see in either direction.

Master Piter was at the far end, shouting instructions over the side of the bridge. Rojer followed his gaze, and saw his apprentices hanging from slings as they warded the underside.

"Piter!" Jessum called when they were halfway across the bridge.

"Ay, Jessum!" the Warder called. Jessum put Rojer down as he and Piter shook hands.

"Bridge is looking good," Jessum noted. Piter had replaced most of his simpler painted wards with intricate etched calligraphy, lacquered and polished.

Piter smiled. "The duke will fill his breeches when he sees my warding," he proclaimed.

Jessum laughed. "Kally's scouring the inn as we speak," he said.

"Make the duke happy and your future's set," Piter said. "A word of praise in the right ears, and we could be plying our trades in Angiers and not this backwater."

"This 'backwater' is my home," Jessum said, scowling. "My grandda was born in Riverbridge, and if I have my say, my grandkids will be, too."

Piter nodded. "No offense meant," he said. "I just miss Angiers."

"So go back," Jessum said. "The road is open, and a single night out on the road is no great feat for a Warder. You don't need the duke for that."

Piter shook his head. "Angiers is teeming with Warders," he said. "I would just be another leaf in the forest. But if I could claim the duke's favor, it would put a line out my door."

"Well, it's my door I'm worried about today," Jessum said. "The wards're peeling off, and Kally don't think they'll last the night. Can you come take a look?"

Piter blew out a breath. "I told you yesterday ... ." he began, but Jessum cut him off.

"I know what you told me, Piter, but I'm telling you it ent enough," he said. "I won't have my boy sleeping behind weak wards so you can make the ones on the bridge a bit artier. Can't you just patch them for the night?"

Piter spat. "You can do that yourself, Jessum. Just trace the lines. I'll give you paint."

"Rojer wards better than me, and that's not at all," Jessum said. "I'd make a botch of it, and Kally would kill me if the corelings didn't."

Piter scowled. He was about to reply when there was a shout from down the road.

"Ay, Riverbridge!"

"Geral!" Jessum called. Rojer looked up in sudden interest, recognizing the Messenger's bulky frame. His mouth watered at the sight. Geral always had a sweet for him.

Another man rode next to him, a stranger, but his Jongleur's motley put the boy at ease. He thought of how the last Jongleur had sung and danced and walked upside down on his hands, and he hopped with excitement. Rojer loved Jongleurs more than anything.

"Little Rojer, gone and grown another six inches!" Geral cried, pulling up his horse and leaping down to pick Rojer up. He was tall and built like a rain barrel, with a round face and grizzled beard. Rojer had been afraid of him once, with his metal shirt and the demon scar that turned his lower lip into an angry pucker, but no more. He laughed as Geral tickled him.

"Which pocket?" Geral asked, holding the boy at arms' length. Rojer pointed immediately. Geral always kept the sweets in the same place.

The big Messenger laughed, retrieving a Rizonan sugar wrapped in a twist of corn husk. Rojer squealed and plopped down on the grass to unwrap it.

"What brings you to Riverbridge this time?" Jessum asked the Messenger.

The Jongleur stepped forward, sweeping his cloak back in a flourish. He was tall, with long hair sun-bleached to gold and a brown beard. His jaw was perfectly squared, and his skin sun-bronzed. Over his motley he wore a fine tabard emblazoned with a cluster of green leaves on a field of brown.

"Arrick Sweetsong," he introduced himself, "Master Jongleur and herald to His Grace, Duke Rhinebeck the Third, guardian of the forest fortress, wearer of the wooden crown, and Lord of all Angiers. I come to inspect the town before His Grace's arrival next week."

"The duke's herald is a Jongleur?" Piter asked Geral, raising an eyebrow.

"None better for the hamlets," Geral replied with a wink.

"Folks are less likely to string a man up for telling them taxes are raised when he's juggling for their kids."

Arrick scowled at him, but Geral only laughed.

"Be a good man and fetch the innkeep to come for our horses," Arrick told Jessum.

"I'm the innkeep," Rojer's father said, holding out his hand. "Jessum Inn. That's my boy, Rojer." He nodded at Rojer.

Arrick ignored the hand and the boy, producing a silver moon as if from thin air and flicking it his way. Jessum caught the coin, looking at it curiously.

"The horses," Arrick said pointedly. Jessum frowned, but he pocketed the coin and moved for the animals. Geral took his own reins and waved him away.

"I still need my wards looked at, Piter," Jessum said. "You'll be sorry if I have to send Kally to shriek at you about it."

"It looks like the bridge still needs a lot of work before His Grace arrives," Arrick noted. Piter stood a bit straighter at that and gave Jessum a sour look.

"Do you wish to sleep behind peeling wards tonight, Master Jongleur?" Jessum asked. Arrick's bronzed skin paled at that.

"I'll take a look at them, if you want," Geral said. "I can patch them if they're not too bad, and I'll fetch Piter myself if they are." He stomped his spear and gave the Warder a hard stare. Piter's eyes widened, and he nodded his understanding.

Geral picked Rojer up and sat him atop his huge destrier. "Hold tight, boy," he said, "we're going for a ride!" Rojer laughed and pulled the destrier's mane as Geral and his father led the horses to the inn. Arrick strode ahead of them like a man followed by servants.

Kally was waiting at the door. "Geral!" she called. "What a pleasant surprise!"

"And who is this?" Arrick asked, his hands flicking quickly to smooth his hair and clothes.

"This is Kally," Jessum said, adding "my wife" when the twinkle in Arrick's eye did not diminish.

Arrick seemed not to hear, striding up to her and throwing his multicolored cloak back as he made a leg.

"A pleasure, madam," he said, kissing her hand. "I am Arrick Sweetsong, Master Jongleur and herald to Duke Rhinebeck the Third, guardian of the forest fortress, wearer of the wooden crown, and Lord of all Angiers. His Grace will be pleased to see such beauty when he visits your fine inn."

Kally covered her mouth, her pale cheeks coloring to match her red hair. She made a clumsy curtsy in return.

"You and Geral must be tired," she said. "Come in and I'll serve some hot soup while I prepare supper."

"We would be delighted, good lady," Arrick said, bowing again.

"Geral promised to look over the wards for us before dark, Kal," Jessum said.

"What?" Kally asked, pulling her eyes from Arrick's handsome smile. "Oh, well you two stake the horses and see to that while I show Master Arrick a room and start supper," she said.

"A lovely idea," Arrick said, offering her an arm as they went inside.

"Keep an eye on Arrick with your wife," Geral muttered. "They call him 'Sweetsong' because his voice will make any woman sweet between the legs, and I've never known him to stop at a wedding vow."

Jessum scowled. "Rojer," he said, pulling him off the horse, "run in and stay with Mum."

Rojer nodded, hitting the ground running.

"The last Jongleur ate fire," Rojer said. "Can you eat fire?"

"That I can," Arrick said, "and spit it back out like a flame demon." Rojer clapped his hands and Arrick turned back to gaze at Kally, who was bending behind the bar to fill him a mug of ale. She had let her hair down.

Rojer pulled his cloak again. The Jongleur tried to tuck it out of reach, but Rojer just tugged on his pant leg instead.

"What is it?" Arrick asked, turning back to him with a scowl.

"Do you sing, too?" Rojer asked. "I like singing."

"Perhaps I will sing for you later," Arrick said, turning away again.

"Oh give him a little song," Kally begged, putting a foaming mug on the counter before him. "It would make him so happy." She smiled, but Arrick's eyes had already drifted down to the top button of her dress, which had mysteriously come undone while she fetched his mug.

"Of course," Arrick said, smiling brightly. "Just a pull of your fine ale to wash the dust from my throat."

He drained the mug in one quaff, eyes never leaving her neckline, and reached for a large multicolored bag on the floor. Kally refilled his mug as he produced his lute.

Arrick's rich alto voice filled the room, clear and beautiful as he gently strummed the lute. He sang a song of a hamlet woman who missed her one chance to love a man before he left for the Free Cities, and forever regretted it. Kally and Rojer stared at him in wonder, mesmerized by the sound. When he finished, they clapped loudly.

"More!" Rojer cried.

"Not now, my boy," Arrick said, ruffling his hair. "Perhaps after supper. Here," he said, reaching into the multicolored bag, "why not try making your own music?" He produced a straw fiddle, several strips of polished rosewood in different lengths set into a lacquered wooden frame. A stout cord attached it to the wand, a six-inch stick with a lathed wooden ball at the end.

"Take this and go play a bit while I speak with your lovely mother," he said.

Rojer squealed in delight, taking the toy and running off to plop down on the wooden floor, striking the strips in different patterns, delighting in the clear sounds each made.

Kally laughed at the sight. "He's going to be a Jongleur one day," she said.

"Not a lot of custom?" Arrick asked, sweeping his hand over the empty tables in the common room.

"Oh, it was crowded enough at lunchtime," Kally said, "but this time of year, we don't get many boarders apart from the occasional Messenger."

"It must get lonely, tending an empty inn," Arrick said.

"Sometimes," Kally said, "but I've Rojer to keep me busy. He's a handful even when it's quiet, and a terror during caravan season, when the drivers get drunk and sing till all hours, keeping him up with their racket."

"I imagine it must be hard for you to sleep through that, too," Arrick said.

"It's hard for me," Kally admitted. "But Jessum can sleep through anything."

"Is that so?" Arrick asked, sliding his hand over hers. Her eyes widened and she stopped breathing, but she didn't pull away.

The front door slammed open. "Wards are patched!" Jessum

called. Kally gasped, snatching her hand away from Arrick's so quickly she spilled his ale across the bar. She grabbed a rag to soak it up.

"Just a patch job?" she asked doubtfully, her eyes down to hide the flush in her cheeks.

"Not by a spear's throw," Geral said. "Honestly, you're lucky they lasted as long as they did. I patched the worst of them, and I'll have a talk with Piter in the morning. I'll see him replace every ward on this inn before sunset if I have to hold him at spearpoint."

"Thank you, Geral," Kally said, casting Jessum a withering look.

"I'm still mucking the barn," Jessum said, "so I staked the horses out in the yard in Geral's portable circle."

"That's fine," Kally said. "Wash up, all of you. Supper will be ready soon."

"Delicious," Arrick proclaimed, drinking copious amounts of ale with his supper. Kally had roasted an herb-crusted shank of lamb, serving the finest cut to the duke's herald.

"I don't suppose you have a sister as beautiful as yourself?" Arrick asked between mouthfuls. "His Grace is in the market for a new bride."

"I thought the duke already had a wife," Kally said, blushing as she leaned to fill his mug.

"He does," Geral grunted. "His fourth."

Arrick snorted. "No more fertile than the others, I'm afraid, if the talk around the palace holds true. Rhinebeck will keep seeking wives until one gives him a son."

"You might have the right of that," Geral admitted.

"How many times will the Tenders let him stand and promise the Creator 'forever'?" Jessum asked.

"As many as he needs," Arrick assured. "Lord Janson keeps the Holy Men in check."

Geral spat. "It's not right, men of the Creator having to debase themselves for that . . ."

Arrick held up a warning finger. "They say even the trees have ears for those who speak out against the first minister."

Geral scowled, but he held his tongue.

"Well, he's not likely to find a bride in Riverbridge," Jessum said. "There ent even women enough for those of us here. I had to go all the way to Cricket Run to find Kally."

"You're Angierian, my dear?" Arrick asked.

"Born, yes," Kally said, "but the Tender had me swear an oath to Miln at the wedding. All Bridgefolk are required to swear to Euchor."

"For now," Arrick said.

"So it's true, what they say," Jessum said. "Rhinebeck is coming to lay claim to Riverbridge."

"Nothing so dramatic," Arrick said. "His Grace simply feels that with half your people of Angierian stock and your bridge built and maintained from Angierian timber, that we should all have a . . ." He eyed Kally as she sat back down. ". . . closer relationship."

"I doubt Euchor will be quick to share Riverbridge," Jessum said. "The Dividing has separated their lands for a thousand years. He'll no sooner yield that border than his own throne."

Arrick shrugged and smiled again. "That is a matter for dukes and ministers," he said, raising his mug. "Small folk such as us need not concern ourselves over such things."

The sun soon set, and outside there were sharp, crackling retorts, punctuated by flashes of light that leaked through the shutters as wards flared. Rojer hated those harsh sounds, and the shrieks that came with them. He sat on the floor, striking his noisemaker harder and harder, trying to drown them out.

"Corelings're hungry tonight," his father mused.

"It's upsetting Rojer," Kally said, rising from her seat to go to him.

"Not to fear," Arrick said, wiping his mouth. He went to his multicolored bag, pulling out a slim fiddle case. "We'll drive those demons off."

He put bow to string, and immediately filled the room with music. Rojer laughed and clapped, his fear vanished. His mother clapped with him, and they found a rhythm to complement Arrick's tune. Even Geral and Jessum began to clap along.

"Dance with me, Rojer!" Kally laughed, taking his hand and pulling him to his feet.

Rojer tried to keep up as she stepped to the beat, but he stumbled and she swept him up in her arms, kissing him as she spun around the room. Rojer laughed in delight.

There was a sudden crash. Arrick's bow slipped from the strings as everyone turned to see the heavy wooden door shaking in its frame. Dust, knocked loose by the impact, drifted lazily to the floor.

Geral was the first to react, the big man moving with surprising speed for the spear and shield he had left by the door. For a long moment, the others stared at him, uncomprehending. There was another crash, and thick black talons burst through the wood. Kally shrieked.

Jessum leapt to the fireplace, snatching up a heavy iron poker. "Get Rojer to the bolt-hole in the kitchen!" he cried, his words punctuated by a roar from beyond the door.

Geral had snatched up his spear by then, and threw his shield to Arrick. "Get Kally and the boy out!" he cried as the door splintered and a seven-foot rock demon burst through. Geral and Jessum turned to meet it. The creature threw back its head and shrieked as small nimble flame demons darted into the room around and between its thick legs.

Arrick caught the shield, but when Kally ran to his protection, Rojer clutched in her arms, he shoved her aside, snatching up his multicolored bag and sprinting to the kitchen.

"Kally!" Jessum cried as she struck the floor, twisting to shield her son from the impact.

"Damn you to the Core, Arrick!" Geral cursed the Jongleur. "May all your dreams turn to dust!" The rock demon struck him a backhand blow, launching him across the room.

A flame demon leapt at her as Kally struggled to her feet, but Jessum struck it hard with the poker, knocking it aside. It coughed fire as it landed, setting the floor alight.

"Go!" he cried as she got her feet under her. From over her shoulder, Rojer watched the demon spit fire on his father as they fled the room. Jessum screamed as his clothes ignited.

His mother clutched him tightly to her breast, moaning as she ran down the hall. Back in the common room, Geral roared in pain.

They burst into the kitchen just as Arrick yanked open the trapdoor and dropped down. His hand reached back, slapping around for the heavy iron ring to pull the warded trap shut.

"Master Arrick!" Kally cried. "Wait for us!"

"Demon!" Rojer screamed as a flame demon scampered into the room, but his warning came too late. The impact as the coreling struck them knocked the breath from his mother, but she kept hold of him even as the creature's talons dug deep into her. She shrieked as it ran up her back, its razor teeth clamping down on her shoulder and slicing through Rojer's right hand. He howled.

"Rojer!" his mother cried, stumbling toward the washing trough before falling to her knees. Screaming in pain, she reached back and got a firm grip on one of the coreling's horns. "You . . . can't . . . have . . . my . . . son!" she screamed, and threw herself forward, pulling on the horn with all her strength. Torn from its perch, the demon took ribbons of flesh with it as Kally flipped it into the trough.

Soaking crockery shattered on impact, and the flame demon gurgled and thrashed, steam filling the air as the water was brought to an instant boil. Kally screamed as her arms burned, but she held the creature under until its thrashes stopped.

"Mum!" Rojer cried, and she turned to see two more of the creatures scamper into the room. She grabbed Rojer and ran for the trap, yanking the heavy door open with one hand. Arrick's wide eyes looked up at her.

Kally fell as a flame demon latched onto her leg, taking a bite of her thigh. "Take him! Please!" she begged, shoving the boy down into Arrick's arms.

"I love you!" she cried to Rojer as she slammed the trap shut, leaving them in darkness.

So close to the Dividing River, houses in Riverbridge were built on great warded blocks to resist flooding. They waited in the darkness, safe enough from corelings so long as the foundation held, but there was smoke everywhere.

"Die from demons or die from smoke," Arrick muttered. He started to move away from the trap, but Rojer clung hard to his leg.

"Let go, boy," Arrick said, kicking his leg in an attempt to shake the boy off.

"Don't leave me!" Rojer cried, weeping uncontrollably.

Arrick frowned. He looked around at the smoke, and spat.

"Hold tight, boy," he said, putting Rojer on his back. He lifted the edges of his cape to seat the boy in a makeshift sling, tying the corners about his waist. He took up Geral's shield and picked his way through the foundation, crouching to crawl out into the night.

"Creator above," he whispered, as he saw the entire village of

Riverbridge in flames. Demons danced in the night, dragging screaming bodies out to feast.

"Seems your parents weren't the only ones Piter shorted," Arrick said. "I hope they drag that bastard down into the Core."

Crouching behind the shield, Arrick made his way around the inn, hiding in the smoke and confusion until they made the main courtyard. There, safe in Geral's portable circle, were the two horses; an island of safety amid the horror.

A flame demon caught sight of them as Arrick broke into a run for the succor, but Geral's shield turned its firespit with a flare of magic. Inside the circle, Arrick dropped Rojer and fell to his knees, gasping. When he recovered, he began to dig at the saddlebags desperately.

"It must be here," he muttered. "I know I left . . . Ah!" He pulled a wineskin free and yanked off the stopper, gulping deeply.

Rojer whimpered, cradling his bloody right hand.

"Eh?" Arrick asked. "You hurt, boy?" He moved over to examine Rojer, and gasped when he saw the boy's hand. Rojer's middle and index fingers were bitten clear away; his remaining fingers still clutched tightly about a lock of red hair, his mother's, severed by the bite.

"No!" Rojer cried, as Arrick tried to take the hair away. "It's mine!"

"I won't take it, boy," Arrick said, "I just need to see the bite." He put the lock in Rojer's other hand, and the boy clenched it tightly.

The wound wasn't bleeding badly, partly cauterized by the flame demon's saliva, but it oozed and stank.

"I'm no Herb Gatherer," Arrick said with a shrug, and squirted it with wine from his skin. Rojer screamed, and Arrick tore a bit of his fine cloak to wrap the wound.

Rojer was crying freely by then, and Arrick wrapped him tightly in his cloak. "There, there, boy," he said, holding him close and stroking his back. "We're alive to tell the tale. That's something, isn't it?"

Rojer kept on weeping, and Arrick began to sing a lullaby. He sang as Riverbridge burned. He sang as the demons danced and feasted. The sound was like a shield around them, and under its protection, Rojer gave in to exhaustion and fell asleep.

CHAPTER 8

TO THE
FREE CITIES
319 AR

ARLEN LEANED MORE HEAVILY on his walking stick as the fever grew in him. He hunched over and retched, but his empty stomach had only bile to yield. Dizzy, he searched for a focal point.

He saw a plume of smoke.

There was a structure off the side of the road far ahead. A stone wall, so overgrown with vines that it was nearly invisible. The smoke was coming from there.

Hope of succor gave strength to his watery limbs, and he stumbled on. He made the wall, leaning against it as he dragged himself along, looking for an entrance. The stone was pitted and cracked; creeping vines threaded into every nook and cranny. Without the vines to support it, the ancient wall might simply collapse, much as Arlen would without the wall to support him.

At last he came to an arch in the wall. Two metal gates, rusted off their hinges, lay before it in the weeds. Time had eaten them away to nothing. The arch opened into a wide courtyard choked with vines and weeds. There was a broken fountain filled with murky rainwater, and a low building so covered in ivy that it could be missed at first glance.

Arlen walked around the yard in awe. Beneath the growth, the ground was cracked stone. Full-sized trees had broken through, overturning giant blocks now covered in moss. Arlen could see deep claw marks in the plain stone.

No wards, he realized in amazement. *This place was from before the Return.* If that was so, it had been abandoned for over three hundred years.

The door to the building had rotted away like the gate. A small stone entryway led into a wide room. Wires hung in a tangle from the walls, the art they had held long disintegrated. A coating of slime on the floor was all that remained of a thick carpet. Ancient grooves were clawed into the walls and furniture, remnants of the fall.

"Hello?" Arlen called. "Is anyone here?"

There was no reply.

His face felt hot, but he was shivering, even in the warm air. He did not think he could manage to search much further, but there had been smoke, and smoke meant life. The thought gave him strength, and finding a crumbling stairwell, he picked his way to the second floor.

Much of the building's top floor was open to sunlight. The roof was cracked and caved in; rusting metal bars jutting from the crumbling stone.

"Is anyone here?" Arlen called. He searched the floor, but found only rot and ruin.

As he was losing hope, he saw the smoke through a window at the far end of the hall. He ran to it, but found only a broken tree limb lying in the rear courtyard. It was clawed and blackened, with small fires still crackling in places, giving off a steady plume.

Crestfallen, he felt his face twist, but he refused to cry. He thought about just sitting and waiting for the demons to come, in hopes they would give him a faster death than the sickness, but he had sworn to give them nothing, and besides, Marea's death had certainly not been quick. He looked down from the window to the stone courtyard.

A fall from here would kill anyone, he mused. A wave of dizziness washed over him, and it felt easy and right to just let himself fall.

Like Cholie? a voice in his head asked.

The noose flashed in his mind, and Arlen snapped back to reality, catching himself and pulling away from the window.

No, he thought, *Cholie's way is no better than Da's. When I die, it will be because something killed me, not because I gave up.*

He could see far from the high window, over the wall and down the road. Off in the distance, he spotted movement, coming his way.

Ragen.

Arlen tapped reserves of strength he didn't know he had, bounding down the steps with something approaching his usual alacrity and running full out through the courtyard.

But his breath gave out as he reached the road, and he fell onto the clay, gasping and clutching a stitch in his side. It felt like there were a thousand splinters in his chest.

He looked up and saw the figures still far down the road, but close enough that they saw him, too. He heard a shout as the world went black.

Arlen awoke in daylight, lying on his stomach. He took a breath, feeling bandages wrapped tightly around him. His back still ached, but it no longer burned, and for the first time in days, his face felt cool. He put his hands under him to rise, but pain shot through him.

"I wouldn't be in any rush to do that," Ragen advised. "You're lucky to be alive."

"What happened?" Arlen asked, looking up at the man who sat nearby.

"Found you passed out on the road," the man said. "The cuts on your back had demon rot. Had to cut you open and drain the poison before I could sew them up."

"Where's Keerin?" Arlen asked.

Ragen laughed. "Inside," he said. "Keerin's been keeping his distance the last couple days. He couldn't handle the gore, and sicked up when we first found you."

"Days?" Arlen asked. He looked around and found himself back in the ancient courtyard. Ragen had made camp there, his portable circles protecting the bedrolls and animals.

"We found you around high sun on Thirday," Ragen said. "It's Fifthday now. You've been delirious the whole time, thrashing around as you sweated out the sickness."

"You cured my demon fever?" Arlen asked in shock.

"That what they call it in the Brook?" Ragen asked. He shrugged. "Good a name as any, I suppose, but it's not some magic disease, boy; just an infection. I found some hogroot not far off the road, so I was able to poultice the cuts. I'll make some tea with it later. If you drink it for the next few days, you should be all right."

"Hogroot?" Arlen asked.

Ragen held up a weed that grew most everywhere. "A staple of every Messenger's herb pouch, though it's best when fresh. Makes you a little dizzy, but for some reason, demon rot can't abide it."

Arlen began to cry. His mother could have been cured by a weed he regularly pulled from Jeph's field? It was just too much.

Ragen waited quietly, giving Arlen space while the tears ran their course. After what seemed an eternity, the flow began to ebb, and his heaving sobs eased. Ragen handed him a cloth wordlessly, and Arlen dried his cheeks.

"Arlen," the Messenger asked finally, "what are you doing all the way out here?"

Arlen looked at him for a long time, trying to decide what to say. When he finally spoke, the tale came spilling out in a rush. He told the Messenger everything, starting with the night his mother was injured and ending with running from his father.

Ragen was quiet while he took in Arlen's tale. "I'm sorry about your mother, Arlen," he said at last. Arlen sniffled and nodded.

Keerin wandered back as Arlen began telling how he had tried to find the road to Sunny Pasture, but had accidentally taken the fork to the Free Cities instead. He paid rapt attention as Arlen described his first night alone, the giant rock demon, and how he had scuffed the ward. The Jongleur went pale when Arlen described the race to repair it before the demon killed him.

"You're the one that cut that demon's arm off?" Ragen asked incredulously, a moment later. Keerin looked ready to sick up again.

"It's not a trick I mean to try again," Arlen said.

"No, I don't suppose it is," Ragen chuckled. "Still, crippling a fifteen-foot rock demon is a deed worth a song or two, eh, Keerin?" He elbowed the Jongleur, but that seemed to push the man over the edge. He covered his mouth and ran off. Ragen shook his head and sighed.

"A giant one-armed rock demon's been haunting us ever since we found you," he explained. "It's hammered the wards harder than any coreling I've ever seen."

"Is he going to be all right?" Arlen asked, watching Keerin double over.

"It'll pass," Ragen grunted. "Let's get some food into you." He helped Arlen sit up against the horse's saddle. The move sent a stab of pain through him, and Ragen saw him wince.

"Chew on this," he advised, handing Arlen a gnarled root. "It will make you a little light-headed, but it should ease the pain."

"Are you an Herb Gatherer?" Arlen asked.

Ragen laughed. "No, but a Messenger needs to know a little of every art, if he wants to survive." He reached into his saddle-bags, pulling out a metal cookpot and some utensils.

"I wish you'd told Coline about hogroot," Arlen lamented.

"I would have," Ragen said, "if I thought for a second she didn't know." He filled the pot, and hung it from the tripod over the firepit. "It's amazing what people have forgotten."

He stoked the flames as Keerin returned, looking pale but relieved. "I'll be sure to mention it when we take you back."

"Back?" Arlen asked.

"Back?" Keerin echoed.

"Of course 'back,'" Ragen said. "Your da will be looking for you, Arlen."

"But I don't want to go back," Arlen said. "I want to go to the Free Cities with you."

"You can't just run away from your problems, Arlen," Ragen said.

"I'm not going back," Arlen said. "You can drag me there, but I'll run again the second you let go."

Ragen stared at him for a long time. Finally, he glanced at Keerin.

"You know what I think," Keerin said. "I've no desire to add five nights, at least, to our trip home."

Ragen frowned at Arlen. "I'll be writing your father when we get to Miln," he warned.

"You'll be wasting your time," Arlen said. "He'll never come for me."

The stone floor of the courtyard and the high wall hid them well that night. A wide portable circle secured the cart, and the animals were staked and hobbled in another. They were in the inner of two concentric rings, with the fire at the center.

Keerin lay huddled in his bedroll, with the blanket over his head. He was shivering though it was not cold, and when the occasional coreling tested the wards, he twitched.

"Why do they keep attacking when they can't get through?" Arlen asked.

"They're looking for flaws in the net," Ragen said. "You'll never see a coreling attack the same spot twice." He tapped his temple. "They remember. Corelings aren't smart enough to study the wards and reason out the weak spots, so they attack the barrier and search that way. They get through rarely, but often enough to make it worth their while."

A wind demon came swooping over the wall and bounced off the wards. Keerin whimpered from under his blanket at the sound.

Ragen looked over at the Jongleur's bedroll and shook his head. "It's like he thinks that if he can't see the corelings, they can't see him," he muttered.

"Is he always like this?" Arlen asked.

"That one-armed demon has him more spooked than usual," Ragen said, "but he wasn't exactly standing at the wards before." He shrugged. "I needed a Jongleur on short notice. The guild gave me Keerin. I don't normally work with ones so green."

"Why bring a Jongleur at all, then?" Arlen asked.

"Oh, you have to bring a Jongleur with you when you're going to the hamlets," Ragen said. "They're apt to stone you if you show up without one."

"Hamlets?"

"Small villages, like Tibbet's Brook," Ragen explained. "Places too far for the dukes to easily control, where most folks can't read."

"What difference does that make?" Arlen asked.

"People that can't read don't have a lot of use for Messengers," Ragen said. "Oh, they're eager enough for their salt, or whatever it is they're shy of, but most won't come out of their way to see you and give you news, and collecting news is a Messenger's first job. But bring a Jongleur with you, and people drop everything to come and see the spectacle. It wasn't just for you that I spread word of Keerin's show.

"Some men," he went on, "can be Merchant, Jongleur, Herb Gatherer, and Messenger all at once, but they're about as common as a friendly coreling. Most Messengers who take the hamlet routes have to hire a Jongleur."

"And you don't usually work the hamlets," Arlen said, remembering.

Ragen winked. "A Jongleur may impress the townies, but he'll only hold you back in a duke's court. The dukes and merchant princes have Jongleurs of their own. All they're interested in is trade and news, and they pay far more than anything old Hog could afford."

Ragen rose before the sun the next morning. Arlen was already awake, and Ragen nodded at him in approval. "Messengers don't have the luxury of sleeping late," he said as he loudly clattered his cookpans to wake Keerin. "Every moment of light is needed."

Arlen was feeling well enough by then to sit next to Keerin in the cart as it trundled toward the tiny lumps on the horizon Ragen called mountains. To pass the time, Ragen told Arlen tales of his travels, and pointed to herbs along the side of the road, saying which to eat and which to avoid, which could poultice a wound, and which would make it worse. He noted the most defensible spots to spend a night and why, and warned about predators.

"Corelings kill the slowest and weakest animals," Ragen said. "So only the biggest and strongest, or those best at hiding, survive. Out on the road, corelings aren't the only thing that will see you as prey."

Keerin looked around nervously.

"What was that place we stayed in the last few nights?" Arlen asked.

Ragen shrugged. "Just some minor lord's keep," he said. "There're hundreds of them in the lands between here and Miln, old ruins picked clean by countless Messengers."

"Messengers?" Arlen asked.

"Of course," Ragen said. "Some Messengers spend weeks hunting for ruins. The ones lucky enough to stumble on ruins no one's ever found can come back with all kinds of loot. Gold, jewels, carvings, sometimes even old wards. But the real prize they're all chasing is *the* old wards, the fighting wards, if they ever really existed."

"Do you think they existed?" Arlen asked.

Ragen nodded. "But I'm not about to risk my neck leaving the road to look for them."

After a couple of hours, Ragen led them off the road to a small cave. "Always best to ward a shelter when you can," he told Arlen. "This cave is one of a few noted in Graig's log."

Ragen and Keerin set up camp, feeding and watering the animals and moving their supplies into the cave. The unhitched cart was put in a circle just outside. While they worked, Arlen inspected the portable circle. "There are wards here I don't know," he noted, tracing the markings with a finger.

"I saw a few in Tibbet's Brook that were new to me, as well," Ragen admitted. "I copied them down in my log. Perhaps tonight you can tell me what they do?" Arlen smiled, pleased that he might offer something in return for Ragen's generosity.

Keerin began shifting uncomfortably as they ate, looking frequently at the darkening sky, but Ragen seemed unhurried as the shadows grew.

"Best to bring the mollies into the cave now," Ragen noted finally. Keerin immediately moved to comply. "Pack animals hate caves," Ragen told Arlen, "so you wait as long as you can before bringing them in. The horse always goes last."

"Doesn't it have a name?" Arlen asked.

Ragen shook his head. "My horses have to earn their names," he said. "The guild trains them special, but plenty of horses still spook when chained outside in a portable circle at night. Only the ones I know won't bolt or panic get names. I bought this one in Angiers, after my garron ran off and got cored. If she makes it to Miln, I'll give her a name."

"She'll make it," Arlen said, stroking the courser's neck. When Keerin had the mollies inside, he took her bridle and led her into the cave.

As the others settled in, Arlen studied the cave mouth. Wards were chiseled into the stone, but not the floor of the entrance. "The wards are incomplete," he said, pointing.

"Course they are," Ragen answered. "Can't ward dirt, can we?" He looked at Arlen curiously. "What would *you* do to complete the circle?" he asked.

Arlen studied the puzzle. The mouth of the cave wasn't a perfect circle, more like an inverted U. Harder to ward, but not *too* hard, and the wards carved on the rock were common enough. Taking a stick, he sketched wards in the dirt, their lines connecting smoothly with those already in place. He checked them thrice, and then slid back, looking at Ragen for approval.

The Messenger was silent a moment as he studied Arlen's work, then nodded.

"Well done," Ragen said, and Arlen beamed. "You plotted the vertices masterfully. I couldn't have woven a tighter web myself, and you did all the equations in your head, no less."

"Uh, thanks," Arlen said, though he had no idea what Ragen was talking about.

Ragen caught the boy's pause. "You *did* do the equations, didn't you?" he asked.

"What's an equation?" Arlen asked. "That line"—he pointed to the nearest ward—"goes to that ward there." He pointed to the wall. "It crosses these lines"—he pointed to other wards—"which crisscross with those here." He pointed to still others. "It's as simple as that."

Ragen was aghast. "You mean you just eyeballed it?" he demanded.

Arlen shrugged as Ragen turned back to him. "Most people use a straightstick to check the lines," he admitted, "but I never bother."

"How Tibbet's Brook isn't swallowed by the night, I have no idea," Ragen said. He pulled a sack from his saddlebag and knelt at the cave mouth, sweeping Arlen's wards away.

"Dirt wards are still foolhardy, however well drawn," he said.

Ragen selected a handful of lacquered wooden ward plates from the sack. Using a straightstick marked with lines, he spaced them out quickly, resealing the net.

It hadn't been dark for more than an hour when the giant one-armed rock demon bounded into the clearing. It gave a great howl, sweeping lesser demons aside as it stomped toward the cave mouth, roaring a challenge. Keerin groaned, retreating to the back of the cave.

"That one has your scent now," Ragen warned. "It will follow you forever, waiting for you to drop your guard."

Arlen looked at the monster for a long moment, considering the Messenger's words. The demon snarled and struck hard at the barrier, but the wards flared and knocked it away. Keerin whimpered, but Arlen rose and walked up to the mouth of the cave. He met the coreling's eyes and slowly raised his hands, bringing them together suddenly in a loud clap, mocking the demon with his two limbs.

"Let it waste its time," he said as the demon howled in impotent rage. "It won't get me."

They continued on the road for almost a week. Ragen turned them north, passing through the foothills of the mountain range, ascending ever higher. Now and again Ragen would stop to hunt, felling small game from great distances with his thin throwing spears.

Most nights they stayed in shelters noted in Graig's log, though twice they simply camped in the road. Like any animal, Ragen's mare was terrified by the stalking demons, but she did not try to pull free from her hobble.

"She deserves a name," Arlen said, for the hundredth time, pointing at the steady horse.

"Fine, fine!" Ragen finally conceded, ruffling Arlen's hair. "You can name her."

Arlen smiled. "Nighteye," he said.

Ragen looked at the horse, and nodded. "It's a good name," he agreed.

CHAPTER 9

FORT MILN
319 AR

THE TERRAIN GREW STEADILY ROCKIER as the tiny lumps on the horizon rose higher and higher. Ragen had not exaggerated when he said a hundred Boggin's Hills could fit in just one mountain, and the range stretched as far as Arlen could see. The air grew cooler as they climbed; strong gusts of wind whipped through the hills. Arlen looked back and saw the whole world spread out before him like a map. He imagined traveling through those lands with only a spear and a Messenger bag.

When they finally caught sight of Fort Miln, Arlen couldn't believe his eyes. Despite Ragen's tales, he had still assumed it would be like Tibbet's Brook, only larger. He nearly fell from the cart as the fortress city rose up before them, looming over the road.

Fort Miln was built into the base of a mountain, overlooking a broad valley. Another mountain, twin to the one Miln abutted, faced the city from across the valley. A circular wall some thirty feet high surrounded the city, though many of the buildings within thrust still higher into the sky. The closer they got to the city, the more it spread out, the wall going for miles in each direction.

The walls were painted with the largest wards Arlen had ever seen. His eyes followed the invisible lines connecting one ward to another, forming a web that would make the wall impervious to corelings.

But despite the triumph of achievement, the walls disappointed Arlen. The "free" cities weren't really free at all. Walls that kept the corelings out also kept the people in. At least in Tibbet's Brook the prison walls were invisible.

"What keeps wind demons from flying over the wall?" Arlen asked.

"The top of the wall is set with wardposts that weave a canopy over the city," Ragen said.

Arlen realized he should have figured that out without Ragen's help. He had more questions, but he kept them to himself, his sharp mind already working on probable solutions.

It was well past high sun when they finally reached the city. Ragen pointed out a column of smoke farther up the mountain, miles above the city.

"The Duke's Mines," he said. "It's a village in itself, larger than your Tibbet's Brook. They're not self-sufficient, but that's how the duke likes it. Caravans come and go most every week. Food goes up, and salt, metal, and coal come down."

A lower wall branched out from the main city, running in a broad swath around the valley. Arlen could make out wardposts and the top of neat green rows. "The great gardens and the Duke's Orchard," Ragen noted.

The gate was open wide as workers came and went, and the guards waved as they approached. They were tall, like Ragen, and wore dented metal helms and old boiled leather over thick woolens. Both carried spears, but they held them more like showpieces than weapons.

"Ay, Messenger!" one cried. "Welcome back!"

"Gaims. Woron." Ragen nodded at them.

"Duke expected you days ago," Gaims said. "We were worried when you didn't arrive."

"Thought the demons got me?" Ragen laughed. "Not a chance! There was a coreling attack in the hamlet I visited on the way back from Angiers. We stayed on a bit to help out."

"Picked up a stray while you were there?" Woron asked with a grin. "A little gift for your wife while she waits for you to make her a Mother?"

Ragen scowled, and the guard drew back. "I meant no offense," he said quickly.

"Then I suggest you avoid saying things that tend to offend, *Servant*," Ragen replied tightly. Woron paled, and nodded quickly.

"I found him out on the road, actually," Ragen said, ruffling Arlen's hair and grinning as if nothing tense had just passed.

Arlen liked that about Ragen. He was quick to laugh, and held no grudges, but he demanded respect, and let you know where you stood. Arlen wanted to be like that one day.

"On the road?" Gaims asked in disbelief.

"Days from anywhere!" Ragen cried. "The boy can ward better than some Messengers I know." Arlen swelled with pride at the compliment.

"And you, Jongleur?" Woron asked Keerin. "Like your first taste of the naked night?"

Keerin scowled, and the guards laughed. "That good, eh?" Woron asked.

"Light's wasting," Ragen said. "Send word to Mother Jone that we'll come to the palace after I deliver the rice and stop home for a bath and a decent meal." The men saluted and let them pass into the city.

Despite his initial disappointment, the grandeur of Miln soon overwhelmed Arlen. Buildings soared into the air, dwarfing anything he had ever seen before, and cobbles covered the streets instead of hard-packed dirt. Corelings couldn't rise through worked stone, but Arlen couldn't imagine the effort needed to cut and fit hundreds of thousands of stones.

In Tibbet's Brook, most every structure was wood, with foundations of piled stone and roofs of thatch with plates for wards. Here, most everything was cut stone, and reeked of age. Despite the warded outer walls, every building was warded individually, some in fantastic works of art, and others in simple functionality.

The air in the city was rank, thick with the stench of garbage, dung fires, and sweat. Arlen tried holding his breath, but soon gave up and settled for breathing through his mouth. Keerin, on the other hand, seemed to breathe comfortably for the first time.

Ragen led the way to a marketplace where Arlen saw more people than he had in his entire life. Hundreds of Rusco Hogs called to him from all sides: "Buy this!" "Try that!" "A special price, just for you!" They were all tall; giants compared to the folk of the Brook.

They passed carts of fruits and vegetables the likes of which Arlen had never seen, and so many sellers of clothes that he thought it must be all the Milnese thought about. There were paintings and carvings, too, so intricate he wondered how anyone had time to make them.

Ragen brought them to a merchant on the far end of the market who bore the symbol of a shield on his tent. "The duke's man," Ragen advised as they pulled up to the cart.

"Ragen!" the merchant called. "What do you have for me today?"

"Marsh rice," Ragen said. "Taxes from the Brook to pay for the duke's salt."

"Been to see Rusco Hog?" the merchant said more than asked. "That crook still robbing the townies blind?"

"You know Hog?" Ragen asked.

The merchant laughed. "I testified before the Mothers' Council ten years ago to have his merchant license pulled, after he tried to pass on a shipment of grain thick with rats," he said. "He left town soon after, and resurfaced at the ends of the world. Heard the same thing happened in Angiers, which is why he was in Miln to begin with."

"Good thing we checked the rice," Ragen muttered.

They haggled for some time over the going rates for rice and salt. Finally, the merchant gave in, admitting that Ragen had gotten the better of Hog. He gave the Messenger a jingling pouch of coins to make up the difference.

"Can Arlen drive the cart from here?" Keerin asked. Ragen glanced at him and nodded. He tossed a purse of coins to Keerin, who caught it deftly and hopped off the cart.

Ragen shook his head as Keerin disappeared into the crowd. "Not the worst Jongleur," he said, "but he doesn't have the stones for the road." He remounted, and led Arlen through the busy streets. Arlen felt suffocated by the press as they moved down a particularly crowded street. He noticed some people dressed only in tattered rags despite the chill mountain air.

"What are they doing?" Arlen asked, watching them hold empty cups out at passersby.

"Begging," Ragen said. "Not everyone in Miln can afford to buy food."

"Can't we just give them some of ours?" Arlen asked.

Ragen sighed. "It's not that simple, Arlen," he said. "The soil here isn't fertile enough to feed even half the people. We need grain from Fort Rizon, fish from Lakton, fruit and livestock from Angiers. The other cities don't just give all that away. It goes to those who work a trade and earn the money to pay for it, the Merchants. Merchants hire Servants to do for them, and feed, clothe, and house them out of their own purse."

He gestured at a man wrapped in rough, filthy cloth holding out a cracked wooden bowl to passersby, who moved to avoid him, refusing eye contact. "So unless you're a Royal or a Holy Man, if you don't work, you end up like that."

Arlen nodded as if he understood, but he didn't really. People ran out of credits at the general store in Tibbet's Brook all the time, but even Hog didn't let them starve.

They came to a house, and Ragen signaled Arlen to stop the cart. It was not a large house compared to many Arlen had seen in Miln, but it was still impressive by Tibbet's Brook standards, made entirely of stone and standing two full stories.

"Is this where you live?" Arlen asked.

Ragen shook his head. He dismounted and went to the door, knocking sharply. A moment later, it was answered by a young woman with long brown hair woven into a tight braid. She was tall and sturdy, like everyone in Miln, and wore a high-necked dress that fell to her ankles and was tight across her bosom. Arlen couldn't tell if she was pretty. He was about to decide that she was not when she smiled, and her whole face changed.

"Ragen!" she cried, throwing her arms around him. "You came! Thank the Creator!"

"Of course I came, Jenya," Ragen said. "We Messengers take care of our own."

"I'm no Messenger," Jenya said.

"You were married to one, and that's the same. Graig died a Messenger, the guild's ruling be damned."

Jenya looked sad, and Ragen changed the subject quickly, striding over to the cart and unloading the remaining stores. "I've brought you good Marsh rice, salt, meat, and fish," he said, carrying the items over and setting them just inside her doorway. Arlen scurried to help.

"And this," Ragen added, pulling the sack of gold and silver he had gotten from Hog out of his belt. He threw in the little pouch from the duke's merchant, as well.

Jenya's eyes widened as she opened it. "Oh, Ragen," she said, "it's too much. I can't . . ."

"You can and you will," Ragen ordered, cutting her off. "It's the least I can do."

Jenya's eyes filled with tears. "I have no way to thank you," she said. "I've been so scared. Penning for the guild doesn't cover everything, and without Graig . . . I thought I might have to go back to begging."

"There, there," Ragen said, patting her shoulder. "My brothers and I will never let that happen. I'll take you into my own household before I let you fall so far," he promised.

"Oh, Ragen, you would do that?" she asked.

"There's one last thing," Ragen said. "A gift from Rusco Hog." He held up the ring. "He wants you to write him, and let him know you got it."

Jenya's eyes began to water again, looking at the beautiful ring.

"Graig was well loved," Ragen said, slipping the ring onto her finger. "Let this ring be a symbol of his memory. The food and money should last your family a good long while. Perhaps, in that time, you'll even find another husband and become a Mother. But if things ever grow so dark that you feel you must sell that ring, you come to me first, you understand?"

Jenya nodded, but her eyes were down, still dripping as she caressed the ring.

"Promise me," Ragen ordered.

"I promise," Jenya said.

Ragen nodded, hugging her one last time. "I'll look in on you when I can," he said. She was still crying as they left. Arlen stared back at her as they went.

"You look confused," Ragen said.

"I guess I am," Arlen agreed.

"Jenya's family were Beggars," Ragen explained. "Her father is blind and her mother sickly. They had the fortune, though, to have a healthy, attractive daughter. She brought herself and her parents up two classes when she married Graig. He took the three of them into his home, and though he never had the choicest routes, he made enough for them to get by and be happy."

He shook his head. "Now, though, she has rent to pay and three mouths to feed on her own. She can't stray far from home, either, because her parents can't do for themselves."

"It's good of you to help her," Arlen said, feeling a little better. "She was pretty when she smiled."

"You can't help everyone, Arlen," Ragen said, "but you should make every effort to help those you can." Arlen nodded. They wound their way up a hill until they reached a large manse. A gated wall six feet high surrounded the sprawling property, and the great house itself was three stories high and had dozens of windows, all reflecting light from their glass. It was bigger than the great hall on Boggin's Hill, and that could hold everyone in Tibbet's Brook for the solstice feast. The manse and the wall around it were painted with brightly colored wards. Such a magnificent place, Arlen decided, must be the home of the duke.

"My mam had a cup of warded glass, hard as steel," he said, looking up at the windows as a thin man came scurrying up from inside the grounds to open the gate. "She kept it hidden, but sometimes she took it out when company came, to show how it glittered." They rode past a garden untouched by coreling mischief, where several hands were digging vegetables.

"This is one of the only manses in Miln with all glass windows," Ragen said proudly. "I'd pay a lot to ward them not to break."

"I know the trick," Arlen said, "but you need a coreling to touch the glass to charge it."

Ragen chuckled and shook his head. "Maybe not, then."

There were smaller buildings on the grounds as well, stone huts with smoking chimneys and people going to and fro, like a tiny village. Dirty children scampered about, and women kept watch over them while tending their chores. They rode to the stables, and a groom was there in a second to take Nighteye's reins. He bowed and scraped to Ragen as if Ragen were a king in a story.

"I thought we were going to stop by your house before visiting the duke," Arlen asked.

Ragen laughed. "This *is* my house, Arlen! Do you think I risk the open road for nothing?"

Arlen looked back at the house, his eyes bulging. "This is all yours?" he asked.

"All of it," Ragen confirmed. "Dukes are free with their coin to those who stare down corelings."

"But Graig's house was so small," Arlen protested.

"Graig was a good man," Ragen said, "but he was never more than a passable Messenger. He was content to make a run to Tibbet's Brook each year, and shuttle to the local hamlets in between. A man like that might support his family, but no more. The only reason there was so much profit for Jenya was that I paid for the extra goods I sold Hog out of my own purse. Graig used to have to borrow from the guild, and they took a hard cut."

A tall man opened the door to the house with a bow. He was stone-faced, wearing a faded blue coat of dyed wool. His face and clothes were clean, a sharp contrast to those in the yard. As soon as they entered, a boy not much older than Arlen sprang to his feet. He ran to a bell rope at the base of a broad, marble stair. Chimes rang through the house.

"I see your luck has held one more time," a woman called a moment later. She had dark hair and piercing blue eyes. She wore a deep blue gown, finer than anything Arlen had ever seen, and her wrists and throat sparkled with jewels. Her smile was cold as she regarded them from the marble balcony above the foyer. Arlen had never seen a woman so beautiful or graceful.

"My wife, Elissa," Ragen advised quietly. "A reason to re-turn . . . and a reason to leave." Arlen was unsure if he was jok-ing. The woman did not seem pleased to see them.

"One of these times, the corelings will have you," Elissa said as she descended the stairs, "and I will finally be free to wed my young lover."

"Never happen," Ragen said with a smile, drawing her close for a kiss. Turning to Arlen, he explained, "Elissa dreams of the day when she will inherit my fortune. I guard against the core-lings as much to spite her as to protect myself."

Elissa laughed, and Arlen relaxed. "Who is this?" she asked. "A stray to save you the work of filling my belly with a child of our own?"

"The only work is melting your frozen petticoats, my dear," Ragen shot back. "May I present Arlen, of Tibbet's Brook. I met him on the road."

"On the road?" Elissa asked. "He's just a child!"

"I'm not a child!" Arlen shouted, then immediately felt fool-ish. Ragen eyed him wryly, and he dropped his gaze.

Elissa gave no sign that she heard the outburst. "Doff your ar-mor and find the bath," she ordered her husband, "you smell like sweat and rust. I'll see to our guest."

As Ragen left, Elissa called a servant to prepare Arlen a snack. Ragen seemed to have more servants than there were people in Tibbet's Brook. They cut him slices of cold ham and a thick crust of bread, with clotted cream and milk to wash it down. Elissa watched him eat, but Arlen couldn't think of anything to say, and kept his attention on his plate.

As he was finishing the cream, a serving woman in a dress of the same blue as the men's jackets entered and bowed to Elissa. "Master Ragen awaits you upstairs," she said.

"Thank you, Mother," Elissa replied. Her face took on a strange cast for a moment, as she absently ran her fingers over her stomach. Then she smiled and looked at Arlen. "Take our guest to the bath," she ordered, "and don't let him up for air until you can tell what color his skin is." She laughed and swept out of the room.

Arlen, used to standing in a trough and dumping cold water over himself, was out of sorts at the sight of Ragen's deep stone tub. He waited as the serving woman, Margrit, poured a kettle of boiling water in to take the chill from his soak. She was tall, like everyone in Miln, with kind eyes and honey-colored hair just hinting at gray peeking from underneath her bonnet. She turned her back while Arlen undressed and got into the tub. She gasped as she saw the stitched wounds on his back, and quickly moved to inspect them.

"Ow!" Arlen shouted as she pinched the uppermost wound.

"Don't be such a baby," she scolded, rubbing her thumb and forefinger together and sniffing at them. Arlen bit down as she repeated the process down his back. "You're luckier than you know," she said at last. "When Ragen told me you were hurt, I thought it must be just a scratch, but this . . ." She tsked at him. "Didn't your mother teach you not to be outside at night?"

Arlen's retort died on a sniffle. He bit his lip, determined not to cry. Margrit noticed, and immediately softened her tone. "These are healing well," she said of his wounds. She took a cake of soap and began to gently wash them. Arlen gritted his teeth. "When you're done in the bath, I'll prepare a poultice and fresh bandages for you."

Arlen nodded. "Are you Elissa's mother?" he asked.

The woman laughed. "Creator, boy, whatever gave you that idea?"

"She called you 'Mother,' " Arlen said.

"Because I am," Margrit said proudly. "Two sons and three daughters, one of them soon to be a Mother herself." She shook her head sadly. "Poor Elissa, all her wealth, and still a Daughter, and her on the dark side of thirty! It breaks the heart."

"Is being a mam so important?" Arlen asked.

The woman regarded him as if he had asked if air were important. "What could be more important than motherhood?" she asked. "It's every woman's duty to produce children to keep the city strong. That's why Mothers get the best rations and first pick of the morning market. It's why all the duke's councilors are Mothers. Men are good for breaking and building, but politics and papers are best left to women who've been to the Mothers' School. Why, it's Mothers that vote to choose a new duke when the old one passes!"

"Then why ent Elissa one?" Arlen asked.

"It's not for lack of trying," Margrit admitted. "I'll wager she's at it right now. Six weeks on the road will make any man a bull, and I brewed fertility tea and left it on her nightstand. Maybe it will help, though any fool knows the best time to make a baby is just before dawn."

"Then why haven't they made one?" Arlen asked. He knew making babies had something to do with the games Renna and Beni had wanted to play, but he was still vague on the process.

"Only the Creator knows," Margrit said. "Elissa might be barren, or it might be Ragen, though that would be a shame. There's a shortage of good men like him. Miln needs his sons."

She sighed. "Elissa's lucky he hasn't left her, or gotten a child on one of the servant girls. Creator knows, they're willing."

"He would leave his wife?" Arlen was aghast.

"Don't look so surprised, boy," Margrit said. "Men need heirs, and they'll get them any way they can. Duke Euchor is on his third wife, and still only daughters to show for it!"

She shook her head. "Not Ragen, though. They fight like corelings sometimes, but he loves Elissa like the sun itself. He'd never leave. Nor Elissa, despite what she's given up."

"Given up?" Arlen asked.

"She was a Noble, you know," Margrit said. "Her mother is on the Duke's Council. Elissa could have served the duke, too, if she'd married another Noble and got with child. But she married down to be with Ragen, against her mother's wishes. They haven't spoken since. Elissa's Merchant now, if well moneyed. Denied the Mothers' School, she'll never hold any position in the city, much less one in the duke's service."

Arlen was quiet while Margrit rinsed out his wounds and collected his clothes off the tiles. She tsked as she inspected the rips and stains. "I'll mend these as best I can while you soak," she promised, and left him to his bath. While she was gone, Arlen tried to make sense of everything she had told him, but there was too much he didn't understand.

Margrit reminded Arlen a little of Catrin Hog, Rusco's daughter. "She'd tell you every secret in the world, if it let her hear her own voice a moment longer," Silvy used to say.

The woman returned later with fresh if ill-fitting clothes. She bandaged his wounds and helped him dress, despite his protests. He had to roll up the tunic sleeves to find his hands, and cuff his breeches to keep from tripping, but Arlen felt clean for the first time in weeks.

He shared an early supper with Ragen and Elissa. Ragen had trimmed his beard, tied back his hair, and donned a fine white shirt with a deep blue suede jacket and breeches.

A pig had been slaughtered on Ragen's arrival, and the table was soon laden with pork chops, ribs, rashers of bacon, and succulent sausage. Flagons of chilled ale and clear, cold water were served. Elissa frowned when Ragen signaled a servant to pour Arlen an ale, but she said nothing. She sipped wine from a glass so delicate Arlen was afraid her slender fingers would break it. There was crusty bread, whiter than he had ever seen, and bowls of boiled turnips and potatoes, thick with butter.

As he looked out over the food, his mouth watering, Arlen couldn't help but remember people out in the city begging for something to eat. Still, his hunger soon overcame his guilt, and he sampled everything, filling his plate again and again.

"Creator, where are you putting it all?" Elissa asked, clapping her hands in amusement as she watched Arlen clean another plate. "Is there a chasm in your belly?"

"Ignore her, Arlen," Ragen advised. "Women will fuss all day in the kitchen, yet fear to take more than a nibble, lest they seem indelicate. Men know better how to appreciate a meal."

"He's right, you know," Elissa said with a roll of her eyes. "Women can hardly appreciate the subtleties of life as men do." Ragen started and spilled his ale, and Arlen realized that she had kicked him under the table. Arlen decided he liked her.

After supper a page appeared, wearing a gray tabard with the duke's shield emblazoned on the front. He reminded Ragen of his appointment, and the Messenger sighed, but assured the page they would be along directly.

"Arlen is hardly dressed to meet the duke," Elissa fussed. "One does not go before His Grace looking like a Beggar."

"There's nothing for it, love," Ragen replied. "We have only a few hours before sunset. We can hardly have a tailor come in time."

Elissa refused to accept that. She stared at the boy for a long moment, then snapped her fingers, striding out of the room. She returned soon after with a blue doublet and a pair of polished leather boots.

"One of our pages is near your age," she told Arlen as she helped him into the jacket and boots. The sleeves of the doublet were short, and the boots pinched his feet, but Lady Elissa seemed satisfied. She ran a comb through his hair and stepped back.

"Good enough," she said with a smile. "Mind your manners before the duke, Arlen," she counseled. Arlen, feeling awkward in the ill-fitting clothes, smiled and nodded.

The Duke's Keep was a warded fortress within the warded fortress of Miln. The outer wall was fitted stone, over twenty feet high, heavily warded and patrolled by armored spearmen. They rode through the gate into a wide courtyard, which circled the palace. Dwarfing Ragen's manse, the palace had four floors, and towers that reached twice that high. Broad, sharp wards marked every stone. The windows glittered with glass.

Men in armor patrolled the yard, and pages in the duke's colors scurried to and fro. A hundred men sweated out in the yard: carpenters, masons, blacksmiths, and butchers. Arlen saw grain stores and livestock, even broad gardens far larger than Ragen's. It seemed to Arlen that if he should close the gate, the duke could last forever in his keep.

The noise and smell of the yard died as the heavy doors of the palace closed behind them. The entrance hall had a wide running carpet, and tapestries on the cool stone walls. Save for a few guards, there were no men to be seen. Dozens of women moved about instead, their wide skirts swishing as they went about their business. Some were doing figures on slates, while others penned the results in heavy books. A few, more richly dressed than the rest, strolled about imperiously, watching the others at their work.

"The duke is in the audience chamber," one of them advised. "He has been expecting you for some time."

A long line of people waited outside the duke's audience chamber. It was mostly women holding quills and sheaves of paper, but there were a few well-dressed men as well.

"Lesser petitioners," Ragen advised, "all hoping for a minute of the duke's time before the Evening Bell rings and they're escorted out."

The lesser petitioners seemed acutely aware that there was little daylight left, and openly argued among themselves as to who ought to go next. But chatter died as they caught sight of Ragen. As the Messenger walked past, bypassing the line completely, all the petitioners fell silent, then followed in his wake like dogs eager for a feeding. They followed right up to the entranceway, where a glare from the guards brought them up short. They crowded around the entrance to listen as Ragen and Arlen entered.

Arlen felt dwarfed by the audience chamber of Duke Euchor of Miln. The domed ceiling of the room was stories high, and ensconced torches rested on the great columns surrounding Euchor's throne. Each column had wards carved into the marble.

"Greater petitioners," Ragen said quietly, indicating the men and women moving about the room. "They tend to cluster." He nodded to a large group of men standing close to the door. "Merchant princes," he said. "Spreading gold around for the right to stand around the palace, sniffing for news, or a Noble to marry off their daughters to."

"There"—he nodded toward a cluster of old women standing ahead of the Merchants—"the Council of Mothers, waiting to give Euchor his day's reports."

Closer to the throne was a group of sandaled men in plain brown robes, standing with quiet dignity. A few spoke in murmurs, as others took down their every word. "Every court needs its Holy Men," Ragen explained.

He pointed at last to a swarm of richly dressed people buzzing about the duke, attended by an army of servants laden with trays of food and drink. "Royals," Ragen said. "The duke's nephews and cousins and second cousins thrice removed, all clamoring for his ear and dreaming of what will happen if Euchor vacates his throne without an heir. The duke hates them."

"Why doesn't he send them away?" Arlen asked.

"Because they're Royals," Ragen said, as if that explained everything.

They were halfway to the duke's throne when a tall woman moved to intercept them. Her hair was kept back in a cloth wrap, and her face was pinched and lined with wrinkles so deep it looked as if wards were carved into her cheeks. She moved with arched dignity, but a little wattle of flesh beneath her chin shook of its own accord. She had Selia's air about her; a woman accustomed to giving orders and having them obeyed without question. She looked down at Arlen and sniffed as if she had smelled a dung heap. Her gaze snapped up at Ragen.

"Euchor's chamberlain, Jone," Ragen muttered while they were still out of earshot. "Mother, Royal, and an eighth breed of coreling. Don't stop walking unless I do, or she'll have you waiting in the stables while I see the duke."

"Your page will have to wait in the hall, Messenger," Jone said, stepping in front of them.

"He's not my page," Ragen said, continuing forward. Arlen kept pace, and the chamberlain was forced to sacrifice her dignity to scurry out of the way.

"His Grace doesn't have time for every stray off the street, Ragen!" she hissed, hurrying to keep pace with the Messenger. "Who is he?"

Ragen stopped, and Arlen stopped with him. He turned and glared at the woman, leaning in. Mother Jone might have been tall, but Ragen was taller, and he outweighed her thrice over. The sheer menace of his presence shrank her back involuntarily.

"He is who I have chosen to bring," he said through his teeth. He thrust a satchel filled with letters at her, and Jone took it reflexively. As she did, the Merchants and Mothers' Council swarmed her, along with the Tenders' acolytes.

The Royals noted the movement, and made comments or gestures to those next to them. Suddenly, half their entourage broke away, and Arlen realized those were just well-dressed servants. The Royals acted as if nothing of note was happening, but their servants shoved as hard as any to get close to that satchel.

Jone passed the letters on to a servant of her own and hurried toward the throne to announce Ragen, though she needn't have bothered. Ragen's entrance had caused enough of a stir that the man could not have failed to note him. Euchor was watching as they approached.

The duke was a heavyset man in his late fifties, with salt-and-pepper hair and a thick beard. He wore a green tunic, freshly stained with grease from his fingers, but richly embroidered with gold thread, and a fur-lined cloak. His fingers glittered with rings, and about his brow he wore a circlet of gold.

"At last, you deign to grace us with your presence," the duke called out, though it seemed he was speaking more to the rest of the room than to Ragen. Indeed, the observation had the Royals nodding and murmuring among themselves, and caused several heads to pop up from the cluster around the mail. "Was my business not pressing enough?" he asked.

Ragen advanced to the dais, meeting the duke's gaze with a stony one of his own. "Forty-five days from here to Angiers and back by way of Tibbet's Brook!" he said loudly. "Thirty and seven nights slept outside, while corelings slashed at my wards!" He never took his eyes from the duke, but Arlen knew he, too, was speaking to the room. Most of those assembled blanched and shuddered at his words.

"Six weeks gone from my home, Your Grace," Ragen said, lowering his voice by half, but still carrying it to all ears. "Do you begrudge me a bath and a meal with my wife?"

The duke hesitated, his eyes flicking about the court. Finally, he gave a great booming laugh. "Of course not!" he called. "An offended duke can make a man's life difficult, but not half so much as an offended wife!"

The tension shattered as the court broke into laughter. "I would speak to my Messenger alone!" the duke commanded, once the laughter faded. There were grumbles from those eager for news, but Jone signaled her servant to leave with the letters, and that took most of the court with her. The Royals lingered a moment, until Jone cracked her hands together. The retort made them jump, and they filed out as quickly as dignity would allow.

"Stay," Ragen murmured to Arlen, stopping a respectful distance from the throne. Jone signaled the guards, who pulled the heavy doors closed, remaining inside. Unlike the men at the gate, these looked alert and professional. Jone moved to stand beside her lord.

"Don't ever do that before my court again!" Euchor growled when the rest were gone.

The Messenger gave a slight bow to acknowledge the command, but it looked insincere, even to Arlen. The boy was in awe. Ragen was utterly fearless.

"There is news from the Brook, Your Grace," Ragen began.

"The Brook?" Euchor burst out. "What do I care about the Brook? What word from Rhinebeck?"

"They've had a rough winter without the salt," Ragen went on as if the duke had not spoken. "And there was an attack . . ."

"Night, Ragen!" Euchor barked. "Rhinebeck's answer could affect all Miln for years to come, so spare me birth lists and harvest counts of some miserable little backwater!"

Arlen gasped and drew protectively behind Ragen, who gripped his arm reassuringly.

Euchor pressed the attack. "Did they discover gold in Tibbet's Brook?" he demanded.

"No, my lord," Ragen replied, "but . . ."

"Did Sunny Pasture open a coal mine?" Euchor cut him off.

"No, my lord."

"Did they rediscover the lost combat wards?"

Ragen shook his head. "Of course not . . ."

"Did you even haul back enough rice to bring me profit to cover the cost of your services to go there and back?" Euchor asked.

"No." Ragen scowled.

"Good," Euchor said, rubbing his hands as if to remove the dust from them. "Then we need not concern ourselves with Tibbet's Brook for another year and a half."

"A year and a half is too long," Ragen dared to persist. "The folk need . . ."

"Go for free, then," the duke cut him off, "so I can afford it."

When Ragen didn't immediately answer, Euchor smiled widely, knowing he had won the exchange. "What word from Angiers?" he demanded.

"I have a letter from Duke Rhinebeck," Ragen sighed, reaching into his coat. He drew forth a slim tube, sealed with wax, but the duke waved at him impatiently.

"Just *tell* me, Ragen! Yes or no?"

Ragen's eyes narrowed. "No, my lord," he said. "His answer is no. The last two shipments were lost, along with all but a handful of the men. Duke Rhinebeck cannot afford to send another. His men can only log so fast, and he needs the timber more than he needs salt."

The duke's face reddened, and Arlen thought it might burst. "Damn it, Ragen!" he shouted, slamming down his fist. "I need that wood!"

"His Grace has decided that he needs it more for the rebuilding of Riverbridge," Ragen said calmly, "on the south side of the Dividing River."

Duke Euchor hissed, and his eyes took on a murderous gleam.

"This is the work of Rhinebeck's first minister," Jone advised. "Janson's been trying to get Rhinebeck a cut of the bridge tolls for years."

"And why settle for a cut when you can have all?" Euchor agreed. "What did you say I would do when you gave me this news?"

Ragen shrugged. "It's not the place of a Messenger to conjecture. What would you have had me say?"

"That people in wooden fortresses shouldn't set fires in other men's yards," Euchor growled. "I don't need to remind you, Ragen, how important that wood is to Miln. Our supply of coal dwindles, and without fuel, all the ore in the mines is useless, and half the city will freeze! I'll torch his new Riverbridge myself before it comes to that!"

Ragen bowed in acknowledgment of the fact. "Duke Rhinebeck knows this," he said. "He empowered me to make a counteroffer."

"And that is?" Euchor asked, raising an eyebrow.

"Materials to rebuild Riverbridge, and half the tolls," Jone guessed before Ragen could open his mouth. She squinted at the Messenger. "And Riverbridge stays on the Angierian side of the Dividing."

Ragen nodded.

"Night!" Euchor swore. "Creator, Ragen, whose side are you on?"

"I am a Messenger," Ragen replied proudly. "I take no sides, I simply report what I have been told."

Duke Euchor surged to his feet. "Then tell me what in the dark of night I pay you for!" he demanded.

Ragen tilted his head. "Would you prefer to go in person, Your Grace?" he asked mildly.

The duke paled at that, and did not reply. Arlen could feel the power of Ragen's simple comment. If possible, his desire to become a Messenger strengthened further.

The duke finally nodded in resignation. "I will think on this," he said at last. "The hour grows late. You are dismissed."

"There is one more thing, my lord," Ragen added, beckoning Arlen to come forward, but Jone signaled the guards to open the doors, and the greater petitioners swarmed back into the room. The duke's attention was already turned away from the Messenger.

Ragen intercepted Jone as she left Euchor's side. "Mother," he said, "about the boy . . ."

"I'm very busy, Messenger," Jone sniffed. "Perhaps you should 'choose' to bring him some time when I am less so." She swept away from them with her head thrown back.

One of the Merchants approached them. He was a bearlike man with only one eye, his other socket a gnarl of scarred flesh. On his breast was a symbol, a man on horseback with spear and satchel. "It's good to see you safe, Ragen," the man said. "You'll be by the guild in the morning to give your report?"

"Guildmaster Malcum," Ragen said, bowing. "I'm glad to see you. I encountered this boy, Arlen, on the road . . ."

"Between cities?" the guildmaster asked in surprise. "You should know better, boy!"

"Several *days* between cities," Ragen clarified. "The boy wards better than many Messengers." Malcum arched his one eyebrow at that.

"He wants to be a Messenger," Ragen pressed.

"You could not ask for a more honorable career," Malcum told Arlen.

"He has no one in Miln," Ragen said. "I thought he might apprentice with the guild . . ."

"Now, Ragen," Malcum said, "you know as well as any that we only apprentice registered Warders. Try Guildmaster Vincin."

"The boy can already ward," Ragen argued, though his tone was more respectful than it had been with Duke Euchor. Guildmaster Malcum was even larger than Ragen, and didn't look like he could be intimidated by talk of nights outside.

"Then he shouldn't have any trouble getting the Warders' Guild to register him," Malcum said, turning away. "I'll see you in the morning," he called over his shoulder.

Ragen looked around, spotting another man in the cluster of Merchants. "Lift your feet, Arlen," he growled, striding across the room. "Guildmaster Vincin!" he called as he walked.

The man looked up at their approach, and moved away from his fellows to greet them. He bowed to Ragen, but it was a bow of respect, not deference. Vincin had an oily black goatee, and hair slicked straight back. Rings glittered on his chubby fingers. The symbol on his breast was a keyward, a ward that served as foundation to all the other wards in a web.

"What can I do for you, Ragen?" the guildmaster asked.

"This boy, Arlen, is from Tibbet's Brook," Ragen said, gesturing to Arlen. "An orphan from a coreling attack, he has no family in Miln, but he wishes to apprentice as a Messenger."

"That's all well, Ragen, but what's it to do with me?" Vincin asked, never more than glancing Arlen's way.

"Malcum won't take him unless he's registered to ward," Ragen said.

"Well, that is a problem," Vincin agreed.

"The boy can already ward," Ragen said. "If you could see your way to . . ."

Vincin was already shaking his head. "I'm sorry, Ragen, but you're not about to convince me that some backwater bumpkin can ward well enough for me to register him."

"The boy's wards cut the arm off a rock demon," Ragen said.

Vincin laughed. "Unless you have the arm with you, Ragen, you can save that tale for the Jongleurs."

"Could you find him an apprenticeship, then?" the Messenger asked.

"Can he pay the apprenticeship fee?" Vincin asked.

"He's an orphan off the road," Ragen protested.

"Perhaps I can find a Warder to take him on as a Servant," the guildmaster offered.

Ragen scowled. "Thanks all the same," he said, ushering Arlen away.

They hurried back to Ragen's manse, the sun fast setting. Arlen watched as the busy streets of Miln emptied, people carefully checking wards and barring their doors. Even with cobbled streets and thick, warded walls, everyone still locked themselves up at night.

"I can't believe you talked to the duke like that," Arlen said as they went.

Ragen chuckled. "First rule of being a Messenger, Arlen," he said. "Merchants and Royals may pay your fee, but they'll walk all over you, if you let them. You need to act like a king in their presence, and never forget who it is risking their life."

"It worked with Euchor," Arlen agreed.

Ragen scowled at the name. "Selfish pig," he spat. "He doesn't care about anything but his own pockets."

"It's okay," Arlen said. "The Brook survived without salt last fall. They can do it again."

"Perhaps," Ragen conceded, "but they shouldn't have to. And you! A good duke would have asked why I brought a boy with me into his chamber. A good duke would have made you a ward of the throne, so you didn't wind up begging on the street. And Malcum was no better! Would it have cored him to test your skill? And Vincin! If you'd had the ripping fee, that greedy bastard would have had a master to apprentice you by sunset! Servant, he says!"

"Ent an apprentice a Servant?" Arlen asked.

"Not in the slightest," Ragen said. "Apprentices are Merchant class. They master a trade and then go into business for themselves, or with another master. Servants will never be anything but, unless they marry up, and I'll be corespawned before I let them turn you into one."

He lapsed into silence, and Arlen, though he was still confused, thought it best not to press him further.

It was full dark not long after they crossed Ragen's wards, and Margrit showed Arlen to a guest room that was half the size of Jeph's entire house. At the center was a bed so high that Arlen had to hop to get in, and having never slept on anything but the ground or a hard straw pallet, he was shocked when he sank into the soft mattress.

He drifted off to slumber quickly, but awoke soon after at the sound of raised voices. He slipped from the bed and left his room, following the sound. The halls of the great manse were empty, the servants having retired for the night. Arlen went to the top of the stairs, the voices becoming clearer. It was Ragen and Elissa.

". . . taking him in, and that's final," he heard Elissa say. "Messaging's no job for a boy anyway!"

"It's what he wants," Ragen insisted.

Elissa snorted. "Pawning Arlen off on someone else won't alleviate your guilt over bringing him to Miln when you should have taken him home."

"Demon dung," Ragen snapped. "You just want someone to mother day and night."

"Don't you dare turn this back on me!" Elissa hissed. "When you decided not to take Arlen back to Tibbet's Brook, *you* took responsibility for him! It's time to own up to that and stop looking for someone else to care for him."

Arlen strained to hear, but there was no response from Ragen for some time. He wanted to go down and barge into the conversation. He knew Elissa meant well, but he was growing tired of adults planning out his life for him.

"Fine," Ragen said at last. "What if I send him to Cob? He won't encourage the boy to be a Messenger. I'll put up the full fee, and we can visit the shop regularly to keep an eye on him."

"I think that's a great idea," Elissa agreed, the peevishness gone from her voice. "But there's no reason Arlen can't stay here, instead of on a hard bench in some cluttered workshop."

"Apprenticeships aren't meant to be comfortable," Ragen said. "He'll need to be there from dawn till dusk if he's to master wardcraft, and if he follows through with his plans to be a Messenger, he'll need all the training he can get."

"Fine," Elissa huffed, but her voice softened a moment later. "Now come put a baby in my belly," she husked.

Arlen hurried back to his room.

As always, Arlen's eyes opened before dawn, but for a moment he thought he was still asleep, drifting on a cloud. Then he remembered where he was and stretched out, feeling the delicious softness of the feathers stuffed into the mattress and pillow, and the warmth of the thick quilt. The fire in the room's hearth had burned down to embers.

The temptation to stay abed was strong, but his bladder helped force him from the soft embrace. He slipped to the cold floor and fetched the pots from under the bed, as Margrit had instructed him. He made his water in one, and waste in the other, leaving them by the door to be collected for use in the gardens. The soil in Miln was stony, and its people wasted nothing.

Arlen went to the window. He had stared at it until his eyes drooped the night before, but the glass still fascinated him. It looked like nothing at all, but was hard and unyielding to the touch, like a wardnet. He traced a finger along the glass, making a line in the morning condensation. Remembering the wards from Ragen's portable circle, he turned the line into one of the symbols. He traced several more, breathing on the glass to clear his work and start anew.

When he finished, he pulled on his clothes and went downstairs, finding Ragen sipping tea by a window, watching the sun rise over the mountains.

"You're up early," Ragen noted with a smile. "You'll be a Messenger yet," he said, and Arlen swelled with pride.

"Today I'm going to introduce you to a friend of mine," Ragen said. "A Warder. He taught me when I was your age, and he's in need of an apprentice."

"Couldn't I just apprentice to you?" Arlen asked hopefully. "I'll work hard."

Ragen chuckled. "I don't doubt it," he said, "but I'm a poor teacher, and spend more time out of town than in. You can learn a lot from Cob. He was a Messenger before I was even born."

Arlen brightened at this. "When can I meet him?" he asked.

"The sun's up," Ragen replied. "Nothing stopping us from going right after breakfast."

Soon after, Elissa joined them in the dining room. Ragen's servants set a grand table, with bacon and ham and bread smeared with honey, eggs and potatoes and big baked apples. Arlen wolfed the meal down, eager to be out in the city. When he finished, he sat staring at Ragen as he ate. Ragen ignored him, eating with maddening slowness as Arlen fidgeted.

Finally, the Messenger put down his fork and wiped his mouth. "Oh, very well," he said, rising. "We can go." Arlen beamed and jumped from his seat.

"Not so fast," Elissa called, stopping both men short. Arlen was unprepared for the chord the words struck in him, an echo of his mother, and bit back a rush of emotion.

"You're not going anywhere until the tailor comes for Arlen's measurements," she said.

"What for?" Arlen asked. "Margrit cleaned my clothes and sewed up all the rips."

"I appreciate the sentiment, love," Ragen said in Arlen's defense, "but there's hardly a rush for new clothes now that the interview with the duke is past."

"This isn't open to debate," Elissa informed them, drawing herself up. "I won't have a guest in our house walking around looking like a pauper."

The Messenger looked at the set of his wife's brow, and sighed. "Let it go, Arlen," he advised quietly. "We're not going anywhere until she's satisfied."

The tailor arrived soon after, a small man with nimble fingers who inspected every inch of Arlen with his knotted strings, carefully marking the information with chalk on a slate. When he was finished, he had a rather animated conversation with Lady Elissa, bowed, and left.

Elissa glided over to Arlen, bending to face him. "That wasn't so bad, was it?" she asked, straightening his shirt and brushing the hair from his face. "Now you can run along with Ragen to meet Master Cob." She caressed his cheek, her hand cool and soft, and for a moment he leaned into the familiar touch, but then pulled back sharply, his eyes wide.

Ragen caught the look, and noted the wounded expression on his wife's face as Arlen backed slowly away from her as if she were a demon.

"I think you hurt Elissa's feelings back there, Arlen," Ragen said as they left his grounds.

"She's not my mam," Arlen said, suppressing his guilt.

"Do you miss her?" Ragen asked. "Your mother, I mean."

"Yes," Arlen answered quietly.

Ragen nodded, and said no more, for which Arlen was thankful. They walked on in silence, and the strangeness of Miln quickly took his mind off the incident. The smell of the dung carts was everywhere, as collectors went from building to building, gathering the night's waste.

"Gah!" Arlen said, holding his nose. "The whole city smells worse than a barn stall! How do you stand it?"

"It's mostly just in the morning, as the collectors go by," Ragen replied. "You get used to it. We had sewers once, tunnels that ran under every home, carrying the waste away, but they were sealed centuries ago, when the corelings used them to get into the city."

"Couldn't you just dig privy pits?" Arlen asked.

"Milnese soil is stony," Ragen said. "Those who don't have private gardens to fertilize are required to put their waste out for collection to use in the Duke's Gardens. It's the law."

"It's a smelly law," Arlen said.

Ragen laughed. "Maybe," he replied. "But it keeps us fed, and drives the economy. The collection guildmaster's manse makes mine look like a hovel."

"I'm sure yours smells better," Arlen said, and Ragen laughed again.

At last they turned a corner and came to a small but sturdy shop, with wards delicately etched around the windows and into the lintel and jamb of the door. Arlen could appreciate the detail of those wards. Whoever made them had a skilled hand.

They entered to a chime of bells, and Arlen's eyes widened at the contents of the shop. Wards of every shape and size, made in every medium, filled the room.

"Wait here," Ragen said, moving across the room to speak with a man sitting on a workbench. Arlen barely noticed him go, wandering around the room. He ran his fingers reverently over wards woven into tapestry, etched into smooth river stones, and molded from metal. There were carved posts for farmers' fields, and a portable circle like Ragen's. He tried to memorize the wards he saw, but there were just too many.

"Arlen, come here!" Ragen called after a few minutes. Arlen started, and rushed over.

"This is Master Cob," Ragen introduced, gesturing to a man who was perhaps sixty. Short for a Milnese, he had the look of a strong man gone to fat. A thick gray beard, shot through with signs of its former black, covered his face, and his close-cropped hair was thin atop his head. His skin was lined and leathern, and his grip swallowed Arlen's hand.

"Ragen tells me you want to be a Warder," Cob said, sitting back heavily on the bench.

"No, sir," Arlen replied. "I want to be a Messenger."

"So does every boy your age," Cob said. "The smart ones wise up before they get themselves killed."

"Weren't you a Messenger once?" Arlen asked, confused at the man's attitude.

"I was," Cob agreed, lifting his sleeve to show a tattoo similar to Ragen's. "I traveled to the five Free Cities and a dozen hamlets, and earned more money than I thought I could ever spend." He paused, letting Arlen's confusion grow. "I also earned this," he said, lifting his shirt to show thick scars running across his stomach, "and this." He slipped a foot from his shoe. A crescent of scarred flesh, long healed, showed where four of his toes had been.

"To this day," Cob said, "I can't sleep more than an hour without starting awake, reaching for my spear. Yes, I was a Messenger. A damned good one and luckier than most, but I still would not wish it on anyone. Messaging may seem glorious, but for every man who lives in a manse and commands respect like Ragen here, there are two dozen rotting on the road."

"I don't care," Arlen said. "It's what I want."

"Then I'll make a deal with you," Cob sighed. "A Messenger must be, above all, a Warder, so I'll apprentice you and teach you to be one. When we have time, I'll teach you what I know of surviving the road. An apprenticeship lasts seven years. If you still wish to be a Messenger then . . . well, you're your own man."

"Seven years?" Arlen gawked.

Cob snorted. "You don't pick up warding in a day, boy."

"I can ward now," Arlen said defiantly.

"So Ragen tells me," Cob said. "He also tells me you do it with no knowledge of geometry or wardtheory. Eyeballing your wards may not get you killed tomorrow, boy, or next week, but it *will* get you killed."

Arlen stomped a foot. Seven years seemed like an eternity, but deep down he knew the master was right. The pain in his back was a constant reminder that he wasn't ready to face the corelings again. He needed the skills this man could teach him. He didn't doubt that there were dozens of Messengers who fell to the demons, and he vowed not to become one of them because he was too stubborn to learn from his mistakes.

"All right," he agreed finally. "Seven years."

SECTION II

MILN
320–325 AR

CHAPTER 10

APPRENTICE
320 AR

"THERE'S OUR FRIEND AGAIN," said Gaims, gesturing into the darkness from their post on the wall.

"Right on time," Woron agreed, coming up next to him. "What do you s'pose he wants?"

"Empty my pockets," Gaims said, "you'll find no answers."

The two guards leaned against the warded rail of the watchtower and watched as the one-armed rock demon materialized before the gate. It was big, even to the eyes of Milnese guards, who saw more of rock demons than any other type.

While the other demons were still getting their bearings, the one-armed demon moved with purpose, snuffling about the gate, searching. Then it straightened and struck the gate, testing the wards. Magic flared and threw the demon back, but it was undeterred. Slowly, the demon moved along the wall, striking again and again, searching for a weakness until it was out of sight.

Hours later, a crackle of energy signaled the demon's return from the opposite direction. The guards at other posts said that the demon circled the city each night, attacking every ward. When it reached the gate once more, it settled back on its haunches, staring patiently at the city.

Gaims and Woron were used to this scene, having witnessed it every night for the past year. They had even begun to look forward to it, passing the time on their watch by betting on how long One Arm took to circle the city, or whether he would head east or west to do so.

"I'm half tempted to let 'im in, just t'see what he's after," Woron mused.

"Don't even joke about that," Gaims warned. "If the watch commander hears talk like that, he'll have both of us in irons, quarrying stone for the next year."

His partner grunted. "Still," he said, "you have to wonder . . ."

That first year in Miln, his twelfth, passed quickly for Arlen as he grew into his role as an apprentice Warder. Cob's first task had been to teach him to read. Arlen knew wards never before seen in Miln, and Cob wanted them committed to paper as soon as possible.

Arlen took to reading voraciously, wondering how he had ever gotten along without it. He disappeared into books for hours at a time, his lips moving slightly at first, but soon he was turning pages rapidly, his eyes darting across the page.

Cob had no cause to complain; Arlen worked harder than any apprentice he had ever known, staying up late in the night etching wards. Cob would often go to his bed thinking of the full day's work to come, only to find it completed when the sun's first light flooded the shop.

After learning his letters, Arlen was put to work cataloguing his personal repertoire of wards, complete with descriptions, into a book the master purchased for him. Paper was expensive in the sparsely wooded lands of Miln, and a whole book was something few commoners ever saw, but Cob scoffed at the price.

"Even the worst grimoire's worth a hundred times the paper it's written on," he said.

"Grimoire?" Arlen asked.

"A book of wards," Cob said. "Every Warder has theirs, and they guard their secrets carefully." Arlen treasured the valuable gift, filling its pages with a slow and steady hand.

When Arlen had finished plumbing his memory, Cob studied the book in shock. "Creator, boy, do you have any idea what this book is worth?" he demanded.

Arlen looked up from the ward he was chiseling into a stone post, and shrugged. "Any graybeard in Tibbet's Brook could teach you those wards," he said.

"That may be," Cob replied, "but what's common in Tibbet's Brook is buried treasure in Miln. This ward here." He pointed to a page. "Can it truly turn firespit into a cool breeze?"

Arlen laughed. "My mam used to love that one," he said. "She wished the flame demons could come right up to the windows on hot summer nights to cool the house with their breath."

"Amazing," Cob said, shaking his head. "I want you to copy this a few more times, Arlen. It's going to make you a very rich man."

"How do you mean?" Arlen asked.

"People would pay a fortune for a copy of this," Cob said. "Maybe we shouldn't even sell at all. We could be the most sought-after Warders in the city if we kept them secret."

Arlen frowned. "It's not right to keep them secret," he said. "My da always said wards are for everyone."

"Every Warder has his secrets, Arlen," Cob said. "This is how we make our living."

"We make our living etching wardposts and painting doorjambs," Arlen disagreed, "not hoarding secrets that can save lives. Should we deny succor to those too poor to pay?"

"Of course not," Cob said, "but this is different."

"How?" Arlen asked. "We didn't have Warders in Tibbet's Brook. We all warded our own homes, and those who were better at it helped those who were worse without asking anything in return. Why should we? It's not us against each other, it's us against the demons!"

"Fort Miln isn't like Tibbet's Brook, boy." Cob scowled. "Here, things cost money. If you don't have any money, you become a Beggar. I have a skill, like any baker or stonemason. Why shouldn't I charge for it?"

Arlen sat quietly for a time. "Cob, why ent you rich?" he asked at last.

"What?"

"Like Ragen," Arlen clarified. "You said you used to be a Messenger for the duke. Why don't you live in a manse and have servants do everything for you? Why do you do this at all?"

Cob blew out a long breath. "Money is a fickle thing, Arlen," he said. "One moment you can have more than you know what to do with, and the next . . . you can find yourself begging food on the street."

Arlen thought of the beggars he saw on his first day in Miln. He had seen many more since, stealing dung to burn for warmth, sleeping in public warded shelters, begging for food.

"What happened to your money, Cob?" he asked.

"I met a man who said he could build a road," Cob said. "A warded road, stretching from here to Angiers." Arlen moved closer and sat on a stool, his attention rapt.

"They've tried to build roads before," Cob went on, "to the Duke's Mines in the mountains, or to Harden's Grove to the south. Short distances, less than a full day, but enough to make a fortune for the builder. They always failed. If there's a hole in a net, no matter how small, corelings will find it eventually. And once they're in . . ." He shook his head. "I told the man this, but he was adamant. He had a plan. It would work. All he needed was money."

Cob looked at Arlen. "Every city is short of something," he said, "and has too much of something else. Miln has metal and stone, but no wood. Angiers, the reverse. Both are short of crops and livestock, while Rizon has more than they need, but no good lumber or metal for tools. Lakton has fish in abundance, but little else.

"I know you must think me a fool," he said, shaking his head, "for considering something everyone from the duke on down had dismissed as impossible, but the idea stuck with me. I kept thinking, *What if he could? Isn't that worth any risk?*"

"I don't think you're a fool," Arlen said.

"Which is why I keep most of your pay in trust," Cob chuckled. "You'd give it away, same as I did."

"What happened to the road?" Arlen pressed.

"Corelings happened," Cob said. "They slaughtered the man and all the workers I hired him, burned the wardposts and plans . . . they destroyed it all. I had invested everything in that road, Arlen. Even letting my servants go wasn't enough to pay my debts. I made barely enough money selling my manse to clear a loan to buy this shop, and I've been here ever since."

They sat for a time, both of them lost in images of what that night must have been like, both of them seeing in their mind's eye the corelings dancing amid the flames and carnage.

"Do you still think the dream was worth the risk?" Arlen asked. "All the cities sharing?"

"To this day," Cob replied. "Even when my back aches from carting wardposts and I can't stand my own cooking."

"This is no different," Arlen said, tapping the book of wards. "If all the Warders shared what they knew, how much better for everyone? Isn't a safer city worth losing a little profit?"

Cob stared at him a long time. Then he came over and put a hand on his shoulder. "You're right, Arlen. I'm sorry. We'll copy the books and sell them to the other Warders."

Arlen slowly began to smile.

"What?" Cob asked suspiciously.

"Why not trade our secrets for theirs?" Arlen asked.

The chimes rang, and Elissa entered the warding shop with a wide smile. She nodded to Cob as she carried a large basket to Arlen, kissing him on the cheek. Arlen grimaced in embarrassment and wiped his cheek, but she took no notice of it.

"I brought you boys some fruit, and fresh bread and cheese," she said, removing the items from the basket. "I expect you've been eating no better than you were upon my last visit."

"Dried meat and hard bread are a Messenger's staples, my lady," Cob said with a smile, not looking up from the keystone he was chiseling.

"Rubbish," Elissa scolded. "You're retired, Cob, and Arlen isn't a Messenger yet. Don't try to glorify your lazy refusal to go to the market. Arlen is a growing boy, and needs better fare." She ruffled Arlen's hair as she spoke, smiling even as he pulled away.

"Come to dinner tonight, Arlen," Elissa said. "Ragen is away, and the manse is lonely without him. I'll feed you something to put meat on your bones, and you can stay in your room."

"I . . . don't think I can," Arlen said, avoiding her eyes. "Cob needs me to finish these wardposts for the Duke's Gardens . . ."

"Nonsense," Cob said, waving his hand. "The wardposts can wait, Arlen. They're not due for another week." He looked up at Lady Elissa with a grin, ignoring Arlen's discomfort. "I'll send him over at the Evening Bell, Lady."

Elissa flashed him a smile. "It's settled, then," she said. "I'll see you tonight, Arlen." She kissed the boy and swept out of the shop.

Cob glanced at Arlen, who was frowning into his work. "I don't see why you choose to spend your nights sleeping on a pallet in the back of the shop when you could have a warm featherbed and a woman like Elissa to dote on you," he said, keeping his eyes on his own work.

"She acts like she's my mam," Arlen complained, "but she's not."

"That's true, she's not," Cob agreed. "But it's clear she wants the job. Would it be so bad to let her have it?"

Arlen said nothing, and Cob, seeing the sad look in the boy's eyes, let the matter drop.

"You're spending too much time inside with your nose buried in books," Cob said, snatching away the volume Arlen was reading. "When was the last time you felt the sun on your skin?"

Arlen's eyes widened. In Tibbet's Brook, he had never spent a moment indoors when he had a choice, but after more than a year in Miln, he could hardly remember his last day outside.

"Go find some mischief!" Cob ordered. "Won't kill you to make a friend your own age!"

Arlen walked out of the city for the first time in a year, and the sun comforted him like an old friend. Away from the dung carts, rotting garbage, and sweaty crowds, the air held a freshness he had forgotten. He found a hilltop overlooking a field filled with playing children and pulled a book from his bag, plopping down to read.

"Hey, bookmole!" someone called.

Arlen looked up to see a group of boys approaching, holding a ball. "C'mon!" one of them cried. "We need one more to make the sides even!"

"I don't know the game," Arlen said. Cob had all but ordered him to play with other boys, but he thought his book far more interesting.

"What's to know?" another boy asked. "You help your side get the ball to the goal, and try to keep the other side from doing it."

Arlen frowned. "All right," he said, moving to join the boy who had spoken.

"I'm Jaik," the boy said. He was slender, with tousled dark hair and a pinched nose. His clothes were patched and dirty. He looked thirteen, like Arlen. "What's your name?"

"Arlen."

"You work for Warder Cob, right?" Jaik asked. "The kid Messenger Ragen found on the road?" When Arlen nodded, Jaik's eyes widened a bit, as if he hadn't believed it. He led the way onto the field, and pointed out the white painted stones that marked the goals.

Arlen quickly caught on to the rules of the game. After a

time, he forgot his book, focusing his attention on the opposing team. He imagined he was a Messenger and they were demons trying to keep him from his circle. Hours melted away, and before he knew it the Evening Bell rang. Everyone hurriedly gathered up their things, fearful of the darkening sky.

Arlen took his time fetching his book. Jaik ran up to him. "You'd better hurry," he said.

Arlen shrugged. "We have plenty of time," he replied.

Jaik looked at the darkening sky, and shuddered. "You play pretty good," he said. "Come back tomorrow. We play ball most afternoons, and on Sixthday we go to the square to see the Jongleur." Arlen nodded noncommittally, and Jaik smiled and sped off.

Arlen headed back through the gate, the now-familiar stink of the city enveloping him. He turned up the hill to Ragen's manse. The Messenger was away again, this time to faraway Lakton, and Arlen was spending the month with Elissa. She would pester him with questions and fuss about his clothes, but he had promised Ragen to "keep her young lovers away."

Margrit had assured Arlen that Elissa had no lovers. In fact, when Ragen was away, she drifted the halls of their manse like a ghost, or spent hours crying in her bedchamber.

But when Arlen was around, the servant said, she changed. More than once, Margrit had begged him to live at the manse full time. He refused, but, he admitted to himself if no one else, he was beginning to like Lady Elissa fussing over him.

"Here he comes," Gaims said that night, watching the massive rock demon rise from the ground. Woron joined him, and they watched from the guard tower as the demon snuffled the ground by the gate. With a howl, it bounded away from the gate to a hilltop. A flame demon danced there, but the rock demon knocked it violently aside, bending low to the ground, seeking something.

"Old One Arm's in a mood tonight," Gaims said as the demon howled again and darted down the hill to a small field, scurrying back and forth, hunched over.

"What do you suppose has gotten into him?" Woron asked. His partner shrugged.

The demon left the field, bounding back up the hill. Its shrieks became almost pained, and when it returned to the gate, it struck at the wards madly, its talons sending showers of sparks as they were repelled by the potent magic.

"Don't see that every night," Woron commented. "Should we report it?"

"Why bother?" Gaims replied. "No one is going to care about the carryings-on of one crazy demon, and what could they do about it if they did?"

"Against that thing?" Woron asked. "Probably just soil themselves."

Pushing away from the workbench, Arlen stretched and got to his feet. The sun was long set, and his stomach growled irritably, but the baker was paying double to have his wards repaired in one night, even though a demon hadn't been spotted on the streets in Creator only knew how long. He hoped Cob had left something for him in the cookpot.

Arlen opened the shop's back door and leaned out, still safely within the warded semicircle around the doorway. He looked both ways, and assured that all was clear, he stepped onto the path, careful not to cover the wards with his foot.

The path from the back of Cob's shop to his small cottage was safer than most houses in Miln, a series of individually warded squares made of poured stone. The stone—crete, Cob called it—was a science left over from the old world, a wonder unheard of in Tibbet's Brook but quite common in Miln. Mixing powdered silicate and lime with water and gravel formed a muddy substance that could be molded and hardened into any shape desired.

It was possible to pour crete, and, as it began to set, carefully scratch wards into its soft substance that hardened into near-permanent protections. Cob had done this, square by square, until a path ran from his home to his shop. Even if one square were somehow compromised, a walker could simply move to the one ahead or behind, and remain safe from corelings.

If we could make a road like this, Arlen thought, *the world would be at our fingertips.*

Inside the cottage, he found Cob hunched over his desk, poring over chalked slates.

"Pot's warm," the master grunted, not looking up. Arlen moved over to the fireplace in the cottage's single room and filled a bowl with Cob's thick stew.

"Creator, boy, you started a mess with this," Cob growled,

straightening and gesturing to the slates. "Half the Warders in Miln are content to keep their secrets, even at the loss of ours, and half of those left keep offering money instead, but the quarter that remain have flooded my desk with lists of wards they're willing to barter. It will be weeks in the sorting!"

"Things will be better for it," Arlen said, using a crust of hard bread as a spoon as he sat on the floor, eating hungrily. The corn and beans were still hard, and the potatoes mushy from overboiling, but he didn't complain. He was accustomed to the tough, stunted vegetables of Miln by now, and Cob could never be bothered to boil them separately.

"I daresay you're right," Cob admitted, "but night! Who thought there were so many different wards right in our own city! Half I've never seen in my life, and I've scrutinized every wardpost and portal in Miln, I assure you!"

He held up a chalked slate. "This one is willing to trade wards that will make a demon turn around and forget what it was doing for your mother's ward to make glass as hard as steel." He shook his head. "And they *all* want the secrets of your forbidding wards, boy. They're easier to draw without a straightstick and a semicircle."

"Crutches for people who can't draw a straight line." Arlen smirked.

"Not everyone is as gifted as you," Cob grunted.

"Gifted?" Arlen asked.

"Don't let it go to your head, boy," Cob said, "but I've never seen anyone pick up warding as quick as you. Eighteen months into your apprenticeship, and you ward like a five-year journeyman."

"I've been thinking about our deal," Arlen said.

Cob looked up at him curiously.

"You promised that if I worked hard," Arlen said, "you'd teach me to survive the road."

They stared at one another a long while. "I've kept my part," Arlen reminded.

Cob blew out a sigh. "I suppose you have," he said. "Have you been practicing your riding?" he asked.

Arlen nodded. "Ragen's groom lets me help exercise the horses."

"Double your efforts," Cob said. "A Messenger's horse is his life. Every night your steed saves you from spending outside is a night out of risk." The old Warder got to his feet, opening a closet and pulling out a thick rolled cloth. "On Seventhdays, when we close the shop," he said, "I'll coach your riding, and I'll teach you to use these."

He laid the cloth on the floor and unrolled it, revealing a number of well-oiled spears. Arlen eyed them hungrily.

Cob looked up at the chimes as a young boy entered his shop. He was about thirteen, with tousled dark curls and a fuzz of mustache at his lip that looked more like dirt than hair.

"Jaik, isn't it?" the Warder asked. "Your family works the mill down by the East Wall, don't they? We quoted you once for new wards, but the miller went with someone else."

"That's right," the boy said, nodding.

"What can I help you with?" Cob asked. "Would your master like another quote?"

Jaik shook his head. "I just came to see if Arlen wants to see the Jongleur today."

Cob could hardly believe his ears. He had never seen Arlen speak to anyone his own age, preferring to spend his time working and reading, or pestering the Messengers and Warders who visited the shop with endless questions. This was a surprise, and one to be encouraged.

"Arlen!" he called.

Arlen came out of the shop's back room, a book in his hand. He practically walked into Jaik before he noticed the boy and pulled up short.

"Jaik's come to take you to see the Jongleur," Cob advised.

"I'd like to go," Arlen told Jaik apologetically, "but I still have to . . ."

"Nothing that can't wait," Cob cut him off. "Go and have fun." He tossed Arlen a small pouch of coins and pushed the two boys out the door.

Soon after, the boys were wandering through the crowded marketplace surrounding the main square of Miln. Arlen spent a silver star to buy meat pies from a vendor, and then, their faces coated with grease, he handed over a few copper lights for a pocketful of sweets from another.

"I'm going to be a Jongleur one day," Jaik said, sucking on a sweet as they made their way to the place where the children gathered.

"Honest word?" Arlen asked.

Jaik nodded. "Watch this," he said, pulling three small wooden balls from his pockets and putting them into the air. Arlen laughed a moment later, when one of the balls struck Jaik's head and the others dropped to the ground in the confusion.

"Still got grease on my fingers," Jaik said as they chased after the balls.

"I guess," Arlen agreed. "I'm going to register at the Messengers' Guild once my apprenticeship with Cob is over."

"I could be your Jongleur!" Jaik shouted. "We could test for the road together!"

Arlen looked at him. "Have you ever even *seen* a demon?" he asked.

"What, you don't think I have the stones for it?" Jaik asked, shoving him.

"Or the brains," Arlen said, shoving back. A moment later, they were scuffling on the ground. Arlen was still small for his age, and Jaik soon pinned him.

"Fine, fine!" Arlen laughed. "I'll let you be my Jongleur!"

"*Your* Jongleur?" Jaik asked, not releasing him. "More like you'll be *my* Messenger!"

"Partners?" Arlen offered. Jaik smiled and offered Arlen a hand up. Soon after, they were sitting atop stone blocks in the town square, watching the apprentices of the Jongleurs' Guild cartwheel and mum, building excitement for the morning's lead performer.

Arlen's jaw dropped when he saw Keerin enter the square. Tall and thin like a redheaded lamppost, the Jongleur was unmistakable. The crowd erupted into a roar.

"It's Keerin!" Jaik said, shaking Arlen's shoulder in excitement. "He's my favorite!"

"Really?" Arlen asked, surprised.

"What, who do you like?" Jaik asked. "Marley? Koy? They're not heroes like Keerin!"

"He didn't seem very heroic when I met him," Arlen said doubtfully.

"You met Keerin?" Jaik asked, his eyes widening.

"He came to Tibbet's Brook once," Arlen said. "He and Ragen found me on the road and brought me to Miln."

"Keerin rescued you?"

"Ragen rescued me," Arlen corrected. "Keerin jumped at every shadow."

"The Core he did," Jaik said. "Do you think he'll remember you?" he asked. "Can you introduce me after the show?"

"Maybe." Arlen shrugged.

Keerin's performance started out much as it had in Tibbet's Brook. He juggled and danced, warming the crowd before telling the tale of the Return to the children and punctuating it with mummery, backflips, and somersaults.

"Sing the song!" Jaik cried. Others in the crowd took up the cry, begging Keerin to sing. He seemed not to notice for a time, until the call was thunderous and punctuated by the pounding of feet. Finally, he laughed and bowed, fetching his lute as the crowd burst into applause.

He gestured, and Arlen saw the apprentices fetch hats and move into the crowd for donations. People gave generously, eager to hear Keerin sing. Finally, he began:

The night was dark
The ground was hard
Succor was leagues away

The cold wind stark
Cutting at our hearts
Only wards kept corelings at bay

"Help me!" we heard
A voice in need
The cry of a frightened child

"Run to us!" I called
"Our circle's wide,
The only succor for miles!"

The boy cried out
"I can't; I fell!"
His call echoed in the black

Catching his shout
I sought to help
But the Messenger held me back

"What good to die?"
He asked me, grim
"For death is all you'll find

"No help you'll provide
'Gainst coreling claws
Just more meat to grind"

I struck him hard
And grabbed his spear
Leaping across the wards

A frantic charge
Strength born of fear
Before the boy be cored

"Stay brave!" I cried
Running hard his way
"Keep your heart strong and true!"

"If you can't stride
To where it's safe
I'll bring the wards to you!"

I reached him quick
But not enough
Corelings gathered round

The demons thick
My work was rough
Scratching wards into the ground

A thunderous roar
Boomed in the night
A demon twenty feet tall

It towered fore
And 'gainst such might
My spear seemed puny and small

Horns like hard spears!
Claws like my arm!
A carapace hard and black!

An avalanche
Promising harm
The beast moved to the attack!

The boy screamed scared
And clutched my leg
Clawed as I drew the last ward!

The magic flared
Creator's gift
The one force demons abhor!

Some will tell you
Only the sun
Can bring a rock demon harm

That night I learned
It could be done
As did the demon One Arm!

He ended with a flourish, and Arlen sat shocked as the audience burst into applause. Keerin took his bows, and the apprentices took in a flood of coin.

"Wasn't that great?" Jaik asked.

"That's not how it happened!" Arlen exclaimed.

"My da says the guards told him a one-armed rock demon attacks the wards every night," Jaik said. "It's looking for Keerin."

"Keerin wasn't even there!" Arlen cried. "*I* cut that demon's arm off!"

Jaik snorted. "Night, Arlen! You can't really expect anyone to believe *that*."

Arlen scowled, standing up and calling, "Liar! Fraud!" Everyone turned to see the speaker, as Arlen leapt off his stone and strode toward Keerin. The Jongleur looked up, and his eyes widened in recognition. "Arlen?" he asked, his face suddenly pale.

Jaik, who'd been running after Arlen, pulled up short. "You do know him," he whispered.

Keerin glanced at the crowd nervously. "Arlen, my boy," he said, opening his arms, "come, let's discuss this in private."

Arlen ignored him. "You didn't cut that demon's arm off!" he screamed for all to hear. "You weren't even there when it happened!"

There was an angry murmur from the crowd. Keerin looked around in fear until someone called "Get that boy out of the square!" and others cheered.

Keerin broke into a wide smile. "No one is going to believe you over me," he sneered.

"I was there!" Arlen cried. "I've got the scars to prove it!" He reached to pull up his shirt, but Keerin snapped his fingers, and suddenly, Arlen and Jaik were surrounded by apprentices.

Trapped, they could do nothing as Keerin walked away, taking the crowd's attention with him as he snatched his lute and quickly launched into another song.

"Why don't you shut it, hey?" a burly apprentice growled. The boy was half again Arlen's size, and all were older than he and Jaik.

"Keerin's a liar," Arlen said.

"A demon's ass, too," the apprentice agreed, holding up the hat of coins. "Think I care?"

Jaik interposed himself. "No need to get angry," he said. "He didn't mean anything . . ."

But before he finished, Arlen sprang forward, driving his fist into the bigger boy's gut. As he crumpled, Arlen whirled to face the rest. He bloodied a nose or two, but he was soon pulled down and pummeled. Dimly, he was aware of Jaik sharing the beating beside him until two guards broke up the fight.

"You know," Jaik said as they limped home, bloody and bruised, "for a bookmole, you're not half bad in a fight. If only you'd pick your enemies better . . ."

"I have worse enemies," Arlen said, thinking of the one-armed demon following him still.

"It wasn't even a good song," Arlen said. "How could he draw wards in the dark?"

"Good enough to get into a fight over," Cob noted, daubing blood from Arlen's face.

"He was *lying,*" Arlen replied, wincing at the sting.

Cob shrugged. "He was just doing what Jongleurs do, making up entertaining stories."

"In Tibbet's Brook, the whole town would come when the Jongleur came," Arlen said. "Selia said they kept the stories of the old world, passing them down one generation to the next."

"And so they do," Cob said. "But even the best ones exaggerate, Arlen. Or did you really believe the first Deliverer killed a hundred rock demons in a single blow?"

"I used to," Arlen said with a sigh. "Now I don't know what to believe."

"Welcome to adulthood," Cob said. "Every child finds a day when they realize that adults can be weak and wrong just like anyone else. After that day, you're an adult, like or not."

"I never thought about it that way," Arlen said, realizing his day had come long before. In his mind's eye, he saw Jeph hiding behind the wards of their porch while his mother was cored.

"Was Keerin's lie really such a bad thing?" Cob asked. "It made people happy. It gave them hope. Hope and happiness are in short supply these days, and much needed."

"He could have done all that with honest word," Arlen said. "But instead he took credit for my deeds just to make more coin."

"Are you after truth, or credit?" Cob asked. "Should credit matter? Isn't the message what's important?"

"People need more than a song," Arlen said. "They need proof that corelings can bleed."

"You sound like a Krasian martyr," Cob said, "ready to throw your life away seeking the Creator's paradise in the next world."

"I read their afterlife is filled with naked women and rivers of wine." Arlen smirked.

"And all you need do to enter is take a demon with you before you're cored," Cob agreed. "But I'll take my chances with this life all the same. The next one will find you no matter where you run. No sense chasing it."

CHAPTER 11

BREACH
321 AR

"THREE MOONS SAYS HE HEADS EAST," Gaims said, jingling the silver coins as One Arm rose.

"Taken," Woron said. "He's gone east three nights running. He's ready for a change."

As always, the rock demon snuffled about before testing the wards at the gate. It moved methodically, never missing a spot. When the gate proved secure, the coreling moved to the east.

"Night," Woron cursed. "I was sure this time he'd do something different." He fished in his pocket for coins as the shrieks of the demon and the crackle of activated wards died out.

Both guardsmen looked over the rail, the bet forgotten, and saw One Arm staring at the wall curiously. Other corelings gathered around, but kept a respectful distance from the giant.

Suddenly, the demon lunged forward with just two talons extended. There was no flare from the wards, and the crack of stone came clearly to the guards' ears. Their blood went cold.

With a roar of triumph, the rock demon struck again, this time with its whole hand. Even in starlight, the guards saw the chunk of stone that came away in its claws.

"The horn," Gaims said, gripping the rail with shaking hands. His leg grew warm, and it took him a moment to realize he had wet himself. "Sound the horn."

There was no movement next to him. He looked over at Woron, and saw his partner staring at the rock demon with his mouth open, a single tear running down the side of his face.

"Sound the ripping horn!" Gaims screamed, and Woron snapped out of his daze, running to the mounted horn. It took him several tries to sound a note. By then, One Arm was spinning and striking the wall with its spiked tail, tearing out more and more rock each time.

Cob shook Arlen awake.

"Who . . . wazzat?" Arlen asked, rubbing his eyes. "Is it morning already?"

"No," Cob said. "The horns are sounding. There's a breach."

Arlen sat bolt upright, his face gone cold. "Breach? There are corelings in the city?"

"There are," Cob agreed, "or soon will be. Up with you!"

The two scrambled to light lamps and gather their tools, pulling on thick cloaks and fingerless gloves to help stave off the cold without impeding their work.

The horns sounded again. "Two blasts," Cob said, "one short, one long. The breach is between the first and second watchposts to the east of the main gate."

A clatter of hooves sounded on the cobblestones outside, followed by a pounding on the door. They opened it to find Ragen in full armor, a long, thick spear in hand. His warded shield was slung on the saddle horn of a heavy destrier. Not a sleek and affectionate courser like Nighteye, this beast was broad and ill-tempered, a warhorse bred for times long gone.

"Elissa is beside herself," the Messenger explained. "She sent me to keep you two alive."

Arlen frowned, but a touch of the fear that gripped him on waking slipped away with Ragen's arrival. They hitched their sturdy garron to the warding cart, and were off, following the shouts, crashes, and flashes of light toward the breach.

The streets were empty, doors and shutters locked tight, but Arlen could see cracks of light around them, and knew the people of Miln were awake, biting nails and praying their wards would hold. He heard weeping, and thought of how dependent the Milnese were upon their wall.

They arrived at a scene of utter chaos. Guardsmen and Warders lay dead and dying on the cobbled streets, spears broken and burning. Three bloodied men-at-arms wrestled with a wind demon, attempting to pin it long enough for a pair of Warder's apprentices to trap it in a portable circle. Others ran to and fro with buckets of water, trying to smother the many small fires as flame demons scampered about in glee, setting alight everything in reach.

Arlen looked at the breach, amazed that a coreling could dig through twenty feet of solid rock. Demons jammed the hole, clawing at each other to be next to pass into the city.

A wind demon squeezed through, getting a running start as it spread its wings. A guard hurled his spear at it, but the missile fell short, and the demon flew into the city unchallenged. A moment later, a flame demon leapt upon the now-unarmed guard and tore his throat out.

"Quickly, boy!" Cob shouted. "The guards are buying us time, but they won't last long against a breach this size. We need to seal it fast!" He sprang from the cart with surprising agility and snatched two portable circles from the back, handing one to Arlen.

With Ragen riding protectively beside them, they sprinted toward the keyward flag of the Warders' Guild, marking the protective circle where the Warders had set up their base. Unarmed Herb Gatherers were tending rows of wounded there, fearlessly darting out of the circle to assist men stumbling toward the sanctuary. They were a scant few to tend so many.

Mother Jone, the duke's advisor, and Master Vincin, the head of the Warders' Guild, greeted them. "Master Cob, good to have you . . ." Jone began.

"Where are we needed?" Cob asked Vincin, ignoring Jone completely.

"The main breach," Vincin said. "Take the posts for fifteen and thirty degrees," he said, pointing toward a stack of wardposts. "And by the Creator, be careful! There's a devil of a rock demon there—the one that made the breach in the first place. They have it trapped from heading further into the city, but you'll have to cross the wards to get into position. It's killed three Warders already, and Creator only knows how many guards."

Cob nodded, and he and Arlen headed over to the pile. "Who was on duty at dusk tonight?" he asked as they took their load.

"Warder Macks and his apprentices," Jone replied. "The duke will hang them for this."

"Then the duke is a fool," Vincin said. "There's no telling what happened out there, and Miln needs every Warder it has and more." He blew out a long breath. "There will be few enough left after tonight, as is."

"Set up your circle first," Cob said for the third time. "When you're safe within, set the post in its stand and wait for the magnesium. It'll be bright as day, so shield your eyes until it comes. Then center yours to the dial on the main post. Don't try to link with the other posts. Trust their Warders to get it right. When it's done, drive stakes between the cobbles to hold it in place."

"And then?" Arlen asked.

"Stay in the corespawned circle until you're told to come out," Cob barked, "no matter what you see, even if you're in there all night! Is that clear?"

Arlen nodded.

"Good," Cob said. He scanned the chaos, waiting, waiting, then shouted "Now!" and they were off, dodging around fires, bodies, and rubble, heading for their positions. In seconds, they cleared a row of buildings and saw the one-armed rock demon towering over a squad of guardsmen and a dozen corpses. Its talons and jaws glistened with blood in the lamplight.

Arlen's blood went cold. He stopped short and looked to Ragen, and the Messenger met his eye for a moment. "Must be after Keerin," Ragen said wryly.

Arlen opened his mouth, but before he could reply, Ragen screamed "Look out!" and swiped his spear Arlen's way.

Arlen fell and dropped his post, banging his knee badly on the cobblestones. He heard the crack as the butt of Ragen's spear took a diving wind demon in the face, and rolled over in time to see the coreling carom off the Messenger's shield and crash to the ground.

Ragen trampled the creature with his warhorse as he kicked into a gallop, grabbing Arlen just as he picked up his post and half dragging, half carrying him over to his position. Cob had already set up his portable circle and was preparing the stand for his wardpost.

Arlen wasted no time setting up his own circle, but his eyes kept flicking back to One Arm. The demon was clawing at the hastily placed wards before it, trying to power through. Arlen could see weaknesses in the net each time it flared, and knew it would not hold forever.

The rock demon sniffed and looked up suddenly, meeting

Arlen's eyes, and the two matched wills for a moment, until it became too much to bear and Arlen dropped his gaze. One Arm shrieked and redoubled its efforts to break through the weakening wards.

"Arlen, stop staring and do your ripping job!" Cob screamed, snapping Arlen out of his daze. Trying his best to block out the shrieks of the coreling and the shouting of guardsmen, he set the collapsible iron stand and placed his wardpost within. He angled it as best he could in the dim flickering light, then placed a hand over his eyes to wait for the magnesium.

The flare went off a moment later, turning night into day. The Warders angled their posts quickly and staked them in place. They waved with white cloths to signal completion.

His work done, Arlen scanned the rest of the area. Several Warders and apprentices were still struggling to set their posts. One post was alight with demonfire. Corelings were screaming and recoiling from the magnesium, terrified that somehow the hated sun had come. Guardsmen surged forward with spears, attempting to drive them back past the wardposts before they activated. Ragen did the same, galloping about upon his destrier, his polished shield reflecting the light and sending corelings scrambling away in fear.

But the false light could not truly hurt the corelings. One Arm did not recoil as a squad of guardsmen, emboldened in the light, sent a row of spears its way. Many of the spear tips broke or skittered off the rock demon's armor, and it grabbed at others, yanking hard and pulling the men past the wards as easily as a child might swing a doll.

Arlen watched the carnage in horror. The demon bit the head off one man and flung his body back into the others, knocking several from their feet. It squashed another man underfoot, and sent a third flying with a sweep of its spiked tail. He landed hard and did not rise.

The wards holding the demon back were buried beneath the bodies and blood, and One Arm bulled forward, killing at will. The guards fell back, some fleeing entirely, but as soon as they backed off, they were forgotten as the giant coreling charged Arlen's portable circle.

"Arlen!" Ragen screamed, wheeling his destrier about. In his panic at the sight of the charging demon, the Messenger seemed to forget the portable circle in which the boy stood. He couched his spear and kicked the horse into a gallop, aiming at One Arm's back.

The rock demon heard his approach and turned at the last moment, setting its feet and taking the spear full in the chest. The weapon splintered, and with a contemptuous swipe of its claws, the giant demon crushed the horse's skull.

The destrier's head twisted to the side and it backpedaled into Cob's circle, knocking him into his wardpost and sending it askew. Ragen had no time to untangle himself, and the animal took him down with it, crushing his leg and pinning him. One Arm moved in for the kill.

Arlen screamed and looked for aid, but there was none to be found. Cob was clutching at his wardpost, trying to pull himself upright. All the other Warders around the breach were signaling. They had replaced the burning post, and only Cob's remained out of place, but there was no one to aid him; the city guard had been decimated in One Arm's last assault. Even if Cob quickly fixed his post, Arlen knew Ragen was doomed. One Arm was on the wrong side of the net.

"Hey!" he cried, stepping from his circle and waving his arms. "Hey, ugly!"

"Arlen, get back in your ripping circle!" Cob screamed, but it was too late. The rock demon's head whipped around at the sound of Arlen's voice.

"Oh yeah, you heard," Arlen murmured, his face flushing hot and then immediately going cold. He glanced past the wardposts. The corelings were growing bold as the magnesium began to die down. Stepping in there would be suicide.

But Arlen remembered his previous encounters with the rock demon, and how it jealously regarded him as its own. With that thought, he turned and ran past the wardposts, catching the attention of a hissing flame demon. The coreling pounced, eyes aflame, but so did One Arm, driving forward to smash the lesser demon.

Even as it whirled back to him, Arlen was diving back past the wardposts. One Arm struck hard at him, but light flared, and it was thwarted. Cob had restored his post, establishing the net. One Arm shrieked in rage, pounding at the barrier, but it was impenetrable.

He ran to Ragen's side. Cob swept him into a hug, and then cuffed him on the ear. "You ever pull a stunt like that again," the master warned, "and I'll break your scrawny neck."

"I was s'posed to protect *you* . . ." Ragen agreed weakly, his mouth twitching in a smile.

There were still corelings loose in the city when Vincin and Jone dismissed the Warders. The remaining guardsmen helped the Herb Gatherers transport the wounded to the city's hospits.

"Shouldn't someone hunt down the ones that got away?" Arlen asked as they eased Ragen into the back of their cart. His leg was splinted, and the Herb Gatherers had given him a tea to numb the pain, leaving him sleepy and distant.

"To what end?" Cob asked. "It would only get the hunters killed, and make no difference in the morning. Better to get inside. The sun will do for any corelings left in Miln."

"The sun is still hours away," Arlen protested as he climbed into the cart.

"What do you propose?" Cob asked, watching warily as they rode. "You saw the full force of the Duke's Guard at work tonight, hundreds of men with spears and shields. Trained Warders, too. Did you see a single demon killed? Of course not. They are immortal."

Arlen shook his head. "They kill each other. I've seen it."

"They are magic, Arlen. They can do to one another what no mortal weapon can."

"The sun kills them," Arlen said.

"The sun is a power beyond you or me," Cob said. "We are simply Warders."

They turned a corner, and gasped. An eviscerated corpse was splayed in the street before them, its blood painting the cobbles red. Parts of it still smoldered; the acrid stench of burned flesh was thick in the air.

"Beggar," Arlen said, noting the ragged clothes. "What was he doing out at night?"

"Two beggars," Cob corrected, holding a cloth over his mouth and nose as he gestured at further carnage not far off. "They must have been turned out of the shelter."

"They can do that?" Arlen asked. "I thought the public shelters had to take everyone."

"Only until they fill up," Cob said. "Those places are scant succor, anyhow. The men will beat each other over food and clothes once the guards lock them in, and they do worse to the women. Many prefer to risk the streets."

"Why doesn't someone do something about it?" Arlen asked.

"Everyone agrees it's a problem," Cob said. "But the citizens say it is the duke's problem, and the duke feels little need to protect those who contribute nothing to his city."

"So better to send the guard home for the night, and let the corelings take care of the problem," Arlen growled. Cob had no reply save to crack the reins, eager to get off the streets.

Two days later, the entire city was summoned to the great square. A gibbet had been erected, and upon it stood Warder Macks, who had been on duty the night of the breach.

Euchor himself was not present, but Jone read his decree: "In the name of Duke Euchor, Light of the Mountains and Lord of Miln, you are found guilty of failing in your duties and allowing a breach in the wardwall. Eight Warders, two Messengers, three Herb Gatherers, thirty-seven guardsmen, and eighteen citizens paid the price for your incompetence."

"As if making it nine Warders will help," Cob muttered. Boos and hisses came from the crowd, and bits of garbage were flung at the Warder, who stood with his head down.

"The sentence is death," Jone said, and hooded men took Macks' arms and led him to the rope, putting the noose around his neck.

A tall, broad-shouldered Tender with a bushy black beard and heavy robes went to him and drew a ward on his forehead. "May the Creator forgive your failing," the Holy Man intoned, "and grant us all the purity of heart and deed to end His Plague and be Delivered."

He backed away, and the trapdoor opened. The crowd cheered as the rope went taut.

"Fools," Cob spat. "One less man to fight the next breach."

"What did he mean?" Arlen asked. "About the Plague and being delivered?"

"Just nonsense to keep the crowd in line," Cob said. "Best not to fill your head with it."

CHAPTER 12

LIBRARY
321 AR

ARLEN WALKED EXCITEDLY behind Cob as they approached the great stone building. It was Seventhday, and normally he would have been annoyed at skipping his spear practice and riding lessons, but today was a treat too fine to miss: his first trip to the Duke's Library.

Ever since he and Cob had begun brokering wards, his master's business had soared, filling a much-needed niche in the city. Their grimoire library had quickly become the largest in Miln, and perhaps the world. At the same time, word had gotten out about their involvement in sealing the breach, and never ones to miss a trend, the Royals had taken notice.

Royals were an irritation to work with, always making ridiculous demands and wanting wards put where they didn't belong. Cob doubled, then tripled his prices, but it made no difference. Having one's manse sealed by Cob the Wardmaster had become a status symbol.

But now, called upon to ward the most valuable building in the city, Arlen knew it had been worth every moment. Few citizens ever saw inside the library. Euchor guarded his collection jealously, granting access only to greater petitioners and their aides.

Built by the Tenders of the Creator before being absorbed by the throne, the library was always run by a Tender, usually one with no flock save the precious books. Indeed, the post carried more weight than presiding over any Holy House save for the Grand Holy House or the duke's own shrine.

They were greeted by an acolyte, and ushered to the office of the head librarian, Tender Ronnell. Arlen's eyes darted everywhere as they walked, taking in the musty shelves and silent scholars who roamed the stacks. Not including grimoires, Cob's collection had contained over thirty books, and Arlen had thought that a treasure. The Duke's Library contained thousands, more than he could read in a lifetime. He hated that the duke kept it all locked away.

Tender Ronnell was young for the coveted position of head librarian, still with more brown in his hair than gray. He greeted them warmly and sat them down, sending a servant to fetch some refreshment.

"Your reputation precedes you, Master Cob," Ronnell said, taking off his wire-rimmed glasses and cleaning them on his brown robe. "I hope you will accept this assignment."

"All the wards I've seen so far are still sharp," Cob noted.

Ronnell replaced his glasses and cleared his throat uncomfortably. "After the recent breach, the duke fears for his collection," he said. "His Grace desires . . . special measures."

"What kind of special measures?" Cob asked suspiciously. Ronnell squirmed, and Arlen could tell that he was as uncomfortable making the request as he expected them to be in filling it.

Finally, Ronnell sighed. "All the tables, benches, and shelves are to be warded against firespit," he said flatly.

Cob's eyes bulged. "That would take months!" he sputtered. "And to what end? Even if a flame demon made it so deep into the city, it could never get past the wards of this building, and if it did, you'd have greater worries than the bookshelves."

Ronnell's eyes hardened at that. "There is no greater worry, Master Cob," he said. "In that, the duke and I agree. You cannot imagine what we lost when the corelings burned the libraries of old. We guard here the last shreds of knowledge that took millennia to accumulate."

"I apologize," Cob said. "I meant no disrespect."

The librarian nodded. "I understand. And you are quite correct, the risk is minimal. Nevertheless, His Grace wants what he wants. I can pay a thousand gold suns."

Arlen ticked the math off in his head. A thousand suns was a lot of money, more than they had ever gotten for a single job, but when accounting for the months of work the job would entail, and the loss of regular business . . .

"I'm afraid I can't help you," Cob said at last. "Too much time away from my business."

"This would garner the duke's favor," Ronnell added.

Cob shrugged. "I messengered for his father. That brought me favor enough. I have little need for more. Try a younger Warder," he suggested. "Someone with something to prove."

"His Grace mentioned your name specifically," Ronnell pressed.

Cob spread his hands helplessly.

"I'll do it," Arlen blurted. Both men turned to him, surprised that he had been so bold.

"I don't think the duke will accept the services of an apprentice," Ronnell said.

Arlen shrugged. "No need to tell him," he said. "My master can plot the wards for the shelves and tables, leaving me to inscribe them." He looked at Cob as he spoke. "If you had taken the job, I would have carved half the wards anyway, if not more."

"An interesting compromise," Ronnell said thoughtfully. "What say you, Master Cob?"

Cob looked at Arlen suspiciously. "I say this is a tedious job of the sort you hate," he said. "What's in it for you, lad?" he asked.

Arlen smiled. "The duke gets to claim that Wardmaster Cob warded the library," he began. "You get a thousand suns, and I"—he turned to Ronnell—"get to use the library whenever I wish."

Ronnell laughed. "A boy after my own heart!" he said. "Have we a deal?" he asked Cob.

Cob smiled, and the men shook hands.

Tender Ronnell led Cob and Arlen on an inspection of the library. As they went, Arlen began to realize what a colossal task he had just undertaken. Even if he skipped the math and plotted the wards by sight, he was looking at the better part of a year's work.

Still, as he turned in place, taking in all the books, he knew it was worth it. Ronnell had promised him full access, day or night, for the rest of his life.

Noting the look of enthusiasm on the boy's face, Ronnell smiled. He had a sudden thought, and took Cob aside while Arlen was too occupied with his own thoughts to notice.

"Is the boy an apprentice or a Servant?" he asked the Warder.

"He's Merchant, if that's what you're asking," Cob said.

Ronnell nodded. "Who are his parents?"

Cob shook his head. "Hasn't any; at least not in Miln."

"You speak for him, then?" Ronnell asked.

"I would say the boy speaks for himself," Cob replied.

"Is he promised?" the Tender asked.

There it was. "You're not the first to ask me that, since my business rose," Cob said. "Even some of the Royals have sent their pretty daughters to sniff at him. But I don't think the Creator has made the girl that can pull his nose out of a book long enough to notice her."

"I know the feeling," Ronnell said, gesturing to a young girl who was sitting at one of the many tables with half a dozen open books scattered before her.

"Mery, come here!" he called. The girl looked up, and then deftly marked her pages and stacked her books before coming over. She looked close to Arlen's fourteen summers, with large brown eyes and long, rich brown hair. She had a soft, round face, and a bright smile. She wore a utilitarian frock, dusty from the library, and she gathered the skirts, dipping a quick curtsy.

"Wardmaster Cob, this is my daughter, Mery," Ronnell said.

The girl looked up, suddenly very interested. "*The* Wardmaster Cob?" she asked.

"Ah, you know my work?" Cob asked.

"No"—Mery shook her head—"but I've heard your grimoire collection is second to none."

Cob laughed. "We might have something here, Tender," he said.

Tender Ronnell bent to his daughter and pointed to Arlen. "Young Arlen there is Master Cob's apprentice. He's going to ward the library for us. Why don't you show him around?"

Mery watched Arlen as the boy gazed about, oblivious to her stare. His dirty blond hair was untrimmed and somewhat long, and his expensive clothes were rumpled and stained, but there was intelligence in his eyes. His features were smooth and symmetrical; not unpleasing. Cob heard Ronnell mutter a prayer as she smoothed her skirts and glided over to him.

Arlen didn't seem to notice Mery as she came over. "Hello," she said.

"Hullo," Arlen replied, squinting to read the print on the spine of a high-shelved book.

Mery frowned. "My name's Mery," she said. "Tender Ronnell is my father."

"Arlen," Arlen said, pulling a book off the shelf and flipping through it slowly.

"My father asked me to show you around the library," Mery said.

"Thanks," Arlen said, putting the book back and walking down a row of shelves to a section of the library that was roped off from the rest. Mery was forced to follow, irritation flashing on her face.

"She's used to ignoring, not being ignored," Ronnell noted, amused.

"BR," Arlen read on the archway over the roped section. "What's BR?" he muttered.

"Before Return," Mery said. "Those are original copies of the books of the old world."

Arlen turned to her as if he had just noticed she existed. "Honest word?" he asked.

"It's forbidden to go back there without the duke's permission," Mery said, watching Arlen's face fall. "Of course," she smiled, "I am allowed, on account of my father."

"Your father?" Arlen asked.

"I'm Tender Ronnell's daughter," she reminded, scowling.

Arlen's eyes widened, and he bowed awkwardly. "Arlen, of Tibbet's Brook," he said.

From across the room, Cob chuckled. "Boy never had a chance," he said.

The months melted together for Arlen as he fell into a familiar routine. Ragen's manse was closer to the library, so he slept there most nights. The Messenger's leg had mended quickly, and he was soon on the road again. Elissa encouraged Arlen to treat the room as his own, and seemed to take a special pleasure at seeing it cluttered with his tools and books. The servants loved his presence as well, claiming Lady Elissa was less of a trial when he was about.

Arlen would rise an hour before the sun, and practice his spear forms by lamplight in the manse's high-ceilinged foyer. When the sun broke the horizon, he slipped into the yard for an hour of target practice and riding. This was followed by a hurried breakfast with Elissa—and Ragen when he was about—before he was off to the library.

It was still early when he arrived, the library empty save for Ronnell's acolytes, who slept in cells beneath the great building. These kept their distance, intimidated by Arlen, who thought nothing of walking up to their master and speaking without summons or permission.

There was a small, isolated room designated as his workshop. It was just big enough for a pair of bookcases, his workbench, and whatever piece of furniture he was working on. One of the cases was filled with paints, brushes, and etching tools. The other was filled with borrowed books. The floor was covered in curled wood shavings, blotched from spilled paint and lacquer.

Arlen took an hour each morning to read, then reluctantly put his book away and got to work. For weeks, he warded nothing but chairs. Then he moved on to benches. The job took even longer than expected, but Arlen didn't mind.

Mery became a welcome sight over these months, sticking her head into his workshop frequently to share a smile or a bit of gossip before scurrying off to resume her duties. Arlen had thought the interruptions from his work and study would grow tiresome, but the opposite proved true. He looked forward to seeing her, even finding his attention wandering on days when she did not visit with her usual frequency. They shared lunches on the library's broad roof, overlooking the city and the mountains beyond.

Mery was different from any girl Arlen had ever known. The daughter of the duke's librarian and chief historian, she was possibly the most educated girl in the city, and Arlen found he could learn as much by talking to her as in the pages of any book. But her position was a lonely one. The acolytes were even more intimidated by her than they were by Arlen, and there was no one else her age in the library. Mery was perfectly comfortable arguing with gray-bearded scholars, but around Arlen she seemed shy and unsure of herself.

Much as he felt around her.

"Creator, Jaik, it's as if you haven't practiced at all," Arlen said, covering his ears.

"Don't be cruel, Arlen," Mery scolded. "Your song was lovely, Jaik," she said.

Jaik frowned. "Then why are you covering your ears, too?" he asked.

"Well," she said, taking her hands away with a bright smile, "my father says music and dancing lead to sin, so I couldn't listen, but I'm sure it was very beautiful."

Arlen laughed, and Jaik frowned, putting his lute away.

"Try your juggling," Mery suggested.

"Are you sure it's not a sin to watch juggling?" Jaik asked.

"Only if it's good," Mery murmured, and Arlen laughed again.

Jaik's lute was old and worn, never seeming to have all its strings at one time. He set it down and pulled colored wooden balls from the small sack he kept his Jongleur's equipment in. The paint was chipped and there were cracks in the wood. He put one ball into the air, then another, and a third. He held that number for several seconds, and Mery clapped her hands.

"Much better!" she said.

Jaik smiled. "Watch this!" he said, reaching for a fourth.

Arlen and Mery both winced as the balls came clattering down to the cobblestones.

Jaik's face colored. "Maybe I should practice more with three," he said.

"You should practice more," Arlen agreed.

"My da doesn't like it," Jaik said. "He says 'if you've nothing to do but juggle, boy, I'll find some chores for you!' "

"My father does that when he catches me dancing," Mery said.

They looked at Arlen expectantly. "My da used to do that, too," he said.

"But not Master Cob?" Jaik asked.

Arlen shook his head. "Why should he? I do all he asks."

"Then when do you find time to practice messengering?" Jaik asked.

"I make time," Arlen said.

"How?" Jaik asked.

Arlen shrugged. "Get up earlier. Stay up later. Sneak away after meals. Whatever you need to do. Or would you rather stay a miller your whole life?"

"There's nothing wrong with being a miller, Arlen," Mery said.

Jaik shook his head. "No, he's right," he said. "If this is what I want, I have to work harder." He looked at Arlen. "I'll practice more," he promised.

"Don't worry," Arlen said. "If you can't entertain the villagers in the hamlets, you can earn your keep scaring off the demons on the road with your singing."

Jaik's eyes narrowed. Mery laughed as he began throwing his juggling balls at Arlen.

"A good Jongleur could hit me!" Arlen taunted, nimbly dodging each throw.

"You're reaching too far," Cob called. To illustrate his point, Ragen let go one hand from his shield and gripped Arlen's spear, just below the tip, before he could retract it. He yanked, and the overbalanced boy went crashing into the snow.

"Ragen, be careful," Elissa admonished, clutching her shawl tightly in the chill morning air. "You'll hurt him."

"He's far gentler than a coreling would be, my lady," Cob said, loud enough for Arlen to hear. "The purpose of the long spear is to hold the demons back at a distance while retreating. It's a defensive weapon. Messengers who get too aggressive with them, like young Arlen here, end up dead. I've seen it happen. There was one time on the road to Lakton . . ."

Arlen scowled. Cob was a good teacher, but he tended to punctuate his lessons with grisly stories of the demise of other Messengers. His intent was to discourage, but his words had the opposite effect, only strengthening Arlen's resolve to succeed where those before him failed. He picked himself up and set his feet more firmly this time, his weight on his heels.

"Enough with the long spears," Cob said. "Let's try the short ones."

Elissa frowned as Arlen placed the eight-foot-long spear on a rack and he and Ragen selected shorter ones, barely three feet long, with points measuring a third of their length. These were designed for close-quarter fighting, stabbing instead of jabbing. He selected a shield as well, and the two of them once again faced off in the snow. Arlen was taller now, broader of the shoulder, fifteen years old with a lean, wiry strength. He was dressed in Ragen's old leather armor. It was big on him, but he was fast growing into it.

"What is the point of this?" Elissa asked in exasperation. "It's not like he's ever going to get that close to a demon and live to tell about it."

"I've seen it happen," Cob disagreed, as he watched Arlen

and Ragen spar. "But there are other things than demons out between the cities, my lady. Wild animals, and even bandits."

"Who would attack a Messenger?" Elissa asked, shocked.

Ragen shot Cob an angry look, but Cob ignored him. "Messengers are wealthy men," he said, "and they carry valuable goods and messages that can decide the fate of Merchants and Royals alike. Most people wouldn't dare bring harm to one, but it can happen. And animals . . . with corelings culling the weak, only the strongest predators remain.

"Arlen!" the Warder called. "What do you do if you're attacked by a bear?"

Without stopping or taking his eyes off Ragen, Arlen called back, "Long spear to the throat, retreat while it bleeds, then strike the vitals when it lowers its guard."

"What else can you do?" Cob called.

"Lie still," Arlen said distastefully. "Bears seldom attack the dead."

"A lion?" Cob asked.

"Medium spear," Arlen called, picking off a stab from Ragen with his shield and countering. "Stab to the shoulder joint and brace as the cat impales itself, then stab with a short spear to the chest or side, as available."

"Wolf?"

"I can't listen to any more of this," Elissa said, storming off toward the manse.

Arlen ignored her. "A good whack to the snout with a medium spear will usually drive off a lone wolf," he said. "Failing that, use the same tactics as for lions."

"What if there's a pack of them?" Cob asked.

"Wolves fear fire," Arlen said.

"And if you encounter a boar?" Cob wanted to know.

Arlen laughed. "I should 'run like all the Core is after me,' " he quoted his instructors.

Arlen awoke atop a pile of books. For a moment he wondered where he was, realizing finally that he had fallen asleep in the library again. He looked out the window, seeing that it was well past dark. He craned his head up, making out the ghostly shape of a wind demon as it passed far above. Elissa would be upset.

The histories he had been reading were ancient, dating back to the Age of Science. They told of the kingdoms of the old world, Albinon, Thesa, Great Linm, and Rusk, and spoke of seas, enormous lakes spanning impossible distances, with yet more kingdoms on the far side. It was staggering. If the books were to be believed, the world was bigger than he had ever imagined.

He paged through the open book he had collapsed upon, and was surprised to find a map. As his eyes scanned the place names, they widened. There, plain as could be, was the duchy of Miln. He looked closer, and saw the river that Fort Miln used for much of its fresh water, and the mountains that stood at its back. Right there was a small star, marking the capital.

He flipped a few pages, reading about ancient Miln. Then, as now, it was a mining and quarrying city, with vassalage spanning dozens of miles. Duke Miln's territory included many towns and villages, ending at the Dividing River, the border of the lands held by Duke Angiers.

Arlen remembered his own journey, and traced back west to the ruins he had found, learning that they had belonged to the earl of Newkirk. Almost shaking with excitement, Arlen looked further, and found what he had been looking for, a small waterway opening into a wide pond.

The barony of Tibbet.

Tibbet, Newkirk, and the others had paid tribute to Miln, who in turn with Duke Angiers owed fealty to the king of Thesa.

"Thesans," Arlen whispered, trying the word on for size. "We're all Thesans."

He took out a pen and began to copy the map.

"That name is not to be spoken again by either of you," Ronnell scolded Arlen and his daughter.

"But . . ." Arlen began.

"You think this wasn't known?" the librarian cut him off. "His Grace has ordered anyone speaking the name of Thesa arrested. Do you want to spend years breaking rocks in his mines?"

"Why?" Arlen asked. "What harm could it bring?"

"Before the duke closed the library," Ronnell said, "some people were obsessed with Thesa, and with soliciting monies to hire Messengers to contact lost dots on the maps."

"What's wrong with that?" Arlen asked.

"The king is three centuries dead, Arlen," Ronnell said, "and the dukes will make war before they bend knee to anyone but themselves. Talk of reunification reminds people of things they ought not remember."

"Better to pretend that the walls of Miln are the entire world?" Arlen asked.

"Until the Creator forgives us and sends his Deliverer to end the Plague," Ronnell said.

"Forgives us for what?" Arlen asked. "What plague?"

Ronnell looked at Arlen, his eyes a mix of shock and indignation. For a moment, Arlen thought the Tender might strike him. He steeled himself for the blow.

Instead, Ronnell turned to his daughter. "Can he really not know?" he asked in disbelief.

Mery nodded. "The Tender in Tibbet's Brook was . . . unconventional," she said.

Ronnell nodded. "I remember," he said. "He was an acolyte whose master was cored, and never completed his training. We always meant to send someone new . . ." He strode to his desk and began penning a letter. "This cannot stand," he said. "What plague, indeed!"

He continued to grumble, and Arlen took it as a cue to edge for the door.

"Not so fast, you two," Ronnell said. "I'm very disappointed in you both. I know Cob is not a religious man, Arlen, but this level of negligence is really quite unforgivable." He looked to Mery. "And you, young lady!" he snapped. "You knew this, and did nothing?"

Mery looked at her feet. "I'm sorry, Father," she said.

"And well you should be," Ronnell said. He drew a thick volume from his desk and handed it to his daughter. "Teach him," he commanded, handing her the Canon. "If Arlen doesn't know the book back and forth in a month, I'll take a strap to both of you!"

Mery took the book, and both of them scampered out as quickly as possible.

"We got off pretty easy," Arlen said.

"Too easy," Mery agreed. "Father was right. I should have said something sooner."

"Don't worry about it," Arlen said. "It's just a book. I'll have it read by morning."

"It's not just a book!" Mery snapped. Arlen looked at her curiously.

"It's the word of the Creator, as penned by the first Deliverer," Mery said.

Arlen raised an eyebrow. "Honest word?" he asked.

Mery nodded. "It's not enough to read it. You have to live it. Every day. It's a guide to bring humanity from the sin that brought about the Plague."

"What plague?" Arlen asked for what felt like the dozenth time.

"The demons, of course," Mery said. "The corelings."

Arlen sat on the library's roof a few days later, his eyes closed as he recited:

> *And man again became prideful and bold,*
> *Turning 'gainst Creator and Deliverer.*
> *He chose not to honor Him who gave life,*
> *Turning his back upon morality.*
>
> *Man's science became his new religion,*
> *Replacing prayer with machine and chemic,*
> *Healing those meant to die,*
> *He thought himself equal to his maker.*
>
> *Brother fought brother, to benefit none.*
> *Evil lacking without, it grew within,*
> *Taking seed in the hearts and souls of men,*
> *Blackening what was once pure and white.*
>
> *And so the Creator, in His wisdom,*
> *Called down a plague upon his lost children,*
> *Opening the Core once again,*
> *To show man the error of his ways.*
>
> *And so it shall be,*
> *Until the day He sends the Deliverer anew.*
> *For when the Deliverer cleanses man,*
> *Corelings will have naught to feed upon.*

And lo, ye shall know the Deliverer
For he shall be marked upon his bare flesh
And the demons will not abide the sight
And they shall flee terrified before him.

"Very good!" Mery congratulated with a smile.

Arlen frowned. "Can I ask you something?" he asked.

"Of course," Mery said.

"Do you really believe that?" he asked. "Tender Harral always said the Deliverer was just a man. A great general, but a mortal man. Cob and Ragen say so, too."

Mery's eyes widened. "You'd best not let my father hear you say that," she warned.

"Do you believe the corelings are our own fault?" Arlen asked. "That we deserve them?"

"Of course I believe," she said. "It is the word of the Creator."

"No," Arlen said. "It's a book. Books are written by men. If the Creator wanted to tell us something, why would he use a book, and not write on the sky with fire?"

"It's hard sometimes to believe there's a Creator up there, watching," Mery said, looking up at the sky, "but how could it be otherwise? The world didn't create itself. What power would wards hold, without a will behind creation?"

"And the Plague?" Arlen asked.

Mery shrugged. "The histories tell of terrible wars," she said. "Maybe we did deserve it."

"Deserve it?" Arlen demanded. "My mam did not *deserve* to die because of some stupid war fought centuries ago!"

"Your mother was taken?" Mery asked, touching his arm. "Arlen, I had no idea . . ."

Arlen yanked his arm away. "It makes no difference," he said, storming toward the door. "I have wards to carve, though I hardly see the point, if we all deserve demons in our beds."

CHAPTER 13

THERE MUST
BE MORE
326 AR

LEESHA BENT IN THE GARDEN, selecting the day's herbs. Some she pulled from the soil root and stalk. Others, she snapped off a few leaves, or used her thumbnail to pop a bud from its stem.

She was proud of the garden behind Bruna's hut. The crone was too old for the work of maintaining the small plot, and Darsy had failed to make the hard dirt yield, but Leesha had the touch. Now many of the herbs that she and Bruna had once spent hours searching for in the wild grew just outside their door, safe within the wardposts.

"You've a sharp mind and a green thumb," Bruna had said when the soil birthed its first sprouts. "You'll be a better Gatherer than I before long."

The pride those words gave Leesha was a new feeling. She might never match Bruna, but the old woman was not one for kind words or empty compliments. She saw something in Leesha that others hadn't, and the girl did not want to disappoint.

Her basket filled, Leesha brushed off and rose to her feet, heading toward the hut—if it could even be called a hut anymore. Erny had refused to see his daughter live in squalor, sending carpenters and roofers to shore up the weak walls and replace the frayed thatch. Soon there was little left that was not new, and additions had more than doubled the structure's size.

Bruna had grumbled about all the noise as the men worked, but her wheezing had eased now that the cold and wet were sealed outside. With Leesha caring for her, the old woman seemed to be getting stronger with the passing years, not weaker.

Leesha, too, was glad the work was completed. The men had begun looking at her differently, toward the end.

Time had given Leesha her mother's lush figure. It was something she had always wanted, but it seemed less an advantage now. The men in town watched her hungrily, and the rumors of her dallying with Gared, though years gone, still sat in the back of many minds, making more than one man think she might be receptive to a lewd, whispered offer. Most of these were dissuaded with a frown, and a few with slaps. Evin had required a puff of pepper and stinkweed to remind him of his pregnant bride. A fistful of the blinding powder was now one of many things Leesha kept in the multitude of pockets in her apron and skirts.

Of course, even if she had been interested in any of the men in town, Gared made sure none could get close to her. Any man other than Erny caught talking to Leesha about more than Herb Gathering received a harsh reminder that in the burly woodcutter's mind she was still promised. Even Child Jona broke out in a sweat whenever Leesha so much as greeted him.

Her apprenticeship would be over soon. Seven years and a day had seemed an eternity when Bruna had said it, but the years had flown, and the end was but days away. Already, Leesha went alone each day to call upon those in town who needed an Herb Gatherer's service, asking Bruna's advice only very rarely, when the need was dire. Bruna needed her rest.

"The duke judges an Herb Gatherer's skill by whether more babies are delivered than people die each year," Bruna had said that first day, "but focus on what's in between, and a year from now the people of Cutter's Hollow won't know how they ever got along without you." It had proven true enough. Bruna brought her everywhere from that moment on, ignoring the request of any for privacy. Her having cared for the unborn of most of the women in town, and brewed pomm tea for half the rest, had them soon paying Leesha every courtesy, and revealing all the failings of their bodies to her without a thought.

But for all that, she was still an outsider. The women talked as if she were invisible, blabbing every secret in the village as freely as if she were no more than a pillow in the night.

"And so you are," Bruna said, when Leesha dared to complain. "It's not for you to judge their lives, only their health. When you put on that pocketed apron, you swear to hold your peace no matter what you hear. An Herb Gatherer needs trust to do her work, and trust must be earned. No secret should ever pass your lips, unless keeping it prevents you healing another."

So Leesha held her tongue, and the women had come to trust her. Once the women were hers, the men soon followed, often with their women prodding at their back. But the apron kept them away, all the same. Leesha knew what almost every man in the village looked like unclothed, but had never been intimate with one; and though the women might sing her praises and send her gifts, there was not a one she could tell her own secrets to.

Yet despite all, Leesha had been far happier in the last seven years than she had been in the thirteen before. Bruna's world was much wider than the one she had been groomed for by her mother. There was grief, when she was forced to close someone's eyes, but there was also the joy of pulling a child from its mother and sparking its first cries with a firm swat.

Soon, her apprenticeship would be over, and Bruna would retire for good. To hear her speak it, she would not live long after that. The thought terrified Leesha in more ways than one.

Bruna was her shield and her spear, her impenetrable ward against the town. What would she do without that ward? Leesha did not have it in her to dominate as Bruna had, barking orders and striking fools. And without Bruna, who would she have that spoke to her as a person and not an Herb Gatherer? Who would weather her tears and witness her doubt? For doubt was a breach of trust as well. People depended on confidence from their Herb Gatherer.

In her most private thoughts, there was even more. Cutter's Hollow seemed small to her now. The doors unlocked by Bruna's lessons were not easily closed—a constant reminder not of what she knew, but of how much she did not. Without Bruna, that journey would end.

She entered the house, seeing Bruna at the table. "Good morning," she said. "I didn't expect you up so early; I would have made tea before going into the garden." She set her basket down and looked to the fire, seeing the steaming kettle near to boil.

"I'm old," Bruna grumbled, "but not so blind and crippled I can't make my own tea."

"Of course not," Leesha said, kissing the old woman's cheek, "you're fit enough to swing an axe alongside the cutters." She laughed at Bruna's grimace and fetched the meal for porridge.

The years together had not softened Bruna's tone, but Leesha seldom noticed it now, hearing only the affection behind the old woman's grumbling, and responding in kind.

"You were out gathering early today," Bruna noted as they ate. "You can still smell the demon stink in the air."

"Only you could be surrounded with fresh flowers and complain of the stink," Leesha replied. Indeed, she kept blooms throughout the hut, filling the air with sweetness.

"Don't change the subject," Bruna said.

"A Messenger came last night," Leesha said. "I heard the horn."

"Not a moment before sundown, too," Bruna grunted. "Reckless." She spat on the floor.

"Bruna!" Leesha scolded. "What have I told you about spitting inside the house?"

The crone looked at her, rheumy eyes narrowing. "You told me this is my ripping home, and I can spit where I please," she said.

Leesha frowned. "I was sure I said something else," she mused.

"Not if you're smarter than your bosom makes people think," Bruna said, sipping her tea.

Leesha let her jaw drop in mock indignation, but she was used to far worse from the old woman. Bruna did and said as she pleased, and no one could tell her differently.

"So it's the Messenger that has you up and about so early," Bruna said. "Hoping it's the handsome one? What's his name? The one that makes puppy eyes at you?"

Leesha smiled wryly. "More like wolf eyes," she said.

"That can be good too!" the old woman cackled, slapping Leesha's knee. Leesha shook her head and rose to clear the table.

"What's his name?" Bruna pressed.

"It's not like that," Leesha said.

"I'm too old for this dance, girl," Bruna said. "Name."

"Marick," Leesha said, rolling her eyes.

"Shall I brew a pot of pomm tea for young Marick's visit?" Bruna asked.

"Is that all anyone thinks about?" Leesha asked. "I like talking to him. That's all."

"I'm not so blind I can't see that boy has more on his mind than talk," Bruna said.

"Oh?" Leesha asked, crossing her arms. "How many fingers am I holding up?"

Bruna snorted. "Not a one," she said, not even turning Leesha's way. "I've been around long enough to know that trick," she said, "just as I know Maverick the Messenger hasn't made eye contact with you once in all your talks."

"His name is Marick," Leesha said again, "and he does, too."

"Only if he doesn't have a clear view of your neckline," the crone said.

"You're impossible," Leesha huffed.

"No cause for shame," Bruna said. "If I had paps like yours, I'd flaunt them too."

"I do *not* flaunt!" Leesha shouted, but Bruna only cackled again.

A horn sounded, not far off.

"That will be young master Marick," Bruna advised. "You'd best hurry and primp."

"It's not like that!" Leesha said again, but Bruna dismissed her with a wave.

"I'll put that tea on, just in case," she said. Leesha threw a rag at the old woman and stuck out her tongue, moving toward the door.

Outside on the porch, she smiled in spite of herself as she waited for the Messenger. Bruna pushed her to find a man nearly as much as her mother did, but the crone did it out of love. She wanted only for Leesha to be happy, and Leesha loved her dearly for it. But despite the old woman's teasing, Leesha was more interested in the letters Marick carried than his wolf eyes.

Ever since she was young, she had loved Messenger days. Cutter's Hollow was a little place, but it was on the road between three major cities and a dozen hamlets, and between the Hollow's timber and Erny's paper, it was a strong part of the region's economy.

Messengers visited the Hollow at least twice a month, and while most mail was left with Smitt, they delivered to Erny and Bruna personally, frequently waiting for replies. Bruna corresponded with Gatherers in Forts Rizon and Angiers, Lakton, and several hamlets. As the crone's eyesight failed, the task of reading the letters and penning Bruna's replies fell to Leesha.

Even from afar, Bruna commanded respect. Indeed, most of

the Herb Gatherers in the area had been students of hers at one time or another. Her advice was frequently sought to cure ailments beyond others' experience, and offers to send her apprentices came with every Messenger. No one wished for her knowledge to pass from the world.

"I'm too old to break in another novice!" Bruna would grouse, waving her hand dismissively, and Leesha would pen a polite refusal, something she had gotten quite used to.

All this gave Leesha many opportunities to talk with Messengers. Most of them leered at her, it was true, or tried to impress her with tales of the Free Cities. Marick was one of those.

But the Messengers' tales struck a chord with Leesha. Their intent might have been to charm their way into her skirts, but the pictures their words painted stayed with her in her dreams. She longed to walk the docks of Lakton, see the great warded fields of Fort Rizon, or catch a glimpse of Angiers, the forest fortress; to read their books and meet their Herb Gatherers. There were other guardians of knowledge of the old world, if she dared seek them out.

She smiled as Marick came into view. Even a ways off, she knew his gait, legs slightly bowed from a life spent on horseback. The Messenger was Angierian, barely as tall as Leesha at five foot seven, but there was a lean hardness about him, and Leesha hadn't exaggerated about his wolf eyes. They roved with predatory calm, searching for threats . . . and prey.

"Ay, Leesha!" he called, lifting his spear toward her.

Leesha lifted her hand in greeting. "Do you really need to carry that thing in broad day?" she called, indicating the spear.

"What if there was a wolf?" Marick replied with a grin. "How would I defend you?"

"We don't see a lot of wolves in Cutter's Hollow," Leesha said, as he drew close. He had longish brown hair and eyes the color of tree bark. She couldn't deny that he was handsome.

"A bear, then," Marick said as he reached the hut. "Or a lion. There are many kinds of predator in the world," he said, eyeing her cleavage.

"Of that, I am well aware," Leesha said, adjusting her shawl to cover the exposed flesh.

Marick laughed, easing his Messenger bag down onto the porch. "Shawls have gone out of style," he advised. "None of the women in Angiers or Rizon wear them anymore."

"Then I'll wager their dresses have higher necks, or their men more subtlety," Leesha replied.

"High necks," Marick agreed with a laugh, bowing low. "I could bring you a high-necked Angierian dress," he whispered, drawing close.

"When would I ever have cause to wear that?" Leesha asked, slipping away before the man could corner her.

"Come to Angiers," the Messenger offered. "Wear it there."

Leesha sighed. "I would like that," she lamented.

"Perhaps you will get the chance," the Messenger said slyly, bowing and sweeping his arm to indicate that Leesha should enter the hut before him. Leesha smiled and went in, but she felt his eyes on her backside as she did.

Bruna was back in her chair when they entered. Marick went to her and bowed low.

"Young master Marick!" Bruna said brightly. "What a pleasant surprise!"

"I bring you greetings from Mistress Jizell of Angiers," Marick said. "She begs your aid in a troubling case." He reached into his bag and produced a roll of paper, tied with stout string.

Bruna motioned for Leesha to take the letter, and sat back, closing her eyes as her apprentice began to read.

"Honored Bruna, Greetings from Fort Angiers in the year 326 AR," Leesha began.

"Jizell yapped like a dog when she was my apprentice, and she writes the same way," Bruna cut her off. "I won't live forever. Skip to the case."

Leesha scanned the page, flipping it over and looking over the back, as well. She was on to the second sheet before she found what she was looking for.

"A boy," Leesha said, "ten years old. Brought into the hospit by his mother, complaining of nausea and weakness. No other symptoms or history of illness. Given grimroot, water, and bed rest. Symptoms increased over three days, with the addition of rash on arms, legs, and chest. Grimroot raised to three ounces over the course of several days.

"Symptoms worsened, adding fever and hard, white boils growing out of the rash. Salves had no effect. Vomiting followed. Given heartleaf and poppy for the pain, soft milk for the stomach. No appetite. Does not appear to be contagious."

Bruna sat a long while, digesting the words. She looked at Marick. "Have you seen the boy?" she asked.

The Messenger nodded.

"Was he sweating?" Bruna asked.

"He was," Marick confirmed, "but shivering, too, like he was both hot and cold."

Bruna grunted. "What color were his fingernails?" she asked.

"Fingernail color," Marick replied with a grin.

"Get smart with me and you'll regret it," Bruna warned.

Marick blanched and nodded. The old woman questioned him for a few minutes more, grunting occasionally at his responses. Messengers were known for their sharp memories and keen observation, and Bruna did not seem to doubt him. Finally, she waved him into silence.

"Anything else of note in the letter?" she asked.

"She wants to send you another apprentice," Leesha said. Bruna scowled.

"I have an apprentice, Vika, who has almost completed her training," Leesha read, "as, your letters tell, do you. If you are not willing to accept a novice, please consider an exchange of adepts." Leesha gasped, and Marick broke into a knowing grin.

"I didn't tell you to stop reading," Bruna rasped.

Leesha cleared her throat. "Vika is most promising," she read, "and well equipped to see to the needs of Cutter's Hollow, as well as look after and learn from wise Bruna. Surely Leesha, too, could learn much ministering to the sick in my hospit. Please, I beg, let at least one more benefit from wise Bruna before she passes from this world."

Bruna was quiet a long while. "I will think on this a while before I reply," she said at last. "Go to your rounds in town, girl. We'll speak on this when you return." To Marick, she said, "You'll have a response tomorrow. Leesha will see to your payment."

The Messenger bowed and backed out of the house as Bruna sat back and closed her eyes. Leesha could feel her heart racing, but she knew better than to interrupt the crone as she sifted through the many decades of her memory for a way to treat the boy. She collected her basket, and left to make her rounds.

Marick was waiting for her when Leesha came outside.

"You knew what was in that letter all along," Leesha accused.

"Of course," Marick agreed. "I was there when she penned it."

"But you said nothing," Leesha said.

Marick grinned. "I offered you a high-necked dress," he said, "and that offer still stands."

"We'll see." Leesha smiled, holding out a pouch of coins. "Your payment," she said.

"I'd rather you pay me with a kiss," he said.

"You flatter me, to say my kisses are worth more than gold," Leesha replied. "I fear to disappoint."

Marick laughed. "My dear, if I braved the demons of the night all the way from Angiers and back and returned with but a kiss from you, I would be the envy of every Messenger ever to pass through Cutter's Hollow."

"Well, in that case," Leesha said with a laugh, "I think I'll keep my kisses a little longer, in hopes of a better price."

"You cut me to the quick," Marick said, clutching his heart. Leesha tossed him the pouch, and he caught it deftly.

"May I at least have the honor of escorting the Herb Gatherer into town?" he asked with a smile. He made a leg and held out his arm for her to take. Leesha smiled in spite of herself.

"We don't do things so quickly in the Hollow," she said, eyeing the arm, "but you may carry my basket." She hooked it on his outstretched arm and headed toward town, leaving him staring after her.

Smitt's market was bustling by the time they reached town. Leesha liked to select early, before the best produce was gone, and place her order with Dug the butcher before making her rounds.

"Good morn, Leesha," said Yon Gray, the oldest man in Cutter's Hollow. His gray beard, a point of pride, was longer than most women's hair. Once a burly cutter, Yon had lost most of his bulk in his latter years, and now leaned heavily on his cane.

"Good morn, Yon," she replied. "How are the joints?"

"Pain me still," Yon replied. "'Specially the hands. Can barely hold my cane some days."

"Yet you find it in you to pinch me whenever I turn 'round," Leesha noted.

Yon cackled. "To an old man like me, girlie, that's worth any pain."

Leesha reached into her basket, pulling forth a small jar. "It's well that I made you more sweetsalve, then," she said. "You've saved me the need to bring it by."

Yon grinned. "You're always welcome to come by and help apply," he said with a wink.

Leesha tried not to laugh, but it was a futile effort. Yon was a lecher, but she liked him well enough. Living with Bruna had taught her that the eccentricities of age were a small price to pay for having a lifetime of experience to draw upon.

"You'll just have to manage yourself, I'm afraid," she said.

"Bah!" Yon waved his cane in mock irritation. "Well, you think on it," he said. He looked to Marick before taking his leave, giving a nod of respect. "Messenger."

Marick nodded back, and the old man moved off.

Everyone at the market had a kind word of greeting for Leesha, and she stopped to ask after the health of each, always working, even while shopping.

Though she and Bruna had plenty of money from selling flamesticks and the like, no one would take so much as a klat in return for her selections. Bruna asked no money for healing, and no one asked money of her for anything else.

Marick stood protectively close as she squeezed fruit and vegetables with a practiced hand. He drew stares, but Leesha thought it was as much because he was with her than it was the presence of a stranger at market. Messengers were common enough in Cutter's Hollow.

She caught the eye of Keet—Stefny's son, if not Smitt's. The boy was nearly eleven, and looked more and more like Tender Michel with each passing day. Stefny had kept her side of the bargain over the years, and not spoken ill of Leesha since she was apprenticed. Her secret was safe as far as Bruna was concerned, but for the life of her, Leesha could not see how Smitt failed to see the truth staring at him from the supper table each night.

She beckoned, and Keet came running. "Bring this bag to Bruna once your chores allow," she said, handing him her selections. She smiled at him and secretly pressed a klat into his hand.

Keet grinned widely at the gift. Adults would never take money from an Herb Gatherer, but Leesha always slipped children something for extra service. The lacquered wooden coin from Angiers was the main currency in Cutter's Hollow, and would buy Rizonan sweets for Keet and his siblings when the next Messenger came.

She was ready to leave when she saw Mairy, and moved to greet her. Her friend had been busy over the years; three children clung to her skirts now. A young glassblower named Benn had left Angiers to find his fortune in Lakton or Fort Rizon. He had stopped in the Hollow to ply his trade and raise a few more klats before the next leg of the journey, but then he met Mairy, and those plans dissolved like sugar in tea.

Now Benn plied his trade in Mairy's father's barn, and business was brisk. He bought bags of sand from Messengers out of Fort Krasia, and turned them into things of both function and beauty. The Hollow had never had a blower before, and everyone wanted glass of their own.

Leesha, too, was pleased by the development, and soon had Benn making the delicate components of distilleries shown in Bruna's books, allowing her to leach the strength from herbs and brew cures far more powerful than the Hollow had ever seen.

Soon after, Benn and Mairy wed, and before long, Leesha was pulling their first child from between Mairy's legs. Two more had followed in short order, and Leesha loved each as if it were her own. She had been honored to tears when they named their youngest after her.

"Good morning, rascals," Leesha said, squatting down and letting Mairy's children fall into her arms. She hugged them tightly and kissed them, slipping them pieces of candy wrapped in paper before rising. She made the candy herself, another thing she had learned from Bruna.

"Good morning, Leesha," Mairy said, dipping a small curtsy. Leesha bit back a frown. She and Mairy had stayed close over the years, but Mairy looked at her differently now that she wore the pocketed apron, and nothing seemed able to change that. The curtsy seemed ingrained.

Still, Leesha treasured her friendship. Saira came secretly to Bruna's hut, begging pomm tea, but their relationship ended there. To hear the women in town tell it, Saira kept well enough entertained. Half the men in the village supposedly knocked on her door at one time or another, and she always had more money than the sewing she and her mother took in could bring.

Brianne was even worse in some ways. She had not spoken to Leesha in the last seven years, but had a bad word to say about her to everyone else. She had taken to seeing Darsy for her cures, and her dalliances with Evin had quickly given her a round belly. When Tender Michel had challenged her, she had named Evin the father rather than face the town alone.

Evin had married Brianne with her father's pitchfork at his back and her brothers to either side, and had committed himself to making her and their son Callen miserable ever since.

Brianne had proven a fit mother and wife, but she never lost the weight she had put on during her pregnancy, and Leesha knew personally how Evin's eyes—and hands—wandered. Gossip had him knocking frequently on Saira's door.

"Good morning, Mairy," she said. "Have you met Messenger Marick?" Leesha turned to introduce the man, only to find he was no longer at her back.

"Oh, no," she said, seeing him facing off with Gared across the market.

At fifteen, Gared had been bigger than any man in the village save his father. Now, at twenty-two, he was gigantic, close to seven feet of packed muscle, hardened by long days at the axe. It was said he must have Milnese blood, for no Angierian had ever been so large.

Word of his lie had spread throughout the village, and since then the girls had kept their distance, afraid to be alone with him. Perhaps that was why he still coveted Leesha; perhaps he would have done so regardless. But Gared had not learned the lessons of the past. His ego had grown with his muscles, and now he was the bully everyone had known he would be. The boys who used to tease him now jumped at his every word, and if he was cruel to them, he was a terror to any unwise enough to cast their eyes upon Leesha.

Gared waited for her still, acting as if Leesha were going to come to her senses one day and realize she belonged with him. Any attempts to convince him otherwise had been met with wood-headed stubbornness.

"You're not local," she heard Gared say, poking Marick hard in the shoulder, "so maybe ya haven't heard that Leesha's spoken for." He loomed over the Messenger like a grown man over a young boy.

But Marick didn't flinch, or move at Gared's poke. He stood stark still, his wolf eyes never leaving Gared's. Leesha prayed he had the sense not to engage.

"Not according to her," Marick replied, and Leesha's hopes fell. She started moving toward them, but already a crowd was forming around the men, denying her a clear path. She wished she had Bruna's stick to help her clear the way.

"Did she say words of promise to you, Messenger?" Gared demanded. "She did to me."

"So I've heard," Marick replied. "I've also heard you're the only fool in the Hollow who thinks those words mean a coreling's piss after you betrayed her."

Gared roared and grabbed at the Messenger, but Marick was quicker, stepping smoothly to the side and snapping up his spear, thrusting the butt right between the woodcutter's eyes. He whipped the spear around in a smooth motion, striking behind Gared's knees as he staggered backward, dropping him hard on his back.

Marick planted his spear back on the ground, standing over Gared, his wolf eyes coldly confident. "I could have used the point," he advised. "You would do well to remember that. Leesha speaks for herself."

Everyone in the crowd was gawking, but Leesha continued her desperate push forward, knowing Gared, and knowing that it was not over.

"Stop this idiocy!" she called. Marick glanced at her, and Gared used that moment to grab the end of his spear. The Messenger's attention snapped back, and he gripped the shaft with both hands to pull the spear free.

It was the last thing he should have done. Gared had a wood demon's strength, and even with him lying prone, none could match it. His corded arms flexed, and Marick found himself flying through the air.

Gared rose, and snapped the six-foot spear in half like a twig. "Let's see how ya fight when yer not hiding behind a spear," he said, dropping the pieces to the dirt.

"Gared, no!" Leesha screamed, pushing past the last of the onlookers and grabbing his arm. He shoved her aside, never taking his eyes off Marick. The simple move sent her reeling back into the crowd, where she crashed into Dug and Niklas, going down in a tangle of bodies.

"Stop!" she cried helplessly, struggling to find her feet.

"No other man will have you," Gared said. "You'll have me, or you'll end up shriveled and alone like Bruna!" He stalked toward Marick, who was only just getting his legs under him.

Gared swung a meaty fist at the Messenger, but again, Marick was quicker. He ducked the blow smoothly, landing two quick punches to Gared's body before retreating well ahead of Gared's wild return swing.

But if Gared even felt the blows, he showed no sign. They repeated the exchange, this time with Marick punching Gared full in the nose. Blood spurted, and Gared laughed, spitting it from his mouth.

"That your best?" he asked.

Marick growled and shot forward, landing a flurry of punches. Gared could not keep up and hardly tried, gritting his teeth and weathering the barrage, his face red with rage.

After a few moments, Marick withdrew, standing in a catlike fighting stance, his fists up and ready. His knuckles were skinned, and he was breathing hard. Gared seemed little the worse for wear. For the first time, there was fear in Marick's wolf eyes.

"That all ya have?" Gared asked, stalking forward again.

The Messenger came at him again, but this time, he was not so quick. He struck once, twice, and then Gared's thick fingers found purchase on his shoulder, gripping hard. The Messenger tried to pull back out of reach, but he was held fast.

Gared drove his fist into the Messenger's stomach, and the wind exploded out of him. He struck again, this time to the head, and Marick hit the ground like a sack of potatoes.

"Not so smug now, are ya!" Gared roared. Marick rose to his hands and knees, struggling to rise, but Gared kicked him hard in the stomach, flipping him over onto his back.

Leesha was darting forward by then, as Gared knelt atop Marick, landing heavy blows.

"Leesha is mine!" he roared. "And any what says otherwise will . . . !"

His words were cut short as Leesha threw a full fist of Bruna's blinding powder in his face. His mouth was already open, and he inhaled reflexively, screaming as it burned into his eyes and throat, his sinuses seizing and his skin feeling as if burned with boiling water. He fell off Marick, rolling on the ground choking and clawing at his face.

Leesha knew she had used too much of the powder. A pinch

would stop most men in their tracks, but a full fist could kill, causing people to choke on their own phlegm.

She scowled and shoved past the gawkers, snatching a bucket of water Stefny had been using to wash potatoes. She dumped it over Gared, and his convulsions eased. He would be blind for hours more, but she would not have his death on her hands.

"Our vows are broken," she told him, "now and forever. I will never be your wife, even if it means dying shriveled and alone! I'd as soon marry a coreling!"

Gared groaned, showing no sign he had heard.

She moved over to Marick, kneeling and helping him to sit up. She took a clean cloth and daubed at the blood on his face. Already he was starting to swell and bruise.

"I guess we showed him, eh?" the Messenger asked, chuckling weakly and wincing at the pain it brought to his face.

Leesha poured some of the harsh alcohol Smitt brewed in his basement onto the cloth.

"Aahhh!" Marick gasped, as she touched him with it.

"Serves you right," Leesha said. "You could have walked away from that fight, and you should have, whether you could have won or not. I didn't need your protection, and I'm no more likely to give my affection to a man who thinks picking a fight is going to gain the favor of an Herb Gatherer than I am the town bully."

"He was the one that started it!" Marick protested.

"I'm disappointed in you, Master Marick," Leesha said. "I thought Messengers came smarter than that." Marick dropped his eyes.

"Take him to his room at Smitt's," she said to some nearby men, and they moved quickly to obey. Most folk in Cutter's Hollow did, these days.

"If you're out of bed before tomorrow morning," Leesha told the Messenger, "I'll hear of it and be even more cross with you."

Marick smiled weakly as the men helped him away.

"That was amazing!" Mairy gasped, when Leesha returned for her basket of herbs.

"It was nothing but stupidity that needed stopping," Leesha snapped.

"Nothing?" Mairy asked. "Two men locked together like bulls, and all you had to do to stop them was throw a handful of herbs!"

"Hurting with herbs is easy," Leesha said, surprised to find Bruna's words on her lips, "it's healing with them that's hard."

It was well past high sun by the time Leesha finished her rounds and made it back to Bruna's hut.

"How are the children?" Bruna asked, as Leesha set her basket down. Leesha smiled. Everyone in Cutter's Hollow was a child in Bruna's eyes.

"Well enough," she said, coming to sit on the low stool by Bruna's chair so the ancient Herb Gatherer could see her clearly. "Yon Gray's joints still ache, but his mind is as young as ever. I gave him fresh sweetsalve. Smitt remains abed, but his cough is lessening. I think the worst is past." She went on, describing her rounds while the crone nodded silently. Bruna would stop her if she had comment; she seldom did anymore.

"Is that all?" Bruna asked. "What of the excitement young Keet tells me went on in the market this morning?"

"Idiocy is more like it," Leesha said.

Bruna dismissed her with a wave. "Boys will be boys," she said. "Even when they're men. It sounds like you dealt with it well enough."

"Bruna, they could have killed each other!" Leesha said.

"Oh, pfaw!" Bruna said. "You're not the first pretty girl to have men fight over her. You may not believe it, but when I was your age, a few bones were broken on my account, as well."

"You were never my age," Leesha teased. "Yon Gray says they called you 'hag' when he was first learning to walk."

Bruna cackled. "So they did, so they did," she said. "But there was a time before then when my paps were as full and smooth as yours, and men fought like corelings to suckle them."

Leesha looked hard at Bruna, trying to peel back the years and see the woman she had been, but it was a hopeless task. Even with all the exaggerations and tampweed tales taken into account, Bruna was a century old, at least. She would never say for sure, answering simply, "I quit counting at a hundred," whenever pressed.

"In any event," Leesha said, "Marick may be a bit swollen in the face, but he'll have no reason not to be on the road tomorrow."

"That's well," Bruna said.

"So you have a cure for Mistress Jizell's young charge?" Leesha asked.

"What would you tell her to do with the boy?" Bruna replied.

"I'm sure I don't know," Leesha said.

"Are you?" Bruna asked. "I'm not. Come now, what would you tell Jizell if you were me? Don't pretend you haven't thought about it."

Leesha took a deep breath. "The grimroot likely interacted poorly with the boy's system," she said. "He needs to be taken off it, and the boils will need to be lanced and drained. Of course, that still leaves his original illness. The fever and nausea could just be a chill, but the dilated eyes and vomit hint at more. I would try monkleaf with lady's brooch and ground adderbark, titrated carefully over a week at least."

Bruna looked at her a long time, then nodded.

"Pack your things and say your good-byes," she said. "You'll bring that advice to Jizell personally."

CHAPTER 14

THE ROAD TO ANGIERS
326 AR

EVERY AFTERNOON WITHOUT FAIL, Erny came up the path to Bruna's hut. The Hollow had six Warders, each with an apprentice, but Erny did not trust his daughter's safety to anyone else. The little papermaker was the best Warder in Cutter's Hollow, and everyone knew it.

Often, he brought gifts his Messengers had secured from far-off places: books and herbs and hand-sewn lace. But gifts were not why Leesha looked forward to his visits. She slept better behind her father's strong wards, and seeing him happy these last seven years was greater than any gift. Elona still caused him grief, of course, but not on the scale she once had.

But today, as Leesha watched the sun cross the sky, she found herself dreading her father's visit. This was going to hurt him deeply.

And her, as well. Erny was a well of support and love that she drew upon whenever things grew too hard for her. What would she do in Angiers without him? Without Bruna? Would any there see past her pocketed apron?

But whatever her fears about loneliness in Angiers, they paled against her greatest fear: that once she tasted the wider world, she would never want to return to Cutter's Hollow.

It wasn't until she saw her father coming up the path that Leesha realized she'd been crying. She dried her eyes and put on her best smile for him, smoothing her skirts nervously.

"Leesha!" her father called, holding out his arms. She fell

into them gratefully, knowing that this might be the last time they played out this little ritual.

"Is everything all right?" Erny asked. "I heard there was some trouble at the market."

There were few secrets in a place as small as Cutter's Hollow. "It's fine," she said. "I took care of it."

"You take care of everyone in Cutter's Hollow, Leesha," Erny said, squeezing her tightly. "I don't know what we'd do without you."

Leesha began to weep. "Now, now, none of that," Erny said, catching a tear off her cheek on his index finger and flicking it away. "Dry your eyes and head on inside. I'll check the wards, and we can talk about what's bothering you over a bowl of your delicious stew."

Leesha smiled. "Mum still burning the food?" she asked.

"When it's not still moving," Erny agreed. Leesha laughed, letting her father check the wards while she laid the table.

"I'm going to Angiers," Leesha said when the bowls were cleared, "to study under one of Bruna's old apprentices."

Erny was quiet a long time. "I see," he said at last. "When?"

"As soon as Marick leaves," Leesha said. "Tomorrow."

Erny shook his head. "No daughter of mine is spending a week on the open road alone with a Messenger," he said. "I'll hire a caravan. It will be safer."

"I'll be careful of the demons, Da," Leesha said.

"It's not just corelings I'm worried about," Erny said pointedly.

"I can handle Messenger Marick," Leesha assured him.

"Keeping a man off you in the dark of night isn't the same as stopping a brawl in the market," Erny said. "You can't leave a Messenger blind if you ever hope to make it off the road alive. Just a few weeks, I beg."

Leesha shook her head. "There's a child I'm needed to treat immediately."

"Then I'll go with you," Erny said.

"You'll do no such thing, Ernal," Bruna cut in. "Leesha needs to do this on her own."

Erny looked at the old woman, and they locked stares and wills. But there was no will in Cutter's Hollow stronger than Bruna's, and Erny soon looked away.

Leesha walked her father out soon after. He did not want to go, nor did she want him to leave, but the sky was filled with color, and already he would have to trot to make it home safely.

"How long will you be gone?" Erny asked, gripping the porch rail tightly and looking off in the direction of Angiers.

Leesha shrugged. "That will depend on how much Mistress Jizell has to teach, and how much the apprentice she's sending here, Vika, has to learn. A couple of years, at least."

"I suppose if Bruna can do without you that long, I can, too," Erny said.

"Promise me you'll check her wards while I'm gone," Leesha said, touching his arm.

"Of course," Erny said, turning to embrace her.

"I love you, Da," she said.

"And I, you, poppet," Erny said, crushing her in his arms. "I'll see you in the morning," he promised before heading down the darkening road.

"Your father makes a fair point," Bruna said, when Leesha came back inside.

"Oh?" Leesha asked.

"Messengers are men like any other," Bruna warned.

"Of that, I have no doubt," Leesha said, remembering the fight in the marketplace.

"Young master Marick may be all charm and smiles now," Bruna said, "but once you're on the road, he'll have his way, no matter what your wishes, and when you reach the forest fortress, Herb Gatherer or no, few will take the word of a young girl over that of a Messenger."

Leesha shook her head. "He'll have what I give him," she said, "and nothing more."

Bruna's eyes narrowed, but she grunted, satisfied that Leesha was wise to the danger.

There was a sharp rap at the door just after first light. Leesha answered, finding her mother standing there, though Elona had not come to the hut since being expelled at the end of Bruna's broom. Her face was a thunderhead as she pushed right past Leesha.

On the sunny side of forty, Elona might still have been the most beautiful woman in the village if not for her daughter. But being autumn to Leesha's summer had not humbled her. She might bow to Erny with gritted teeth, but she carried herself like a duchess to all others.

"Not enough you steal my daughter, you have to send her away?" she demanded.

"Good morn to you as well, Mother," Leesha said, closing the door.

"You stay out of this!" Elona snapped. "The witch has twisted your mind!"

Bruna cackled into her porridge. Leesha interposed herself between the two, just as Bruna was pushing her half-finished bowl away and wiping her sleeve across her mouth to retort. "Finish your breakfast," Leesha ordered, pushing the bowl back in front of her, and turning back to Elona. "I'm going because I want to, Mother. And when I return, I'll bring healing the likes of which Cutter's Hollow has not seen since Bruna was young."

"And how long will it take this time?" Elona demanded. "You've already wasted your best breeding years with your nose buried in dusty old books."

"My best . . . !" Leesha stuttered. "Mother, I'm barely twenty!"

"Exactly!" Elona shouted. "You should have three children by now, like your friend the scarecrow. Instead, I watch as you pull babes from every womb in the village but your own."

"At least she was wise enough not to shrivel hers with pomm tea," Bruna muttered.

Leesha whirled on her. "I told you to finish your porridge!" she said, and Bruna's eyes widened. She looked ready to retort, then grunted and turned her attention back to her bowl.

"I'm not a brood mare, Mother," Leesha said. "There's more in life for me than that."

"What more?" Elona pressed. "What could be more important?"

"I don't know," Leesha said honestly. "But I'll know when I find it."

"And in the meantime, you leave the care of Cutter's Hollow to a girl you've never met and ham-hand Darsy, who nearly killed Ande, and half a dozen since."

"It's only for a few years," Leesha said. "My whole life, you called me useless, but now I'm supposed to believe the Hollow can't get on a few years without me?"

"What if something happens to you?" Elona demanded. "What if you're cored on the road? What would I do?"

"What would *you* do?" Leesha asked. "For seven years, you've barely said a word to me, apart from pressing me to forgive Gared. You don't know anything about me anymore, Mother. You haven't bothered. So don't pretend now that my death would be some great loss to you. If you want Gared's child on your knee so badly, you'll have to bear it yourself."

Elona's eyes widened, and as when Leesha was a willful child, her response was swift. "I forbid it!" she shouted, her open hand flying at Leesha's face.

But Leesha was not a child anymore. She was of a size with her mother, faster and stronger. She caught Elona's wrist and held it fast. "The days when your word carried weight with me are long past, Mother," Leesha said.

Elona tried to pull away, but Leesha held on a bit, if only to show she could. When she was finally released, Elona rubbed her wrist and looked scornfully at her daughter. "You'll be back one day, Leesha," she swore. "Mark my words! And it will be much worse for you then!"

"I think it's time you left, Mother," Leesha said, opening the door just as Marick was raising his hand to knock. Elona snarled and pushed past him, stomping down the path.

"Apologies if I'm intruding," Marick said. "I came for Mistress Bruna's response. I'm bound for Angiers by midmorning."

Leesha looked at Marick. His jaw was bruised, but his thick tan hid it well, and the herbs she had applied to his split lip and eye had kept the swelling down.

"You seem well recovered," she said.

"Quick healers go far in my line of work," Marick said.

"Well then fetch your horse," Leesha said, "and return in an hour. I will deliver Bruna's response personally."

Marick smiled widely.

"It is good that you go," Bruna said, when they were alone at last. "Cutter's Hollow holds no more challenges for you, and you're far too young to stagnate."

"If you think that wasn't a challenge," Leesha said, "then you weren't paying attention."

"A challenge, perhaps," Bruna said, "but the outcome was never in doubt. You've grown too strong for the likes of Elona."

Strong, she thought. *Is that what I've become?* It didn't feel that way most of the time, but it was true, none of the inhabitants of Cutter's Hollow frightened her anymore.

Leesha gathered her bags, small and seemingly inadequate; a few dresses and books, some money, her herb pouch, a bedroll, and food. She left her pretties, the gifts her father had given her and other possessions near to her heart. Messengers traveled light, and Marick would not take well to having his horse overburdened. Bruna had said Jizell would provide for her during her training, but still, it seemed precious little to start a new life with.

A new life. For all the stress of the idea, it brought excitement, as well. Leesha had read every book in Bruna's collection, but Jizell had a great many more, and the other Herb Gatherers in Angiers, if they could be persuaded to share, held more still.

But as the hour drew to a close, Leesha felt as if the breath were being squeezed from her. Where was her father? Would he not see her off?

"It's nearly time," Bruna said. Leesha looked up and realized her eyes were wet.

"We'd best say our good-byes," Bruna said. "Odds are, we'll never have another chance."

"Bruna, what are you saying?" Leesha asked.

"Don't play the fool with me, girl," Bruna said. "You know what I mean. I've lived my share twice over, but I'm not going to last forever."

"Bruna," Leesha said, "I don't have to go . . ."

"Pfagh!" Bruna said with a wave of her hand. "You've mastered all I can teach you, girl, so let these years be my last gift to you. Go," she prodded, "see and learn as much as you can."

She held out her arms, and Leesha fell into them. "Just promise me that you'll look after my children when I'm gone. They can be stupid and willful, but there's good in them, when the night is dark."

"I will," Leesha promised. "And I'll make you proud."

"You could never do otherwise," the old woman said.

Leesha sobbed into Bruna's rough shawl. "I'm scared, Bruna," she said.

"You'd be a fool not to be," Bruna said, "but I've seen a good piece of the world myself, and I've never seen a thing you couldn't handle."

Marick led his horse up the path not long after. The Messenger had a fresh spear in his hand, and his warded shield slung over the horn of his saddle. If the pummeling he had taken the day before pained him in any way, he gave no sign.

"Ay, Leesha!" he called when he saw her. "Ready to begin your adventure?"

Adventure. The word cut past sadness and fear, sending a thrill through her.

Marick took Leesha's bags, slinging them atop his lean Angierian courser as Leesha turned to Bruna one last time. "I'm too old for good-byes that last half the day," Bruna said. "Take care of yourself, girl."

The old woman pressed a pouch into her hands, and Leesha heard the clink of Milnese coin, worth a fortune in Angiers. Bruna turned and went inside before Leesha could protest.

She pocketed the pouch quickly. The sight of metal coin this far from Miln could tempt any man, even a Messenger. They walked on opposite sides of the horse down the path to town, where the main road led on to Angiers. Leesha called to her father as they passed his house, but there was no reply. Elona saw them pass and went inside, slamming the door behind her.

Leesha hung her head. She had been counting on seeing her father one last time. She thought of all the villagers she saw every day, and how she hadn't had time to part with them all properly. The letters she had left with Bruna seemed woefully inadequate.

As they reached the center of town, though, Leesha gasped. Her father was waiting there, and behind him, lining the road, was the entire town. They went to her one by one as she passed, some kissing her and others pressing gifts into her hands. "Remember us well and return," Erny said, and Leesha hugged him tightly, squeezing her eyes shut to ward off tears.

"The Hollowers love you," Marick remarked as they rode through the woods. Cutter's Hollow was hours behind them, and the day's shadows were growing long. Leesha sat before him on his courser's wide saddle, and the beast seemed to bear it and their baggage well.

"There are times," Leesha said, "when I even believe it myself."

"Why shouldn't you believe it?" Marick asked. "A beauty like the dawn who can cure all ills? I doubt any could help but love you."

Leesha laughed. "A beauty like the dawn?" she asked. "Find the poor Jongleur you stole that line from and tell him never to use it again."

Marick laughed, his arms tightening around her. "You know," he said in her ear, "we never discussed my fee for escorting you."

"I have money," Leesha said, wondering how far her coin would go in Angiers.

"So do I," Marick laughed. "I'm not interested in money."

"Then what kind of price did you have in mind, Master Marick?" Leesha asked. "Is this another play for a kiss?"

Marick chuckled, his wolf eyes glinting. "A kiss was the price to bring you a letter. Bringing you safely to Angiers will be much more . . . expensive." He shifted his hips behind her, and his meaning was clear.

"Always ahead of yourself," Leesha said. "You'll be lucky to get the kiss at this rate."

"We'll see," Marick said.

They made camp soon after. Leesha prepared supper while Marick set the wards. When the stew was ready, she crumbled a few extra herbs into Marick's bowl before handing it to him.

"Eat quick," Marick said, taking the bowl and shoveling a large spoonful into his mouth. "You'll want to get in the tent before the corelings rise. Seeing them up close can be scary."

Leesha looked over at the tent Marick had pitched, barely big enough for one.

"It's small," he winked, "but we'll be able to warm each other in the chill of night."

"It's summer," she reminded him.

"Yet I still feel a cold breeze whenever you speak," Marick chuckled. "Perhaps we can find a way to melt that. Besides"—he gestured past the circle, where misty forms of corelings had already begun to rise—"it's not as if you can go far."

He was stronger than her, and her struggles against him did as little good as her refusals. With the cries of corelings as their backdrop, she suffered his kisses and pawing at her, hands fumbling and rough. And when his manhood failed him, she comforted him with soothing words, offering remedies of herb and root that only worsened his condition.

Sometimes he grew angry, and she was afraid he might strike her. Other times he wept, for what kind of man could not spread his seed? Leesha weathered it all, for the trial was not too high a price for passage to Angiers.

I am saving him from himself, she thought each time she dosed his food, for what man wished to be a rapist? But the truth was, she felt little remorse. She took no pleasure in using her skills to break his weapon, but deep down, there *was* a cold satisfaction, as if all her female ancestors throughout the untold ages since the first man who forced a woman to the ground were nodding in grim approval that she had unmanned him before he could unmaiden her.

The days passed slowly, with Marick's mood shifting from sour to spoiled as each night's failure mounted upon him. The last night, he drank deep from his wineskin, and seemed ready to leap from the circle and let the demons have him. Leesha's relief was palpable when she saw the forest fortress spread out before them in the wood. She gasped at the sight of the high walls, their lacquered wards hard and strong, large enough to encompass Cutter's Hollow many times over.

The streets of Angiers were covered with wood to prevent demons from rising inside; the entire city was a boardwalk. Marick took her deep into the city, and set her down outside Jizell's hospit. He gripped her arm as she turned to go, squeezing hard, hurting her.

"What happened out beyond the walls," he said, "stays out there."

"I won't tell anyone," Leesha said.

"See that you don't," Marick said. "Because if you do, I'll kill you."

"I swear," Leesha said. "Gatherer's word."

Marick grunted and released her, pulling hard on his courser's bridle and cantering off.

A smile touched the corners of Leesha's mouth as she gathered her things and headed toward the hospit.

CHAPTER 15

FIDDLE ME
A FORTUNE
325 AR

THERE WAS SMOKE, and fire, and a woman screamed above the corelings' shrieks.

I love you!

Rojer started awake, his heart racing. Dawn had broken over the high walls of Fort Angiers, soft light filtering in through the cracks in the shutters. He held his talisman tightly in his good hand as the light grew, waiting for his heart to still. The tiny doll, a child's creation of wood and string topped with her lock of red hair, was all he had left of his mother.

He didn't remember her face, lost in the smoke, or much else about that night, but he remembered her last words to him. He heard them over and over in his dreams.

I love you!

He rubbed the hair between the thumb and ring finger of his crippled hand. Only a jagged scar remained where his first two fingers had been, but because of her, he had lost nothing else.

I love you!

The talisman was Rojer's secret ward, something he didn't even share with Arrick, who had been like a father to him. It helped him through the long nights when darkness closed heavily around him and the coreling screams made him shake with fear.

But day had come, and the light made him feel safe again. He kissed the tiny doll and returned it to the secret pocket he had sewn into the waistband of his motley pants. Just knowing it was there made him feel brave. He was ten years old.

Rising from his straw mattress, Rojer stretched and stumbled out of the tiny room, yawning. His heart fell as he saw Arrick passed out at the table. His master was slumped over an empty bottle, his hand wrapped tightly around its neck as if to choke a few last drops from it.

They both had their talismans.

Rojer went over and pried the bottle from his master's fingers.

"Who? Wazzat?" Arrick demanded, half lifting his head.

"You fell asleep at the table again," Rojer said.

"Oh, 's you, boy," Arrick grunted. "Thought it 'uz tha' ripping landlord again."

"The rent's past due," Rojer said. "We're set to play Small Square this morning."

"The rent," Arrick grumbled. "Always the rent."

"If we don't pay today," Rojer reminded, "Master Keven promised he'd throw us out."

"So we'll perform," Arrick said, rising. He lost his balance and attempted to catch himself on the chair, but he only served to bring it down on top of him as he hit the floor.

Rojer went to help him up, but Arrick pushed him away. "I'm fine!" he shouted, as if daring Rojer to differ as he rose unsteadily to his feet. "I could do a backflip!" he said, looking behind him to see if there was room. His eyes made it clear he was regretting the boast.

"We should save that for the performance," Rojer said quickly.

Arrick looked back at him. "You're probably right," he agreed, both of them relieved.

"My throat's dry," Arrick said. "I'll need a drink before I sing."

Rojer nodded, running to fill a wooden cup from the pitcher of water.

"Not water," Arrick said. "Bring me wine. I need a claw from the demon that cored me."

"We're out of wine," Rojer said.

"Then run and get me some," Arrick ordered. He stumbled to his purse, tripping as he did and just barely catching himself. Rojer ran over to support him.

Arrick fumbled with the strings a moment, then lifted the whole purse and slammed it back down on the wood. There was no retort as the cloth struck, and Arrick growled.

"Not a klat!" he shouted in frustration, throwing the purse. The act took his balance, and he turned a full circle trying to right himself before dropping to the floor with a thud.

He gained his hands and knees by the time Rojer got to him, but he retched, spilling wine and bile all over the floor. He made fists and convulsed, and Rojer thought he would retch again, but after a moment he realized his master was sobbing.

"It was never like this when I worked for the duke," Arrick moaned. "Money was spilling from my pockets, then."

Only because the duke paid for your wine, Rojer thought, but he was wise enough to keep it to himself. Telling Arrick he drank too much was the surest way to provoke him into a rage.

He cleaned his master up and supported the heavy man to his mattress. Once he was passed out on the straw, Rojer got a rag to clean the floor. There would be no performance today.

He wondered if Master Keven would really put them out, and where they would go if he did. The Angierian wardwall was strong, but there were holes in the net above, and wind demons were not unheard of. The thought of a night on the street terrified him.

He looked at their meager possessions, wondering if there was something he could sell. Arrick had sold Geral's destrier and warded shield when times had turned sour, but the Messenger's portable circle remained. It would fetch a fair price, but Rojer would not dare sell it. Arrick would drink and gamble with the money, and there would be nothing left to protect them when they were finally put out in the night for real.

Rojer, too, missed the days when Arrick worked for the duke. Arrick was loved by Rhinebeck's whores, and they had treated Rojer like he was their own. Hugged against a dozen perfumed bosoms a day, he had been given sweets and taught to help them paint and preen. He hadn't seen his master as much then; Arrick had often left him in the brothel when he journeyed to the hamlets, his sweet voice delivering ducal edicts far and wide.

But the duke hadn't cared for finding a young boy curled in the bed when he stumbled into his favorite whore's chambers one night, drunk and aroused. He wanted Rojer gone, and Arrick with him. Rojer knew it was his fault that they lived so poorly now. Arrick, like his parents, had sacrificed everything to care for him.

But unlike with his parents, Rojer could give something back to Arrick.

Rojer ran for all he was worth, hoping the crowd was still there. Even now, many would come to an advertised engagement of the Sweetsong, but they wouldn't wait forever.

Over his shoulder he carried Arrick's "bag of marvels." Like their clothes, the bag was made from a Jongleur's motley of colored patches, faded and threadbare. The bag was filled with the instruments of a Jongleur's art. Rojer had mastered them all, save the colored juggling balls.

His bare, callused feet slapped the boardwalk. Rojer had boots and gloves to match his motley, but he left them behind. He preferred the firm grip of his toes to the worn soles of his bell-tipped, motley boots, and he hated the gloves.

Arrick had stuffed the fingers of the right glove with cotton to hide the ones Rojer was missing. Slender thread connected the false digits to the remaining ones, making them bend as one. It was a clever bit of trickery, but Rojer was ashamed each time he pulled the constrictive thing onto his crippled hand. Arrick insisted he wear them, but his master couldn't hit him for something he didn't know about.

A grumbling crowd milled about Small Square as Rojer arrived; perhaps a score of people, some of those children. Rojer could remember a time when word that Arrick Sweetsong might appear drew hundreds from all ends of the city and even the hamlets nearby. He would have been singing in the temple to the Creator then, or the duke's amphitheater. Now Small Square was the best the guild would give him, and he couldn't even fill that.

But any money was better than none. If even a dozen left Rojer a klat apiece, it might buy another night from Master Keven, so long as the Jongleurs' Guild did not catch him performing without his master. If they did, overdue rent would be the least of their troubles.

With a "Whoot!" he danced through the crowd, throwing handfuls of dyed wingseeds from the bag. The seedpods spun and fluttered in his wake, leaving a trail of bright color.

"Arrick's apprentice!" one crowd member called. "The Sweetsong will be here after all!"

There was applause, and Rojer felt his stomach lurch. He

wanted to tell the truth, but Arrick's first rule of jongling was never to say or do anything to break a crowd's good mood.

The stage at Small Square had three tiers. The back was a wooden shell designed to amplify sound and keep inclement weather off the performers. There were wards inscribed into the wood, but they were faded and old. Rojer wondered if they would grant succor to him and his master, should they be put out tonight.

He raced up the steps, handspringing across the stage and throwing the collection hat just in front of the crowd with a precise snap of his wrist.

Rojer warmed every crowd for his master, and for a few minutes, he fell into that routine, cartwheeling about and telling jokes, performing magic tricks, and mumming the foibles of well-known authority figures. Laughter. Applause. Slowly, the crowd began to swell. Thirty. Fifty. But more and more began to murmur, impatient for the appearance of Arrick Sweetsong. Rojer's stomach tightened, and he touched the talisman in its secret pocket for strength.

Staving off the inevitable as long as he could, he called the children forward to tell them the story of the Return. He mummed the parts well, and some nodded in approval, but there was disappointment on many faces. Didn't Arrick usually sing the tale? Wasn't that why they came?

"Where is the Sweetsong?" someone called from the back. He was shushed by his neighbors, but his words hung in the air. By the time Rojer had finished with the children, there were general grumbles of discontent.

"I came to hear a song!" the same man called, and this time others nodded in agreement.

Rojer knew better than to oblige. His voice had never been strong, and it cracked whenever he held a note for more than a few breaths. The crowd would turn ugly if he sang.

He turned to the bag of marvels for another option, passing over the juggling balls in shame. He could catch and throw well enough with his crippled right hand, but with no index finger to put the correct spin on the ball and only half a hand to catch with, the complex interplay between both hands when juggling was beyond him.

"What kind of Jongleur can't sing and can't juggle?" Arrick would shout sometimes. Not much of one, Rojer knew.

He was better with the knives in the bag, but calling audience members up to stand by the wall while he threw required a special license from the guild. Arrick always chose a buxom girl to assist, who more often than not ended up in his bed after the performance.

"I don't think he's coming," he heard that same man say. Rojer cursed him silently.

Many of the other crowd members were slipping away, as well. A few tossed klats in the hat out of pity, but if Rojer didn't do something soon, they would never have enough to satisfy Master Keven. His eyes settled on the fiddle case, and he snatched it quickly, seeing that only a few onlookers remained. He pulled out the bow, and as always, there was a rightness in the way it fit his crippled hand. His missing fingers weren't needed here.

No sooner than he put bow to string, music filled the square. Some of those who were turning away stopped to listen, but Rojer paid them no mind.

Rojer didn't remember much about his father, but he had a clear memory of Jessum clapping and laughing as Arrick fiddled. When he played, Rojer felt his father's love, as he did his mother's when he held his talisman. Safe in that love, he let fear fall away and he lost himself in the vibrating caress of the strings.

Usually he played only an accompaniment to Arrick's singing, but this time Rojer reached beyond that, letting his music fill the space Sweetsong would have occupied. The fingers of his good left hand were a blur on the frets, and soon the crowd began clapping a tempo for him to weave the music around. He played faster and faster as the tempo grew louder, dancing around the stage in time to the music. When he put his foot on one of the steps on the stage and pushed off into a backflip without missing a note, the crowd roared.

The sound broke his trance, and he saw that the square was filled, with people even crowded outside to hear. It had been some time since even Arrick drew such a crowd! Rojer almost missed a stroke in his shock, and gritted his teeth to hold on to the music until it became his world again.

"That was a good performance," a voice congratulated as Rojer counted the lacquered wooden coins in the hat. Nearly three hundred klats! Keven would not pester them for a month.

"Thank you . . ." Rojer began, but his voice caught in his throat as he looked up. Masters Jasin and Edum stood before him. Guildsmen.

"Where's your master, Rojer?" Edum asked sternly. He was a master actor and mummer whose plays were said to draw audience members from as far as Fort Rizon.

Rojer swallowed hard, his face flushing hot. He looked down, hoping they would take his fear and guilt as shame. "I . . . I don't know," he said. "He was supposed to be here."

"Drunk again, I'll wager," Jasin snorted. Also known as Goldentone, a name he was said to have given himself, he was a singer of some note, but more importantly, he was the nephew of Janson, Duke Rhinebeck's first minister, and made sure the entire world knew it. "Old Sweetsong is pickled sour these days."

"It's a wonder he's kept his license this long," Edum said. "I heard he soiled himself in the middle of his act last month."

"That's not true!" Rojer said.

"I'd be more worried about myself, if I were you, boy," Jasin said, pointing a long finger in Rojer's face. "Do you know the penalty for collecting money for an unlicensed performance?"

Rojer paled. Arrick could lose his license over this. If the guild brought the matter to the magistrate as well, they could both find themselves chopping wood with chained ankles.

Edum laughed. "Don't worry, boy," he said. "So long as the guild has its cut"—he helped himself to a large portion of the wooden coins Rojer had collected—"I don't think we need to make further note of this incident."

Rojer knew better than to protest as the men divided and pocketed over half the take. Little, if any, would actually find its way to the coffers of the Jongleurs' Guild.

"You've got talent, boy," Jasin said as they turned to go. "You might want to consider a master with better prospects. Come see me if you tire of cleaning up after old Soursong."

Rojer's disappointment lasted only until he shook the collection hat. Even half was more than he had ever hoped to make. He hurried back to the inn, pausing only to make a single stop. He made his way to Master Keven, whose face was a thunderhead as the boy approached.

"You'd better not be here to beg for your master, boy," he said.

Rojer shook his head, handing the man a purse. "My master says there's enough there for a tenday," he said.

Keven's surprise was evident as he hefted the bag and heard the satisfying clack of wooden coins within. He hesitated a moment, then grunted and pocketed the purse with a shrug.

Arrick was still asleep when he returned. Rojer knew his master would never realize the innkeep had been paid. He would avoid the man assiduously, and congratulate himself on making it ten days without paying.

He left the few remaining coins in Arrick's purse. He would tell his master he had found them loose in the bag of marvels. It was rare for that to happen since money became tight, but Arrick wouldn't question his fortune once he saw what else Rojer had bought.

Rojer placed the wine bottle by Arrick's side as he slept.

Arrick was up before Rojer the next morning, checking his makeup in a cracked hand mirror. He wasn't a young man, but neither was he so old that the tools in a Jongleur's paintbox couldn't make him look so. His long, sun-bleached hair was still more gold than gray, and his brown beard, darkened with dye, concealed the growing wattle beneath his chin. The paint matched his tanned skin so closely that the wrinkles around his blue eyes were all but invisible.

"We got lucky last night, m'boy," he said, contorting his face to see how the paint held, "but we can't avoid Keven forever. That hairy badger will catch us sooner or later, and when he does, I'd like more than . . ." He reached into the purse, pulling out the coins and flicking the lot into the air. ". . . six klats to our name." His hands moved too fast to follow, snatching the coins out of the air and putting them into a comfortable rhythm in the air above him.

"Have you been at your juggling, boy?" he asked.

Before Rojer could open his mouth to reply, Arrick flicked one of the klats his way. Rojer was wise to the ruse, but ready or not, he felt a stab of fear as he caught the coin in his left hand and tossed it up into the air. More coins followed in rapid succession, and he fought for control as he caught them with his crippled hand and tossed them to the other to be put into the air again.

By the time he had four coins going, he was terrified. When

Arrick added a fifth, Rojer had to dance wildly to keep them all moving. Arrick thought better of tossing the sixth and waited patiently instead. Sure enough, Rojer fell to the floor in a clatter of coins a moment later.

Rojer cringed in anticipation of his master's tirade, but Arrick only sighed deeply. "Put your gloves on," he said. "We need to go out and fill our purse."

The sigh cut even deeper than a shout and a cuff on the ear. Anger meant Arrick expected better. A sigh meant his master had given up.

"No," he said. The word slipped out before he could stop it, but once it hung there in the air between them, Rojer felt the rightness of it, like the fit of the bow in his crippled hand.

Arrick blustered through his mustache, shocked at the boy's audacity.

"The gloves, I mean," Rojer clarified, and saw Arrick's expression change from anger to curiosity. "I don't want to wear them anymore. I hate them."

Arrick sighed and uncorked his new bottle of wine, pouring a cup.

"Didn't we agree," he said, pointing at Rojer with the bottle, "that people would be less likely to hire you if they knew your infirmity?" he asked.

"We never agreed," Rojer said. "You just told me to start wearing the gloves one day."

Arrick chuckled. "Hate to disillusion you, boy, but that's how it is between masters and apprentices. No one wants a crippled Jongleur."

"So that's all I am?" Rojer asked. "A cripple?"

"Of course not," Arrick said. "I wouldn't trade you for any apprentice in Angiers. But not everyone will look past your demon scars to see the man within. They will label you with some mocking name, and you'll find them laughing at you and not with."

"I don't care," Rojer said. "The gloves make me feel like a fraud, and my hand is bad enough without the fake fingers making it clumsier. What does it matter why they laugh, if they come and pay klats to do it?"

Arrick looked at him a long time, tapping his cup. "Let me see the gloves," he said at last.

They were black, and reached halfway up his forearm.

Bright-colored triangles of cloth were sewn to the ends, with bells attached. Rojer tossed them to his master with a frown.

Arrick caught the gloves, looked at them for half a moment, and then tossed them out the window, brushing his hands together as if touching the gloves had left them unclean.

"Grab your boots and let's go," he said, tossing back the remains of his cup.

"I don't really like the boots either," Rojer dared.

Arrick smiled at the boy. "Don't push your luck," he warned with a wink.

Guild law allowed licensed Jongleurs to perform on any street corner, so long as they did not block traffic or hinder commerce. Some vendors even hired them to attract attention to their booths, or the common rooms of taverns.

Arrick's drinking had alienated most of the latter, so they performed in the street. Arrick was a late sleeper, and the best spots had long since been staked out by other Jongleurs. The space they found wasn't ideal: a corner on a side street far from the main lanes of traffic.

"It'll do," Arrick grunted. "Drum up some business, boy, while I set up."

Rojer nodded and ran off. Whenever he found a likely cluster of people, he cartwheeled by them, or walked by on his hands, the bells sewn into his motley ringing an invitation.

"Jongleur show!" he cried. "Come see Arrick Sweetsong perform!"

Between his acrobatics and the weight still carried by his master's name, he drew a fair bit of attention. Some even followed him on his rounds, clapping and laughing at his antics.

One man elbowed his wife. "Look, it's the crippled boy from Small Square!"

"Are you sure?" she asked.

"Just look at his hand!" the man said.

Rojer pretended not to hear, moving on in search of more customers. He soon brought his small following to his master, finding Arrick juggling a butcher knife, a meat cleaver, a hand axe, a small stool, and an arrow in easy rhythm, joking with a growing crowd of his own.

"And here comes my assistant," Arrick called to the crowd, "Rojer Halfgrip!"

Rojer was already running forward when the name registered. What was Arrick doing?

It was too late to slow, though, so he put his arms out and flung himself forward, cartwheeling into a triple backflip to stand a few yards from his master. Arrick snatched the butcher knife from the deadly array in the air before him and flicked it Rojer's way.

Fully expecting the move, Rojer went into a spin, catching the blunt and specially weighted knife easily in his good left hand. As he completed the circuit, he uncoiled and threw, sending the blade spinning right at Arrick's head.

Arrick, too, went into a spin, and came out of the circuit with the blade held tightly in his teeth. The crowd cheered, and as the blade went back up into rhythm with the other implements, a wave of klats clicked into the hat.

"Rojer Halfgrip!" Arrick called. "With only ten years and eight fingers, he's still deadlier with a knife than any grown man!"

The crowd applauded. Rojer held his crippled hand up for all to see, and the crowd ooohed and aahed over it. Already, Arrick's suggestion had most of them believing he made that catch and throw with his crippled hand. They would tell others, and exaggerate in the telling. Rather than risk Rojer being labeled by the crowd, Arrick had labeled him first.

"Rojer Halfgrip," he murmured, tasting the name on his tongue.

"Hup!" Arrick called, and Rojer turned as his master flung the arrow at him. He slapped his hands together, catching the missile just before it struck his face. He spun again, putting his back to the crowd. With his good hand, he threw the arrow between his legs back toward his master, but when he finished the move and faced the crowd, his crippled right hand was extended. "Hup!" he called back.

Arrick feigned fear, dropping the blades he was juggling, but the stool fell into his hands just in time for the arrow to stick in its center. Arrick studied it as if amazed at his own good fortune. He flicked his wrist as he pulled the arrow free, and it became a bouquet of flowers, which he bestowed on the prettiest woman in the crowd. More coins clattered into the hat.

Seeing his master moving on to magic, Rojer ran to the bag of marvels for the implements Arrick would need for his tricks. As he did, there came a cry from the crowd.

"Play your fiddle!" a man called. As he did, there was a general buzz of agreement. Rojer looked up to see the same man who had called so loudly for Sweetsong the day before.

"In the mood for music, are we?" Arrick asked the crowd, not missing a beat. He was answered with a cheer, so Arrick went to the bag and took the fiddle, tucking it under his chin and turning back to the audience. But before he could put bow to string, the man cried out.

"Not you, the boy!" he bellowed. "Let Halfgrip play!"

Arrick looked to Rojer, his face a mask of irritation as the crowd began chanting "Halfgrip! Halfgrip!" Finally he shrugged, handing his apprentice the instrument.

Rojer took the fiddle with shaking hands. "Never upstage your master" was a rule apprentices learned early. But the crowd was calling for him to play, and again the bow felt so right in his crippled hand, free of the cursed glove. He closed his eyes, feeling the stillness of the strings under his fingertips, and then brought them to a low hum. The crowd quieted as he played softly for a few moments, stroking the strings like the back of a cat, making it purr.

The fiddle came alive in his hands, then, and he led it out like a partner in a reel, sweeping it into a whirlwind of music. He forgot the crowd. He forgot Arrick. Alone with his music, he explored new harmonies even as he maintained a constant melody, improvising in time to the tempo of clapping that seemed a world removed.

He had no idea how long it went on. He could have stayed in that world forever, but there was a sharp twang, and something stung his hand. He shook his head to clear it and looked up at the wide-eyed and silent crowd.

"String broke," he said sheepishly. He glanced at his master, who stood in the same shock as the other onlookers. Arrick raised his hands slowly and began to clap.

The crowd followed soon after, and it was thunderous.

"You're going to make us rich with that fiddling, boy," Arrick said, counting their take. "Rich!"

"Rich enough to pay the back dues you owe the guild?" a voice asked.

They turned to see Master Jasin leaning against the wall. His two apprentices, Sali and Abrum, stood close by. Sali sang soprano with a clear voice as beautiful as she was ugly. Arrick sometimes joked that if she wore a horned helmet, audiences would mistake her for a rock demon. Abrum sang bass, his voice a deep thrum that made the planked streets vibrate. He was tall and lean, with gigantic hands and feet. If Sali was a rock demon, he was surely a wood.

Like Arrick, Master Jasin was an alto, his voice rich and pure. He wore expensive clothes of fine blue wool and gold thread, spurning the motley that most of his profession wore. His long black hair and mustache were oiled and meticulously groomed.

Jasin was a man of average size, but that made him no less dangerous. He had once stabbed a Jongleur in the eye during an argument over a particular corner. The magistrate ruled it self-defense, but that wasn't how the talk in the apprentice room of the guildhouse told it.

"The payment of my guild dues is no concern of yours, Jasin," Arrick said, quickly dumping the coins in the bag of marvels.

"Your apprentice may have talked your way out of missing that performance yesterday, Soursong, but his fiddle can't succor you forever." As he spoke, Abrum snatched Rojer's fiddle from his hands and broke it over his knee. "Sooner or later, the guild will have your license."

"The guild would never give up Arrick Sweetsong," Arrick said, "but even if they did, Jasin would still be known as 'Secondsong.' "

Jasin scowled, for many in the guild already used that name, and the master was known to fly into rages at its utterance. He and Sali advanced on Arrick, who held the bag protectively. Abrum backed Rojer against a wall, keeping him from going to his master's aid.

But this wasn't the first time they had needed to fight to defend their take. Rojer dropped straight down on his back, coiling like a spring and kicking straight up. Abrum screamed, his normally deep voice taking on a different pitch.

"I thought your apprentice was a bass, not a soprano," Arrick said. When Jasin and Sali spared a glance to their companion, his quick hands darted into the bag of marvels, sending a fistful of wingseeds spinning in the air before them.

Jasin lunged through the cloud, but Arrick sidestepped and

tripped him easily, bringing the bag around in a hard swing at Sali, hitting the bulky woman full in the chest. She might have kept her feet, but Rojer was in position, kneeling behind her. She fell hard, and before the three could recover, Arrick and Rojer ran off down the boardwalk.

CHAPTER 16

ATTACHMENTS
323–325 AR

THE ROOF OF THE DUKE'S LIBRARY in Miln was a magical place for Arlen. On a clear day, the world spread out below him, a world unrestrained by walls and wards, stretching on into infinity. It was also the place where Arlen first looked at Mery, and truly saw her.

His work in the library was nearly complete, and he would soon be returning to Cob's shop. He watched the sun play over the snowcapped mountains and fall on the valley below, trying to memorize the sight forever, and when he turned to Mery, he wanted to do the same for her. She was fifteen, and more beautiful by far than mountains and snow.

Mery had been his closest friend for over a year, but Arlen had never thought more of her than that. Now, seeing her limned in sunlight, cold mountain wind blowing the long brown hair from her face as she hugged her arms against the swell of her bosom to ward off the chill, she was suddenly a young woman, and he a young man. His pulse quickened at the way her skirts flared in the breeze, edges of lace hinting of petticoats beneath.

He said nothing as he stepped forward, but she caught the look in his eyes, and smiled. "It's about time," she said.

He reached out, tentatively, and traced the back of his hand down her cheek. She leaned in to the touch, and he tasted her sweet breath, kissing her. It was soft at first, hesitant, but it deepened as she responded, becoming something with a life of its own, something hungry and passionate, something that had been building inside him for over a year without his knowing.

Some time later, their lips parted with a soft pop, and they smiled nervously. Arms around one another, they looked out over Miln, sharing in the glow of young love.

"You're always staring out into the valley," Mery said. She ran her fingers through his hair, and kissed his temple. "Tell me what you dream about, when your eyes have that faraway look."

Arlen was quiet for some time. "I dream of freeing the world from the corelings," he said.

Her thoughts having gone another way, Mery laughed at the unexpected response. She did not mean to be cruel, but the sound cut at him like a lash. "You think yourself the Deliverer, then?" she asked. "How will you do this?"

Arlen drew away from her a little, feeling suddenly vulnerable. "I don't know," he admitted. "I'll start by messaging. I've already saved enough money for armor and a horse."

Mery shook her head. "That will never do, if we're to marry," she said.

"We're to marry?" Arlen asked in surprise, amazed at the tightness in his throat.

"What, am I not good enough?" Mery asked, pulling away and looking indignant.

"No! I never said . . ." Arlen stuttered.

"Well, then," she said. "Messaging may bring money and honor, but it's too dangerous, especially once we have children."

"We're having children now?" Arlen squeaked.

Mery looked at him as if he were an idiot. "No, it will never do," she went on, ignoring him as she thought things through. "You'll need to be a Warder, like Cob. You'll still get to fight demons, but you'll be safe with me instead of riding down some coreling-infested road."

"I don't want to be a Warder," Arlen said. "It was never more than a means to an end."

"What end?" Mery asked. "Lying dead on the road?"

"No," Arlen said. "That won't happen to me."

"What will you gain as a Messenger that you can't as a Warder?"

"Escape," Arlen said without thinking.

Mery fell silent. She turned her head to avoid his eyes, and after a few moments, slipped her arm from his. She sat quietly, and Arlen found sadness only made her more beautiful still.

"Escape from what?" she asked at last. "From me?"

Arlen looked at her, drawn in ways he was only just beginning to understand, and his throat caught. Would it be so bad to stay? What were the chances of finding another like Mery?

But was that enough? He'd never wanted family. They were attachments he did not need. If he had wanted marriage and children, he might as well have stayed in Tibbet's Brook with Renna. He'd thought Mery was different . . .

Arlen called to mind the image that had sustained him for the last three years, seeing himself riding down the road, free to roam. As always, the thought swelled him, until he turned to look again at Mery. The fantasy fled, and all he could think about was kissing her again.

"Not you," he said, taking her hands. "Never you." Their lips met again, and for a time, his thoughts touched on nothing else.

"I have an assignment to Harden's Grove," Ragen said, referring to a small farming hamlet a full day's ride from Fort Miln. "Would you care to join me, Arlen?"

"Ragen, no!" Elissa cried.

Arlen glared, but Ragen grabbed his arm before he could speak. "Arlen, may I have a moment alone with my wife?" he asked gently. Arlen wiped his mouth and excused himself.

Ragen closed the door after him, but Arlen refused to let his fate be decided out of his hands, and circled around through the kitchen, listening at the servants' entrance. The cook looked at him, but Arlen looked right back, and the man kept to his own business.

"He's too young!" Elissa was saying.

"Lissa, he'll always be too young for you," Ragen said. "Arlen is sixteen, and he's old enough to make a simple day trip."

"You're encouraging him!"

"You know full well Arlen needs no encouragement from me," Ragen said.

"Enabling him, then," Elissa snapped. "He's safer here!"

"He'll be safe enough with me," Ragen said. "Isn't it better that he makes his first few trips with someone to supervise him?"

"I'd rather he not make his first few trips at all," Elissa said acidly. "If you cared about him, you'd feel the same."

"Night, Lissa, it's not like we'll even *see* a demon. We'll reach the Grove before sunset and leave after sunrise. Regular folk make the trip all the time."

"I don't care," Elissa said. "I don't want him going."

"It's not your choice," Ragen reminded.

"I forbid it!" Elissa shouted.

"You can't!" Ragen shouted back. Arlen had never heard him raise his voice to her.

"Just you watch me," Elissa snarled. "I'll drug your horses! I'll chop every spear in two! I'll throw your armor in the well to rust!"

"Take away every tool you want," Ragen said through gritted teeth, "and Arlen and I will *still* leave for Harden's Grove tomorrow, on *foot,* if need be."

"I'll leave you," Elissa said quietly.

"What?"

"You heard me," she said. "Take Arlen out of here, and I'll be gone before you get back."

"You can't be serious," Ragen said.

"I've never been more serious in my life," Elissa said. "Take him and I go."

Ragen was quiet a long time. "Look, Lissa," he said finally. "I know how upset you've been that you haven't gotten pregnant . . ."

"Don't you dare bring that into this!" Elissa growled.

"Arlen is not your son!" Ragen shouted. "No amount of smothering will ever make it so! He is our *guest,* not our child!"

"Of course he's not our child!" Elissa shouted. "How could he be when you're out delivering ripping letters whenever I cycle?"

"You knew what I was when you married me," Ragen reminded her.

"I know," Elissa replied, "and I'm realizing that I should have listened to my mother."

"What's that supposed to mean?" Ragen demanded.

"It means I can't do this anymore," Elissa said, starting to cry. "The constant waiting, wondering if you'll ever come home; the scars you claim are nothing. The praying that the scant few times we make love will conceive before I'm too old. And now, this!

"I knew what you were when we married," she sobbed, "and I thought I had learned to handle it. But this . . . Ragen, I just can't bear the thought of losing you both. I can't!"

A hand rested on Arlen's shoulder, giving him a start. Margrit stood there, a stern look on her face. "You shouldn't be listening to this," she said, and Arlen felt ashamed for his spying. He was about to leave when he caught the Messenger's words.

"All right," Ragen said. "I'll tell Arlen he can't come, and stop encouraging him."

"Really?" Elissa sniffled.

"I promise," Ragen said. "And when I get back from Harden's Grove," he added, "I'll take a few months off and keep you so fertilized that something can't help but grow."

"Oh, Ragen!" Elissa laughed, and Arlen heard her fall into his arms.

"You're right," Arlen told Margrit. "I had no right to listen to that." He swallowed the angry lump in his throat. "But they had no right to discuss it in the first place."

He went up to his room and began packing his things. Better to sleep on a hard pallet in Cob's shop than in a soft bed that came at the cost of his right to make his own decisions.

For months, Arlen avoided Ragen and Elissa. They stopped by Cob's shop often to see him, but he was not to be found. They sent servants to make overtures, but the results were the same.

Without use of Ragen's stable, Arlen bought his own horse and practiced riding in the fields outside the city. Mery and Jaik often accompanied him, the three of them growing closer. Mery frowned upon the practice, but they were all still young, and the simple joy of galloping a horse about the fields drove other feelings away.

Arlen worked with increasing autonomy in Cob's shop, taking calls and new customers unsupervised. His name became known in warding circles, and Cob's profits grew. He hired servants and took on more apprentices, leaving the bulk of their training to Arlen.

Most evenings, Arlen and Mery walked together, taking in the colors of the sky. Their kisses grew hungrier, both wanting more, but Mery always pulled away before it went too far.

"You'll be done with your apprenticeship in another year," she kept saying. "We can marry the next day, if you wish, and you can ravish me every night from then on."

One morning when Cob was away from the shop, Elissa paid a visit. Arlen, busy talking to a customer, didn't notice her until it was too late.

"Hello, Arlen," she said when the customer left.

"Hello, Lady Elissa," he replied.

"There's no need to be so formal," Elissa said.

"I think informality confused the nature of our relationship," Arlen replied. "I don't want to repeat the error."

"I've apologized again and again, Arlen," Elissa said. "What will it take for you to forgive me?"

"Mean it," Arlen answered. The two apprentices at the workbench looked at one another, then got up in unison and left the room.

Elissa took no notice of them. "I do," she said.

"You don't," Arlen replied, gathering some books from the counter and moving to put them away. "You're sorry that I overheard, and took offense. You're sorry that I left. The only thing you're *not* sorry about is what you did, making Ragen refuse to take me."

"It's a dangerous trip," Elissa said carefully.

Arlen slammed down the books, and met Elissa's eyes for the first time. "I've made the trip a dozen times in the last six months," he said.

"Arlen!" Elissa gasped.

"I've been to the Duke's Mines, as well," Arlen went on. "And the South Quarries. Everywhere within a day of the city. I've made my circles, and the Messengers' Guild's been courting me ever since I gave them my application, taking me wherever I want to go. You've accomplished nothing. I won't be caged, Elissa. Not by you, not by anyone."

"I never wanted to cage you, Arlen, only to protect you," Elissa said softly.

"That was never your place," Arlen said, turning back to his work.

"Perhaps not," Elissa sighed, "but I only did it because I care. Because I love you."

Arlen paused, refusing to look at her.

"Would it be so bad, Arlen?" Elissa asked. "Cob isn't young, and he loves you like a son. Would it be such a curse to take over his shop and marry that pretty girl I've seen you with?"

Arlen shook his head. "I'm not going to be a Warder, not ever."

"What about when you retire, like Cob?"

"I'll be dead before then," Arlen said.

"Arlen! What a terrible thing to say!"

"Why?" Arlen asked. "It's the truth. No Messenger keeps working and manages to die of old age."

"But if you know it's going to kill you, then why do it?" Elissa demanded.

"Because I'd rather live a few years knowing I'm free than spend decades in a prison."

"Miln is hardly a prison, Arlen," Elissa said.

"It is," he insisted. "We convince ourselves that it's the whole world, but it isn't. We tell ourselves that there's nothing out there we don't have here, but there is. Why do you think Ragen keeps messaging? He has all the money he could ever spend."

"Ragen is in service to the duke. He has a duty to do the job, because no one else can."

Arlen snorted. "There are other Messengers, Elissa, and Ragen looks at the duke like he was a bug. He doesn't do it out of loyalty, or honor. He does it because he knows the truth."

"What truth?"

"That there's more out there than there is in here," Arlen said.

"I'm pregnant, Arlen," Elissa said. "Do you think Ragen will find *that* somewhere else?"

Arlen paused. "Congratulations," he said at last. "I know how much you wanted it."

"That's all you have to say?"

"I suppose you'll expect Ragen to retire, then. A father can't risk himself, can he?"

"There are other ways to fight demons, Arlen. Every birth is a victory against them."

"You sound just like my father," Arlen said.

Elissa's eyes widened. As long as she had known Arlen, he'd never spoken of his parents.

"He sounds like a wise man," she said softly.

She'd said the wrong thing. Elissa knew it immediately. Arlen's face hardened into something she had never seen before; something frightening.

"He wasn't wise!" Arlen shouted, throwing a cup of brushes to the floor. It shattered, sending inky droplets everywhere. "He was a coward! He let my mother die! He let her die . . ." His face screwed up into an anguished grimace, and he stumbled, clenching his fists. Elissa rushed to him, not knowing what to do or say, only knowing that she wanted to hold him.

"He let her die because he was scared of the night," Arlen

whispered. He tried to resist as her arms encircled him, but she held on tightly as he wept.

She held him a long time, stroking his hair. Finally, she whispered, "Come home, Arlen."

Arlen spent the last year of his apprenticeship living with Ragen and Elissa, but the nature of their relationship had changed. He was his own man now, and not even Elissa tried to fight it any longer. To her surprise, her surrender only brought them closer. Arlen doted on her as her belly grew, he and Ragen scheduling their excursions so that she was never alone.

Arlen also spent a great deal of time with Elissa's Herb Gatherer midwife. Ragen said a Messenger needed to know something of a Gatherer's art, so Arlen sought plants and roots that grew beyond the city walls for the woman, and she taught him something of her craft.

Ragen stayed close to Miln in those months, and when his daughter, Marya, was born, he hung up his spear for good. He and Cob spent that entire night drinking and toasting.

Arlen sat with them, but he stared at his glass, lost in thought.

"We should make plans," Mery said one evening, as she and Arlen walked to her father's house.

"Plans?" Arlen asked.

"For the wedding, goose," Mery laughed. "My father would never let me marry an apprentice, but he'll speak of nothing else once you're a Warder."

"Messenger," Arlen corrected.

Mery looked at him for a long time. "It's time to put your trips aside, Arlen," she said. "You'll be a father soon."

"What has that got to do with it?" Arlen asked. "Lots of Messengers are fathers."

"I won't marry a Messenger," Mery said flatly. "You know that. You've always known."

"Just as you've always known that's what I am," Arlen replied. "Yet here you are."

"I thought you could change," Mery said. "I thought you could escape this delusion that you're somehow trapped, that you need to risk your life to be free. I thought you loved me!"

"I do," Arlen said.

"But not enough to give this up," she said. Arlen was quiet.

"How can you love me and still do this?" Mery demanded.

"Ragen loves Elissa," Arlen said. "It's possible to do both."

"Elissa hates what Ragen does," Mery countered. "You said so yourself."

"And yet they've been married fifteen years," Arlen said.

"Is that what you condemn me to?" Mery asked. "Sleepless nights alone, not knowing if you'll ever come back? Wondering if you're dead, or if you've met some minx in another city?"

"That won't happen," Arlen said.

"You're corespawned right it won't," Mery said, as tears began to flow down her cheeks. "I won't let it. We're done."

"Mery, please," Arlen said, reaching out to her, but she drew back, evading his grasp.

"We have nothing more to say." She whirled and ran off toward her father's house.

Arlen stood there a long time, staring after her. The shadows grew long, and the sun dipped below the horizon, but still he stood, even at Last Bell. He shuffled his boots on the cobbled street, wishing the corelings could rise through the worked stone and consume him.

"Arlen! Creator, what are you doing here?" Elissa cried, rushing to him as he entered the manse. "When the sun went down, we thought you were staying at Cob's!"

"I just needed some time to think," Arlen mumbled.

"Outside in the dark?"

Arlen shrugged. "The city is warded. There were no corelings about."

Elissa opened her mouth to speak, but she caught the look in Arlen's eyes, and the reprimand died on her lips. "Arlen, what's happened?" she asked softly.

"I told Mery what I told you," Arlen said, laughing numbly. "She didn't take it as well."

"I don't recall taking it very well myself," Elissa said.

"There you'll find my meaning," Arlen agreed, heading up the stairs. He went to his room and threw open the window, breathing the cold night air and looking out into the darkness.

In the morning, he went to see Guildmaster Malcum.

Marya cried before dawn the next morning, but the sound brought relief rather than irritation. Elissa had heard stories of children dying in the night, and the thought filled her with such terror that the child had to be pried from her arms at bedtime and her dreams were filled with knotting anxiety.

Elissa swung her feet out of bed and into her slippers as she freed a breast for nursing. Marya pinched the nipple hard, but even the pain was welcome, a sign of strength in her beloved child. "That's it, light," she cooed, "drink and grow strong."

She paced as the child nursed, already dreading being parted from her. Ragen snored contentedly in the bed. After only a few weeks' retirement, he was sleeping better, his nightmares less frequent, and she and Marya kept his days filled, that the road might not tempt him.

When Marya finally let go, she burped contently and dozed off. Elissa kissed her and put her back into her nest, going to the door. Margrit was waiting there, as always.

"G'morning, Mother Elissa," the woman said. The title, and the genuine affection with which it was said, still filled Elissa with joy. Even though Margrit had been her servant, they had never before been peers in the way that counted most in Miln.

"Heard the darling's cries," Margrit said. "She's a strong one."

"I need to go out," Elissa said. "Please prepare a bath and have my blue dress and ermine cloak laid out." The woman nodded, and Elissa went back to her child's side. When she was bathed and dressed, Elissa reluctantly handed the baby to Margrit and went out into the city before her husband awoke. Ragen would reprimand her for meddling, but Elissa knew that Arlen was teetering on an edge, and she would not let him fall because she failed to act.

She glanced about, fearing that Arlen might see her as she entered the library. She didn't find Mery in any of the cells or stacks, but was hardly surprised. Like many of the things personal to him, Arlen did not speak of Mery often, but Elissa listened intently when he did. She knew there was a place that was special to them, and knew the girl would be drawn there.

Elissa found Mery on the library's roof, weeping.

"Mother Elissa!" Mery gasped, hurriedly wiping her tears. "You startled me!"

"I'm sorry, dear," Elissa said, going over to her. "If you want me to go, I will, but I thought you might need someone to talk to."

"Did Arlen send you?" Mery asked.

"No," Elissa replied. "But I saw how upset he was, and knew it must be as hard for you."

"He was upset?" Mery sniffed.

"He wandered the streets in the dark for hours," Elissa said. "I was worried sick."

Mery shook her head. "Determined to get himself killed," she murmured.

"I think it's just the opposite," Elissa said. "I think he's trying desperately to feel alive." Mery looked at her curiously, and she sat down next to the girl.

"For years," Elissa said, "I could not understand why my husband felt the need to wander far from home, staring down corelings and risking his life over a few parcels and papers. He'd made money enough to keep us in luxury for two lifetimes. Why keep at it?

"People describe Messengers with words like duty, honor, and self-sacrifice. They convince themselves that this is why Messengers do what they do."

"It's not?" Mery asked.

"For a time I thought it was," Elissa said, "but I see things more clearly now. There are times in life when we feel so very alive that when they pass, we feel . . . diminished. When that happens, we'll do almost anything to feel so alive again."

"I've never felt diminished," Mery said.

"Neither had I," Elissa replied. "Not until I became pregnant. Suddenly, I was responsible for a life within me. Everything I ate, everything I did, affected it. I had waited so long that I was terrified of losing the child, as many women my age do."

"You're not so old," Mery protested. Elissa only smiled.

"I could feel Marya's life pulsing within me," Elissa continued, "and mine pulsing in harmony. I'd never felt anything like it. Now, with the baby born, I despair I might never feel it again. I cling to her desperately, but that connection will never be the same."

"What does this have to do with Arlen?" Mery asked.

"I'm telling you how I think Messengers feel when they travel," Elissa said. "For Ragen, I think that the risk of losing his life made him appreciate how precious it is, and sparked an instinct in him that would never allow him to die.

"For Arlen, it's different. The corelings have taken a lot from him, Mery, and he blames himself. I think, deep down, he even hates himself. He blames the corelings for making him feel that way, and only in defying them can he gain peace."

"Oh, Arlen," Mery whispered, tears brimming in her eyes once more.

Elissa reached out and touched her cheek. "But he loves you," she said. "I hear it when he talks about you. I think, sometimes, when he's busy loving you, he forgets to hate himself."

"How have you done it, Mother?" Mery asked. "How have you managed to endure all these years, married to a Messenger?"

Elissa sighed. "Because Ragen is kindhearted and strong at the same time, and I know how rare that kind of a man is. Because I never doubted that he loved me, and would come back. But most of all, because the moments I had with him were worth all the ones apart."

She put her arms around Mery, holding the girl tightly. "Give him something to come home to, Mery, and I think Arlen will learn that his life is worth something, after all."

"I don't want him to go at all," Mery said quietly.

"I know," Elissa agreed. "Neither do I. But I don't think I can love him less if he does."

Mery sighed. "Neither can I," she said.

Arlen was waiting that morning when Jaik left for the mill. He had his horse with him, a bay courser with a black mane named Dawn Runner, and his armor on.

"What's this?" Jaik asked. "Off to Harden's Grove?"

"And beyond," Arlen said. "I have a commission from the guild to message to Lakton."

"Lakton!?" Jaik gaped. "It will take you weeks to get there!"

"You could come with me," Arlen offered.

"What?" Jaik asked.

"As my Jongleur," Arlen said.

"Arlen, I'm not ready to . . ." Jaik began.

"Cob says you learn things best by doing them," Arlen cut him off. "Come with me, and we'll learn together! Do you want to work in the mill forever?"

Jaik dropped his eyes to the cobbled street. "Milling's not so bad," he said, shifting his weight from foot to foot.

Arlen looked at him a moment, and nodded. "You take care of yourself, Jaik," he said, mounting Dawn Runner.

"When will you be back?" Jaik asked.

Arlen shrugged. "I don't know," he said, looking toward the city gates. "Maybe never."

Elissa and Mery returned to the manse later that morning, to wait for Arlen's return. "Don't give in *too* easily," Elissa advised as they walked. "You don't want to give *all* your power away. Make him fight for you, or he'll never understand what you're worth."

"Do you think he will?" Mery asked.

"Oh," Elissa smiled, "I *know* he will."

"Have you seen Arlen this morning?" Elissa asked Margrit when they arrived.

"Yes, Mother," the woman replied. "A few hours ago. Spent some time with Marya, then left carrying a bag."

"A bag?" Elissa asked.

Margrit shrugged. "Prob'ly off to Harden's Grove, or some such."

Elissa nodded, not surprised that Arlen had chosen to leave town for a day or two. "He'll be gone through tomorrow, at least," she told Mery. "Come and see the baby before you go."

They headed upstairs. Elissa cooed as she approached Marya's nest, eager to hold her daughter, but she stopped short when she saw the folded paper tucked partially beneath the baby.

Her hands shaking, Elissa lifted the scrap of parchment and read aloud:

> *Dear Elissa and Ragen,*
> *I have taken assignment to Lakton from the Messengers'*
> *Guild. By the time you read this, I will be on the road.*
> *I'm sorry I could not be what everyone wanted.*
> *Thank you for everything. I will never forget you.*
> *—Arlen*

"No!" Mery cried. She turned and fled the room, leaving the house at a run.

"Ragen!" Elissa cried. "Ragen!!"

Her husband came rushing to her side, and he shook his head sadly as he read the note. "Always running from his problems," he muttered.

"Well?" Elissa demanded.

"Well, what?" Ragen asked.

"Go and find him!" Elissa cried. "Bring him back!"

Ragen fixed his wife with a stern look, and without a word spoken they argued. Elissa knew it was a losing battle from the start, and soon lowered her eyes.

"Too soon," she whispered. "Why couldn't he have waited one more day?" Ragen put his arms around her as she started to weep.

"Arlen!" Mery cried as she ran. All pretense of calm had flown from her, all interest in seeming strong, in making Arlen fight. All she wanted now was to find him before he left and tell him that she loved him, and that she would continue loving him no matter what he chose to do.

She reached the city gate in record time, panting from exertion, but it was too late. The guards reported that he had left the city hours earlier.

Mery knew in her heart he was not coming back. If she wanted him, she would have to go after him. She knew how to ride. She could get a horse from Ragen, and ride after him. He would surely succor in Harden's Grove the first night. If she hurried, she could get there in time.

She sprinted back to the manse, terror at the thought of losing him giving her fresh strength. "He's gone!" she shouted to Elissa and Ragen. "I need to borrow a horse!"

Ragen shook his head. "It's past midday. You'll never make it in time. You'll get halfway there, and the corelings will tear you to pieces," he said.

"I don't care!" Mery cried. "I have to try!" She darted for the stables, but Ragen caught her fast. She cried and beat at him, but he was stone, and nothing she did could loosen his grip.

Suddenly, Mery understood what Arlen had meant when he said Miln was a prison. And she knew what it was like to feel diminished.

It was late before Cob found the simple letter, stuck in the ledger on his countertop. In it, Arlen apologized for leaving early, before his seven years were up. He hoped Cob could understand.

Cob read the letter again and again, memorizing every word, and the meanings between the lines.

"Creator, Arlen," he said. "Of course I understand."

Then he wept.

SECTION III

KRASIA

328 AR

CHAPTER 17

RUINS
328 AR

WHAT ARE YOU DOING, ARLEN? he asked himself as his torch-light flickered invitingly on the stone stairs leading down into the dark. The sun was dipping low, and it would take several minutes to get back to his camp, but the stairs called to him in a way he could not explain.

Cob and Ragen had warned him about this. The thought of treasures that might be found in ruins was too much for some Messengers, and they took risks. Stupid risks. Arlen knew he was one of these, but he could never resist exploring the "lost dots on the map," as Tender Ronnell had put it. The money he made messaging paid for these excursions, sometimes taking him days from the nearest road. But for all his effort, he had found only dregs.

His thoughts flashed back to the pile of books from the old world that crumbled to dust when he tried to pick them up. The rusted blade that gashed his hand and infected it so badly he felt his arm was on fire. The wine cellar that caved in and trapped him for three days until he dug himself out without a bottle to show for it. Ruin hunting never paid off, and one day, he knew, it would be the death of him.

Go back, he urged himself. *Have a bite. Check your wards. Get some rest.*

"The night take you," Arlen cursed himself, and headed down the stairs.

But for all his self-loathing, Arlen's heart pounded with excitement. He felt free and alive beyond anything the Free Cities could offer. *This* was why he became a Messenger.

He reached the bottom of the stairs, and dragged a sleeve

across his sweating brow, taking a brief pull from his waterskin. Hot as it was, it was hard to imagine that after sunset the desert above would drop to near-freezing temperatures.

He moved along a gritty corridor of fitted stones, his torch-light dancing along the walls like shadow demons. *Are there shadow demons?* he wondered. *That would be just my luck.* He sighed. There was so much he still didn't know.

He had learned much in the last three years, soaking up knowledge of other cultures and their struggles with the corelings like a sponge. In the Angierian forest, he had spent weeks studying wood demons. In Lakton, he learned of boats beyond the small, two-man canoes used in Tibbet's Brook, and paid for his curiosity about water demons with a puckered scar on his arm. He had been lucky, able to plant his feet and haul on the tentacle, dragging the coreling from the water. Unable to abide the air, the nightmarish creature had let go and slipped beneath the surface once more. He spent months there, learning water wards.

Fort Rizon was much like home, less a city than a cluster of farming communities, each helping one another to ease the inevitable losses to corelings who bypassed the wardposts.

But Fort Krasia, the Desert Spear, was Arlen's favorite. Krasia of the stinging wind, where the days burned and the cold nights brought forth sand demons from the dunes.

Krasia, where they still fought.

The men of Fort Krasia had not allowed themselves to succumb to despair. They waged a nightly battle against the corelings, locking away their wives and children and taking up spear and net. Their weapons, like those Arlen carried, could do little to pierce the tough skin of a coreling, but they stung the demons, and were enough to harass them into warded traps until the desert sun rose to reduce them to ashes. Their determination was an inspiration.

But for all he had learned, Arlen only hungered for more. Every city had taught him something unknown in the others. Somewhere out there had to be the answers he sought.

Thus, this latest ruin. Half buried in sand, almost forgotten save for a crumbling Krasian map Arlen had discovered, the city of Anoch Sun had stood untouched for hundreds of years. Much of the surface was collapsed or worn down by wind and sand, but the lower levels, cut deep into the ground, were intact.

Arlen turned a corner, and his breath caught. Up ahead, in the dim flickering light, he saw pitted symbols cut into the stone pillars to either side of the corridor. Wards.

Holding the torch close, Arlen inspected them. They were old. Ancient. The very air about them was stale with the weight of centuries. He took paper and charcoal from his satchel to make rubbings, then, swallowing hard, continued on, lightly stirring the dust of ages.

He came to a stone door at the end of the hall. It was painted with faded and chipped wards, few of which Arlen recognized. He pulled out his notebook and copied those intact enough to be made out, then moved to inspect the door.

It was more a slab than a door, and Arlen soon realized that nothing held it in place save its own weight. Taking up his spear to use as a lever, he wedged the metal tip into the seam between the slab and the wall, and heaved. The point of the spear snapped off.

"Night!" Arlen cursed. This far from Miln, metal was rare and expensive. Refusing to be balked, he took a hammer and chisel from his pack and hacked at the wall itself. The sandstone cut easily, and soon he had carved a nook wide enough to work the shaft of his spear into the room beyond. The spear was thick and sturdy, and this time when Arlen threw his weight against the lever, he felt the great slab shift slightly. Still, the wood would break before it moved.

Using the chisel, Arlen pried up the floor stones at the door's base, digging a deep groove for it to tip into. If he could shift the stone that far, its own inertia would keep it in motion.

Moving back to the spear, he heaved once more. The stone resisted, but Arlen persevered, grinding his teeth with the effort. Finally, with a thunderous impact, the slab toppled to the ground, leaving a narrow gap in the wall, choked with dust.

Arlen moved into what appeared to be a burial chamber. The air reeked of age, but already fresher air was flooding the chamber from the corridor. Holding up his torch, he saw that the walls were brightly painted with tiny, stylized figures, depicting countless battles of humans against demons.

Battles that the humans seemed to be winning.

In the center of the room stood an obsidian coffin, cut roughly in the shape of a man holding a spear. Arlen approached the coffin, noting the wards along its length. He reached out to touch them, and realized his hands were shaking.

He knew there was little time remaining before sunset, but Arlen could not have turned away now if all the demons in the Core rose up against him. Breathing deeply, he moved to the head of the sarcophagus and pushed hard, forcing the lid down so that it would tilt to the floor without breaking. Arlen knew he should have copied the wards before trying this, but taking the time to copy them would have meant coming back in the morning, and he simply could not wait.

The heavy stone moved slowly, and Arlen's face reddened with the strain as he pushed, his muscles knotted and bunched. The wall was close behind him, and he braced a foot against it for leverage. With a scream that echoed down the corridor, he shoved with all his might, and the cover slid off, crashing to the ground.

Arlen paid the lid no mind, staring at the contents of the great coffin. The wrapped body inside was remarkably intact, but it could not hold his attention. All Arlen could see was the object clutched in its bandaged hands. A metal spear.

Sliding the weapon reverently from the corpse's stubborn grasp, Arlen marveled at its lightness. It was seven feet long from tip to tip, and the shaft was more than an inch in diameter. The point was still sharp enough to draw blood after so many years. The metal was unknown to Arlen, but that fact flew from his thoughts as he noted something else.

The spear was warded. All along its silvery surface the etchings ran, a level of craftsmanship unknown in modern times. The wards were unlike anything he had ever seen.

As Arlen became aware of the enormity of his find, he realized, too, the danger he was in. The sun was setting above. Nothing he had found here would matter if he died before bringing it back to civilization.

Snatching up his torch, Arlen bolted out of the burial chamber and sprinted down the hall, taking the steps three at a time. He darted through the maze of passages on instinct, praying that his twists and turns were true.

Finally, he saw the exit to the dusty, half-buried streets, but not a sliver of light could be seen through the doorway. As he reached the exit, he saw that the sky was still tinged with color. The sun had only just set. His camp was in sight, and the corelings were just beginning to rise.

Without pausing to consider his actions, Arlen dropped his

torch and charged out of the building, scattering the sand as he zigzagged around the rising sand demons.

Cousins to rock demons, sand demons were smaller and more nimble, but still among the strongest and most armored of the coreling breeds. They had small, sharp scales, a dirty yellow almost indistinguishable from the grit, instead of the large charcoal gray plates of their rock-demon cousins, and they ran on all fours where rock demons stood hunched on two legs.

But their faces were the same; rows of segmented teeth jutted out on their jaws like a snout, while their nostril slits rested far back, just below their large, lidless eyes. Thick bones from their brows curved upward and back, cutting through the scales as sharp horns. Their brows twitched continually as they squeezed down, displacing the ever-blowing sand.

And even more frightening than their larger cousins, sand demons hunted in packs. They would work together to see him cored.

His heart pounding and his discovery forgotten, Arlen moved through the ruins with incredible speed and alacrity, vaulting fallen pillars and crumbled rock while dodging right and left around the solidifying corelings.

Demons needed a moment to get their bearings on the surface, and Arlen took full advantage of that as he sprinted toward his circle. He kicked one demon in the back of the knees, knocking it down just long enough for him to get past. Another he charged directly, only to spin out of the way at the last moment, the coreling's claws slashing through empty air.

He picked up speed as the circle neared, but one demon stood in his way, and there was no way around it. The creature was nearly four feet tall, and its initial confusion was past. It crouched at the ready, directly in his path, hissing hatred.

Arlen was so close—his precious circle just a few feet away. He could only hope to barrel through the smaller creature and roll into his circle before it could kill him.

He charged right in, instinctively stabbing with his new spear as he bowled the creature over. There was a flash upon impact, and Arlen struck the ground hard, coming up in a spray of sand and continuing on, not daring to look back. He leapt for his circle, and was safe.

Panting with exertion, Arlen looked up at the sand demons surrounding him, outlined in desert twilight. They hissed and clawed at his wards, talons bringing bright flashes of magic.

In the flickering light, Arlen caught sight of the demon he had crashed into. It was slowly dragging itself away from Arlen and its fellows, leaving an inky black trail in the sand.

Arlen's eyes widened. Slowly, he glanced down at the spear he still clutched in his hands.

The tip was coated in demon ichor.

Suppressing the urge to laugh aloud, Arlen looked back at the injured coreling. One by one, its fellows paused in their assault on Arlen's wards, sniffing the air. They turned, glancing down at the trail of ichor, and then at the injured demon.

With a shriek, the pack fell upon the creature, tearing it apart.

The cold of the desert night eventually forced Arlen to take his eyes off the metal spear. He had laid a fire when he made camp earlier, so he struck spark to it and coaxed the flames to life, warming himself and a bit of dinner. Dawn Runner had been hobbled and blanketed in his circle, brushed and fed before Arlen left to explore the ruins that afternoon.

As it had every night for the last three years, One Arm showed up soon after moonrise, bounding over the dunes and scattering the smaller corelings to stand before Arlen's circle. Arlen greeted it as always with a clap of his two hands. One Arm roared its hatred in return.

When he first left Miln, Arlen had wondered if he would ever find a way to sleep through the sound of One Arm hammering at his wards, but it was second nature to him now. His warding circle had been proven time and again, and Arlen maintained it religiously, keeping the plates freshly lacquered and the rope mended.

He hated the demon, though. The years had brought none of the kinship the guards on the wall of Fort Miln had felt. As One Arm remembered who had crippled it, so too did Arlen recall who had given him the puckered scars across his back and almost cost him his life. He remembered, too, nine Warders, thirty-seven guardsmen, two Messengers, three Herb Gatherers, and eighteen citizens of Miln who had lost their lives because of it. He gazed at the demon now, absently stroking his new spear.

What would happen if he struck? The weapon had wounded a sand demon. Would the wards affect a rock demon as well?

It took all his willpower to resist the urge to leap from his circle and find out.

Arlen had hardly slept when the sun drove the demons back into the Core, but he rose with high spirits. After breakfast, he took out his notebook and examined the spear, painstakingly copying every ward and studying the patterns they formed along the shaft and head.

When he finished, the sun was high in the sky. Taking another torch, he went back down into the catacombs, making rubbings of the wards cut into the stone. There were other tombs, and he was tempted to ignore all sense and explore every one. But if he stayed even another day, his food would run out before he reached the Oasis of Dawn. He had gambled on finding a well in the ruins of Anoch Sun, and indeed he had, but vegetation was scant and inedible.

Arlen sighed. The ruins had stood for centuries. They would be there when he returned, hopefully with a team of Krasian Warders at his back.

By the time he came back outside, the day was wearing on. Arlen took time to exercise and feed Dawn Runner, then prepared a meal for himself, his mind turned inward.

The Krasians would demand proof, of course. Proof the spear could kill. They were warriors, not ruin hunters, and would not give up a single able-bodied man for an expedition without good reason.

Proof, he thought. And it was only right that it come from him.

With barely an hour before sunset, Arlen began to ready his camp. He hobbled his horse again, checking the portable circle around it. He prepared his ten-foot circle as usual, then took a series of wardstones from his bags and began to lay them around it in a wide outer ring some forty feet in diameter. He placed the stones slightly farther apart than usual, carefully lining them up with their fellows. There was a third portable circle in the saddlebags—Arlen always kept a spare—and he set that one in the camp as well, off to the side in the larger circle, by its edge.

When he was finished, Arlen knelt in his center circle, the spear at his side, and breathed deeply, clearing his mind of distractions. He didn't watch as the sun dipped and the sand glowed on the horizon before going dark.

The nimble sand demons rose first, and Arlen heard the wards of his outer circle spark and crackle, keeping them back. Moments later, he heard the roar of One Arm, scattering lesser demons from its path as it approached Arlen's outer ring. Arlen ignored it, continuing to breathe, his eyes closed, his mind calm. The lack of reaction served only to anger the demon further, and it struck hard against the warding.

Magic flared, visible even through his closed eyelids, but the demon did not immediately continue its assault. He opened his eyes, watching One Arm cock its head curiously. Arlen allowed himself a humorless smile.

One Arm struck the wards again, and again it paused. This time, the demon let out a piercing cry and set its feet, thrusting its good arm at the warding, talons spread. As if it were pressing against a wall of glass, the demon leaned forward, shrieking against the pain as it doubled and tripled the pressure against the wards. Angry magic spiderwebbed out from where its claws met the barrier, and as the demon pressed, the magic bowed visibly in the air.

With a sound that chilled even Arlen's calm mind, the rock demon flexed its armored legs and smashed through the wardnet, tumbling into the inner ring. Dawn Runner whinnied and pulled at his hobble.

Arlen rose as One Arm did, their eyes meeting. The weaker sand demons tried desperately to replicate One Arm's feat, but the wardstones were precisely spaced, and none of them could muster the strength to cross. They shrieked their frustration at the barrier as they bore witness to the confrontation within the circle.

Though he had grown since they first met, Arlen felt no less dwarfed by One Arm now than he had that first, terrifying night. The rock demon stood over fifteen feet tall from its clawed feet to the tips of its horns, more than twice a man's height. Arlen was forced to crane his head upward to meet the coreling's eyes, locked unwaveringly on his own.

One Arm's snout split wide to reveal rows of razor-sharp teeth, running with drool, and it flexed its daggerlike talons teasingly. Its armored chest was thrown out, the black carapace impenetrable to known weapons, and its spiked tail whipped back and forth, heavy enough to smash a horse with a single blow. Its body was smoking and scorched from crossing the net, but the obvious hurt only made the coreling seem more dangerous, a titan mad with pain.

Arlen's fingers tightened on the metal spear as he stepped from the circle.

CHAPTER 18

RITE OF PASSAGE
328 AR

ONE ARM SHRIEKED into the night, its vengeance finally at hand. Arlen forced himself to breathe deeply, fighting to keep his heart from pounding right out of his chest. Even if the magic of the spear could harm the demon—and he had nothing more than his hopes that it could—it would not be enough to win this battle. He needed all his wits about him, all his training.

His feet slowly slid apart into a battle stance. The sand would slow him, but it would slow One Arm as well. He kept eye contact, and made no sudden moves as the coreling savored the moment. Its reach far exceeded his own, even with the spear. Let it come to him.

Arlen felt as if his entire life had been rushing toward this moment without his ever realizing it. He wasn't sure if he was ready for this test, but after being hounded by this demon for more than ten years, he found the thought of putting it off any longer intolerable. Even now, he could step back into the protective circle, safe from the rock demon's attacks. Deliberately, he moved away from it, committing himself to the contest.

One Arm watched him circle, its muzzle curling in a snarl. A low rumbling echoed in the coreling's throat. Its tail flicked faster, and Arlen knew it was getting ready to strike.

With a roar, the demon lunged, its talons splayed as they cut the air. Arlen darted straight forward, ducking the blow and moving inside the coreling's reach. He kept on, going right between its legs, stabbing his spear into its tail as he rolled aside. There was a satisfying flash of magic as he struck, and the demon howled as the weapon broke through its armor and pierced flesh.

Arlen was expecting the return slash of the demon's tail, but it came quicker than he anticipated. He threw himself flat to the ground as the appendage whooshed by, the spikes inches from his head. He was up again in a flash, but One Arm was already turning, using its tail's momentum to speed its pivot. For all its size, the coreling was agile and quick.

One Arm struck again, and Arlen could not dodge in time. He whipped the shaft of his spear perpendicular to the blow in parry, but he knew the demon was far too powerful to block. He had let his emotions get the better of him; had entered this contest too soon. He cursed himself for a fool.

But as the demon's talons struck the metal of the spear, the wards etched along its length flared. Arlen hardly felt the blow, but One Arm was deflected as if it had struck a warded circle. The demon was thrown back as its own power rebounded, but it recovered fast, unharmed.

Arlen forced himself to overcome his shock and move, understanding the blessing for what it was and determined to make the most of it. One Arm charged him madly, determined to power through this new obstacle.

Scattering sand as he ran, Arlen vaulted the fallen remains of a thick stone pillar, taking shelter behind it and preparing to dodge left or right, depending on how the demon approached.

One Arm struck hard at the pillar, almost four feet in diameter, and broke it in half, throwing one side out of its way with a flex of its sinewy arm. The raw display of power was terrifying, and Arlen bolted for his circle, needing a moment to recover.

The demon anticipated his reaction, though, and its legs twitched, launching it into the air. It landed in between Arlen and his succor.

Arlen stopped short, and One Arm again shrieked in triumph. It had tested Arlen's mettle, and found him wanting. It respected the spear's bite, but there was no fear in the coreling's eyes as it advanced. Arlen gave ground slowly, deliberately, not wanting to provoke the creature with a sudden move. He backed up as far as he could before crossing his outer wardstones and coming into the reach of the sand demons clustered to watch the battle.

One Arm saw his predicament, and roared, its thunderous charge terrible to behold. Arlen set himself firmly, his legs coiled. He did not bother to raise the spear to block. Instead, he cocked it back, ready to stab.

The rock demon's blow was powerful enough to crush a lion's skull, but it never struck home. Arlen had allowed the demon to back him into his spare portable circle, unnoticed in the sand. The wards flared to life, reflecting the demon's attack back on it, and Arlen was ready, leaping forward and skewering the demon in the belly with his warded spear.

One Arm's shriek pierced the night, a deafening, horrifying sound. To Arlen, it was like music. He pulled back on the spear, but it held fast, caught in the rock demon's thick black carapace. He yanked again, and this time it nearly cost him his life as One Arm lashed out and struck him a glancing blow, its claws digging deep into his shoulder and chest.

Arlen was sent spinning away, but he wrenched himself toward his spare circle, collapsing in the protective ring. As he clutched his wounds, he watched the giant rock demon stumble about. Again and again, One Arm attempted to grasp the spear and pull it free of the wound, but the wards along its length thwarted the demon. And all along, the magic continued to work, sparking in the wound and sending killing waves through the coreling's body.

Arlen allowed himself a slight smile as One Arm collapsed to the ground, thrashing. But as he watched the demon's flailing slow to twitching, he felt a great emptiness grow inside of him. He had dreamt of this moment countless times, of how it would feel, of what he would say, but it wasn't like he imagined. Instead of elation, he felt depression and loss.

"That was for you, Mam," he whispered as the great demon ceased to move. He tried to picture her, desperate to feel her approval, and he was shocked and ashamed when he could not remember her face. He screamed, feeling wretched and small under the stars.

Giving the demon a wide berth, Arlen made his way back to his supplies, binding his wounds. The stitches he made were crooked, but they held his wounds closed, and the hogroot poultice burned, the pain evidence of its need. Already the wound was infecting.

He found no sleep that night. If the pain of his wounds and the ache of his heart had not been sufficient to drive slumber away, a chapter of his life was about to end, and he was determined to see it through.

When the sun crested the dunes, it flooded Arlen's camp with a speed that could only be found in the desert. The sand demons had already melted away, fleeing at the first hint of dawn. Arlen winced as he stood up, making his way from the circle to stand over One Arm, retrieving his spear.

Wherever the sun's light touched, the black carapace smoked, then sparked and ignited. Soon the demon's body was a funeral pyre, and Arlen stood watching, mesmerized. As the rock demon collapsed into ashes soon borne on the morning wind, he saw hope for the human race.

CHAPTER 19

THE FIRST WARRIOR
OF KRASIA
328 AR

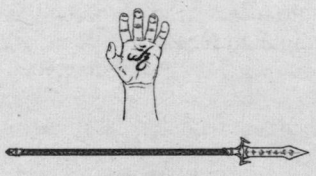

THE DESERT ROAD wasn't really a road at all, simply a string of ancient signposts, some clawed and jagged, others half buried in sand, keeping a traveler from losing his way. It wasn't all sand, as Ragen had once said, though there was enough of that to wander for days seeing naught else. On the outskirts ran hundreds of miles of hard, dust-choked flats, with sparse bits of dead vegetation clinging to cracked clay, too dry to rot. Apart from the shadows cast by dunes in the sea of sand, there was no shelter from the beating sun, so hot Arlen could not imagine it was the same body that brought cold light to Fort Miln. The wind blew continually, and he had to cover his face to keep from inhaling sand, his throat raw and dry.

The nights were worse, the heat leaching from the ground moments after the sun dipped below the horizon, welcoming the corelings into a cold, desolate place.

But even here, there was life. Snakes and lizards hunted tiny rodents. Carrion birds sought the corpses of creatures slain by corelings, or that wandered into the desert and could not find their way back out. There were at least two large oases, where a large body of water caused the surrounding soil to grow dense with edible vegetation, and others where a trickle from the rock or a pool of water no wider than a man's stride supported a host of stunted plants and small creatures. Arlen had witnessed these desert dwellers burying themselves in the sand at night, resisting the cold with conserved heat and hiding from the demons that stalked the sands.

There were no rock demons in the desert, for there was not enough prey. No flame demons, because there was little to burn. Wood demons had no bark to blend into, no limbs to climb. Water demons could not swim through sand, and wind demons could find no perch. The dunes and desert flats belonged to sand demons alone. Even they were sparse in the deep desert, clustering mostly about the oases, but the sight of a fire would draw them from miles around.

Five weeks from Fort Rizon to Krasia, more than half of it through the desert, was more than many of the hardiest Messengers cared to contemplate. Despite Northern merchants offering exorbitant sums for Krasian silks and spice, few were desperate—or crazy—enough to go there.

For his own part, Arlen found the trip peaceful. He slept in his saddle during the hottest parts of the day, carefully wrapped in loose white cloth. He watered his horse frequently, and spread tarps beneath his portable circles at night to keep the wards from becoming obscured in the sand. He was tempted to lash out at the circling sand demons, but his wound had made his grip weak, and he knew that should the spear be pulled from his grasp, a common wind might lose it in the sand more surely than hundreds of years in a buried tomb.

Despite the cries of the sand demons, the nights seemed quiet to Arlen, used to the great roars of One Arm. He slept more peacefully on those nights than any spent outside before.

For the first time in his life, Arlen saw his path extend beyond being a glorified errand boy. He had always known he was destined for more than messaging; he was destined to fight. But he now realized it was more than that: He was destined to bring *others* to fight.

He was certain he could duplicate the warded spear, and was already pondering ways to adapt its wards to other weapons; arrows, staves, slingstones, the possibilities were endless.

In all the places he had seen, only the Krasians refused to live in terror of the corelings, and for that reason Arlen respected them above all. There were no people more deserving of this gift. He would show them the spear, and they would supply him with everything he needed to build them weapons to turn the tide of their nightly war.

The thoughts fled as Arlen caught sight of the oasis. The sand could reflect the sky's blue and trick a man into rushing off the road to water that did not exist, but when his horse picked up the pace, Arlen knew it was real. Dawn Runner could smell the water.

Their water had been depleted the day before, and by the time they reached the small pool, both Arlen and his horse were sick with thirst. In unison, they dropped their heads to the cool water, drinking deeply.

When they had drunk their fill, Arlen refilled their waterskins and set them in the shade beneath one of the sandstone monoliths standing silent guard around the oasis. He inspected the wards cut into the stone, finding them intact, but with some signs of wear. The eternally blowing sand scratched at them little by little, wearing down the edges over time. He took out his etching tools, deepening and sharpening them to maintain the net.

While Dawn Runner grazed on scrub grass and the leaves of stunted bushes, Arlen harvested dates, figs, and other fruit from the oasis trees. He ate his fill, and set the rest where they could dry in the sun.

An underground river fed the oasis, and in years beyond memory, men had dug away the sand and cut the stone beneath, finally reaching the running water. Arlen descended the stone steps into a cool underground chamber and collected the nets stored there, tossing them into the water. When he left, he carried a satisfying catch of fish. He set aside a choice few for himself and cleaned the others, salting them and setting them alongside the fruit to dry.

Taking a forked tool from the oasis stores, he then searched around the stones, at last spotting telltale grooves in the sand. Soon he had a snake pinned with the forked stick, and snatched it by the tail, cracking it like a whip to kill it. There was likely a cache of eggs nearby, but he did not search them out. It would be dishonorable to deplete the oasis more than necessary. Again, he put part of the snake aside for his own uses, and set the rest to dry.

In a carved nook in one of the great sandstones, marked with the sigils of many Messengers, Arlen retrieved a cache of tough, dried fruits, fish, and meat left by the previous Messenger, and refilled his saddlebags. Once his harvest dried, he would replenish the nook for the next Messenger to succor here.

It was impossible to cross the desert without stopping at the Oasis of Dawn. The only source of water for over a hundred miles, it was the destination of every desert traveler in either direction. Most of these were Messengers, and therefore Warders, and over the years that exclusive society had marked their passing on the abundant sandstone. Dozens of names were cut into the stones; some were simply scratched print, while others were masterworks of calligraphy. Many Messengers included more than just their names, listing the cities they had visited, or the number of times they had succored at the Oasis of Dawn.

On his eleventh trip through the oasis, Arlen had long since finished carving his name and those of the living cities and villages he had visited, but he never stopped exploring, and always had something to add. Slowly, using beautiful scrolling letters, Arlen reverently inscribed "Anoch Sun" into the list of ruins he had seen. No other Messenger's mark in the oasis made such a claim, and that filled him with pride.

The next day, Arlen continued to increase the oasis' stores. It was a matter of honor among Messengers to leave the oasis stocked better than it was found, against the day when one of their number should stumble in too injured or sunstruck to gather for themselves.

That night, he composed a letter to Cob. He had written many such; they sat in his saddlebag, unsent. His words always felt inadequate to make up for abandoning his duties, but this news was too great not to share. He illustrated the wards on the spear's tip precisely, knowing Cob could spread the knowledge to every Warder in Miln in short order.

He left the Oasis of Dawn first thing the next morning, heading southwest. For five days, he saw little more than yellow dunes and sand demons, but early on the sixth, the city of Fort Krasia, the Desert Spear, came into view, framed by the mountains beyond.

From afar, it seemed just another dune, sandstone walls blending with their surroundings. It was built around an oasis much larger than the Oasis of Dawn, fed, the ancient maps said, by the same great underground river. Its warded walls, carved rather than painted, stood proudly in the sun. High above the city flew Krasia's banner, crossed spears over a rising sun.

The guards at the gate wore the black robes of *dal'Sharum*, the Krasian warrior caste, veiled against the ruthless sand. While not as tall as Milnese, Krasians were a head taller than most Angierians or Laktonians, hard with wiry muscle. Arlen nodded to them as he passed.

The guards raised their spears in return. Among Krasian men, this was the barest courtesy, but Arlen had worked hard to earn the gesture. In Krasia, a man was judged by the number of scars he carried and *alagai*—corelings—he had killed. Outsiders, or *chin,* as the Krasians called them, even Messengers, were considered cowards who had given up the fight, and were unworthy of any courtesy from *dal'Sharum.* The word *"chin"* was an insult.

But Arlen had shocked the Krasians with his requests to fight alongside them, and after he had taught their warriors new wards and assisted in many kills, they now called him Par'chin, which meant "brave outsider." He would never be considered an equal, but the *dal'Sharum* had stopped spitting at his feet, and he had even made a few true friends.

Through the gate, Arlen entered the Maze, a wide inner yard before the wall of the city proper, filled with walls, trenches, and pits. Each night, their families locked safe behind the inner walls, the *dal'Sharum* engaged in *alagai'sharak,* Holy War against demonkind. They lured corelings into the Maze, ambushing and harrying them into warded pits to await the sun. Casualties were high, but Krasians believed that dying in *alagai'sharak* assured them a place at the side of Everam, the Creator, and went gladly into the killing zone.

Soon, Arlen thought, *it will be only corelings that die here.*

Just inside the main gate was the Great Bazaar, where merchants hawked over hundreds of laden carts, the air thick with hot Krasian spices, incense, and exotic perfumes. Rugs, bolts of fine cloth, and beautiful painted pottery sat beside mounds of fruit and bleating livestock. It was a noisy and crowded place, filled with shouted haggling.

Every other marketplace Arlen had ever seen teemed with men, but the Great Bazaar of Krasia was filled almost entirely with women, covered head to toe in thick black cloth. They bustled about, selling and buying, shouting at each other vigorously and handing over their worn golden coins only grudgingly.

Jewelry and bright cloth were sold in abundance in the bazaar, but Arlen had never seen it worn. Men had told him the women wore the adornments under their black, but only their husbands knew for sure.

Krasian men above the age of sixteen were almost all warriors. A small few were *dama,* the Holy Men who were also

Krasia's secular leaders. No other vocation was considered honorable. Those who took a craft were called *khaffit,* and considered contemptible, barely above women in Krasian society. The women did all the day-to-day work in the city, from farming and cooking to child care. They dug clay and made pottery, built and repaired homes, trained and slaughtered animals, and haggled in the markets. In short, they did everything but fight.

Yet despite their unending labor, they were utterly subservient to the men. A man's wives and unmarried daughters were his property, and he could do with them as he pleased, even kill them. A man could take many wives, but if a woman so much as let a man who was not her husband look at her unveiled, she could—and often would—be put to death. Krasian women were considered expendable. Men were not.

Without their women, Arlen knew, the Krasian men would be lost, but the women treated men in general with reverence, and their husbands with near-worship. They came each morning to find the dead from the night's *alagai'sharak,* and wailed over the bodies of their men, collecting their precious tears in tiny vials. Water was coin in Krasia, and a warrior's status in life could be measured by the number of tear bottles filled upon his death.

If a man was killed, it was expected that his brothers or friends would take his wives, so they would always have a man to serve. Once, in the Maze, Arlen had held a dying warrior who offered him his three wives. "They are beautiful, Par'chin," he had assured, "and fertile. They will give you many sons. Promise you will take them!"

Arlen promised they would be cared for, and then found another willing to take them on. He was curious about what lay under the Krasian women's robes, but not enough to trade his portable circle for a clay building, his freedom for a family.

Following behind almost every woman were several tan-clad children; the girls' hair wrapped, the boys in rag caps. As early as eleven, the girls would begin to marry and take on the black clothes of women, while the boys were taken to the training grounds even younger. Most would take on the black robes of *dal'Sharum.* Some few would come to wear the white of *dama,* and devote their lives to serving Everam. Those who failed at both professions would be *khaffit,* and wear tan in shame until they died.

The women caught sight of Arlen as he rode through the

market, and began whispering to one another excitedly. He watched them, amused, for none would look him in the eye, or approach him. They hungered for the goods in his saddlebags—fine Rizonan wool, Milnese jewels, Angierian paper, and other treasures of the North—but he was a man, and worse, a *chin,* and they dared not approach. The eyes of the *dama* were everywhere.

"Par'chin!" a familiar voice called, and Arlen turned to see his friend Abban approach, the fat merchant limping and leaning heavily on his crutch.

Lame since childhood, Abban was *khaffit,* unable to stand among the warriors and unworthy to be a Holy Man. He had done well for himself, though, doing trade with Messengers from the North. He was clean-shaven, and wore the tan cap and shirt of *khaffit,* but over that he wore a rich headcloth, vest, and pantaloons of bright silk, stitched in many colors. He claimed his wives were as beautiful as those of any *dal'Sharum.*

"By Everam, it is good to see you, son of Jeph!" Abban called in flawless Thesan, slapping Arlen on the shoulder. "The sun always shines brighter when you grace our city!"

Arlen wished he had never told the merchant his father's name. In Krasia, the name of a man's father was more important than one's own. He wondered what they would think if they knew his father was a coward.

But he clapped Abban on the shoulder in return, his smile genuine. "And you, my friend," he said. He would never have mastered the Krasian tongue, or learned to navigate its strange and often dangerous culture, without the lame merchant's aid.

"Come, come!" Abban said. "Rest your feet in my shade and wash the dust from your throat with my water!" He led Arlen to a bright and colorful tent pitched behind his carts in the bazaar. He clapped his hands, and his wives and daughters—Arlen could never tell the difference—scurried to open the flaps and tend to Dawn Runner. Arlen had to force himself not to help as they took the heavily laden saddlebags and carried them into the tent, knowing that the Krasians found the sight of a man laboring unseemly. One of the women reached for the warded spear, wrapped in cloth and slung from his saddle horn, but Arlen snatched it away before she could touch it. She bowed deeply, afraid she had given some insult.

The inside of the tent was filled with colorful silk pillows and intricately woven carpets. Arlen left his dusty boots by the flap and breathed deeply of the cool, scented air. He eased down onto the pillows on the floor as Abban's women knelt before him with water and fruit.

When he was refreshed, Abban clapped his hands, and the women brought them tea and honeyed pastries. "Your trip through the desert passed well?" Abban asked.

"Oh, yes." Arlen smiled. "Very well indeed."

They made small talk for some time afterward. Abban never failed in this formality, but his eyes kept flicking to Arlen's saddlebags, and he rubbed his hands together absently.

"To business then?" Arlen asked as soon as he judged it polite.

"Of course, the Par'chin is a busy man," Abban agreed, snapping his fingers. The women quickly brought out an array of spices, perfume, silks, jewelry, rugs, and other Krasian craft.

Abban examined the goods from Arlen's clients in the North while Arlen perused the items proposed for trade. Abban found fault with everything, scowling. "You crossed the desert just to trade this lot?" he asked in disgust when he was done. "It hardly seems worth the trip."

Arlen hid his grin as they sat and were served fresh tea. Bidding always started this way.

"Nonsense," he replied. "A blind man could see I have brought some of the finest treasures Thesa has to offer. Better by far than the sorry goods your women have brought before me. I hope you have more hidden away, because"—he fingered one carpet, a masterwork of weaving—"I've seen better carpets rotting in ruins."

"You wound me!" Abban cried. "I, who give you water and shade! Woe am I, that a guest in my tent should treat me so!" he lamented. "My wives worked the loom day and night to make that, using only the finest wool! A better carpet you will never see!"

After that, it was only a matter of haggling, and Arlen had not forgotten the lessons learned watching old Hog and Ragen a lifetime ago. As always, the session ended with both men acting as if they had been robbed, but inwardly feeling they had gotten the better of the other.

"My daughters will pack up your goods and hold them for your departure," Abban said at last. "Will you sup with us tonight? My wives prepare a table none in your North can match!"

Arlen shook his head regretfully. "I go to fight tonight," he said.

Abban shook his head. "I fear you have learned our ways too well, Par'chin. You seek the same death."

Arlen shook his head. "I have no intent to die, and expect no paradise in the next life."

"Ah, my friend, no one intends to go to Everam in the flower of their youth, but that is the fate that awaits those who go to *alagai'sharak.* I can recall a time when there were as many of us as there are grains of sand in the desert, but now . . ." He shook his head sadly. "The city is practically empty. We keep the bellies of our wives fat with children, but still more die in the night than are born in the day. If we don't change our ways, a decade from now Krasia will be consumed by the sand."

"What if I told you I had come to change that?" Arlen asked.

"The son of Jeph's heart is true," Abban said, "but the *Damaji* will not listen to you. Everam demands war, they say, and no *chin* is going to change their minds." The *Damaji* were the city's ruling council, made up of the highest-ranked *dama* of each of the twelve Krasian tribes. They served the Andrah, Everam's most-favored *dama,* whose word was absolute.

Arlen smiled. "I can't turn them from *alagai'sharak,*" he agreed, "but I can help them win it." He uncovered his spear and held it out to Abban.

Abban's eyes widened slightly at the sight of the magnificent weapon, but he raised his palm and shook his head. "I am *khaffit,* Par'chin. The spear is forbidden to my unclean touch."

Arlen drew the weapon back and bowed low in apology. "I meant no offense," he said.

"Ha!" Abban laughed. "You may be the only man ever to bow to me! Even the Par'chin need not fear offending *khaffit.*"

Arlen scowled. "You are a man like any other," he said.

"With that attitude, you will ever be *chin,*" Abban said, but he smiled. "You're not the first man to ward a spear," he said. "Without the combat wards of old, it makes no difference."

"They *are* the wards of old," Arlen said. "I found this in the ruins of Anoch Sun."

Abban blanched. "You found the lost city?" he asked. "The map was accurate?"

"Why do you sound so surprised?" Arlen asked. "I thought you said it was guaranteed!"

Abban coughed. "Yes, well," he said, "I trusted our source, of course, but no one has been there in more than three hundred years. Who is to say how accurate the map was?" He smiled. "Besides, it's not like you were likely to come back for a refund if I was wrong." They both laughed.

"By Everam, it is a fine tale, Par'chin," Abban said when Arlen finished describing his adventure in the lost city, "but if you value your life, you will not tell the *Damaji* that you looted the holy city of Anoch Sun."

"I won't," Arlen promised, "but surely they will see the value in the spear, regardless."

Abban shook his head. "Even if they agree to grant you audience, Par'chin," he said, "and I doubt they will, they will refuse to see value in anything a *chin* brings them."

"You may be right," Arlen said, "but I should at least try. I have messages to deliver to the Andrah's palace, anyway. Walk with me."

Abban held up his crutch. "It is a long way to the palace, Par'chin," he said.

"I'll walk slowly," Arlen said, knowing the crutch had nothing to do with the refusal.

"You don't want to be seen with me outside the market, my friend," Abban warned. "That alone may cost you the respect you've earned in the Maze."

"Then I'll earn more," Arlen said. "What good is respect, if I can't walk with my friend?"

Abban bowed deeply. "One day," he said, "I wish to see the land that makes noble men like the son of Jeph."

Arlen smiled. "When that day comes, Abban, I will take you across the desert myself."

Abban grabbed Arlen's arm. "Stop walking," he ordered.

Arlen obeyed, trusting in his friend though he saw nothing amiss. Women walked the street carrying heavy loads, and a group of *dal'Sharum* walked ahead of them. Another group was approaching from the other direction. Each was led by a *dama* in white robes.

"Kaji tribe," Abban said, pointing with his chin at the warriors ahead of them. "The others are Majah. It would be best for us to wait here a bit."

Arlen squinted at the two groups. Both were clad in the same black, and their spears were simple and unadorned. "How can you tell the difference?" he asked.

Abban shrugged. "How can you not?" he replied.

As they watched, one of the *dama* called something to the other. They faced off, and began to argue. "What do you suppose they're arguing about?" Arlen asked.

"Always the same thing," Abban said. "The Kaji *dama* believe sand demons reside on the third layer of Hell, and wind demons on the fourth. The Majah say the opposite. The Evejah is vague on the point," he added, referring to the Krasian holy canon.

"What difference does that make?" Arlen asked.

"Those on the lower levels are furthest from Everam's sight," Abban said, "and should be killed first."

The *dama* were screaming now, and the *dal'Sharum* on either side were clenching their spears in rage, ready to defend their leaders.

"They'll fight one another over which demons to kill first?" Arlen asked, incredulous.

Abban spat in the dust. "The Kaji will fight the Majah over far less, Par'chin."

"But there will be real enemies to fight once the sun sets!" Arlen protested.

Abban nodded. "And when it does, the Kaji and Majah will stand united," he said. "As we say, 'By night, my enemy becomes my brother.' But sunset is still hours away."

One of the Kaji *dal'Sharum* struck a Majah warrior across the face with the butt of his spear, knocking the man down. In seconds, all the warriors on each side were locked in combat. Their *dama* stood off to the side, unconcerned by and uninvolved in the violence, continuing to shout at one another.

"Why is this tolerated?" Arlen asked. "Can't the Andrah forbid it?"

Abban shook his head. "The Andrah is supposed to be of all tribes and none, but in truth, he will always favor the tribe he was raised from. And even if he didn't, not even he can end every blood feud in Krasia. You can't forbid men from being men."

"They're acting more like children," Arlen said.

"The *dal'Sharum* know only the spear, and the *dama* the Evejah," Abban agreed sadly.

The men were not using the points of their weapons . . . yet, but the violence was escalating quickly. If someone did not intervene, there would surely be death.

"Don't even think about it," Abban said, gripping Arlen's arm as he started forward.

Arlen turned to argue, but his friend, looking over his shoulder, gasped and fell to one knee. He yanked on Arlen's arm to do the same.

"Kneel, if you value your hide," he hissed.

Arlen looked around, spotting the source of Abban's fear. A woman walked down the road, swathed in holy white. *"Dama'ting,"* he murmured. The mysterious Herb Gatherers of Krasia were seldom seen.

He cast his eyes down as she passed, but did not kneel. It made no difference; she took no notice of either of them, proceeding serenely toward the melee, unnoticed until she was almost upon the men. The *dama* blanched when they saw her, shouting something to their men. At once, the fighting stopped, and the warriors fell over themselves to clear a path for the *dama'ting* to pass. The warriors and *dama* quickly dispersed in her wake, and traffic on the road resumed as if nothing out of the ordinary had happened.

"Are you brave, Par'chin, or mad?" Abban asked, when she was gone.

"Since when do men kneel to women?" Arlen asked, perplexed.

"Men don't kneel to *dama'ting,* but *khaffit* and *chin* do, if they are wise," Abban said. "Even the *dama* and *dal'Sharum* fear them. It is said they see the future, knowing which men will live through the night and which will die."

Arlen shrugged. "So what if they do?" he asked, clearly doubtful. A *dama'ting* had cast his fortune the first night he had gone into the Maze, but there had been nothing about the experience to make him believe she could actually see the future.

"To offend a *dama'ting* is to offend fate," Abban said as if Arlen were a fool.

Arlen shook his head. "We make our own fates," he said, "even if the *dama'ting* can cast their bones and see them in advance."

"Well, I don't envy the fate you will make if you offend one," Abban said.

They resumed walking and soon reached the Andrah's palace, an enormous domed structure of white stone that was likely as old as the city itself. Its wards were painted in gold, and glittered in the bright sunlight that fell upon its great spires.

But they had not set foot on the palace steps before a *dama* came rushing down to them. "Begone, *khaffit!*" he shouted.

"So sorry," Abban apologized, bowing deeply, eyes on the ground, and backed away. Arlen stood his ground.

"I am Arlen, son of Jeph, Messenger from the North, known as Par'chin," he said in Krasian. He planted his spear on the ground, and even wrapped it was clear what it was. "I bring letters and gifts for the Andrah and his ministers," Arlen went on, holding up his satchel.

"You keep poor company for one who speaks our tongue, Northerner," the *dama* said, still scowling at Abban, who groveled in the dust.

An angry retort came to Arlen's lips, but he bit it back.

"The Par'chin needed directions," Abban said to the dirt, "I only sought to guide . . ."

"I did not ask you to speak, *khaffit!*" the *dama* shouted, kicking Abban hard in the side. Arlen's muscles bunched, but a warning glare from his friend kept him in place.

The *dama* turned back as if nothing had happened. "I will take your messages," he said.

"The duke of Rizon asked that I deliver a gift to the *Damaji* personally," Arlen dared.

"Not in this life will I let a *chin* and a *khaffit* enter the palace," the *dama* scoffed.

The response was disappointing, but not unexpected. Arlen had never managed to see a *Damaji*. He handed over his letters and packages, scowling as the *dama* ascended the steps.

"I am sorry to say I told you so, my friend," Abban said. "It did not help that I was with you, but I speak true that the *Damaji* would not suffer an outsider in their presence, even if he was the duke of your Rizon himself. You would have been politely asked to wait, and left forgotten on some silk pillow to lose face."

Arlen gritted his teeth. He wondered what Ragen had done

when he visited the Desert Spear. Had his mentor tolerated such handling?

"Now will you sup with me?" Abban asked. "I have a daughter, just fifteen and beautiful. She would make you a good wife in the North, keeping your home for you while you travel."

What home? Arlen wondered, thinking of the tiny apartment full of books in Fort Angiers that he hadn't been to in over a year. He looked at Abban, knowing his scheming friend was more interested in the trade contacts he could make with a daughter in the North than in her happiness or the upkeep of Arlen's home, in any event.

"You honor me, my friend," he replied, "but I'm not ready to quit just yet."

"No, I rather thought not," Abban sighed. "I suppose you will go to see *him*?"

"Yes," Arlen said.

"He is no more tolerant of my presence than the *dama*," Abban warned.

"He knows your value," Arlen disagreed.

Abban shook his head. "He tolerates my existence because of you," he said. "The Sharum Ka has wanted lessons in the Northern tongue ever since you were first allowed into the Maze."

"And, Abban is the only man in Krasia who knows it," Arlen said, "making him valuable to the First Warrior, despite being *khaffit*." Abban bowed, but looked unconvinced.

They headed for the training grounds located not far from the palace. The city's center was neutral territory for all tribes, where they gathered to worship and prepare for *alagai'sharak*.

It was late afternoon, and the camp bustled with activity. Arlen and Abban passed first through the workshops of the weaponsmiths and Warders, whose crafts were the only ones considered worthy of *dal'Sharum*. Beyond that stood the open grounds, where drillmasters shouted and men trained.

On the far side was the palace of the Sharum Ka and his lieutenants, the *kai'Sharum*. Second only to the immense palace of the Andrah, this great dome housed the most honored of all, men who had proven their valor on the battlefield time and time again. Below the palace was said to be a great harem, where they might pass on their brave blood to future generations.

There were stares and muttered curses as Abban limped by on

his crutch, but none dared bar their way. Abban was under the protection of the Sharum Ka.

They passed lines of men doing spear forms in lockstep, and others practicing the brutal, efficient movements of *sharusahk,* Krasian hand combat. Warriors practiced marksmanship or threw nets at running spear boys, honing their skills for the night's coming battle. Deep in the midst of this was a great pavilion, where they found Jardir going over plans with one of his men.

Ahmann asu Hoshkamin am'Jardir was the Sharum Ka of Krasia, a title that translated into Thesan as "First Warrior." He was a tall man, well over six feet, wrapped in black cloth and wearing a white turban. In some way Arlen did not fully understand, the title Sharum Ka was a religious one as well, signified by the turban.

His skin was a deep copper color, his eyes dark as his black hair, oiled back and hanging down his neck. His black beard was forked and impeccably trimmed, but there was nothing soft about the man. He moved like a raptor, swift and sure, and his wide sleeves were rolled back to reveal hard, muscular arms, crisscrossed with scars. He was not much past thirty.

One of the pavilion guards caught sight of Arlen and Abban as they approached, and bent to whisper in Jardir's ear. The First Warrior turned from the chalked slate he was studying.

"Par'chin!" he called, spreading his arms with a smile and rising to meet them. "Welcome back to the Desert Spear!" He spoke in Thesan, his vocabulary and accent much improved since Arlen's last visit. He caught Arlen in a firm embrace and kissed his cheeks. "I did not know you had returned. The *alagai* will quail in fear tonight!"

Upon his first visit to Krasia, the First Warrior had taken an interest in Arlen as an oddity, if nothing more, but they had bled for one another in the Maze, and in Krasia, that meant everything.

Jardir turned to Abban. "What are you doing here among men, *khaffit?*" he asked disgustedly. "I have not summoned you."

"He's with me," Arlen said.

"He *was* with you," Jardir said pointedly. Abban bowed deeply and scurried off as quickly as his lame leg would allow.

"I don't know why you waste your time with that *khaffit,* Par'chin," Jardir spat.

"Where I come from, a man's worth does not end with lifting the spear," Arlen said.

Jardir laughed. "Where you come from, Par'chin, they do not lift the spear at all!"

"Your Thesan is much improved," Arlen noted.

Jardir grunted. "Your *chin* tongue is not easy, and twice as hard for needing a *khaffit* to practice it when you are away." He watched Abban limp away, sneering at his bright silks. "Look at that one. He dresses like a woman."

Arlen glanced across the yard at a black-swathed woman carrying water. "I've never seen a woman dressed like that," he said.

"Only because you won't let me find you a wife whose veils you can lift." Jardir grinned.

"I doubt the *dama* would allow one of your women to marry a tribeless *chin*," Arlen said.

Jardir waved his hand. "Nonsense," he said. "We have shed blood together in the Maze, my brother. If I take you into my tribe, not even the Andrah himself would dare protest!"

Arlen wasn't so sure about that, but he knew better than to argue. Krasians had a way of becoming violent if you challenged their boasts, and it might even be so. Jardir seemed equal to a *Damaji*, at least. Warriors obeyed him without question, even over their *dama*.

But Arlen had no desire to join Jardir's tribe or any other. He made the Krasians uncomfortable; a *chin* who practiced *alagai'sharak* and yet kept company with *khaffit*. Joining a tribe would ease that discomfort, but the moment he did, he would be subject to the tribe's *Damaji*, embroiled in their every blood feud, and never allowed to leave the city again.

"I don't think I'm ready for a wife just yet," he said.

"Well don't wait too long, or men will think you *push'ting*," Jardir said, laughing and punching Arlen's shoulder. Arlen wasn't sure what the word meant, but he nodded anyway.

"How long have you been in the city, my friend?" Jardir asked.

"Only a few hours," Arlen said. "I just delivered my messages to the palace."

"And already you come to offer your spear! By Everam," Jardir cried to his fellows, "the Par'chin must have Krasian blood in him!" His men joined in his laughter.

"Walk with me," Jardir said, putting his arm on Arlen's shoulder and moving away from the others. Arlen knew Jardir was already trying to decide where he would best fit in the night's battle. "The Bajin lost a Pit Warder last night," he said. "You could fill in there."

Pit Warders were among the most important of the Krasian soldiers, warding the demon pits used to trap corelings, and assuring that the wards activated after the demons fell in. It was risky work, for if the tarps used to disguise the pits didn't fall in and reveal the wards fully, there was little to prevent a sand demon from climbing out and killing the Warder as he tried to uncover them. There was only one position with a higher mortality rate.

"Push Guard, I would prefer," Arlen replied.

Jardir shook his head, but he was smiling. "Always the most dangerous duty for you," he chided. "If you are killed, who will carry our letters?"

Arlen understood the sarcasm, even through Jardir's thick accent. Letters meant little to him. Few *dal'Sharum* could even read.

"Not so dangerous, this night," Arlen said. Unable to contain his excitement, he unrolled his new spear, holding it up to the First Warrior proudly.

"A kingly weapon," Jardir agreed, "but it is the warrior that wins through in the night, Par'chin, not the spear." He put his hand on Arlen's shoulder and looked him in the eyes. "Do not put too much faith in your weapon. I have seen warriors more seasoned than you paint their spears and come to a bitter end."

"I did not make it," Arlen said. "I found it in the ruins of Anoch Sun."

"The birthplace of the Deliverer?" Jardir laughed. "The Spear of Kaji is a myth, Par'chin, and the lost city has been reclaimed by the sands."

Arlen shook his head. "I've been there," he said. "I can take you there."

"I am Sharum Ka of the Desert Spear, Par'chin," Jardir replied. "I cannot just pack a camel and ride off into the sand looking for a city that exists only in ancient texts."

"I think I will convince you when night falls," Arlen said.

Jardir smiled patiently. "Promise me that you will not try anything foolish," he said. "Warded spear or no, you are not the Deliverer. It would be sad to bury you."

"I promise," Arlen said.

"Good, then!" Jardir clapped him on the shoulder. "Come, my friend, the hour grows late. You shall sup in my palace tonight, before we muster outside Sharik Hora!"

They supped on spiced meats, ground peas, and the paper-thin layers of bread the Krasian women made by spreading wet meal on hot, polished rocks. Arlen had a place of honor next to Jardir, surrounded by *kai'Sharum* and served by Jardir's own wives. Arlen never understood why Jardir paid him so much respect, but after his treatment at the Andrah's palace, it was most welcome.

The men begged stories of him, calling for the tale of One Arm's crippling, though they had heard it many times. Always it was tales of One Arm, or Alagai Ka, as they called him. Rock demons were rare in Krasia, and as Arlen complied, his audience sat entranced by the tale.

"We built a new scorpion after your last visit, Par'chin," one of the *kai'Sharum* told him as they sipped their nectar after the meal. "It can punch a spear through a sandstone wall. We will find a way to pierce Alagai Ka's hide yet."

Arlen chuckled and shook his head. "I'm afraid you will not see One Arm tonight," he said, "or ever again. He has seen the sun."

The eyes of the *kai'Sharum* bulged. "Alagai Ka is dead?" one asked. "How did you manage this?"

Arlen smiled. "I will tell you the tale after tonight's victory," he said. He stroked the spear next to him gently as he did, a gesture the First Warrior did not miss.

CHAPTER 20

ALAGAI'SHARAK
328 AR

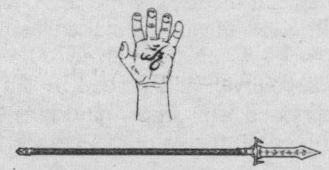

"GREAT KAJI, SPEAR OF EVERAM, grant strength to your warriors' arms and courage to their hearts this night, as they go forth to your holy work."

Arlen shifted uneasily as the *Damaji* bestowed the blessings of Kaji, the first Deliverer, on the *dal'Sharum*. In the North, claiming the Deliverer was just a mortal man might get you in a fistfight, but it was no crime. In Krasia, such heresy was punishable by death. Kaji was Everam's Messenger, come to unite all mankind against the *alagai*. They called him Shar'Dama Ka, First Warrior-Priest, and said he would return to unite man again one day, when they were worthy of *Sharak Ka,* the First War. Any who suggested otherwise came to a quick and brutal end.

Arlen was not such a fool as to voice his doubts about Kaji's divinity, but the Holy Men still unnerved him. They always seemed to be looking for an excuse to take offense at him, the outsider, and giving offense in Krasia usually meant death for the offender.

But whatever discomfort Arlen might feel around the *Damaji,* he always swelled at the sight of Sharik Hora, the enormous domed temple to Everam. Literally meaning "Heroes' Bones," Sharik Hora was a reminder of what humanity was capable of, a building dwarfing any structure Arlen had ever seen. The Duke's Library in Miln was tiny by comparison.

But Sharik Hora was impressive for more than its size. It was a symbol of courage beyond death, for it had been decorated with the bleached bones of every warrior who had died in *alagai'sharak.* They ran up the support beams and framed the windows. The great altar was made entirely of skulls, the pews out of leg bones. The chalice that worshippers drank water from was a hollowed skull resting in two skeletal hands, its stem the forearms, and its base a pair of feet. Each gigantic chandelier was made from dozens of skulls and hundreds of ribs, and the great domed ceiling, two hundred feet above, was covered in the skulls of the Krasians' warrior ancestors, looking down and judging, demanding honor.

Arlen once tried to calculate how many warriors decorated the hall, but the task defeated him. All the cities and hamlets in Thesa, perhaps two hundred fifty thousand souls, could not have decorated a fraction of Sharik Hora. The Krasians were numberless, once.

Now all of Krasia's warriors, perhaps four thousand in all, fit into Sharik Hora with room to spare. They gathered there twice each day, once at dawn and once at dusk, to honor Everam; to thank Him for corelings killed the previous night, and to beg His strength in killing them in the night to come. Most of all, though, they prayed for the Shar'Dama Ka to come again and begin *Sharak Ka*. To a one, they would follow him down into the Core itself.

Screams borne on the desert wind reached Arlen in the ambush pocket where he waited anxiously for the corelings to come. The warriors around him shifted their feet, offering prayers to Everam. Elsewhere in the Maze, *alagai'sharak* had begun.

They heard the reports as the Mehnding tribe positioned on the city walls cranked and fired their weapons, launching heavy stones and giant spears into the demon ranks. Some of these struck sand demons, killing or injuring them enough for their fellows to turn upon them, but the true purpose of the attack was to anger the corelings, stirring them into a frenzy. Demons were easily enraged, and once so, could be herded like sheep at the sight of prey.

When the corelings were boiling, the outer gates of the city opened, disabling the outer wardnet. Sand and flame demons charged through, wind demons gliding above them. Several dozen were usually allowed entrance before the gates closed and the net was reestablished.

Inside the gates stood a group of warriors, banging spear against shield. These men, known as Baiters, were mostly old and weak, expendable, but their honor knew no bounds. With shouts and whoops, they scattered at the demons' charge, splitting up in a prearranged fashion to divide the demons and lead them deeper into the Maze.

Watchers atop the Maze walls took down wind demons with bolas and weighted nets. As they crashed to the ground, Stakers emerged from tiny, warded alcoves to pin them before they could free themselves, shackling their limbs to warded stakes that were hammered into the ground, preventing them from returning to the Core to flee the dawn.

Meanwhile, the Baiters ran on, leading the sand and occasional flame demons to their end. The demons could run faster, but they could not negotiate the sharp turns of the Maze as easily as men who knew every twist. When a demon got too close, the Watchers attempted to slow it with nets. Many of these attempts were successful. Many were not.

Arlen and the others in the Push Guard tensed, hearing the shouts as their Baiters approached. "Ware!" a Watcher called from above. "I count nine!"

Nine sand demons were far more than the usual two or three that reached an ambush point. Baiters attempted to whittle their numbers as they split up, so that an ambush seldom faced more than five. Arlen tightened his grip on the warded spear as the eyes of the *dal'Sharum* went wild with excitement. To die in *alagai'sharak* was to win entry into paradise.

"Lights!" came the call from above. As the Baiters led the demons into the ambush point, the Watchers lit blazing oil fires before angled mirrors, flooding the area with light.

Caught unawares, the corelings shrieked and recoiled. The light could not harm them, but it gave the exhausted Baiters time to escape. Prepared for the light, they flowed with practiced precision around the demon pits, dropping into shallow, warded trenches.

The sand demons recovered quickly and resumed their charge, oblivious to the path the Baiters had taken. Three of them ran right onto the sand-colored tarps that covered the two wide demon pits, shrieking as they fell into the twenty-foot holes.

The traps sprung, the Push Guard shouted and charged from their ambush pockets, spears leveled between circular, warded shields to drive the remaining corelings into the pits.

Arlen roared past his fears as he charged with the others,

caught up in the beautiful madness of Krasia. This was how he imagined the warriors of old, shouting down the instinct to run and hide as they leapt into battle. For a moment, he forgot who and where he was.

But then his spear struck a sand demon and the wards flared to life, streaking silver lightning into the creature. It shrieked in agony, but was swept away by the longer spears to either side of Arlen. Dazzled by the flare of defensive wards, none of the other men even noticed.

Arlen's group drove the two remaining demons they faced into the open pit on their side of the ambush point. The pit's wards were a one-way kind known only in Krasia. Corelings could enter the ring, but not escape. Under the packed dirt of the pit floor lay quarried stone, cutting off their path to the Core and trapping them in the pits until dawn took them.

Looking up, Arlen saw the opposite side was not doing nearly so well. The tarp had snagged as it fell into their pit, leaving some of the wards covered. Before the Pit Warder could clear the block, the two corelings that had fallen in climbed through the gap, killing him.

The Push Guard on the far side of the ambush point had erupted into chaos, faced with five sand demons and lacking a working demon pit to drive them into. There were only ten men in that unit, and the demons were in their midst, slashing and biting.

"Retreat to the pocket!" the *kai'Sharum* on Arlen's side ordered.

"The Core I will!" Arlen cried, charging across to aid the other group. Seeing an outsider display such courage, the *dal'Sharum* followed, the commander shouting at their backs.

Arlen paused only long enough to kick the tarp away from the demon pit and activate the circle. Barely missing a beat, he leapt into the melee, the warded spear alive in his hand.

He stabbed the first demon in the side, and this time the other men could not miss the flash of magic as the weapon struck home. The sand demon fell to the ground, mortally wounded, and Arlen felt a rush of wild energy flow through him.

He caught movement out of the corner of his eye and pivoted, his spear in line to block the razor teeth of another sand demon. The defensive wards along the spear's length activated before the coreling could bite down, locking its mouth open. Arlen gave the spear a sharp twist and the magic flared, snapping the creature's jaw.

A third demon charged, but Arlen's limbs surged with power. He whipped the butt of his spear across, and the wards on its end sheared off half the coreling's face. As it fell, he dropped his shield and twirled the spear in his hands, bringing it down hard to pierce the demon's heart.

Arlen roared and looked about for another demon to fight, but the others had been driven into the pit. All about, men were staring at him in awe.

"What are we waiting for?" he cried, charging into the Maze. "We've *alagai* to hunt!"

The *dal'Sharum,* chanting, "Par'chin! Par'chin!" followed.

Their first encounter was a wind demon that swooped in, tearing the throat from one of Arlen's followers. Before the creature could climb skyward again, Arlen threw his spear, blasting through the coreling's head with a shower of sparks and dropping it to the ground.

Arlen retrieved his weapon and ran on, the wild magic of the spear sweeping him along like a berserker out of legend. As his band scoured the Maze, their numbers grew, and as Arlen slew demon after demon, more and more took up the chant of "Par'chin! Par'chin!"

Forgotten were the warded ambush pockets and escape pits. Gone was the fear and respect of the night. With his metal spear, Arlen seemed invulnerable, and the confidence he exuded was like a drug to the Krasians.

Flushed with the thrill of victory, Arlen felt as if he had broken from a chrysalis, made anew by the ancient weapon. He felt no fatigue, though he had been running and fighting for hours. He felt no pain, though he bore many scrapes and cuts. His thoughts were focused only on the next encounter, the next demon to kill. Each time he felt the surge of magic punch through a coreling's armor, the same thought rang in his head.

Every man must have one.

Jardir appeared before him, and Arlen, covered in demon ichor, thrust the spear high to salute the First Warrior. *"Sharum Ka!"* he cried. "No demon will escape your Maze alive tonight!"

Jardir laughed, thrusting his own spear into the air in response. He came and embraced Arlen like a brother.

"I underestimated you, Par'chin," he said. "I won't do so again."

Arlen smiled. "You say that every time," he replied.

Jardir nodded to the two sand demons Arlen had just slain. "This time, for sure," he promised, returning the grin. Then he turned to the men following Arlen.

"Dal'Sharum!" he called, gesturing to the dead corelings. "Gather up these filthy things and haul them atop the outer wall! Our sling teams need target practice! Let the corelings beyond the walls see the folly of attacking Fort Krasia!"

A cheer rose from the men, and they hastened to his bidding. As they did, Jardir turned to Arlen. "The Watchers report there is still battle in one of the eastern ambush points," he said. "Have you any fight left in you, Par'chin?"

Arlen's smile was feral. "Lead the way," he replied, and the two men ran off, leaving the others to their work.

They sprinted for some time, out to one of the farthest edges of the Maze. "Just ahead," Jardir called, as they banked around a sharp corner into an ambush point. Arlen gave no thought to the quiet, his head filled with the stomp of his feet and the pounding of his blood.

But as he turned the corner, a leg shot out from the side, hooking his foot and sending him sprawling to the ground. He rolled as he struck, keeping a grip on his precious weapon, but by the time he regained his feet, men had blocked the point's only exit.

Arlen looked around in confusion, seeing no sign of demons or fighting. He had found an ambush, but it was not for the corelings.

CHAPTER 21

ONLY A *CHIN*
328 AR

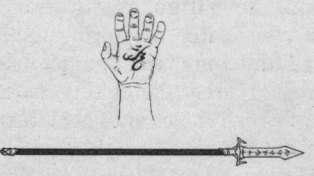

SHARUM MOVED IN TO SURROUND ARLEN: Jardir's elite. Arlen knew them all, men he had supped and laughed with that very evening, and fought beside many times before.

"What is this?" Arlen asked, though in his heart he knew full well.

"The Spear of Kaji belongs in the hands of the Shar'Dama Ka," Jardir replied as he approached. "You are not he."

Arlen clutched the spear as if afraid it might fly from his hands. The men that closed on him were the same warriors he had eaten with a few hours before, but there was no friendship in their eyes now. Jardir had done well in separating him from his supporters.

"It need not be this way," Arlen said, backing away until the demon pit at the point's center was at his heels. Distantly, he noted the hiss of a sand demon trapped within.

"I can make more of these," he went on. "One for every *dal'Sharum*. That's why I came."

"We're capable of doing that ourselves." Jardir smiled, a cold split to his bearded face. His teeth flashed in the moonlight. "You cannot be our savior. You are only a *chin*."

"I don't want to fight you," Arlen said.

"Then don't, my friend," Jardir said softly. "Give me the weapon, take your horse, and go with the dawn, never to return."

Arlen hesitated. He had no doubt Krasia's Warders could replicate the spear as well as he. In no time at all, the Krasians could turn the tide of their Holy War. Thousands of lives saved, thousands of demons killed. Did it matter who took the credit?

But there was more at stake than just credit. The spear was a gift not for Krasia, but for *all* men. Would the Krasians share their knowledge with others? If this scene was anything to go by, Arlen thought not.

"No," he said. "I think I'll have to keep it a little longer. Let me make one for you, and I'll go. You'll never see me again, and you'll have what you want."

Jardir snapped his fingers, and the men closed in on Arlen.

"Please," Arlen begged. "I don't want to hurt any of you."

Jardir's elite warriors laughed at that. They had all devoted their lives to the spear.

But so had Arlen.

"The corelings are the enemy!" he screamed as they charged. "Not me!" But even as he protested, he spun, diverting two spear tips with a twist of his weapon and kicking hard into the ribs of one of the men, sending him crashing into another. He dove into the rush, coming up in their midst, whirling his spear like a staff, refusing to use the point.

He cracked the end across one warrior's face, feeling his jaw break, and dropped low as he followed through, smashing the metal spear like a club into another man's knee. A spear thrust cut the air just above him as the warrior dropped screaming to the ground.

But unlike when he fought the corelings, the weapon now felt heavy in Arlen's hands, the endless energy that had driven him through the Maze extinguished. Against men, it was just a spear. Arlen planted it on the ground and leapt into the air in a high kick to a man's throat. The butt of the spear struck another's stomach, doubling him over. The point gashed a third man's thigh, making him drop his weapon to clutch the wound. Arlen retreated from the responding press, putting the demon pit at his back so they could not surround him.

"Again I underestimate you, though I promised I would not," Jardir said. He waved, and more men came forward to add to the press.

Arlen fought hard, but the outcome was never in doubt. A shaft struck the side of his head, knocking him down, and the warriors fell on him savagely, raining blows upon him until he let go of the spear to cover his head with his arms.

As quickly as that, the beating stopped. Arlen was hauled to his feet, his hands pinned behind him by two thickly muscled

warriors, as he watched Jardir bend over and pick up his spear.
The First Warrior clutched his prize tightly and looked Arlen in
the eyes.

"I am truly sorry, my friend," he said. "I wish there could be
another way."

Arlen spat in his face. "Everam is watching your betrayal!"
he shouted.

Jardir only smiled, wiping the spittle away. "Do not speak of
Everam, *chin*. I am his Sharum Ka, not you. Without me, Krasia falls. Who will miss you, Par'chin? You will not fill so much
as a single tear bottle."

He looked to the men holding Arlen. "Throw him into the pit."

Arlen had not recovered from the shock of impact when Jardir's
own fine spear dropped down to stick quivering in the dirt in
front of him. Looking up the sheer twenty-foot walls of the pit,
he saw the First Warrior looking down on him.

"You lived with honor, Par'chin," Jardir said, "and so you
may keep it in death. Die fighting, and you will awaken in paradise."

Arlen snarled, looking at the sand demon on the other side of
the pit as it rose into a crouch. A low growl issued from its muzzle as it bared rows of razor-sharp teeth.

Arlen rose to his feet, ignoring the pain in his bruised muscles. He reached slowly for the spear, keeping his eyes locked
with the demon's. His stance, neither threatening nor fearful,
confused the creature, and it paced back and forth on all fours,
unsure.

It was possible to kill a sand demon with an unwarded spear.
Their small lidless eyes, normally protected by the bony ridges of
their brow, went wide when they pounced. A precise thrust to that
one vulnerable spot, if driven hard into the brain beyond, could
kill the creature instantly. But demons healed with magical speed,
and an imprecise thrust, or one that did not penetrate fully, would
only enrage it further. Without a shield, in the dim light of the
moon and oil lamps above, it was a nearly impossible task.

While the demon puzzled out his behavior, Arlen began to
slowly drag the point of the spear in the dirt, scratching lines of
warding directly in front of him, the coreling's most likely path.
The creature would quickly find its way around, but it might
buy him time. Stroke by stroke, he cut the symbols into the dirt.

The sand demon drifted back to the pit walls, where the shadows thrown by the lamplight above were greatest. Its tan scales blended with the clay, making it nearly invisible. Only its wide, black eyes stood out, reflecting the scant light back at him.

Arlen saw the attack before it came. The demon's corded muscles bunched and twitched as it tamped down its hind legs. He carefully positioned himself behind his completed wards and then broke eye contact, as if in submission.

With a growl that erupted into a roar, the coreling launched itself at him, more than a hundred pounds of talon, fang, and armored muscle. Arlen waited until it struck the wards, and as soon as they flared to life he thrust hard at the exposed eyes, the demon's momentum adding power to his blow.

Watching from above, the Krasians cheered.

Arlen felt the spear point dig in, but not deeply enough before the thrust and the flare of magic threw the creature back across the pit, shrieking in pain. Arlen glanced at the spear, and saw the point had broken off. He saw it glinting in the moonlight from the demon's eye as it shook off its pain and got its feet back under it. It clawed at its face, and the point came free. Already the bleeding had stopped.

The coreling growled low and began to slither toward him, crawling on its belly across the pit's floor. Arlen let it stalk, racing to complete his semicircle. The demon pounced again, and again the makeshift wards flared, stopping it cold. Arlen thrust again, this time attempting to drive the broken point of the spear down its maw to the more vulnerable flesh of its throat. The coreling was too quick, catching Arlen's spear in its jaws and pulling it from his grasp as it was thrown back again.

"Night," Arlen cursed. His circle was far from complete, and without the spear, he had no hope of finishing it.

Recovering from the blow, the sand demon was completely unprepared as Arlen leapt from behind his wards and tackled it. Above, the spectators roared.

The coreling scratched and bit, but Arlen was quicker, maneuvering behind it to put his forearms under its armpits, locking his fingers behind its head. He drew himself up to his full height, lifting the demon from the ground.

Arlen was larger and heavier than the sand demon, but he could not match the sinewy strength of the coreling as it thrashed. Its muscles felt like the cables used in the quarries of

Miln, and its back claws threatened to cut his legs to ribbons. He swung the creature about, slamming it into the wall of the pit. Before it could recover from the impact, he drew back and slammed it again. His grip was weakening against the powerful creature's onslaught, so he threw his weight about one more time, hurling it into his wards. Magic brightened the pit, jolting the demon on impact, and Arlen snatched up the spear and darted back behind his wards before it could recover.

The enraged demon launched itself at the wards repeatedly, but Arlen quickly completed a makeshift semicircle with the pit wall at his back. There were holes in the net, but he hoped they were too small for the demon to find and squeeze through.

But hope failed a moment later, as the coreling leapt onto the pit wall, its talons digging into the clay. It moved along the side of the wall toward Arlen, bared fangs wet with drool.

Arlen's hasty wards were weak, with a short radius of protection, not much higher than the demon could jump. It wouldn't take the coreling long to realize it could climb above them.

Steeling himself, Arlen placed his foot over the ward nearest the wall, cutting off its magic. He kept his foot an inch off the floor, so as not to scuff the marking. He waited until the demon leapt, then stepped back, uncovering the ward.

The demon was halfway across when the net reactivated, banishing coreling flesh from its line. Half the creature fell into the circle with Arlen. Half dropped with a thump outside.

Even severed from its hindquarters, the coreling clawed and bit at Arlen as he scrambled away, keeping it back with his spear. He crossed the wards, trapping the sand demon's torso in the semicircle, still twitching as it oozed black ichor into the dirt.

Arlen looked up, seeing the Krasians staring at him open-mouthed. He scowled and snapped the spear over his knee. Inspired by the demon, he jabbed the broken end high into the soft clay of the pit wall. He pulled hard, his biceps bulging, and as he began to rise, he swung his other arm up, sticking the spear's broken head farther up the wall.

Hand over hand, Arlen climbed the twenty-foot wall of the pit. He gave no thought to what lay behind, or what waited above. He focused only on the task at hand, ignoring the burning strain of his muscles, the tearing of his flesh.

As he crested the edge of the pit, the Krasians backed away, their eyes wide. Many of them invoked Everam and touched their foreheads and hearts, while others drew wards in the air to protect them as if he were a demon himself.

His limbs like jelly, Arlen struggled to his feet. He looked at the First Warrior through blurry eyes. "If you want me dead," he growled, "you'll have to kill me yourself. There are no more corelings left in the Maze to do your work for you."

Jardir took a step forward, but hesitated at a murmur of disapproval from some of his men. Arlen had proven himself a warrior. Killing him now would not be honorable.

Arlen was counting on that, but before the men had time to think it through, Jardir snapped forward, striking him on the temple with the butt of the warded spear.

Arlen was knocked to the ground, his head ringing and the world spinning, but he spat and put his hands under himself, pushing hard against the ground to regain his feet. He looked up, only to see Jardir moving again. He felt the metal spear strike his face, and knew no more.

CHAPTER 22

PLAY THE HAMLETS
329 AR

ROJER DANCED AS THEY WALKED, four brightly painted wooden balls orbiting his head. Juggling standing still was beyond him, but Rojer Halfgrip had a reputation to maintain, and so he had learned to work around the limitation, moving with fluid grace to keep his crippled hand in position to catch and throw.

Even at fourteen he was small, barely passing five feet, with carrot-red hair, green eyes, and a round face, fair and freckled. He ducked and stretched and turned full circles, his feet moving in tempo with the balls. His soft, split-toed boots were covered in dust from the road, and the cloud he kicked up hung around them, making every breath taste of dry dirt.

"Is it even worth it, if you can't stay still?" Arrick asked irritably. "You look like an amateur, and your audiences won't care for breathing dirt any more than I do."

"I won't be performing in the road," Rojer said.

"In the hamlets you may," Arrick disagreed, "there are no boardwalks there."

Rojer missed a beat, and Arrick stopped as the boy frantically tried to recover. He regained control of the balls eventually, but Arrick still tsked.

"With no boardwalks, how do they stop demons rising inside the walls?" Rojer asked.

"No walls, either," Arrick said. "Maintaining a net around even a small hamlet would take a dozen Warders. If a village has two and an apprentice, they count themselves lucky."

Rojer swallowed back the taste of bile in his mouth, feeling faint. Screams over a decade old rang out in his head, and he stumbled, falling on his backside as balls rained down on him. He slapped his crippled hand against the dirt angrily.

"Best leave juggling to me and focus on other skills," Arrick said. "If you spent half the time practicing singing as you do juggling, you might last three notes before your voice breaks."

"You always said, 'A Jongleur who can't juggle is no Jongleur at all,' " Rojer said.

"Never mind what I said!" Arrick snapped. "Do you think Jasin ripping Goldentone juggles? You've got talent. Once we build your name, you'll have apprentices to juggle for you."

"Why would I want someone to do my tricks for me?" Rojer asked, picking up the balls and slipping them into the pouch at his waist. As he did, he caressed the reassuring lump of his talisman, tucked safely away in its secret pocket, drawing strength.

"Because petty tricks aren't where the money is, boy," Arrick said, drawing on his ever-present wineskin. "Jugglers make klats. Build a name, and you earn soft Milnese gold, like I used to." He drank again, more deeply this time. "But to build a name, you have to play the hamlets."

"Goldentone never played the hamlets," Rojer said.

"Exactly my point!" Arrick shouted, gesticulating wildly. "His uncle might be able to pull strings in Angiers, but he has no sway in the hamlets. When we make your name, we're going to bury him!"

"He's no match for Sweetsong and Halfgrip," Rojer said quickly, placing his master's name first, though the buzz on the streets of Angiers of late had them reversed.

"Yes!" Arrick shouted, clicking his heels and dancing a quick jig.

Rojer had deflected Arrick's irritation in time. His master had become increasingly prone to fits of rage over the last few years, drinking more and more as Rojer's moon waxed and his own waned. His song was no longer so sweet, and he knew it.

"How far to Cricket Run?" Rojer asked.

"We should be there by lunchtime tomorrow," Arrick said.

"I thought the hamlets could only be a day apart," Rojer asked.

Arrick grunted. "The duke's decree was that villages stand no farther apart than a man *on a good horse* might go in a day," he said. "A fair bit farther than you get on foot."

Rojer's hopes fell. Arrick really meant to spend a night on the road with nothing between them and the corelings but Geral's old portable circle, which hadn't seen use in a decade.

But Angiers was no longer entirely safe for them. As their popularity grew, Master Jasin had taken a special interest in thwarting them. His apprentices had broken Arrick's arm the year previous, and stolen the take more than once after a big show. Between that and Arrick's drinking and whoring, he and Rojer rarely had two klats to click together. Perhaps the hamlets could indeed offer better fortune.

Making a name in the hamlets was a rite of passage for Jongleurs, and had seemed a grand adventure while they were safe in Angiers. Now Rojer looked at the sky and swallowed hard.

Rojer sat on a stone, sewing a bright patch onto his cloak. Like his other clothes, the original cloth had long since worn away, replaced a patch at a time until only the patches remained.

"Settup th'circle when yur done, boy," Arrick said, wobbling a bit. His wineskin was nearly empty. Rojer looked at the setting sun and winced, moving quickly to comply.

The circle was small, only ten feet in diameter. Just big enough for two men to lie with a fire between them. Rojer put a stake at the center of the camp and used a five-foot string hooked to it to draw a smooth circle in the dirt. He laid the portable circle out along its perimeter, using a straightstick to insure that the warded plates lined up properly, but he was no Warder, and couldn't be sure he had done it right.

When he was finished, Arrick stumbled over to inspect his work.

"Looksh right," his master slurred, barely glancing at the circle. Rojer felt a chill on his spine and went over everything again to be sure, and a third time, to be positive. Still, he was uneasy as he built a fire and prepared supper, the sun dipping ever lower.

Rojer had never seen a demon. At least, not that he remembered clearly. The clawed hand that had burst through his parents' door was etched forever in his mind, but the rest, even the coreling that had crippled him, was only a haze of smoke and teeth and horn.

His blood ran cold as the woods began to cast long shadows on the road. It wasn't long before a ghostlike form rose up out of the ground not far from their fire. The wood demon was no bigger than an average man, with knobbed and barklike skin stretched hard over wiry sinew. The creature saw their fire and roared, throwing back its horned head and revealing rows of sharp teeth. It flexed its claws, limbering them for killing. Other shapes flitted on the edge of the firelight, slowly surrounding them.

Rojer's eyes flicked to Arrick, who was drawing hard on his wineskin. He had hoped that his master, who had slept in portable circles before, might be calm, but the fear in Arrick's eyes said differently. With a shaking hand, Rojer reached into his secret pocket and took out his talisman, gripping it tightly.

The wood demon lowered its horns and charged, and something surfaced in Rojer's mind, a memory long suppressed. Suddenly he was three years old, watching over his mother's shoulder as death approached.

It all came back to him in that instant. His father taking up the poker and standing his ground with Geral to buy time for his mother and Arrick to escape with him. Arrick shoving them aside as he ran to the bolt-hole. The bite that took his fingers. His mother's sacrifice.

I love you!

Rojer gripped the talisman, and felt his mother's spirit around him like a physical presence. He trusted it to protect him more than the wards as the coreling bore down on them.

The demon struck the wards hard. Rojer and Arrick both jumped as the magic flared. Geral's web was etched in silver fire in the air for a brief instant, and the coreling was thrown back, stunned.

Relief was short-lived. The sound and light drew the attention of other woodies, and they charged in turn, testing the net from all sides.

But Geral's lacquered wards held fast. One by one or in groups, the wood demons were thrown back, forced to circle angrily, searching in vain for weaknesses.

But even as corelings continued to throw themselves at him, Rojer's mind was in another place. Again and again he saw his parents die, his father burned and his mother drowning the flame demon before shoving him into the bolt-hole. And over and over, he saw Arrick shove them aside.

Arrick had killed his mother. As surely as if he had done the deed himself. Rojer brought the talisman to his lips, kissing her red hair.

"What's that you're holding?" Arrick asked softly, when it became clear the demons could not break through.

At any other time, Rojer would have felt a stab of panic at his talisman's discovery, but he was in a different place now, reliving a nightmare and desperately trying to sort out what it meant. Arrick had been like a father to him for over ten years. Could these memories really be true?

He opened his hand, letting Arrick see the tiny wooden doll with its bright red hair. "My mum," he said.

Arrick looked sadly at the doll, and something in his expression told Rojer all he needed to know. His memory was true. Angry words came to Rojer's lips, and he tensed, ready to charge his master, throw him from the circle and let the corelings have him.

Arrick lowered his eyes and cleared his throat, beginning to sing. His voice, soured by years of drink, took on something of its old sweetness as he sang a soft lullaby, one that tickled Rojer's memory just as the sight of the wood demon had. Suddenly he remembered how Arrick had held him in the very circle they now sat in, singing the same lullaby as Riverbridge burned.

Like his talisman, the song wrapped itself around Rojer, reminding him how safe it had made him feel that night. Arrick had been a coward, it was true, but he had honored Kally's request to take care of him, though it had cost him his royal commission and ruined his career.

He tucked his talisman away in its secret pocket and stared out into the night as images over a decade old flashed in his mind and he tried desperately to make sense of them.

Eventually, Arrick's singing trailed off, and Rojer pulled himself from contemplation and fetched their cooking utensils. They fried sausages and tomatoes in a small skillet, eating them with hard, crusty bread. After supper, they practiced. Rojer took out his fiddle, and Arrick wet his lips with the last drops from his wineskin. They faced one another, doing their best to ignore the corelings stalking about the circle.

Rojer began to play, and all his doubts and fears fell away as the vibration of the strings became his world. He caressed a melody forth, and nodded when he was ready. Arrick joined him with a soft hum, waiting for another nod before beginning to sing. They played thus for some time, falling into a comfortable harmony honed by years of practice and performance.

Much later, Arrick broke off suddenly, looking around.

"What is it?" Rojer asked.

"I don't think a demon has struck the wards since we started," Arrick said.

Rojer stopped playing, looking out into the night. It was true, he realized, wondering how he hadn't noticed it before. The wood demons were crouched about the circle, motionless, but as Rojer met the eyes of one, it sprang at him.

Rojer screamed and fell back as the coreling struck the wards and was repelled. All around them the magic flared as the rest of the creatures shook off their daze and attacked.

"It was the music!" Arrick said. "The music held them back!"

Seeing the confused look on the boy's face, Arrick cleared his throat, and began to sing.

His voice was strong, and carried far down the road, drowning out the demon roars with its beautiful sound, but it did nothing to keep the demons at bay. On the contrary, the corelings shrieked all the louder and clawed at the barrier, as if desperate to silence him.

Arrick's thick eyebrows furrowed, and he changed tune, singing the last song he and Rojer had been practicing, but the corelings still swiped at the wards. Rojer felt a stab of fear. What if the demons found a weakness in the wards, like they had . . .

"The fiddle, boy!" Arrick called. Rojer looked dumbly down at the fiddle and bow still clutched in his hands. "Play it, fool!" Arrick commanded.

But Rojer's crippled hand shook, and the bow touched string with a piercing whine, like fingernails on slate. The corelings shrieked, and backed a step away. Emboldened, Rojer played more jarring and sour notes, driving the demons farther and farther off. They howled and put clawed hands to their heads as if in pain.

But they did not flee. The demons backed away from the circle slowly until they found a tolerable distance. There they waited, black eyes reflecting the firelight.

The sight chilled Rojer's heart. They knew he couldn't play forever.

Arrick had not been exaggerating when he said they would be treated as heroes in the hamlets. The people of Cricket Run had no Jongleurs of their own, and many remembered Arrick from his time as the duke's herald, a decade gone.

There was a small inn for housing cattle drivers and produce farmers heading to and from Woodsend and Shepherd's Dale, and they were welcomed there and given free room and board. The whole town showed up to watch them perform, drinking enough ale to more than repay the innkeep. In fact, everything went flawlessly, until it came time to pass the hat.

"An ear of corn!" Arrick shouted, shaking it in Rojer's face. "Whar we sposa to do wi'that?"

"We could always eat it," Rojer offered. His master glared at him and continued to pace.

Rojer had liked Cricket Run. The people there were simple and good-hearted, and knew how to enjoy life. In Angiers, crowds pressed close to hear his fiddle, nodding and clapping, but he had never seen folk so quick to dance as the Runners. Before his fiddle was halfway from its case, they were backing up, making room. Before long, they were reeling and spinning and laughing uproariously, embracing his music fully and flowing wherever it took them.

They cried without shame at Arrick's sad ballads, and laughed hysterically at their bawdy jokes and mummery. They were, in Rojer's estimation, everything one could ask in an audience.

When the act was over, chants of "Sweetsong and Halfgrip!" were deafening. They were inundated with offers of lodging, and the wine and food overflowed. Rojer was swept behind a haystack by a pair of raven-eyed Runner girls, sharing kisses until his head spun.

Arrick was less pleased.

"How could I have forgotten what it was like?" he lamented.

He was referring, of course, to the collection hat. There was no coin in the hamlets, or little enough. What there was went for necessities, seed and tools and wardposts. A pair of wooden klats settled to the bottom of the hat, but that wasn't even enough to pay for the wine Arrick had drunk on the journey from Angiers. For the most part, the Runners paid in grain, with the occasional bag of salt or spice thrown in.

"Barter!" Arrick spat the word like a curse. "No vintner in Angiersh will take payment in bagsh of barley!"

The Runners had paid in more than just grain. They gave gifts of salted meat and fresh bread, a horn of clotted cream and a basket of fruit. Warm quilts. Fresh patches for their boots. Whatever good or service they could spare was offered with gratitude. Rojer hadn't eaten so well since the duke's palace, and for the life of him he could not understand his master's distress. What was coin for, if not to buy the very things that the Runners gave in abundance?

"Leasht they had wine," Arrick grumbled. Rojer eyed the skin nervously as his master took a pull, knowing it would only amplify Arrick's distress, but he said nothing. No amount of wine could distress Arrick so much as the suggestion that he should not drink so much wine.

"I liked it there," Rojer dared. "I wish we could have stayed longer."

"What d'you know?" Arrick snapped. "You're jussa stupid boy." He groaned as if in pain. "Woodsend'll be no better," he lamented, looking down the road, "and Sheepshagger's Dale'll be worsht of all! What wash I thinking, keeping this stupid circle?"

He kicked at the precious plates of the portable circle, knocking the wards askew, but he did not seem to notice or care, stumbling drunkenly about the fire.

Rojer gasped. Sunset was mere moments away, but he said nothing, darting over to the spot and frantically correcting the damage, glancing fearfully at the horizon.

He finished not a moment too soon. The corelings rose as he was still smoothing the rope. He fell back as the first coreling leapt at him, crying out as the wards flared to life.

"Damn you!" Arrick screamed at a demon as it charged him. The drunken Jongleur stuck his chin out in defiance and cackled as the coreling smashed against the wardnet.

"Master, please," Rojer begged, taking Arrick's arm and pulling him toward the center of the ring.

"Oh, Halfgrip knowsh besht, now?" he sneered, yanking his arm away and almost falling down in the process. "Poor drunk Shweetsong dun't know t'keep away from coreling clawsh?"

"It's not like that," Rojer protested.

"Then wha's it like?" Arrick demanded. "Y'think tha' 'cos the crowds cheer yur name that y'd be anything without me?"

"No," Rojer said.

"Damn right," Arrick muttered, pulling again on his skin and stumbling away.

Rojer's throat tightened, and he reached into his secret pocket for his talisman. He rubbed the smooth wood and silky hair with his thumb, trying to call upon its power.

"Tha's right, call yer mum!" Arrick shouted, turning back and pointing at the little doll. "F'get who raised you, who taught you everything y'know! I gave up my life for you!"

Rojer gripped his talisman tighter, feeling his mother's presence, hearing her last words. He thought again of how Arrick had shoved her to the ground, and an angry lump formed in his throat. "No," he said. "You were the only one who didn't."

Arrick scowled and advanced on the boy. Rojer shrank back, but the circle was small, and there was nowhere to go. Outside the circle, demons paced hungrily.

"Gimme that!" Arrick shouted angrily, grabbing at Rojer's hands.

"It's mine!" Rojer cried. They struggled for a moment, but Arrick was larger and stronger, and had two full hands. He snatched the talisman away at last and threw it into the fire.

"No!" Rojer shouted, diving toward the flames, but it was too late. The red hair ignited immediately, and before he could find a twig to fish the talisman out, the wood caught. Rojer knelt in the dirt and watched it burn, dumbfounded. His hands began to shake.

Arrick ignored him, stumbling up to a wood demon that was hunched at the circle's edge, clawing at the wards. "It's your fault thish happened t'me!" he screamed. "Your fault I wash shaddled with an ungrateful boy and lost my commishon! Yoursh!"

The coreling shrieked at him, revealing rows of razor-sharp teeth. Arrick roared right back, smashing his wineskin over the creature's head. The skin burst, spraying them both with blood-red wine and tanned leather.

"My wine!" Arrick cried, realizing suddenly what he had done. He moved to cross the wards as if he could in some way undo the damage.

"Master, no!" Rojer cried. He dove into a tumble, reaching up with his good hand to grab Arrick's ratty ponytail as he kicked at the backs of his master's knees. Arrick was yanked back away from the wards and landed heavily atop his apprentice.

"Get'cher handsh offa me!" Arrick cried, not realizing that Rojer had just saved his life. He gripped the boy's shirt as he lurched to his feet, shoving him right out of the circle.

Coreling and human alike froze in that moment. Awareness dawned on Arrick's face even as a wood demon shrieked in triumph and tamped down, launching itself at the boy.

Rojer screamed and fell back, having no hope of getting back across the wards in time. He brought up his hands in a feeble attempt to fend the creature off, but before the coreling struck, there was a cry, and Arrick tackled the demon, knocking it away.

"Get back to the circle!" Arrick cried. The demon roared and struck back hard, launching the Jongleur through the air. He bounced as he hit the ground, a flailing limb snagging the rope of the portable circle and pulling the plates out of alignment.

All around the clearing, other corelings began to race to the breach. They were both going to die, Rojer realized. The first demon made to charge at him again, but again Arrick grabbed at it, turning it aside.

"Your fiddle!" he cried. "You can drive them back!" As the words left his lips, though, the coreling's talons dug deep into his chest, and he spit a thick bubble of blood.

"Master!" Rojer screamed. He glanced at his fiddle doubtfully.

"Save yourself!" Arrick gasped just before the demon tore out his throat.

By the time dawn banished the demons back to the Core, the fingers of Rojer's good hand were cut and bleeding. It was only with great effort that he straightened them and released the fiddle.

He had played through the long night, cowering in the darkness as the fire died, sending discordant notes into the air to keep at bay the corelings he knew were waiting in thc black.

There had been no beauty, no melody to fall into as he played, just screeches and dissonance; nothing to turn his thoughts from the horror around him. But now, looking at the scattered bits of flesh and bloody cloth that were all that remained of his master, a new horror struck, and he fell to his knees, retching.

After a time, his heaving eased, and he stared at his cramped and bloody hands, willing them to stop shaking. He felt flushed and hot, but his face was cold in the morning air, drained of blood. His stomach continued to roil, but there was nothing left in it to expel. He wiped his mouth with a motley sleeve and forced himself to rise.

He tried to collect enough of Arrick to bury, but there was little to be found. A clump of hair. A boot, torn open to get at the meat within. Blood. Corelings disdained neither bone nor offal, and they had fed in a frenzy.

The Tenders taught that corelings ate their victims body and soul, but Arrick had always said Holy Men were bigger liars than Jongleurs, and his master could spin a whopper. Rojer thought of his talisman, and the feeling of his mother's spirit it brought. How could he feel her if her soul had been consumed?

He looked to the cold ashes of the fire. The little doll was there, blackened and split, but it crumbled away in his hands. Not far away, lying in the dirt, were the remains of Arrick's ponytail. Rojer took the hair, more gray than gold now, and put it in his pocket.

He would make a new talisman.

Woodsend came into sight well before dusk, much to Rojer's relief. He didn't think he had the strength to last another night outside.

He had thought of turning back to Cricket Run and begging passage with a Messenger back to Angiers, but it would have meant explaining what happened, and Rojer wasn't ready for that. Besides, what was there for him in Angiers? Without a license, he couldn't perform, and Arrick had made enemies of any that might have completed his apprenticeship. Better to keep on to the ends of the world, where no one would know him and the guild could not reach.

Like Cricket Run, Woodsend was filled with good, solid folk who welcomed a Jongleur with open arms, too pleased to question the fortune that had brought an entertainer to their town.

Rojer accepted their hospitality with gratitude. He felt a fraud, claiming to be a Jongleur when he was only an unlicensed apprentice, but he doubted the Enders would care much if they knew. Would they refuse to dance to his fiddle, or laugh less at his mummery?

But Rojer didn't dare touch the colored balls in the bag of marvels, and begged off from song. He flipped instead, tumbling and hand walking, using everything in his repertoire to hide his inadequacies.

The Enders didn't press him, and that was enough for now.

CHAPTER 23

REBIRTH
328 AR

THE BRIGHT SUN BROUGHT Arlen back to consciousness. Sand stuck to his face as he lifted his head and spit grit from his mouth. Struggling to his knees, he looked around, but all he saw was sand.

They had carried him out onto the dunes and left him to die.

"Cowards!" he cried. "Letting the desert do your work does not absolve you!"

He quivered on his knees, trying to find the strength to stand while his body screamed at him to lie back down and die. His head was spinning.

He had come to help the Krasians. How could they betray him like this?

Don't lie to yourself, a voice in his head said. *You've done your share of betrayal. You ran from your father when he needed you most. Abandoned Cob before your apprenticeship was up. Left Ragen and Elissa without so much as an embrace. And Mery . . .*

"Who will miss you, Par'chin?" Jardir had asked. "You will not fill so much as a single tear bottle."

And he was right.

If he were to die here, Arlen knew, the only ones who were likely to notice would be merchants more concerned with a loss of profit than his life. Perhaps this was what he deserved for abandoning everyone who had ever loved him. Perhaps he *should* just lie down and die.

His knees buckled. The sand seemed to pull at him, calling him to its embrace. He was about to give in when something caught his eye.

A few feet away, a skin of water rested in the sand. Had Jardir's conscience gotten the better of him, or had one of his men looked back and taken pity on the betrayed Messenger?

Arlen crawled to the skin, clutching it like a lifeline. Someone might mourn him after all.

But it made little difference. Even if he returned to Krasia, no one would believe a *chin* over the Sharum Ka. On Jardir's word, the *dal'Sharum* would kill Arlen without a thought.

So you should let them keep the spear you risked your life for? he asked himself. *Let them keep Dawn Runner, your portable circles, and everything else you own?*

The thought had Arlen clutching at his waist, and he realized with relief that he had not lost everything. There, still safe, was the simple leather bag he carried when fighting in the Maze. In it he kept a small warding kit, his herb pouch . . . and his notebook.

The notebook changed everything. Arlen had lost his other books, but all of them together were not worth this one. Since the day he left Miln, Arlen had copied every new ward he had learned into his notebook.

Including those on the spear.

Let them keep the ripping thing, they want it so much, Arlen thought. *I can make another.*

With a heave, he brought himself to his feet. He took the warm skin of water and allowed himself a short pull, then put it over his shoulder and climbed to the top of the nearest dune.

Shielding his eyes, he could see Krasia like a mirage in the distance, giving him bearings to head for the Oasis of Dawn. Without his horse, the trip would mean a week of sleeping unwarded in the desert. His water would be gone long before then, but he doubted it would matter. The sand demons would get him before he died of thirst.

Arlen chewed hogroot as he walked. It was bitter and made his stomach churn, but he was covered in demon scratches, and it helped keep them from infecting. Besides, without food, even nausea was preferable to pangs of hunger.

He drank sparingly, though his throat was dry and swollen. His shirt was tied around his head to ward off the sun, leaving his back vulnerable. His skin was blotched yellow and blue from the beating he had taken, and burned red atop that. Every step was agony.

Arlen kept moving until the sun was nearly set. He felt as if he had made no progress at all, but the long line of tracks blowing away behind him showed a surprising distance covered.

Night came, bringing corelings and bitter cold. Either was enough to kill him, so Arlen hid from both, burying himself in the sand to preserve body heat and hide from the demons. He tore a sheet from his notebook, rolling the paper into a slender breathing tube, but still he felt as if he were suffocating as he lay, terrified that the corelings might find him. When the sun rose and warmed the sand, he dug free of his sandy grave and stumbled on, feeling as if he had not rested at all.

So it went, day after day, night after night. He grew weaker as the days went by without food, rest, or more than a splash of water. His skin cracked and bled, but he ignored the damage and walked on. The sun beat down with increasing weight, and the flat horizon grew no closer.

At some point, he lost his boots. He wasn't sure how or when. His feet were scraped raw from the hot sand, bleeding and blistered. He tore the sleeves from his shirt to bind them.

He fell with increasing frequency, sometimes getting right back to his feet, other times passing out and rising minutes or hours later. Sometimes, he would fall and continue tumbling all the way down a dune. Exhausted, he took it as a blessing, saving himself painful steps.

By the time the water ran out, he had lost count of the days. He was still on the desert path, but had no idea how far there was yet to go. His lips were split and dry, and even his cuts and blisters had ceased to ooze, as if all the liquid in his body had evaporated.

He fell again, and struggled to find a reason to get back up.

Arlen awoke with a start, his face wet. It was nighttime, and that should have filled him with terror, but he lacked the strength to fear.

He looked down, and saw that his face had been resting on the edge of the pool in the Oasis of Dawn, his hand in the water.

He wondered how he had gotten to be there. His last memory . . . he had no idea what his last memory was. The trip through the desert was a blur, but he didn't care. He had made it. That was all that mattered. Within the warded obelisks of the oasis, he was safe.

Arlen drank greedily from the pool. A moment later, he vomited it up, and forced himself to sip slowly after that. When his thirst was quenched, he closed his eyes again, and slept soundly for the first time in over a week.

When he woke, Arlen raided the oasis' stores. There were supplies as well as food: blankets, herbs, a spare warding kit. Too weak to forage, he spent several days simply eating the dried stores, drinking cool water, and cleansing his wounds. By then, he was able to gather fresh fruit. After a week, he found the strength to fish. Two, he could stand and stretch without pain.

The oasis had stores enough to get him out of the desert. He might be half dead when he crawled from the scorched clay flats, but he would be half alive, as well.

There were a handful of spears in the oasis' stores, but compared to the magnificent metal weapon he had lost, sharpened wood seemed woefully inadequate. Without lacquer to harden the symbols, carved wards would mar with the first thrust through hard coreling scales.

What, then? He had wards that could burn the life from demons, but what good were they without a weapon to affix them to?

He considered painting stones with the attack wards. He could throw them, or even press them against the corelings by hand . . .

Arlen laughed. If he was going to get that close to a demon, he might as well paint the wards right onto his hands.

His laughter died as the thought germinated. Could it work? If so, he would have a weapon no one could steal, one no coreling could knock from his grasp or catch him without.

Arlen took out his notebook, studying the wards on the spear's tip, and those at its butt. Those were the offensive wards; the wards on the shaft were defensive. He noted that the wards on the butt did not form a line by linking with others, as did the wards along the edge of the tip. They stood alone, the same symbol repeated around the circumference of the spear, and on the flat of its end. Perhaps the difference was one of cutting versus bludgeoning.

As the sun dipped lower, Arlen copied the bludgeoning ward in the dirt, over and over, until he felt confident. He took a brush and a paint bowl from his warding kit, carefully painting the ward onto the palm of his left hand. He blew on it softly until it was dry.

Painting his right hand was trickier, but Arlen knew from experience that with concentration, he could ward equally well with his left hand, though it took longer.

As darkness descended, Arlen gently flexed his hands, making sure the movement would not crack or peel the paint. Satisfied, he went to the stone obelisks that warded the oasis, watching the demons circle the barrier, smelling prey just beyond their reach.

The first coreling to catch sight of him was a specimen of no particular note: a sand demon about four feet in length, with long arms and bunched, muscular legs. Its barbed tail slithered back and forth as it met Arlen's eyes.

A moment later, it launched itself at the wardnet. As it leapt, Arlen stepped aside and reached out, partially covering two wards. The net broke and the coreling tumbled past him, confused at the lack of resistance. He quickly drew his hand back, reestablishing the net. Whatever happened, the demon would not survive. Either it would perish fighting Arlen, or it would kill him and die when the sun rose and it could not escape the heavily warded oasis.

The demon righted itself and turned back, hissing as it bared rows of teeth. It circled, its corded muscles tensing as its tail flicked sharply. Then, with a catlike roar, it pounced again.

Arlen met it head-on, holding his hands with palms out, his arms longer than the demon's. The creature's scaled chest struck the wards, and with a flash and a howl of agony, the coreling was thrown back. It struck the ground hard, and Arlen could see thin wisps of smoke rising from the point of contact. He smiled.

The demon got back to its feet and began circling again, this time more cautiously. It was unaccustomed to prey fighting back, but it soon regained its courage, leaping to the attack again.

Arlen caught the coreling's wrists and fell back, kicking it in the stomach and flipping it over him. As he made contact, the wards flared, and he could feel the magic working. It did not burn him, though the coreling's flesh sizzled at the touch, but there was a tingle of energy in his hands, as if they had lost circulation and gone prickly. The feeling shot up his arms like a shiver.

They both rose quickly, and Arlen returned the coreling's growl with one of his own. The demon licked at its scorched wrists, trying to soothe them, and Arlen could see grudging respect in its eyes. Respect and fear. This time, *he* was the predator.

His confidence was almost the death of him. The demon shrieked and lunged, and this time, Arlen was too slow. Black talons raked across his chest as he tried to twist out of the way.

He punched out in desperation, forgetting that the wards were on his palms. His knuckles scraped against the coreling's gritty scales, tearing skin, but the blow had little effect. With a backhanded swat, the sand demon sent him sprawling to the ground.

The next moments were desperate, as Arlen scrambled and rolled to avoid its slashing claws, razor teeth, and whipping spiked tail. He started to rise, but the demon coiled and pounced on him, bearing him back to the ground. Arlen managed to get his knee between them, holding the creature back, but its hot, fetid breath washed across his face as its fangs closed not an inch from his face.

Arlen bared his own teeth in as he boxed the demon's ears. The coreling shrieked in pain as the wards flared, but Arlen held on tightly. Smoke began to drift from the grip as the light brightened. The demon thrashed madly, claws tearing at him in a desperate attempt to escape.

But Arlen had it now, and he would not let go. Every moment he held on, the tingling in his palms grew in intensity, as if gaining momentum. He squeezed his hands together, and was amazed when they grew closer, as if the creature's skull was softening, liquefying.

The coreling's assault slowed, and Arlen rolled to the side, reversing the pin. The demon's claws closed weakly about his arms, trying to pull them away, but it was no use.

With a final flex of his muscles, Arlen brought his hands together, crushing the coreling's head in an explosion of gore.

CHAPTER 24

NEEDLES
AND INK
328 AR

ARLEN COULDN'T SLEEP THAT NIGHT, though it was not from the throbbing of his wounds. All his life he had dreamt of the heroes in Jongleurs' tales, donning armor and fighting corelings with warded weapons. When he found the spear, he thought that dream was within his grasp, but when he reached for it, it slipped through his fingers and he stumbled into something new.

Nothing, not even that night in the Maze when he had felt invincible, could compare with the sensation of facing a coreling on its own terms and feeling the tingle in his flesh as his magic burned its life away. He hungered for that feeling again, and that hunger put all his former desires in a new light.

Looking back at his visit to Krasia, Arlen realized that it wasn't as magnanimous as he had believed. Whatever he had told himself, he had wanted to be more than a weaponsmith, or one fighter among many. He had wanted glory. Fame. He had wanted to go down in the histories as the man who had given men back the fight.

As the Deliverer, even?

The thought disturbed him. For the salvation of humanity to mean anything, for it to last, it had to come from everyone, not just one man.

But did humanity even *want* to be saved? Did they deserve it? Arlen didn't know anymore. Men like his father had lost the will to fight, content to hide behind wards, and what he had seen in Krasia, what he now saw in himself, made Arlen wonder about those who had not.

There could never be peace between Arlen and the corelings. He knew in his heart he could never sit safe behind his wards and let them dance in peace now that he had another choice. But who would stand by his side and fight? Jeph had struck him at the idea. Elissa had scolded him. Mery had shunned him. The Krasians had tried to kill him.

Ever since the night he had seen Jeph watch his wife be cored from the safety of his porch wards, Arlen had known that the corelings' greatest weapon was fear. What he hadn't understood was that fear took many forms. For all his attempts to prove otherwise, Arlen was terrified of being alone. He wanted someone, anyone, to believe in what he was doing. Someone to fight with, and for.

But there was no one. He saw that now. If he wanted companionship, he would have to slink back to the cities and accept it on their terms. If he wanted to fight, he had to do it alone.

The sense of power and elation, so fresh in his mind, faded. He curled up slowly, gripping his knees, and stared out over the desert, looking for a road where there was none.

Arlen rose with the sun and padded to the pool to rinse his wounds. He had stitched and poulticed them before bedding down, but one could never be too careful with wounds from a coreling. As he splashed the cool water on his face, his tattoo caught his eye.

All Messengers had tattoos, marking their city of origin. It was a symbol of how far they had traveled. Arlen remembered that first day when Ragen showed him his, the city in the mountains that graced the flag of Miln. Arlen had meant to get that same tattoo when he completed his first job. He went to a tattooist, ready to be marked forever a Messenger, but he had hesitated. Fort Miln was home to him in many ways, but it was not where he had come from.

Tibbet's Brook had no flag, so Arlen took the crest of Earl Tibbet himself, lush fields split by a stream that fed a small lake. The tattooist took his needles and imprinted that reminder of home on Arlen's shoulder for all time.

For all time. The notion lingered in Arlen's mind. He had watched the tattooist closely. The man's art was not so different from that of a Warder: precise markings, painstakingly placed with no room for error. There were needles in Arlen's herb pouch, and ink in his warding kit.

Arlen started a small fire, recalling every moment spent with the tattooist. He passed his needles through the flames, and poured a bit of thick, viscous ink into a small bowl. He wrapped thread about the needles to prevent them from piercing too deeply, and carefully studied the contours of his left hand, noticing every wrinkle and shift as it flexed. When he was ready, he took a needle, dipped it in the ink, and set to work.

It was slow going. He was forced to pause frequently to wipe his palm clear of blood and excess ink. He had nothing but time, though, so he worked with care, his hand steady. By midmorning, he was satisfied with his warding. He poulticed the hand and wrapped it carefully, then went about replenishing the oasis' stores. He worked hard the rest of the day, and the day after that, knowing that he would need as much as he could carry before he left.

Arlen remained in the oasis for another week, warding his skin in the mornings and gathering food in the afternoons. The tattoos on his palms healed rapidly, but Arlen did not stop there. Remembering the skinned knuckles from punching the sand demon, he warded those of his left hand, waiting only for the scabs on his right to fall away before he did those as well. No coreling would ever shrug away one of his punches again.

As he worked, he ran through his battle with the sand demon repeatedly, remembering how it moved, its strength and speed, the nature of its attacks, and the signals that heralded them. He made careful notes of his recollections, studying them and considering how his reactions could have been better. He could not afford to stumble anymore.

The Krasians had honed the brutal yet precise moves of *sharusahk* into an art form. He began to adapt the moves, and the placement of his tattoos, so the two would act as one.

When Arlen finally left the Oasis of Dawn, he ignored the path entirely, cutting straight across the sand toward the lost city of Anoch Sun. He took as much dried food as he could carry. Anoch Sun had a well, but no food, and he planned to be there for some time.

Even as he left, Arlen knew that his water would not last all the way to the lost city. Spare skins at the oasis were few, and it might take as much as two weeks to reach the city on foot. His water wouldn't last a week.

But never once did he look back. *There's nothing behind me,* he thought. *I can only go forward.*

As dusk spread darkness across the sand, Arlen took a deep breath and continued on, not bothering to set camp. The stars were clear over the cloudless desert, and it was easy to keep his sense of direction; easier, in fact, than it was during the day.

There were few corelings so far out in the desert. They tended to congregate where there was prey, and prey was scarce on the barren sands. Arlen walked for hours in the cold moonlight before a demon caught his scent. He heard its cries long before the creature appeared, but he did not flee, for he knew it could track him, nor did he try to hide, for he had much farther to go that night. He stood his ground as the sand demon came bounding over the dunes.

When Arlen met the creature's gaze calmly, the coreling paused, confused. It growled at him, clawing the sand, but Arlen only smiled. It roared a challenge, but Arlen did not react at all. Instead, he focused on his surroundings: the flashes of movement in the periphery of his vision; the whisper of the wind and the scrape of sand; the scent upon the cold night air.

Sand demons hunted in packs. Arlen had never seen one of them alone before, and he doubted this one was now. Sure enough, while his attention had been fixed upon the snarling, shrieking creature before him, two more demons, as silent as death, had circled around to either side, nearly invisible in the darkness. Arlen pretended not to notice them, keeping eye contact with the coreling in front of him as it drew closer and closer.

The attack came, as expected, not from the posturing sand demon before him, but from those off to the sides. Arlen was impressed with the cunning the corelings showed. Out on the sands, he supposed, where one could see far in every direction and the slightest sound could carry miles on the wind, it was necessary to develop instincts for misdirection when on the hunt.

But while Arlen had not yet become the hunter, neither was he easy prey. As the two sand demons leapt at him from either side, foretalons reaching, he darted forward, toward the demon that had been serving as the distraction.

The two attacking demons veered off, barely avoiding a collision, while the other backed away in surprise. It was fast, but not as fast as Arlen's left hook. The wards on his knuckles flared, a sizzling blow that rocked the demon back on its heels, but Arlen did not stop there. He snapped his right hand onto the coreling's face, pressing the ward tattooed on his palm against its eyes. The ward activated, burning, and the creature shrieked and lashed out blindly.

Anticipating the move, Arlen threw himself backward. He hit the ground in a roll and came back up a few feet away from the blinded creature, facing the other two corelings as they launched themselves his way.

Again, Arlen was impressed. Not to be fooled twice, the corelings did not attack in unison, staggering their strikes so he could not play them against one another.

The tactic worked against the demons, though, for it allowed Arlen to focus upon them one at a time. As the first reached for him, he stepped right up, inside its grasp, and boxed its ears. The explosion of magic collapsed the demon to the sand, where it shrieked and writhed in agony, clutching at its head.

The second demon was close behind the first, and Arlen had no time to dodge or strike. Instead, remembering another trick from the last encounter, he caught the creature's wrists and threw himself onto his back, kicking upward. The sharp scales of the sand demon's abdomen cut through the wrappings on his feet and into the flesh beneath, but it did not prevent Arlen from using the creature's own momentum to hurl it away. The one he had blinded continued to flail about, but it was little threat.

Before the thrown demon could recover, Arlen pounced on the one writhing on the ground, digging his knees into its back and ignoring the pain as its scales cut into him. He caught the coreling about the throat with one hand, and pressed the other hard into the back of its head. He felt the magic beginning to build, but was forced to relinquish his hold too soon in order to roll out of the way as the coreling he had thrown renewed its assault.

Arlen came back to his feet, and he and the sand demon circled one another warily. It charged, and Arlen bent his knees, ready to sidestep the slashing claws, but the demon stopped short, snapping its stout, powerful frame about like a whip. Its thick tail collided with Arlen's side, sending him sprawling.

He hit the ground and rolled to the side just in time as the heavy, ridged end of the tail thudded into the sand where his head had been. He rolled back, narrowly avoiding the next blow. As the sand demon retracted its tail for another strike, Arlen managed to grasp it. He squeezed, feeling the ward tingle in his palm, then grow warm as the magic gathered. The demon howled and thrashed, but Arlen held fast, locking his other hand just below the first. He quickstepped to keep out of reach as the magic intensified, finally burning right through the tail, popping the ridged end off in an ichorous splatter.

Arlen was thrown by the severance, and the coreling, free again, whirled on him and attacked. Arlen caught one of its wrists in his left hand and jabbed his right elbow into the creature's throat, but the unwarded blow had little effect. The demon flexed its sinewy arms, and Arlen again found himself flying through the air.

As the creature pounced, Arlen called upon his last reserves of strength and met it head-on, locking his hands around its throat and bearing it backward. The coreling's talons ripped at his arms, but Arlen's limbs were longer, and it could not reach his body. They struck the ground hard, and Arlen brought his knees up to the coreling's arm joints, pinning the limbs with his weight as he continued to choke, feeling the magic swell with every passing second.

The coreling thrashed about, but Arlen only squeezed harder, burning through its scales and into the vulnerable flesh beneath. Bones cracked, and his fists closed.

He rose from the now-headless demon, and looked to the others. The one whose ears he had boxed was crawling weakly away, its will for the fight gone. The blind demon had vanished, but Arlen was untroubled by that fact. He didn't envy the crippled creature its trip back to the Core. Most likely, its fellows would tear it to pieces.

He finished off the demon limping pathetically in the sand, bandaged his wounds, and then, after a short rest, picked up his roll of provisions and headed on toward Anoch Sun.

Arlen traveled night and day, taking his sleep in the shadow of the dunes when the sun was highest. On only two other nights was he forced to fight; once against another pack of sand demons, and once against a lone wind demon. The others he passed unmolested.

Without the weight of the sun upon him, he covered more distance by night than by day. He was windburned and raw by his seventh day out of the oasis, his feet blistered and bleeding and his water gone, but new strength flowed into him as Anoch Sun came into view.

Arlen refilled his skins at one of the few working wells, drinking deeply, and then set to warding the building that led into the catacombs where he had found the spear. In some of the nearby collapsed buildings, wooden support beams were left exposed, and in the dryness of the desert, they remained intact. Arlen harvested these, along with the sparse scrub brush, for fires. The three torches left at the oasis and the handful of candles in his warding kit would not last long, and there was no natural light below.

He rationed his dwindling supply of food carefully. The edge of the desert, and the nearest hope of more, was at least five days from Anoch Sun on foot, perhaps three if he traveled at night as well as day. That didn't give him much time, and there was a lot to do.

For the next week, Arlen explored the catacombs, carefully copying new wards wherever he found them. He found more of the stone coffins, but none contained weapons like the first one he'd found. Still, there was an abundance of wards etched upon the coffins and pillars, and more were painted into stories upon the walls. Arlen could not read the pictograms, but he understood much from the body language and expressions on the sequential images. The works were so intricate that he could make out some of the wards on the weapons the warriors carried.

There were new breeds of corelings in the pictures, as well. A series of images showed men killed by demons that looked human, save for their teeth and claws. One central image showed a thin coreling with spindly limbs and a scrawny chest, its head enormous for its body, standing before a host of demons. The coreling faced off against a robed man who stood before a like number of human warriors. The faces of the two were contorted as if in a contest of wills, but they stood well apart. A halo of light surrounded them, as their respective armies looked on.

Perhaps most striking about the image, the man held no weapon. The light emanating from him seemed to be from a ward painted—tattooed?—upon his forehead. Arlen looked to the next image, and saw the demon and its host flee as the humans raised their spears in triumph.

Arlen copied the ward from the man's forehead carefully into his notebook.

Days passed, and food dwindled. If he stayed in Anoch Sun any longer, he would starve before he found more. He decided to leave at first light for Fort Rizon. Once he reached the city, he could secure a bank note against his accounts to cover a horse and supplies to return.

But it galled him to leave having barely scratched the surface of Anoch Sun. Many tunnels had collapsed, requiring time to dig through, and there were many more buildings that might have entrances to underground chambers. The ruins held the key to destroying demonkind, and this was the second time his stomach had forced him to abandon them.

The corelings rose while he was lost in thought. They came in numbers to Anoch Sun, despite the lack of prey. Perhaps they thought the buildings might one day attract more men, or perhaps they took pleasure in dominating a place that had once stood in defiance of their kind.

Arlen rose and walked to the edge of his wards, watching the corelings dance in the moonlight. His stomach rumbled, and he wondered, not for the first time, at the nature of demons. They were magical creatures, immortal and inhuman. They destroyed, but they did not create. Even their corpses burned away instead of rotting to feed the soil. But he had seen them feed, seen them shit and piss. Was their nature entirely outside the natural order?

A sand demon hissed at him. "What are you?" Arlen asked, but the creature only swiped at the wards, growling in frustration and stalking away when they flared.

Arlen watched it go, his thoughts dark. "To the Core with it," he muttered, leaping out from the protection of his wards. The coreling turned just in time to take a blow from Arlen's warded knuckles. His punches struck the unsuspecting creature like thunderbolts. Before it knew what had hit it, the demon was dead.

Other corelings approached at the sound, but they moved warily, and Arlen was able to dart back to the building and cover his wards long enough to drag his victim through.

"Let's see if you can't give something back, after all," Arlen told the dead creature. Using cutting wards painted onto a sharp piece of obsidian, he opened up the sand demon, surprised to find that beneath the hard armor its flesh was as vulnerable as his. The muscle and sinew was tough, but not so much more than that of any beast.

The stench of the creature was terrible. The black ichor that served as its blood stank so badly that Arlen's eyes teared and he gagged. Holding his breath, he cut meat from the creature, and shook it vigorously to remove the excess fluid before setting it over his small fire. The ichor smoked and eventually burned away, the smell of the cooking flesh becoming tolerable.

When it was cooked through, Arlen held up the dark, foul meat, and the years melted away, casting him back to Tibbet's Brook, and the words of Coline Trigg. He had caught a fish that day, but its scales were brown and sickly, and the Herb Gatherer had made him throw it back. "Never eat something that looks sick," Coline had said. "What you put in your mouth becomes a part of you."

Will this become a part of me, too? he wondered. He looked at the meat, mustered his nerve, and put it in his mouth.

SECTION IV

CUTTER'S HOLLOW
331–332 AR

CHAPTER 25

A NEW VENUE
331 AR

THE RAIN INCREASED to a steady pour, and Rojer picked up his pace, cursing his luck. He had been planning to leave Shepherd's Dale for some time, but hadn't expected it to be under such hurried and unpleasant circumstances.

He supposed he couldn't blame the shepherd. True, the man spent more time tending to his flock than his wife, and it was she who made the advance, but coming home early to beat the rain and finding a boy in bed with your wife didn't tend to put men in a reasoning mood.

In a way, he was thankful for the rain. Without it, the man might well have raised half the men in the Dale to give chase. Dalesmen were a possessive lot; probably because their women were often left alone while they took their precious herds to graze. The shepherds were serious folk, about their herds and about their wives. Interfere with either one . . .

After a frantic chase around the room, the shepherd's wife had jumped upon her husband's back, restraining him long enough for Rojer to snatch up his bags and dart out the door. Rojer's bags were always packed. Arrick had taught him that.

"Night," he muttered, as his boot sucked into a thick mud puddle. The cold and wet seeped right in through the soft leather, but he dared not stop and try to build a fire just yet.

He drew his motley cloak tighter, wondering why he always seemed to be running from something. Over the last two years, he had moved on almost every season, living in Cricket Run, Woodsend, and Shepherd's Dale three times each, at least, but he still felt like an outsider. Most villagers went their whole lives without ever leaving their town, and were forever attempting to persuade Rojer to do the same.

Marry me. Marry my daughter. Stay at my inn and we'll paint your name over the door to attract custom. Keep me warm while my husband's afield. Help us harvest and stay the winter.

They said it a hundred ways, but they all meant, "Give up the road and plant roots here."

Every time it was said, Rojer found himself on the road. It was nice to be wanted, but as what? A husband? A father? A farmhand? Rojer was a Jongleur, and he could not imagine being anything else. The first time he lifted a finger at harvest or helped chase down a lost sheep he knew he would be starting down a road that would quickly make him otherwise.

He touched the golden-haired talisman in its secret pocket, feeling Arrick's spirit watching over him. He knew he would feel his master's disappointment keenly if he ever put his motley aside. Arrick had died a Jongleur, and Rojer would, too.

True to Arrick's words, the hamlets had sharpened Rojer's skills. Two years of constant performing had made him into more than just a fiddler and tumbler. Without Arrick to lead, Rojer had been forced to broaden and grow, coming up with innovative ways to entertain alone. He was constantly perfecting some new magic trick or bit of music, but as much as his tricks and fiddling, he had become known for his storytelling.

Everyone in the hamlets loved a good story, especially one that told of faraway places. Rojer obliged, telling of places he'd seen and places he hadn't, towns that sat over the next hill and ones that existed only in his imagination. The stories grew bigger with every telling, his characters coming alive in people's minds as they went on their adventures. Jak Scaletongue, who could speak to corelings, and was forever tricking the stupid beasts with false promises. Marko Rover, who crossed the Milnese mountains and found a rich land on the other side where corelings were worshipped like gods. And of course, the Warded Man.

The duke's Jongleurs passed through the hamlets to make decrees every spring, and the latest had told tales of a feral man who wandered the wilderness, killing demons and feasting on their flesh. He claimed it was honest word from a tattooist who had put wards on the man's back, and that others had confirmed the tale. The audience's attention had been rapt, and when folk had asked Rojer to retell the story another night, he had obliged, adding embellishments all his own.

Listeners loved to ask questions and attempt to catch him in contradiction, but Rojer delighted in the dance of words, keeping the bumpkins convinced of his outlandish tales.

Ironically, the most difficult boast to sell was that he could make the corelings dance with his fiddle. He could have proved it at any time, of course, but as Arrick used to say, "The moment you get up to prove one thing, you'll be expected to prove them all."

Rojer looked up at the sky. *I'll be playing for the corelings soon enough,* he thought. It had been overcast all day, and was getting steadily darker. In the cities, where high walls made it so that most people never saw an actual coreling, it was believed to be a tampweed tale that they could rise under dark clouds, but living outside the walls in the hamlets for two years had taught Rojer better. Most would wait until full sunset to rise, but if the clouds grew thick enough, a few bold demons would test the false night.

Cold and wet and in no mood to take the risk, he cast about for a suitable campsite. He'd be lucky to make Woodsend the next day. More likely, he would be two nights on the road. The thought made his stomach churn.

And Woodsend would be no better than the Dale. Or Cricket Run, for that matter. Sooner or later, he would get some woman with child, or worse, fall in love, and before he knew it, he would only be taking his fiddle from its case on festival days. Until he needed to barter it to fix the plow or buy seed, that was. Then he would be just like everyone else.

Or you could go home.

Rojer often thought of returning to Angiers, but was forever coming up with reasons to put it off another season. After all, what did the city have to offer? Narrow streets, choked with people and animals, wooden planks infused with the stench of manure and garbage. Beggars and thieves and the ever-present worry about money. People who ignored each other as an art.

Normal people, Roger thought, and sighed. Villagers were always seeking to know everything about their neighbors, and opened their homes to strangers without a thought. It was commendable, but Rojer was a city boy at heart.

Returning to Angiers would mean dealing with the guild again. An unlicensed Jongleur's days were numbered, but a guildsman in good standing's business was assured. His experience in the hamlets should be enough to win him a license, especially if he found a guildsman to speak for him. Arrick had alienated most of those, but Rojer might find one to take pity on him upon hearing of his master's fate.

He found a tree that gave some shelter from the rain, and after setting up his circle, managed to collect enough dry tinder from beneath its boughs to start a small fire. He fed it carefully, but the wind and wet extinguished it before long.

"Bugger the hamlets," Rojer said as the darkness enveloped him, broken only by the occasional flare of magic as a demon tested his wards.

"Bugger them all."

Angiers hadn't changed much since he'd been gone. It seemed smaller, but Rojer had been living in wide-open places for some time, and had grown a few inches since he had been there last. He was sixteen now, a man by anyone's standards. He stood outside the city for some time, staring at the gate and wondering if he was making a mistake.

He had a little coin, sifted carefully from his collection hat over the years and hoarded against his return, and some food in his pack. It wasn't much, but it would keep him out of the shelters for a few nights at least.

If all I want is a full belly and a roof, I can always go back to the hamlets, he thought. He could head south to Farmer's Stump and Cutter's Hollow, or north, to where the duke had rebuilt Riverbridge on the Angierian side of the river.

If, he told himself again, mustering his courage and walking through the gate.

He found an inn that was cheap enough, and unpacked his best motley, heading back out as soon as he was changed. The Jongleurs' Guildhouse was located near the center of town, where its residents could easily make engagements in any part of the city. Any licensed Jongleur could live in the house, provided they took the jobs assigned to them without complaint, and paid half their earnings to the guild.

"Fools," Arrick called them. "Any Jongleur willing to give half his take for a roof and three communal servings of gruel isn't worthy of the name."

It was true enough. Only the oldest and least skilled Jongleurs lived in the house, ready to take the jobs others turned down. Still, it was better than destitution, and safer than public shelters. The wards on the guildhouse were strong, and its residents less apt to rob one another.

Rojer headed for the residences, and a few inquiries soon had him knocking on a particular door.

"Eh?" the old man asked, squinting into the hall as he opened his door. "Who's that?"

"Rojer Halfgrip, sir," Rojer said, and seeing no recognition in the rheumy eyes, added, "I was apprentice to Arrick Sweetsong."

The confused look soured in an instant, and the man moved to close the door.

"Master Jaycob, please," Rojer said, placing his hand on the door.

The old man sighed, but made no effort to close the door as he moved back into the small chamber and sat down heavily. Rojer entered, closing the door behind them.

"What is it you want?" Jaycob asked. "I'm an old man and don't have time for games."

"I need a sponsor to apply for a guild license," Rojer said.

Jaycob spat on the floor. "Arrick's become a dead weight?" he asked. "His drinking slowing down your success, so you're leaving him to rot and striking out on your own?" He grunted. "Fitting. S'what he did to me, twenty-five years ago."

He looked up at Rojer. "But fitting or no, if you think I'm to help in your betrayal . . ."

"Master Jaycob," Rojer said, holding up his hands to forestall the coming tirade, "Arrick is dead. Cored on the road to Woodsend, two years gone."

"Keep your back straight, boy," Jaycob said as they walked down the hall. "Remember to look the guildmaster in the eye, and don't speak until you're spoken to."

He had already said these things a dozen times, but Rojer only nodded. He was young to get his own license, but Jaycob said there had been some in the guild's history who were younger still. It was talent and skill that would win a license, not years.

It wasn't easy to get an appointment with the guildmaster, even with a sponsor. Jaycob hadn't had the strength to perform in years, and while the guildsmen were politely respectful of his advanced years, he was more ignored than venerated in the office wing of the guildhouse.

The guildmaster's secretary left them waiting outside his office for several hours, watching in despair as other appointments came and went. Rojer sat with his back straight, resisting the urge to shift or slump, as the light from the window slowly crossed the room.

"Guildmaster Cholls will see you now," the clerk said at last, and Rojer snapped back to attention. He stood quickly, lending Jaycob a hand to help the old man to his feet.

The guildmaster's office was like nothing Rojer had seen since his time in the duke's palace. Thick warm carpet covered the floors, patterned and bright, and elaborate oil lamps with colored glass hung from the oak walls between paintings of great battles, beautiful women, and still lifes. His desk was dark polished walnut, with small, intricate statuettes for paperweights, mirroring the larger statues on pedestals throughout the room. Behind the desk was the symbol of the Jongleurs' Guild, three colored balls, in a large seal on the wall.

"I don't have a lot of time, Master Jaycob," Guildmaster Cholls said, not even bothering to look up from the sheaf of papers on his desk. He was a heavy man, fifty summers at least, dressed in the embroidered cloth of a merchant or noble, rather than Jongleur's motley.

"This one is worth your time," Jaycob said. "The apprentice of Arrick Sweetsong."

Cholls looked up at last, if only to glance askew at Jaycob. "Didn't realize you and Arrick were still in touch," he said, ignoring Rojer entirely. "Heard you broke on bad terms."

"The years have a way of softening such things," Jaycob said stiffly, as close to a lie as he was willing to go. "I've made my peace with Arrick."

"It seems you're the only one," Cholls said with a chuckle. "Most of the men in this building would as soon throttle the man as look at him."

"They'd be a little late," Jaycob said. "Arrick is dead."

Cholls sobered at that. "I'm saddened to hear that," he said. "Every one of us is precious. Was it the drink, in the end?"

Jaycob shook his head. "Corelings."

The guildmaster scowled, and spat into a brass bucket by his desk that seemed there for no other purpose. "When and where?" he asked.

"Two years, on the road to Woodsend."

Cholls shook his head sadly. "I recall his apprentice was something of a fiddler," he said at last, glancing Rojer's way.

"Indeed," Jaycob agreed. "That and more. I present to you Rojer Halfgrip." Rojer bowed.

"Halfgrip?" the guildmaster asked, with sudden interest. "I've heard tales of a Halfgrip playing the Western hamlets. That you, boy?"

Rojer's eyes widened, but he nodded. Arrick had said that reputations carried quickly from the hamlets, but it was still a shock. He wondered if his reputation was good or ill.

"Don't let it go to your head," Cholls said, as if reading his mind. "Yokels exaggerate."

Rojer nodded, keeping eye contact with the guildmaster. "Yes, sir. I understand."

"Well then, let's get on with this," Cholls said. "Show me what you have."

"Here?" Rojer asked doubtfully. The office was large and private, but with its thick carpets and expensive furniture, it hardly seemed suited to tumbling and knife throwing.

Cholls waved at him impatiently. "You performed with Arrick for years, so I'll accept that you can juggle and sing," he said. Rojer swallowed hard. "Earning a license means showing a focus skill beyond those basics."

"Fiddle him, boy, just like you did me," Jaycob said confidently. Rojer nodded. His hands shook slightly as he took his fiddle from its case, but when his fingers closed about the smooth wood, the fear washed away like dust in a bath. He began to play, the guildmaster forgotten as he fell into the music.

He played a short while before a shout broke the music's spell. His bow slipped from the strings, and in the silence that followed, a voice thundered outside the door.

"No, I will not wait for some worthless apprentice to finish his test! Move aside!" There were sounds of a scuffle before the door burst open and Master Jasin stormed into the room.

"I'm sorry, Guildmaster," the clerk apologized, "he refused to wait."

Cholls waved the clerk away as Jasin stormed up to him. "You gave the Duke's Ball to Edum?" he demanded. "That's been my performance for ten years! My uncle will hear of this!"

Cholls stood his ground, arms crossed. "The duke himself requested the change," he said. "If your uncle has a problem, suggest he take it up with His Grace."

Jasin scowled. It was doubtful even First Minister Janson would intercede with the duke over a performance for his nephew.

"If that's all you came to discuss, Jasin, you'll have to excuse us," Cholls went on. "Young Rojer here is testing for his license."

Jasin's eyes snapped over to Rojer, flaring with recognition. "I see you've ditched the drunk," he sneered. "Hope you didn't trade him for this old relic." He thrust his chin at Jaycob. "The offer stands, you want to work for me. Let Arrick beg for *your* scraps for a change, eh?"

"Master Arrick was cored on the road two years ago," Cholls said.

Jasin glanced back at the guildmaster, then laughed out loud. "Fabulous!" he cried. "That news makes up for losing the Duke's Ball, and to spare!"

Rojer hit him.

He didn't even realize what he'd done until he was standing over the master, his knuckles tingling and wet. He'd felt the brittle crunch as his fist struck Jasin's nose, and he knew his chances of winning his license were now gone, but at that moment, he didn't care.

Jaycob grabbed him and pulled him back as Jasin surged to his feet, swinging wildly.

"I'll kill you for thad, you little . . . !"

Cholls was between them in an instant. Jasin thrashed in his grasp, but the guildmaster's bulk was more than enough to restrain him. "That's enough, Jasin!" he barked. "You're not killing anyone!"

"You saw whad he did!" Jasin cried, as blood streamed from his nose.

"And I heard what you said!" Cholls shouted back. "I was tempted to hit you myself!"

"How ab I subbosed to sig tonide?" Jasin demanded. His nose had already begun to swell, and his words became less understandable with every moment.

Cholls scowled. "I'll get someone to perform in your stead," he said. "The guild will cover the loss. Daved!" The clerk stuck his head in the door. "Escort Master Jasin to an Herb Gatherer, and have the bill sent here."

Daved nodded, moving to assist Jasin. The master shoved him away. "Thid idn't ober," he promised Rojer as he left.

Cholls blew out a long breath as the door closed. "Well, boy, you've gone and done it now. That's an enemy I wouldn't wish on anyone."

"He was already my enemy," Rojer said. "You heard what he said."

Cholls nodded. "I did," he said, "but you still should have restrained yourself. What will you do if a patron insults you next? Or the duke himself? Guildsmen can't go around punching anyone that angers them."

Rojer hung his head. "I understand," he said.

"You've just cost me a fair bit of coin, though," Cholls said. "I'll be throwing money and prime performances at Jasin for weeks to keep him appeased, and with that fiddling of yours, I'd be a fool not to make you earn it back."

Rojer looked up hopefully.

"Probationary license," Cholls said, taking a sheet of paper and a quill. "You're only to perform under the supervision of a master of the guild, paid from your take, and half of your gross earnings will come to this office until I consider your debt closed. Understood?"

"Absolutely, sir!" Rojer said eagerly.

"And you'll hold your temper," Cholls warned, "or I'll tear up this license and you'll never perform in Angiers again."

Rojer worked his fiddle, but out of the corner of his eye he was watching Abrum, Jasin's burly apprentice. Jasin usually had one of his apprentices watching Rojer's performances. It made him uneasy, knowing that they were watching him for their master, who meant him only ill, but it had been months since the incident in the guildmaster's office, and nothing had ever seemed to come of it. Master Jasin had recovered quickly and was soon performing again, raking in accolades at every high-society event in Angiers.

Rojer might have dared to hope the episode was behind them, save that the apprentices came back almost every day. Sometimes it was Abrum the wood demon lurking in a crowd, and others it was Sali the rock demon sipping a drink at the back of a tavern, but however innocuous they might seem, it was no coincidence.

Rojer ended his performance with a flourish, whipping the bow from his fiddle into the air. He took his time to bow, straightening just in time to catch it. The crowd burst into applause, and Rojer's sharp ears caught the clink of metal coins in the hat as Jaycob moved about the crowd with it. Rojer couldn't suppress a smile. The old man looked almost spry.

He scanned the dispersing crowd as they collected their equipment, but Abrum had vanished. Still, they packed up quickly and took a roundabout path to their inn to make sure they could not be easily followed. The sun was soon to set, and the streets were emptying rapidly. Winter was on the wane, but the boardwalks still held patches of ice and snow, and few stayed out unless they had business to.

"Even without Cholls' cut, the rent is paid with days to spare," Jaycob said, jingling the purse with their take. "When the debt's paid, you'll be rich!"

"*We'll* be rich," Rojer corrected, and Jaycob laughed, kicking his heels and slapping Rojer on the back.

"Look at you," Rojer said, shaking his head. "What happened to the shuffling and half-blind old man that opened his door to me a few months gone?"

"It's performing again that's done it," Jaycob said, giving Rojer a toothless grin. "I know I'm not singing or throwing knives, but even passing the hat has gotten my dusty blood pumping like it hasn't in twenty years. I feel I could even . . ." He looked away.

"What?" Rojer asked.

"Just . . ." Jaycob said, "I don't know, spin a tale, perhaps? Or play dim while you throw punch lines my way? Nothing to steal your shine . . ."

"Of course," Rojer said. "I would have asked, but I felt I was imposing too much already, dragging you all over town to supervise my performances."

"Boy," Jaycob said, "I can't remember the last time I've been so happy."

They were grinning as they turned a corner and walked right into Abrum and Sali. Behind them, Jasin smiled broadly.

"It's good to see you, my friend!" Jasin said, as Abrum

clapped Rojer's shoulder. The wind suddenly exploded from Rojer's stomach, the punch doubling him over and knocking him to the frozen boardwalk. Before he could rise, Sali delivered a heavy kick to his jaw.

"Leave him alone!" Jaycob cried, throwing himself at Sali. The heavy soprano only laughed, grabbing him and swinging him hard against the wall of a building.

"Oh, there's plenty for you too, old man!" Jasin said, as Sali landed heavy blows to his body. Rojer could hear the crunch of brittle bone, and the weak, wet gasps that escaped the master's lips. Only the wall held him upright.

The wooden planks beneath his hands were spinning, but Rojer wrenched himself to his feet, holding his fiddle by the neck with both hands, swinging the makeshift club wildly. "You won't get away with this!" he cried.

Jasin laughed. "Who will you go to?" he asked. "Will the city magistrates take the obviously false accusations of a petty street performer over the word of the first minister's nephew? Go to the guard, and it's you they'll hang."

Abrum caught the fiddle easily, twisting Rojer's arm hard as he drove a knee into his crotch. Rojer felt his arm break even as his groin caught fire, and the fiddle came down hard on the back of his head, shattering as it hammered him to the boardwalk again.

Even through the ringing in his ears, Rojer heard Jaycob's continued grunts of pain. Abrum stood over him, smiling as he lifted a heavy club.

CHAPTER 26

HOSPIT

332 AR

"AY, JIZELL!" Skot cried as the old Herb Gatherer came to him with her bowl. "Why not let your apprentice take the task for once?" He nodded at Leesha, changing another man's dressing.

"Ha!" Jizell barked. She was a heavyset woman, with short gray hair and a voice that carried. "If I let her give the rag baths, I'd have half of Angiers crying plague within a week."

Leesha shook her head as the others in the room laughed, but she was smiling as she did. Skot was harmless. He was a Messenger whose horse had thrown him on the road. Lucky to be alive, especially with two broken arms, he had somehow managed to track down his horse and get back in the saddle. He had no wife to care for him, and so the Messengers' Guild had produced the klats to put him up in Jizell's hospit until he could do for himself.

Jizell soaked her rag in the warm, soapy bowl and lifted the man's sheet, her hand moving with firm efficiency. The Messenger gave a yelp as she was finishing up, and Jizell laughed. "Just as well I give the baths," she said loudly, glancing down. "We wouldn't want to disappoint poor Leesha."

The others in their beds all had a laugh at the man's expense. It was a full room, and all were a little bed-bored.

"I think she'd likely find it in different form than you," Skot grumbled, blushing furiously, but Jizell only laughed again.

"Poor Skot has a shine on you," Jizell told Leesha later, when they were in the pharmacy grinding herbs.

"A shine?" laughed Kadie, one of the younger apprentices. "He's not shining, he's in loooove!" The other apprentices in earshot burst into giggles.

"I think he's cute," Roni volunteered.

"You think everyone is cute," Leesha said. Roni was just flowering, and boy-crazed. "But I hope you have better taste than to fall for a man that begs you for a rag bath."

"Don't give her ideas," Jizell said. "Roni had her way, she'd be rag-bathing every man in the hospit." The girls all giggled, and even Roni didn't disagree.

"At least have the decency to blush," Leesha told her, and the girls tittered again.

"Enough! Off with you giggleboxes!" Jizell laughed. "I want a word with Leesha."

"Most every man that comes in here shines on you," Jizell said when they were gone. "It wouldn't kill you to talk to one apart from asking after his health."

"You sound like my mum," Leesha said.

Jizell slammed her pestle down on the counter. "I sound like no such thing," she said, having heard all about Elona over the years. "I just don't want you to die an old maid to spite her. There's no crime in liking men."

"I like men," Leesha protested.

"Not that I've seen," Jizell said.

"So I should have jumped to offer Skot a rag bath?" Leesha asked.

"Certainly not," Jizell said. "At least, not in front of everyone," she added with a wink.

"Now you sound like Bruna," Leesha groaned. "It will take more than crude comments to win my heart." Requests like Skot's were nothing new to Leesha. She had her mother's body, and that meant a great deal of male attention, whether she invited it or not.

"Then what does it take?" Jizell asked. "What man could pass your heart wards?"

"A man I can trust," Leesha said. "One I can kiss on the cheek without him bragging to his friends the next day that he stuck me behind the barn."

Jizell snorted. "You'll sooner find a friendly coreling," she said.

Leesha shrugged.

"I think you're scared," Jizell accused. "You've waited so long to lose your flower that you've taken a simple, natural thing every girl does and built it up into some unscalable wall."

"That's ridiculous," Leesha said.

"Is it?" Jizell asked. "I've seen you when ladies come asking your advice on bed matters, grasping and guessing as you blush furiously. How can you advise others about their bodies when you don't even know your own?"

"I'm quite sure I know what goes where," Leesha said wryly.

"You know what I mean," Jizell said.

"What do you suggest I do about it?" Leesha demanded. "Pick some man at random, just to get it over with?"

"If that's what it takes," Jizell said.

Leesha glared at her, but Jizell met the gaze and didn't flinch. "You've guarded that flower so long that no man will ever be worthy to take it in your eyes," she said. "What good is a flower hidden away for no one to see? Who will remember its beauty when it wilts?"

Leesha let out a choked sob, and Jizell was there in an instant, holding her tightly as she cried. "There, there, poppet," she soothed, stroking Leesha's hair, "it's not as bad as all that."

After supper, when the wards were checked and the apprentices sent to their studies, Leesha and Jizell finally had time to brew a pot of herb tea and open the satchel from the morning Messenger. A lamp sat on the table, full and trimmed for long use.

"Patients all day and letters all night," Jizell sighed. "Thank light Herb Gatherers don't need sleep, eh?" She upended the bag, spilling parchment all over the table.

They quickly separated out correspondence meant for the patients, and then Jizell grabbed a bundle at random, glancing at the hail. "These are yours," she said, passing the bundle to Leesha and snatching another letter off the pile, which she opened and began to read.

"This one's from Kimber," she said after a moment. Kimber was another of Jizell's apprentices sent abroad, this one to Farmer's Stump, a day's ride south. "The cooper's rash has gotten worse, and spread again."

"She's brewing the tea wrong; I just know it," Leesha groaned. "She never lets it steep long enough, and then wonders at her weak cures. If I have to go to Farmer's Stump and brew it for her, I'll give her such a thumping!"

"She knows it," Jizell laughed. "That's why she wrote to me this time!"

The laughter was infectious, and Leesha soon joined in. Leesha loved Jizell. She could be as hard as Bruna when the occasion demanded, but she was always quick to laugh.

Leesha missed Bruna dearly, and the thought turned her back to the bundle. It was Fourthday, when the weekly Messenger arrived from Farmer's Stump, Cutter's Hollow, and points south. Sure enough, the hail of the first letter in the stack was in her father's neat script.

There was a letter from Vika, as well, and Leesha read that one first, her hands clenching as always until she was assured that Bruna, older than ancient, was still well.

"Vika's given birth," she noted. "A boy, Jame. Six pounds eleven ounces."

"Is that the third?" Jizell asked.

"Fourth," Leesha said. Vika had married Child Jona—Tender Jona, now—not long after arriving in Cutter's Hollow, and wasted no time in bearing him children.

"Not much chance of her coming back to Angiers, then," Jizell lamented.

Leesha laughed. "I thought that was given after the first," she said.

It was hard to believe seven years had passed since she and Vika exchanged places. The temporary arrangement was proving permanent, which didn't entirely displease Leesha.

Regardless of what Leesha did, Vika would stay in Cutter's Hollow, and seemed better liked there than Bruna, Leesha, and Darsy combined. The thought gave Leesha a sense of freedom she never dreamt existed. She'd promised to return one day to ensure the Hollow had the Gatherer it needed, but the Creator had seen to that for her. Her future was hers to choose.

Her father wrote that he had caught a chill, but Vika was tending him, and he expected to recover quickly. The next letter was from Mairy; her eldest daughter already flowered and promised, Mairy would likely be a grandmother soon. Leesha sighed.

There were two more letters in the bundle. Leesha corresponded with Mairy, Vika, and her father almost every week, but her mother wrote less often, and oftentimes in a fit of pique.

"All well?" Jizell asked, glancing up from her own reading to see Leesha's scowl.

"Just my mum," Leesha said, reading. "The tone changes with her humors, but the message stays the same: 'Come home and have children before you grow too old and the Creator takes the chance from you.' " Jizell grunted and shook her head.

Tucked in with Elona's letter was another sheet, supposedly from Gared, though the missive was in her mother's hand, for Gared knew no letters. But whatever pains she took to make it seem dictated, Leesha was sure at least half the words were her mother's alone, and most likely the other half as well. The content, as with her mother's letters, never changed. Gared was well. Gared missed her. Gared was waiting for her. Gared loved her.

"My mother must think me very stupid," Leesha said wryly as she read, "to believe Gared would ever even attempt a poem, much less one that didn't rhyme."

Jizell laughed, but it died prematurely when she saw that Leesha had not joined her.

"What if she's right?" Leesha asked suddenly. "Dark as it is to think Elona right about anything, I do want children one day, and you don't need to be an Herb Gatherer to know that my days to do it are fewer ahead than behind. You said yourself I've wasted my best years."

"That was hardly what I said," Jizell replied.

"It's true enough," Leesha said sadly. "I've never bothered to look for men; they always had a way of finding me whether I wanted it or not. I just always thought one day I'd be found by one that fit into my life, rather than expecting me to fit into his."

"We all dream that sometimes, dear," Jizell said, "and it's a nice enough fantasy once in a while, when you're staring at the wall, but you can't hang your hopes on it."

Leesha squeezed the letter in her hand, crumpling it a bit.

"So you're thinking of going back and marrying this Gared?" Jizell asked.

"Oh, Creator, no!" Leesha cried. "Of course not!"

Jizell grunted. "Good. You've saved me the trouble of thumping you on the head."

"Much as my belly longs for a child," Leesha said, "I'll die a maid before I let Gared give me one. Problem is, he'd have at any other man in the Hollow that tried."

"Easily solved," Jizell said. "Have children here."

"What?" Leesha asked.

"Cutter's Hollow is in good hands with Vika," Jizell said. "I trained the girl myself, and her heart is there now in any event."

She leaned in, putting a meaty hand atop Leesha's. "Stay," she said. "Make Angiers your home and take over the hospit when I retire."

Leesha's eyes widened. She opened her mouth, but no sound came out.

"You've taught me as much as I've taught you these years," Jizell went on. "There's no one else I trust to run my business, even if Vika returned tomorrow."

"I don't know what to say," Leesha managed.

"No rush to say anything," Jizell said, patting Leesha's hand. "I daresay I don't plan to retire any day soon. Just think on it."

Leesha nodded. Jizell opened her arms, and she fell into them, embracing the older woman tightly. As they parted, a shout from outside made them jump.

"Help! Help!" someone cried. They both glanced at the window. It was past dark.

Opening one's shutters at night in Angiers was a crime punishable by whipping, but Leesha and Jizell gave it no thought as they threw open the bar, seeing a trio of city guardsmen running down the boardwalk, two of them each carrying another man.

"Ay, the hospit!" the lead guard called, seeing the shutters open on the lamplit room. "Open your doors! Succor! Succor and healing!"

As one, Leesha and Jizell bolted for the stairs, nearly tumbling down in their haste to get to the door. It was winter, and though the city's Warders worked diligently to keep the wardnet clear of snow, ice, and dead leaves, a few wind demons invariably found their way in each night, hunting homeless beggars and waiting for the occasional fool that dared defy curfew and the law. A wind demon could drop like a silent stone and then spread its taloned wings in a sudden snap, eviscerating a victim before grasping the body in its rear claws and swooping away with it.

They made it to the landing and threw open the door, watching as the men approached. The lintels were warded; they and their patients were safe enough even without the door.

"What's happening?" Kadie cried, sticking her head out over the balcony at the top of the stairs. Behind her, the other apprentices were pouring out of their room.

"Put your aprons back on and get down here!" Leesha ordered, and the younger girls scrambled to obey.

The men were still a ways off, but running hard. Leesha's stomach clenched as she heard shrieks in the sky. There were wind demons about, drawn to the light and commotion.

But the guards were closing the distance fast, and Leesha dared to hope that they would make it unscathed until one of the men slipped on a patch of ice and went down hard. He screamed, and the man he was carrying tumbled to the boardwalk.

The guard still with a man over his shoulder shouted something to the other, and put his head down, picking up speed. The unburdened man turned and rushed back to his fallen comrade.

A sudden flap of leathery wings was the only warning before the head of the hapless guard flew free of his body, rolling across the boardwalk. Kadie screamed. Before blood even began to spurt from the wound, the wind demon gave a shriek and launched skyward, hauling the dead man's body into the air.

The laden guard passed the wards, hauling his charge to safety. Leesha looked back to the remaining man, struggling to rise, and her brow set.

"Leesha, no!" Jizell cried, grabbing at her, but Leesha stepped nimbly aside and bolted out onto the boardwalk.

She ran in sharp zigzag as the shrieks of wind demons rang out in the cold air above. One coreling attempted a dive attack anyway and missed her completely, if only by a few inches. It tumbled into the boardwalk with a crash, but quickly righted itself, its thick hide unharmed by the impact. Leesha spun away, hurling a fistful of Bruna's blinding powder into its eyes. The creature roared in pain, and Leesha ran on.

"Save him, not me!" the guard called as she drew near, pointing to the still form lying on the boardwalk. The guard's ankle was at an odd angle, clearly broken. Leesha glanced at the other form, prone on the boardwalk. She could not carry them both.

"Not me!" the guard called again as she drew close.

Leesha shook her head. "I've a better chance of getting you to safety," she said, in a tone that brooked no debate. She got under his arm and heaved.

"Keep low," the guard gasped. "Windies are less apt to dive at things low to the ground."

She hunched as much as she could, staggering under the big man's weight, and knew they were not going to make it at the shuffling pace, low or not.

"Now!" Jizell cried, and Leesha looked up to see Kadie and the other apprentices run out onto the boardwalk, holding the edges of white sheets above their heads. The fluttering cloth was almost everywhere, making it impossible for the wind demons to pick a target.

Under this cover, Mistress Jizell and the first guard came rushing up to them. Jizell helped Leesha as the guard fetched the unconscious man. Fear gave them all strength, and they covered the remaining distance quickly, retreating into the hospit and barring the door.

"This one's dead," Jizell said, her voice cold. "I'd wager he's been gone over an hour."

"I almost sacrificed myself for a dead man?" the guard with the broken ankle exclaimed. Leesha ignored him, moving over to the other injured man.

With his round, freckled face and slender form, he seemed more a boy than a man. He had been badly beaten, but he was breathing, and his heart was strong. Leesha inspected him swiftly, cutting away his bright patchwork clothes as she probed for broken bones and searched for the sources of the blood that soaked his motley.

"What happened?" Jizell asked the injured guard, as she inspected the break in his ankle.

"We werc headin' in from last patrol," the guard said through gritted teeth. "Found these two, Jongleurs by their look, lyin' on the walk. Must'a been robbed after a show. They was both alive, but in a bad way. It was dark by then, but neither of them looked like they'd last the night without a Gatherer to tend them. I remembered this hospit, and we ran hard as we could, tryin' to stay under eaves, outta sight from windies."

Jizell nodded. "You did the right thing," she said.

"Tell that to poor Jonsin," the guard said. "Creator, what will I tell his wife?"

"That's a worry for the morrow," Jizell said, lifting a flask to the man's lips. "Drink this."

The guard looked at her dubiously. "What is it?" he asked.

"It will put you to sleep," Jizell said. "I need to set your ankle, and I promise you, you don't want to be awake when I do."

The guard quaffed the potion quickly.

Leesha was cleaning out the younger one's wounds when he

started awake with a gasp, sitting up. One of his eyes was swollen shut, but the other was a bright green, and darted about wildly. "Jaycob!" he cried.

He thrashed wildly, and it took Leesha, Kadie, and the last guard to wrestle him back down. He turned his one piercing eye on Leesha. "Where is Jaycob?" he asked. "Is he all right?"

"The older man who was found with you?" Leesha asked, and he nodded.

Leesha hesitated, picking her words, but the pause was answer enough, and he screamed, thrashing again. The guard pinned him hard, looking him in the eyes.

"Did you see who did this to you?" he asked.

"He's in no condition . . ." Leesha began, but the man cut her off with a glare.

"I lost a man tonight," he said. "I don't have time to wait." He turned back to the boy. "Well?" he asked.

The boy looked at him with eyes filling with tears. Finally, he shook his head, but the guard didn't let up. "You must have seen *some*thing," he pressed.

"That's enough," Leesha said, grabbing the man's wrists and pulling hard. He resisted for a moment, and then let go. "Wait in the other room," she ordered. He scowled, but complied.

The boy was weeping openly when Leesha turned back to him. "Just put me back out into the night," he said, holding up a crippled hand. "I was meant to die a long time ago, and everyone that tries to save me ends up dead."

Leesha took the crippled hand in hers and looked him in the eye. "I'll take my chances," she said, squeezing. "We survivors have to look out for one another." She put the flask of sleeping draught to his lips, and held his hand, lending him strength until his eyes slipped closed.

The sound of fiddling filled the hospit. Patients clapped their hands, and the apprentices danced as they went about their tasks. Even Leesha and Jizell had a spring in their step.

"To think young Rojer was worried he had no way to pay," Jizell said as they prepared lunch. "I've half a mind to pay him to come entertain the patients after he's back on his feet."

"The patients and the girls love him," Leesha agreed.

"I've seen you dancing when you think no one is looking," Jizell said.

Leesha smiled. When he wasn't fiddling, Rojer spun tales that had the apprentices clustered at the foot of his bed, or taught them makeup tricks he claimed came from the duke's own courtesans. Jizell mothered him constantly, and the apprentices all shined and doted on him.

"An extra-thick slice of beef for him, then," Leesha said, cutting the meat and laying it on a platter already overladen with potatoes and fruit.

Jizell shook her head. "I don't know where that boy puts it," she said. "You and the others have been stuffing him for a full moon and more, and he's still thin as a reed."

"Lunch!" she bellowed, and the girls filtered in to collect the trays. Roni moved directly for the overladen one, but Leesha swept it out of reach. "I'll take this one myself," she said, smiling at the looks of disappointment around the kitchen.

"Rojer needs to take a break and eat something, not spin private tales while you girls cut his meat," Jizell said. "You can all fawn on him later."

"Intermission!" Leesha called as she swept into the room, but she needn't have bothered. The bow slipped from the fiddle strings with a squeak the moment she appeared. Rojer smiled and waved, knocking over a wooden cup as he tried to set his fiddle aside. His broken fingers and arm had mended neatly, but his leg casts were still on strings, and he could not easily reach the bedstand.

"You must be hungry today," she laughed, setting the tray across his lap and taking the fiddle. Rojer looked at the tray dubiously, smiling up at her.

"I don't suppose you could help me cut?" he asked, holding up his crippled hand.

Leesha raised her eyebrows at him. "Your fingers seem nimble enough when you work your fiddle," she said. "Why are they deficient now?"

"Because I hate eating alone," Rojer laughed.

Leesha smiled, sitting on the side of the bed and taking the knife and fork. She cut a thick bite of meat, dragging it through the gravy and potatoes before bringing it up to Rojer's mouth. He smiled at her, and a bit of gravy leaked from his mouth, making Leesha titter. Rojer blushed, his fair cheeks turning as red as his hair.

"I can lift the fork myself," he said.

"You want me to just cut up the meat and leave?" Leesha asked, and Rojer shook his head vigorously. "Then hush," she said, lifting another forkful to his mouth.

"It's not my fiddle, you know," Rojer said, glancing back to the instrument after a few moments of silence. "It's Jaycob's. Mine was broken when . . ."

Leesha frowned as he trailed off. After more than a month, he still refused to speak of the attack, even when pressed by the guard. He'd sent for his few possessions, but so far as she knew, he hadn't even contacted the Jongleurs' Guild to tell them what had happened.

"It wasn't your fault," Leesha said, seeing his eyes go distant. "You didn't attack him."

"I might as well have," Rojer said.

"What do you mean?" Leesha asked.

Rojer looked away. "I mean . . . by forcing him from retirement. He'd still be alive if . . ."

"You said he told you coming out of retirement was the best thing that had happened to him in twenty years," Leesha argued. "It sounds like he lived more in that short time than he would have in years spent in that cell in the guildhouse."

Rojer nodded, but his eyes grew wet. Leesha squeezed his hand. "Herb Gatherers see death often," she told him. "No one, no one, ever goes to the Creator with all their business complete. We all get a different length of time, but it needs to be enough, regardless."

"It just seems to come early for the people who cross my path," Rojer sighed.

"I've seen it come early for a great many who have never heard of Rojer Halfgrip," Leesha said. "Would you like to shoulder the blame for their deaths, as well?"

Rojer looked at her, and she pressed another forkful into his mouth. "It doesn't serve the dead to stop living yourself, out of guilt," she said.

Leesha had her hands full of linens when the Messenger arrived. She slipped the letter from Vika into her apron, and left the rest for later. She finished putting away the laundry, but then a girl ran up to tell her a patient had coughed blood. After that, she had to set a broken arm, and give the apprentices their lesson.

Before she knew it, the sun had set, and the apprentices were all in bed. She turned the wicks down to a dim orange glow, and made a last sweep through the rows of beds, making sure the patients were comfortable before she went upstairs for the night. She met Rojer's eyes as she passed, and he beckoned, but she smiled and shook her head. She pointed to him, then put her hands together as if praying, leaned her cheek against them, and closed her eyes.

Rojer frowned, but she winked at him and kept on, knowing he wouldn't follow. His casts had come off, but Rojer complained of pain and weakness despite the clean mend.

At the end of the room, she took the time to pour herself a cup of water. It was a warm spring night, and the pitcher was damp with condensation. She brushed her hand against her apron absently to dry it, and there was a crinkle of paper. She remembered Vika's letter and pulled it out, breaking the seal with her thumb and tilting the page toward the lamp as she drank.

A moment later, she dropped her cup. She didn't notice, or hear the ceramic shatter. She clutched the paper tightly and fled the room.

Leesha was sobbing quietly in the darkened kitchen when Rojer found her.

"Are you all right?" he asked quietly, leaning heavily on his cane.

"Rojer?" she sniffed. "Why aren't you in bed?"

Rojer didn't answer, coming to sit beside her. "Bad news from home?" he asked.

Leesha looked at him a moment, then nodded. "That chill my father caught?" she asked, waiting for Rojer to nod his recollection before going on. "He seemed to get better, but it came back with a vengeance. Turns out it was a flux that's run from one end of the Hollow to the other. Most seem to be pulling through it, but the weaker ones . . ." She began to weep again.

"Someone you know?" Rojer asked, cursing himself as he said it. Of course it was someone she knew. Everyone knew everyone in the hamlets.

Leesha didn't notice the slip. "My mentor, Bruna," she said, fat teardrops falling onto her apron. "A few others, as well, and two children I never had the chance to meet. Over a dozen in all, and more than half the town still laid up. My father worst amongst them."

"I'm sorry," Rojer said.

"Don't feel sorry for me; it's my fault," Leesha said.

"What?" Rojer asked.

"I should have been there," Leesha said. "I haven't been Jizell's apprentice in years. I promised to return to Cutter's Hollow when my studies were done. If I had kept my promise, I would have been there, and perhaps . . ."

"I saw the flux kill some people in Woodsend once," Rojer said. "Would you like to add those to your conscience? Or those that die in this very city, because you can't tend them all?"

"That's not the same and you know it," Leesha said.

"Isn't it?" Rojer asked. "You said yourself that it does nothing to serve the dead if you stop living yourself out of guilt."

Leesha looked at him, her eyes round and wet.

"So what do you want to do?" Rojer asked. "Spend the night crying, or start packing?"

"Packing?" Leesha asked.

"I have a Messenger's portable circle," Rojer said. "We can leave for Cutter's Hollow in the morning."

"Rojer, you can barely walk!" Leesha said.

Rojer lifted his cane, set it on the counter, and stood. He walked a bit stiffly, but unaided.

"Been faking to keep your warm bed and doting women a bit longer?" Leesha asked.

"I never!" Rojer blushed. "I'm . . . just not ready to perform yet."

"But you're fit to walk all the way to Cutter's Hollow?" Leesha asked. "It would take a week without a horse."

"I doubt I'll need to do any backflips on the way," Rojer said. "I can do it."

Leesha crossed her arms and shook her head. "No. I absolutely forbid it."

"I'm not some apprentice you can forbid," Rojer said.

"You're my patient," Leesha shot back, "and I'll forbid anything that puts your healing in jeopardy. I'll hire a Messenger to take me."

"Good luck finding one," Rojer said. "The weekly man south will have left today, and at this time of year, most of the others will be booked. It'll cost a fortune to convince one to drop everything and take you to Cutter's Hollow. Besides, I can drive corelings away with my fiddle. No Messenger can offer you that."

"I'm sure you could," Leesha said, her tone making it clear she was sure of no such thing, "but what I need is a swift Messenger's horse, not a magic fiddle." She ignored his protests, ushering him back to bed, and then went upstairs to pack her things.

"So you're sure about this?" Jizell asked the next morning.

"I have to go," Leesha said. "It's too much for Vika and Darsy to handle alone."

Jizell nodded. "Rojer seems to think he's taking you," she said.

"Well he's not," Leesha said. "I'm hiring a Messenger."

"He's been packing his things all morning," Jizell said.

"He's barely healed," Leesha said.

"Bah!" Jizell said. "It's near three moons. I haven't seen him use his cane all morning. I think it's been nothing more than a reason to be around you for some time."

Leesha's eyes bulged. "You think that Rojer . . . ?"

Jizell shrugged. "I'm just saying, it isn't every day a man comes along who'll brave corelings for your sake."

"Jizell, I'm old enough to be his mother!" Leesha said.

"Bah!" Jizell scoffed. "You're only twenty-seven, and Rojer says he's twenty."

"Rojer says a lot of things that aren't so," Leesha said.

Jizell shrugged again.

"You say you're nothing like my mum," Leesha said, "but you both find a way to turn every tragedy into a discussion about my love life."

Jizell opened her mouth to reply, but Leesha held up a hand to stay her. "If you'll excuse me," she said, "I have a Messenger to hire." She left the kitchen in a fume, and Rojer, listening at the door, barely managed to get out of her way and out of sight.

Between her father's arrangements and her earnings from Jizell, Leesha was able to acquire a promissory note from the Duke's Bank for one hundred fifty Milnese suns. It was a sum beyond the dreams of Angierian peasantry, but Messengers didn't risk their lives for klats. She'd hoped it would be enough, but Rojer's words proved prophetic, or a curse.

Spring trade was on in full, and even the worst Messengers had assignments. Skot was out of the city, and the secretary at the Messengers' Guild flat-out refused to help her. The best they could offer was next week's man south, a full six days away.

"I could walk there in that time!" she shouted at the clerk.

"Then I suggest you get started," the man said dryly.

Leesha bit her tongue and stomped off. She thought she would lose her mind if she had to wait a week to leave. If her father died in that week . . .

"Leesha?" a voice called. She stopped short, turning slowly.

"It is you!" Marick called, striding up to her with his arms outspread. "I didn't realize you were still in the city!" Shocked, Leesha let him embrace her.

"What are you doing in the guildhouse?" Marick asked, backing up to eye her appreciatively. He was still handsome, with his wolf eyes.

"I need an escort to take me back to Cutter's Hollow," she said. "There's a flux sweeping the town, and they need my help."

"I could take you, I suppose," Marick said. "I'll need to call a favor to cover my run to Riverbridge tomorrow, but that should be easy enough."

"I have money," Leesha said.

"You know I don't take money for escort work," Marick said, leering at her as he swept in close. "There's only one payment that interests me." His hand reached around to squeeze her buttock, and Leesha resisted the urge to pull away. She thought of the people that needed her, and more, she thought of what Jizell had said about flowers no one saw. Perhaps it was the Creator's plan that she should meet Marick this day. She swallowed hard and nodded at him.

Marick swept Leesha into a shadowed alcove off the main hall. He pushed her against the wall behind a wooden statue and kissed her deeply. After a moment, she returned the kiss, putting her arms around his shoulders, his tongue warm in her mouth.

"I won't have that problem this time," Marick promised, taking her hand and placing it on his rigid manhood.

Leesha smiled timidly. "I could come to your inn before dark," she said. "We could . . . spend the night, and leave in the morning."

Marick looked from side to side, and shook his head. He pushed her against the wall again, reaching down with one hand to unbuckle his belt. "I've waited for this too long," he grunted. "I'm ready now, and I'm not letting it get away!"

"I'm not doing it in a hallway!" Leesha hissed, pushing him back. "Someone will see!"

"No one will see," Marick said, pressing in and kissing her again. He produced his stiff member, and started pulling up her skirts. "You're here, like magic," he said, "and this time, so am I. What more could you want?"

"Privacy?" Leesha asked. "A bed? A pair of candles? Anything!"

"A Jongleur singing outside the window?" Marick mocked, his fingers probing between her legs to find her opening. "You sound like a virgin."

"I *am* a virgin!" Leesha hissed.

Marick pulled away, his erection still in his hand, and looked at her wryly. "Everyone in Cutter's Hollow knows you stuck that ape Gared a dozen times at least," he said. "Are you still lying about it after all this time?"

Leesha scowled and drove her knee hard into his crotch, storming out of the guildhouse while Marick was still groaning on the ground.

"No one would take you?" Rojer asked that night.

"No one I wouldn't have to bed in exchange," Leesha grunted, leaving out that she had indeed been willing to go that far. Even now, she worried that she'd made a huge mistake. Part of her wished she had just let Marick have his way, but even if Jizell was right and her maidenhead wasn't the most precious thing in all the world, it was surely worth more than that.

She scrunched up her eyes too late, only serving to squeeze out the tears she sought to prevent. Rojer touched her face, and she looked at him. He smiled and reached out, producing a brightly colored handkerchief as if from her ear. She laughed in spite of herself, and took the kerchief to dry her eyes.

"I could still take you," he said. "I walked all the way from here to Shepherd's Dale. If I can do that, I can get you to Cutter's Hollow."

"Truly?" Leesha asked, sniffing. "That's not just one of your Jak Scaletongue stories, like being able to charm corelings with your fiddle?"

"Truly," Rojer said.

"Why would you do that for me?" Leesha asked.

Rojer smiled, taking her hand in his crippled one. "We're survivors, aren't we?" he asked. "Someone once told me that survivors have to look out for one another."

Leesha sobbed, and hugged him.

Am I going mad? Rojer asked himself as they left the gates of Angiers behind. Leesha had purchased a horse for the trip, but Rojer had no riding experience, and Leesha little more. He sat behind her as she guided the beast at a pace barely faster than they could walk.

Even then, the horse jarred his stiff legs painfully, but Rojer did not complain. If he said anything before they were out of sight of the city, Leesha would make them turn back.

Which is what you should do anyway, he thought. *You're a Jongleur, not a Messenger.*

But Leesha needed him, and he knew from the first time he saw her that he could never refuse her anything. He knew she saw him as a child, but that would change when he brought her home. She would see there was more to him; that he could take care of himself, and her as well.

And what was there for him in Angiers, anyway? Jaycob was gone, and the guild likely thought he was dead, as well, which was probably for the best. "If you go to the guard, it's you they'll hang," Jasin had said, but Rojer was smart enough to know that if Goldentone ever learned he was alive, he would never get the chance to tell tales.

He looked at the road ahead, though, and his gut clenched. Like Cricket Run, Farmer's Stump was just a day away on horseback, but Cutter's Hollow was much farther, perhaps four nights even with the horse. Rojer had never spent more than two nights outside, and that just the once. Arrick's death flashed in his mind. Could he handle losing Leesha, too?

"Are you all right?" Leesha asked.

"What?" Rojer replied.

"Your hands are shaking," Leesha said.

He looked at his hands on her waist, and saw that she was right. "It's nothing," he managed. "I just felt a chill out of nowhere."

"I hate that," Leesha said, but Rojer barely heard. He stared at his hands, trying to will them to stillness.

You're an actor! he scolded himself. *Act brave!*

He thought of Marko Rover, the brave explorer in his stories. Rojer had described the man and mummed his adventures so many times, every trait and mannerism was second nature to him. His back straightened, and his hands ceased to shake.

"Let me know when you get tired," he said, "and I'll take over the reins."

"I thought you've never ridden before," Leesha said.

"You learn things by doing them," Rojer said, quoting the line Marko Rover used whenever he encountered something new.

Marko Rover was never afraid to do things he'd never done before.

With Rojer at the reins, they made better time, but even so, they barely made it to Farmer's Stump before dusk. They stabled the horse and made their way to the inn.

"You a Jongleur?" the innkeep asked, taking in Rojer's motley.

"Rojer Halfgrip," Rojer said, "out of Angiers and points west."

"Never heard of you," the innkeep grunted, "but the room's free if you put on a show."

Rojer looked to Leesha, and when she shrugged and nodded, he smiled, pulling out his bag of marvels.

Farmer's Stump was a small cluster of buildings and houses, all connected by warded boardwalks. Unlike any other village Rojer had ever been to, the Stumpers went outside at night, walking freely—if hastily—from building to building.

The freedom meant a full taproom, which pleased Rojer well. He performed for the first time in months, but it felt natural, and he soon had the entire room clapping and laughing at tales of Jak Scaletongue and the Warded Man.

When he returned to his seat, Leesha's face was a little flushed with wine. "You were wonderful," she said. "I knew you would be."

Rojer beamed, and was about to say something when a pair of men came over, bearing a handful of pitchers. They handed one to Rojer, and another to Leesha.

"Just a thanks for the show," the lead man said. "I know it ent much . . ."

"It's wonderful, thank you," Rojer said. "Please, join us." He gestured to the empty seats at their table. The two men sat.

"What brings you through the Stump?" the first man asked. He was short, with a thick black beard. His companion was taller, burlier, and mute.

"We're heading to Cutter's Hollow," Rojer said. "Leesha is an Herb Gatherer, going to help them fight the flux."

"Hollow's a long way," the man with the black beard said. "How'll you last the nights?"

"Don't fear for us," Rojer said. "We have a Messenger's circle."

"Portable circle?" the man asked in surprise. "That must'a cost a pretty pile."

Rojer nodded. "More than you know," he said.

"Well, we won't keep you from yer beds," the man said, he and his companion rising from the table. "You'll want an early start." They moved away, going to join a third man at another table as Rojer and Leesha finished their drinks and headed to their room.

CHAPTER 27

NIGHTFALL
332 AR

"LOOK AT ME! I'm a Jongleur!" said one of the men, plopping the belled motley cap on his head and prancing around the road. The black-bearded man barked a laugh, but their third companion, larger than both of them combined, said nothing. All were smiling.

"I'd like to know what that witch threw at me," the black-bearded man said. "Dunked my whole head in the stream, and it still feels like my eyes are on fire." He held up the circle and the reins of the horse, grinning. "Still, an easy take like that only comes along once a'life."

"Be months before we need t'work again," the man in the motley cap agreed, jingling the purse of coins, "and not a scratch on us!" He jumped up and clicked his heels.

"Maybe not a scratch on *you*," chuckled the black-bearded man, "but I've a few on my back! That arse was worth nearly as much as the circle, even if that dust she threw in my eyes made it so I could barely see what went where." The man in the motley cap laughed, and their giant mute companion clapped his hands with a grin.

"Should've taken her with us," the man in the motley cap said. "Gets cold in that miserable cave."

"Don't be stupid," the black-bearded man said. "We got a horse and a Messenger circle, now. We don't need to stay in the cave no more, and that's best. Word in the Stump's that the duke's noticin' them just leaving the town gettin' hit. We go south first thing come morning, before we've got Rhinebeck's guards on our heels."

The men were so busy with their discussion, they didn't

notice the man riding down the road toward them until he was just a dozen yards away. In the waning light, he seemed wraith-like, wrapped in flowing robes and astride a dark horse, moving in the shadow of the trees beside the forest road.

When they did take note of him, the mirth on their faces fell away, replaced with looks of challenge. The black-bearded man dropped the portable circle to the ground and pulled a heavy cudgel from the horse, advancing on the stranger. He was squat and thickly set, with thinning hair above his long, unkempt beard. Behind him, the mute raised a club the size of a small tree, and the man in the motley cap brandished a spear, the head nicked and burred.

"This here's our road," the black-bearded man explained to the stranger. "We're fine to share, like, but there's a tax."

In answer, the stranger stepped his horse from the shadows.

A quiver of heavy arrows hung from his saddle, the bow strung and in easy reach. A spear as long as a lance rested in a harness on the other side, a rounded shield beside it. Strapped behind his seat, several shorter spears jutted, their points glittering wickedly in the setting sun.

But the stranger reached for no weapon, merely letting his hood slip back a bit. The men's eyes widened, and their leader backed away, scooping up the portable circle.

"Might let you pass just the once," he amended, glancing back at the others. Even the giant had gone pale with fear. They kept their weapons ready, but carefully edged around the giant horse and backed down the road.

"We'd best not see you on this road again!" the black-bearded man called, when they were a safe distance away.

The stranger rode on, unconcerned.

Rojer fought his terror as their voices receded. They had told him they would kill him if he tried to rise again. He reached into his secret pocket to take hold of his talisman, but all he found were some broken bits of wood and a clump of yellow-gray hair. It must have broken when the mute kicked him in the gut. He let the remnants fall from his numb fingers into the mud.

The sound of Leesha's sobs cut into him, making him afraid to look up. He had made that mistake before, when the giant had gotten off his back to take his turn with Leesha. One of the others had quickly taken his place, using Rojer's back as a bench to watch the fun.

There was little intelligence in the giant's eyes, but if he lacked the sadism of his companions, his dumb lust was a terror in itself; the urges of an animal in the body of a rock demon. If Rojer could have removed the image of him atop Leesha from his mind by clawing out his eyes, he would not have hesitated.

He had been a fool, advertising their path and valuables like that. Too much time spent in the Western hamlets had dulled his natural, city-bred distrust of strangers.

Marko Rover wouldn't have trusted them, he thought.

But that wasn't entirely true. Marko was forever getting tricked or clubbed on the head and left for dead. He survived by keeping his wits afterward.

He survives because it's a story and you control the ending, Rojer reminded himself.

But the image of Marko Rover picking himself up and dusting himself off stuck with him, and eventually, Rojer gathered his strength and his nerve, forcing himself to his knees. Pain shot through him, but he did not think they had broken any bones. His left eye was so swollen he could barely see out of it, and he tasted blood in his mouth from his thickened lip. He was covered in bruises, but Abrum had done worse.

But there were no guardsmen, this time, to haul him to safety. No mother or master to put themselves in a demon's path.

Leesha whimpered again, and guilt shook him. He had fought to save her honor, but they had been three, all armed and stronger than him. What could he have done?

I wish they'd killed me, he thought to himself, slumping. *Better dead than to have seen . . .*

Coward, a voice in the back of his head snarled. *Get up. She needs you.*

Rojer staggered to his feet, looking around. Leesha was curled up in the dirt of the forest road, sobbing, without even the strength to cover her shame. There was no sign of the bandits.

Of course, it hardly mattered. They had taken his portable circle, and without it he and Leesha were as good as dead. Farmer's Stump was almost a full day behind them, and there was nothing ahead on the road for several days' walk. It would be dark in little more than an hour.

Rojer ran to Leesha's side, falling to his knees beside her.

"Leesha, are you all right?" he asked, cursing himself for the crack in his voice. She needed him to be strong.

"Leesha, please answer me," he begged, squeezing her shoulder.

Leesha ignored him, curled up tight, shaking as she wept. Rojer stroked her back and whispered comfort to her, subtly tugging her dress back down. Whatever place her mind had retreated to in order to withstand the ordeal, she was reluctant to leave it. He tried to hold her in his arms, but she shoved him violently away, curling right back up, wracked with tears.

Leaving her side, Rojer picked through the dirt, gathering what few things had been left them. The bandits had dug through their bags, taking what they wanted and tossing the rest, mocking and destroying their personal effects. Leesha's clothing lay scattered in the road, and Rojer found Arrick's brightly colored bag of marvels trampled in the muck. Much of what it had contained was taken or smashed. The painted wooden juggling balls were stuck in the mud, but Rojer left them where they lay.

Off the road where the mute had kicked it, he spied his fiddle case, and dared to hope they might survive. He rushed over to find the case broken open. The fiddle itself was salvageable with a little tuning and some new strings, but the bow was nowhere to be found.

Rojer looked as long as he dared, throwing leaves and underbrush in every direction with mounting panic, but to no avail. It was gone. He put the fiddle back in its case and spread out one of Leesha's long skirts, bundling the few salvageable items within.

A strong breeze broke the stillness, rustling the leaves of the trees. Rojer looked up at the setting sun, and realized suddenly, in a way he had not before, that they were going to die. What did it matter if he had a bowless fiddle and some clothes with him when it happened?

He shook his head. They weren't dead yet, and it was possible to avoid corelings for a night, if you kept your wits. He squeezed his fiddle case reassuringly. If they lived through the night, he could cut off a lock of Leesha's hair and make a new bow. The corelings couldn't hurt them if he had his fiddle.

To either side of the road, the woods loomed dark and dangerous, but Rojer knew corelings hunted men above all other creatures. They would stalk the road. The woods were their best hope to find a hiding place, or a secluded spot to prepare a circle.

How? that hated voice asked again. *You never bothered to learn.*

He moved back to Leesha, kneeling gently by her side. She was still shuddering, crying silently. "Leesha," he said quietly, "we need to get off the road."

She ignored him.

"Leesha, we need to find a place to hide." He shook her.

Still no response.

"Leesha, the sun is setting!"

The sobbing stopped, and Leesha raised wide, frightened eyes. She looked at his concerned, bruised face, and her face screwed up as her crying resumed.

But Rojer knew he had touched her for a moment, and refused to let that go. He could think of few things worse than what had happened to her, but getting torn apart by corelings was one of them. He gripped her shoulders and shook her violently.

"Leesha, you need to get ahold of yourself!" he shouted. "If we don't find a place to hide soon, the sun is going to find us scattered all over the road!"

It was a graphic image, intentionally so, and it had the desired effect as Leesha came up for air, gasping but no longer crying. Rojer dried her tears with his sleeve.

"What are we going to do?" Leesha squeaked, gripping his arms painfully tight.

Again, Rojer called upon the image of Marko Rover, and this time it came readily. "First, we're going to get off the road," he said, sounding confident when he was not. Sounding as if he had a plan when he did not. Leesha nodded, and let him help her stand. She winced in pain, and it cut right through him.

With Rojer supporting Leesha, they stumbled off the road and into the woods. The remaining light dropped dramatically under the forest canopy, and the ground crackled beneath their feet with twigs and dry leaves. The place smelled sickly sweet with rotting vegetation. Rojer hated the woods.

He scoured his mind for the tales of people who had survived the naked night, sifting for words with a ring of truth, searching for something, anything, that could help them.

Caves were best, the tales all agreed. Corelings preferred to hunt in the open, and a cave with even simple wards across the front was safer than attempting to hide. Rojer could recall at least three consecutive wards from his circle. Perhaps enough to ward a cave mouth.

But Rojer knew of no caves nearby, and had no idea what to look for. He cast about helplessly, and caught the sound of running water. Immediately, he pulled Leesha in that direction. Corelings tracked by sight, sound, and smell. Barring true succor, the best way to avoid them was to mask those things. Perhaps they could dig into the mud on the water's bank.

But when he found the source of the sound, it was only a trickling stream with no bank to speak of. Rojer grabbed a smooth rock from the water and threw it, growling in frustration.

He turned back to find Leesha squatting in the ankle-deep water, weeping again as she scooped up handfuls and splashed herself. Her face. Her breasts. Between her legs.

"Leesha, we have to go . . ." he said, reaching out to take her arm, but she shrieked and pulled away, bending for more water.

"Leesha, we don't have time for this!" he screamed, grabbing her and yanking her to her feet. He dragged her back into the woods, having no idea what he was looking for.

Finally he gave up, spotting a small clearing. There was nowhere to hide, so their only hope was to ward a circle. He let Leesha go and moved quickly into the clearing, brushing away a bed of rotting leaves to find the soft, moist dirt beneath.

Leesha's blurry eyes slowly came into focus as she watched Rojer scraping leaves from the forest floor. She leaned heavily on a tree, her legs still weak.

Only minutes ago, she had thought that she would never recover from her ordeal, but the corelings about to rise were too immediate a threat, and she found, almost gratefully, that they kept her mind from replaying her assault again and again, as it had been since the men had taken their spoils and left.

Her pale cheeks were smudged with dirt and streaked with tears. She tried to smooth her torn dress, to regain some sense of dignity, but the ache between her legs was a constant reminder that her dignity was scarred forever.

"It's almost dark!" she moaned. "What are we going to do?"

"I'll draw a circle in the dirt," Rojer said. "It will be all right. I'll make everything all right," he promised.

"Do you even know how?" she asked.

"Sure . . . I guess," Rojer said unconvincingly. "I had that portable one for years. I can remember the symbols." He picked up a stick, and started to scratch lines in the dirt, glancing up to the darkening sky again and again as he worked.

He was being brave for her. Leesha looked at Rojer, and felt a stab of guilt for getting him into this. He claimed to be twenty, but she knew that for a lie with years to spare. She should never have brought him along on such a dangerous journey.

He looked much like he had the first time she had seen him, his face puffy and bruised, blood oozing from his nose and mouth. He wiped at it with his sleeve and pretended it did not affect him. Leesha saw through the act easily, knew he was as frantic as she, but his effort was comforting, nonetheless.

"I don't think you're doing that right," she said, looking over his shoulder.

"It'll be fine," Rojer snapped.

"I'm sure the corelings will love it," she shot back, annoyed by his dismissive tone, "since it won't hinder them in the least." She looked around. "We could climb a tree," she suggested.

"Corelings can climb better than we can," Rojer said.

"What about finding someplace to hide?" she asked.

"We looked as long as we could," Rojer said. "We barely have time to make this circle, but it should keep us safe."

"I doubt it," Leesha said, looking at the shaky lines in the dirt.

"If only I had my fiddle . . ." Rojer began.

"Not that pile of dung again," Leesha snapped, sharp irritation rising to drive back humiliation and fear. "It's one thing to brag to the apprentices in the light of day that you can charm demons with your fiddle, but what do you gain in carrying a lie to your grave?"

"I'm not lying!" Rojer insisted.

"Have it your way," Leesha sighed, crossing her arms.

"It will be all right," Rojer said again.

"Creator, can't you stop lying, even for a moment?" Leesha cried. "It's not going to be all right and you know it. Corelings aren't bandits, Rojer. They won't be satisfied with just . . ." She looked down at her torn skirts, and her voice trailed off.

Rojer's face screwed up in pain, and Leesha knew she had

been too harsh. She wanted to lash out at something, and it was easy to blame Rojer and his inflated promises for what happened. But in her heart, she knew it was more her fault than his. He left Angiers for *her*.

She looked at the darkening sky and wondered if she would have time to apologize before they were torn to pieces.

Movement in the trees and scrub behind them sent them both whirling around in fear. A man, swathed in gray robes, stepped into the clearing. His face was hidden in the shadows of his hood, and though he carried no weapons, Leesha could tell from his bearing that he was dangerous. If Marick was a wolf, this man was a lion.

She steeled herself, ravishment fresh in her mind, and honestly wondered for a moment which would be worse: another rape, or the demons.

Rojer was up in an instant, grabbing her arm and thrusting her behind him. He brandished the stick before him like a spear, his face twisted in a snarl.

The man ignored them both, moving over to inspect Rojer's circle. "You have holes in your net there, there, and there," he said, pointing, "and this," he kicked the dirt by one crude symbol, "this isn't even a ward."

"Can you fix it?" Leesha asked hopefully, pulling free from Rojer's grasp and moving toward the man.

"Leesha, no," Rojer whispered urgently, but she ignored him.

The man didn't even glance her way. "There's no time," he replied, pointing to the corelings already beginning to rise at the edge of the clearing.

"Oh, no," Leesha whimpered, her face draining of color.

The first to solidify was a wind demon. It hissed at the sight of them and crouched as if to spring, but the man gave it no time. As Leesha watched in amazement, he leapt right at the coreling, grabbing its arms to prevent it from spreading its wings. The demon's flesh hissed and smoked at his touch.

The wind demon shrieked and opened its maw, filled with needle-sharp teeth. The man snapped his head back, flipping off his hood, then drove forward, slamming the top of his bald head into the coreling's snout. There was a flash of energy, and the demon was thrown backward. It struck the ground, stunned. The man stiffened his fingers, driving them into the coreling's throat. There was another flash, and black ichor erupted in a spray.

The man turned sharply, wiping the ichor from his fingers as he strode past Rojer and Leesha. She could see his face now, though there was little human about it. His head was completely shaved, even his eyebrows, and in place of the lost hair were tattoos. They circled his eyes and rested atop his head, lined his ears and covered his cheeks, even running along his jaw and around his lips.

"My camp is near," he said, ignoring their stares. "Come with me if you want to see the dawn."

"What about the demons?" Leesha asked, as they fell in behind him. As if to accentuate her point, a pair of wood demons, knobby and barklike, rose up to block their path.

The man pulled off his robe, stripping down to a loincloth, and Leesha saw that the tattoos were not limited to his head. Wards ran along his rippling arms and legs in intricate patterns, with larger ones on his elbows and knees. A circle of protection covered his back, and another large tattoo stood at the center of his muscular chest. Every inch of him was warded.

"The Warded Man," Rojer breathed. Leesha found the name dimly familiar.

"I'll handle the demons," the man said. "Take this," he ordered, handing Leesha his robe.

He sprinted at the corelings, tumbling into a somersault and uncoiling to strike both demons in the chest with his heels. Magic exploded from the blow, blasting the wood demons from their path.

The race through the trees was a blur. The Warded Man set a brutal pace, unhindered by the corelings that leapt at them from all sides. A wood demon sprang at Leesha from the trees, but the man was there, driving a warded elbow into its skull with explosive force. A wind demon swooped in to slash its talons at Rojer, but the Warded Man tackled it away, punching right through one of its wings, grounding it.

Before Rojer could thank him, the Warded Man was off again, picking their path through the trees. Rojer helped Leesha keep up, untangling her skirts when they caught in the brush.

They burst from the trees, and Leesha could see a fire across the road: the Warded Man's camp. Standing between them and succor, though, was a group of corelings, including a massive, eight-foot-tall rock demon.

The rock demon roared and beat its thick, armored chest

with gigantic fists, its horned tail lashing back and forth. It knocked the other corelings aside, claiming the prey for itself.

The Warded Man showed no fear as he approached the monster. He gave a high-pitched whistle, and set his feet, ready to spring when the demon attacked.

But before the rock demon could strike, two massive spikes burst from its breast, sizzling and sparking with magic. The Warded Man struck quickly, driving his warded heel into the coreling's knee and collapsing the monster to the ground.

As it fell, Leesha saw a monstrous black form behind it. The beast kicked away, pulling its horns free, and then reared up with a whinny, driving its hooves into the coreling's back with a thunderclap of magic.

The Warded Man charged the remaining demons, but the corelings scattered at his approach. A flame demon spat fire at him, but the man held up his spread hands, and the blast became a cool breeze as it passed through his warded fingers. Shaking with fear, Rojer and Leesha followed him into his camp, stepping into his circle of protection with enormous relief.

"Twilight Dancer!" the Warded Man called, whistling again. The great horse ceased its attack on the prone demon and galloped after them, leaping into the ring.

Like its master, Twilight Dancer looked like something out of a nightmare. The stallion was enormous, bigger by far than any horse Leesha had ever seen. Its coat was thick, shining ebony, and its body was armored in warded metal. The barding about its head had been fitted with a long pair of metal horns, etched with wards, and even its black hooves had been carved with the magic symbols, painted silver. The towering beast looked more demon than horse.

Hanging from its black leather saddle were various harnesses for weapons, including a yew bow and a quiver of arrows, long knives, a bola, and spears of various lengths. A polished metal shield, circular and convex, was hooked over the saddle horn, ready to be snatched up in an instant. Its rim was etched with intricate wards.

Twilight Dancer stood quietly as the Warded Man checked it for wounds, seeming unconcerned with the demons that lurked just a few feet away. When he was assured that his mount was unharmed, the Warded Man turned back to Leesha and Rojer, who stood nervously in the center of the circle, still reeling from the events of the last few minutes.

"Stoke the fire," the man told Rojer. "I've some meat we can put on, and a loaf of bread." He moved toward his supplies, rubbing at his shoulder.

"You're hurt," Leesha said, coming out of her shock and rushing over to inspect his wounds. There was a cut on his shoulder, and another, deeper gash on his thigh. His skin was hard, and crisscrossed with scars, giving it a rough texture, but not unpleasant to the touch. There was a slight tingle in her fingertips as she touched him, like static from a carpet.

"It's nothing," the Warded Man said. "Sometimes a coreling gets lucky and catches a talon on flesh before the wards drive it away." He tried to pull away, reaching for his robe, but she was not to be put off.

"No wound from a demon is 'nothing,' " Leesha said. "Sit down and I'll dress these," she ordered, ushering him over to sit against a large stone. In truth, she was almost as frightened of the man as she was of the corelings, but she had dedicated her life to helping the injured, and the familiar work took her mind away from the pain that still threatened to consume her.

"I've an herb pouch in that saddlebag," the man said, gesturing. Leesha opened the bag and found the pouch. She bent to the fire's light as she rooted through the contents.

"I don't suppose you have any pomm leaves?" she asked.

The man looked at her. "No," he said. "Why? There's plenty of hogroot."

"It's nothing," Leesha mumbled. "I swear, you Messengers seem to think that hogroot is a cure for everything." She took the pouch, along with a mortar and pestle and a skin of water, and knelt beside the man, grinding the hogroot and a few other herbs into a paste.

"What makes you think I'm a Messenger?" the Warded Man asked.

"Who else would be out on the road alone?" Leesha asked.

"I haven't been a Messenger in years," the man said, not flinching at all as she cleaned out the wounds and applied the stinging paste. Rojer narrowed his eyes as he watched her spread the salve on his thick muscles.

"Are you an Herb Gatherer?" the Warded Man asked, as she passed a needle through the fire and threaded it.

Leesha nodded, but kept her eyes on her work, brushing a thick lock of hair behind her ear as she set to stitching the gash in his thigh. When the Warded Man made no further comment, she flicked her eyes up to meet his. They were dark, the wards around the sockets giving them a gaunt, deep-set look. Leesha couldn't hold that gaze for long, and quickly looked away.

"I'm Leesha," she said, "and that's Rojer making supper. He's a Jongleur." The man nodded Rojer's way, but like Leesha, Rojer could not meet his gaze for long.

"Thank you for saving our lives," Leesha said. The man only grunted in response. She paused briefly, waiting for him to return the introduction, but he made no effort to do so.

"Don't you have a name?" she asked at last.

"None I've used in some time," the man answered.

"But you do have one," Leesha pressed. The man only shrugged.

"Well then what shall we call you?" she asked.

"I don't see that you need to call me anything," the man replied. He noted that her work was finished, and pulled away from her touch, again covering himself from head to foot in his gray robes. "You owe me nothing. I would have helped anyone in your position. Tomorrow I'll see you safely to Farmer's Stump."

Leesha looked to Rojer by the fire, then back at the Warded Man. "We just left the Stump," she said. "We need to get to Cutter's Hollow. Can you take us there?" The gray hood shook back and forth.

"Going back to the Stump will cost us a week at least!" Leesha cried.

The Warded Man shrugged. "That's not my problem."

"We can pay," Leesha blurted. The man glanced at her, and she looked away guiltily. "Not now, of course," she amended. "We were attacked by bandits on the road. They took our horse, circle, money, even our food." Her voice softened. "They took . . . everything." She looked up. "But once I get to Cutter's Hollow, I'll be able to pay."

"I have no need of money," the Warded Man said.

"Please!" Leesha begged. "It's urgent!"

"I'm sorry," the Warded Man said.

Rojer came over to them, scowling. "It's fine, Leesha," he said. "If this cold heart won't help us, we'll find our own way."

"What way is that?" Leesha snapped. "The way of being killed while you attempt to hold off demons with your stupid fiddle?"

Rojer turned away, stung, but Leesha ignored him, turning back to the man.

"Please," she begged, grabbing his arm as he, too, turned away from her. "A Messenger came to Angiers three days ago with word of a flux that spread through the Hollow. It's killed a dozen people so far, including the greatest Herb Gatherer that ever lived. The Gatherers left in the town can't possibly treat everyone. They need my help."

"So you want me to not only put aside my own path, but to go *into* a village rife with flux?" the Warded Man asked, sounding anything but willing.

Leesha began to weep, falling to her knees as she clutched at his robes. "My father is very sick," she whispered. "If I don't get there soon, he may die."

The Warded Man reached out, tentatively, and put a hand on her shoulder. Leesha was unsure of how she had reached him, but she sensed that she had. "Please," she said again.

The Warded Man stared at her for a long time. "All right," he said at last.

Cutter's Hollow was six days' ride from Fort Angiers, on the southern outskirts of the Angierian forest. The Warded Man told them it would take four more nights to reach the village. Three, if they pressed hard and made good time. He rode alongside them, slowing his great stallion to their pace on foot.

"I'm going to scout up the road," he said after a while. "I'll be back in an hour or so."

Leesha felt a stab of cold fear as he kicked his stallion's flanks and galloped off down the road. The Warded Man scared her almost as much as the bandits or the corelings, but at least in his presence she was safe from those other threats.

She hadn't slept at all, and her lip throbbed from all the times she had bitten it to keep from crying. She had scrubbed every inch of herself after they fell asleep, but still she felt soiled.

"I've heard stories of this man," Rojer said. "Spun a few myself. I thought he was only a myth, but there can't be two men painted like that, who kill corelings with their bare hands."

"You called him the Warded Man," Leesha said, remembering.

Rojer nodded. "That's what he's called in the tales. No one knows his real name," he said. "I heard of him over a year ago when one of the duke's Jongleurs passed through the Western hamlets. I thought he was just an ale story, but it seems the duke's man was telling true."

"What did he say?" Leesha asked.

"That the Warded Man wanders the naked night, hunting demons," Rojer said. "He shuns human contact, appearing only when he needs supplies and paying with ancient gold. From time to time, you hear tales of him rescuing someone on the road."

"Well, we can bear witness to that," Leesha said. "But if he can kill demons, why has no one tried to learn his secrets?"

Rojer shrugged. "According to the tales, no one dares. Even the dukes themselves are terrified of him, especially after what happened in Lakton."

"What happened?" Leesha asked.

"The story goes that the dockmasters of Lakton sent spies to steal his combat wards," Rojer said. "A dozen men, all armed and armored. Those he didn't kill were crippled for life."

"Creator!" Leesha gasped, covering her mouth. "What kind of monster are we traveling with?"

"Some say he's part demon himself," Rojer agreed, "the result of a coreling raping a woman on the road."

He started suddenly, his face coloring as he realized what he'd said, but his thoughtless words had the opposite effect, breaking the spell of her fear. "That's ridiculous," she said, shaking her head.

"Others say he's no demon at all," Rojer pressed on, "but the Deliverer himself, come to lift the Plague. Tenders have prayed to him and begged his blessings."

"I'd sooner believe he's half coreling," Leesha said, though she sounded less than sure.

They traveled on in uncomfortable silence. A day ago, Leesha had been unable to get a moment's peace from Rojer, the Jongleur constantly trying to impress her with his tales and music, but now he kept his eyes down, brooding. Leesha knew he was hurting, and part of her wanted to offer comfort, but a bigger part needed comfort of her own. She had nothing to give.

Soon after, the Warded Man rode back to them. "You two walk too slow," he said, dismounting. "If we want to save ourselves a fourth night on the road, we'll need to cover thirty miles today. You two ride. I'll run alongside."

"You shouldn't be running," Leesha said. "You'll tear the stitches I put in your thigh."

"It's all healed," the Warded Man said. "Just needed a night's rest."

"Nonsense," Leesha said, "that gash was an inch deep." As if to prove her point, she went over to him and knelt, lifting the loose robe away from his muscular, tattooed leg.

But when she removed the bandage to examine the wound, her eyes widened in shock. New, pink flesh had already grown to knit the wound together, her stitches poking from otherwise healthy skin.

"That's impossible," she said.

"It was just a scratch," the Warded Man said, sliding a wicked blade through the stitches and picking them out one by one. Leesha opened her mouth, but the Warded Man rose and went back to Twilight Dancer, taking the reins and holding them out to her.

"Thank you," she said numbly, taking the reins. In one moment, everything she knew about healing had been called into question. Who was this man? *What* was he?

Twilight Dancer cantered down the road, and the Warded Man ran alongside in long, tireless strides, easily keeping pace with the horse as the miles melted away under his warded feet. When they rested, it was from Rojer and Leesha's desire and not his. Leesha watched him subtly, searching for signs of fatigue, but there were none. When they made camp at last, his breath was smooth and regular as he fed and watered his horse, even as she and Rojer groaned and rubbed the aches from their limbs.

There was an awkward silence about the campfire. It was well past dark, but the Warded Man walked freely about the camp, collecting firewood and removing Twilight Dancer's barding, brushing the great stallion down. He moved from the horse's circle to their own without a thought to the wood demons lurking about. One leapt at him from the cover of the brush, but the Warded Man paid no mind as it slammed into the wards barely an inch from his back.

While Leesha prepared supper, Rojer limped bowlegged around the circle, attempting to walk off the stiffness of a day's hard riding.

"I think my stones are crushed from all that bouncing," he groaned.

"I'll have a look, if you like," Leesha said. The Warded Man snorted.

Rojer looked at her ruefully. "I'll be all right," he managed, continuing to pace. He stopped suddenly a moment later, staring down the road.

They all looked up, seeing the eerie orange light of the flame demon's mouth and eyes long before the coreling itself came into sight, shrieking and running hard on all fours.

"How is it that the flame demons don't burn the entire forest down?" Rojer wondered, watching the trailing wisps of fire behind the creature.

"You're about to find out," the Warded Man said. Rojer found the amusement in his voice even more unsettling than his usual monotone.

The words were barely spoken before howls heralded the approach of a pack of wood demons, three strong, barreling down the road after the flame demon. One of them had another flame demon hanging limply from its jaws, dripping black ichor.

So occupied was the flame demon with outrunning its pursuers, it failed to notice the other wood demons gathering in the scrub at the edges of the road until one pounced, pinning the hapless creature and eviscerating it with its back talons. It shrieked horribly, and Leesha covered her ears from the sound.

"Woodies hate flame demons," the Warded Man explained when it was over, his eyes glinting in pleasure at the kill.

"Why?" Rojer asked.

"Because wood demons are vulnerable to demonfire," Leesha said. The Warded Man looked up at her in surprise, then nodded.

"Then why don't the flame demons set them on fire?" Rojer asked.

The Warded Man laughed. "Sometimes they do," he said, "but flammable or no, there isn't a flame demon alive that's a match in a fight with a wood demon. Woodies are second only to rock demons in strength, and they're nearly invisible within the borders of the forest."

"The Creator's Great Plan," Leesha said. "Checks and balances."

"Nonsense," the Warded Man countered. "If the flame

demons burned everything away, there would be nothing left for them to hunt. Nature found a way to solve the problem."

"You don't believe in the Creator?" Rojer asked.

"We have enough problems already," the Warded Man answered, and his scowl made it clear that he had no desire to pursue the subject.

"There are some that call you the Deliverer," Rojer dared.

The Warded Man snorted. "There's no Deliverer coming to save us, Jongleur," he said. "You want demons dead in this world, you have to kill them yourself."

As if in response, a wind demon bounced off Twilight Dancer's wardnet, filling the area with a brief flash of light. The stallion dug at the dirt with his hooves, as if eager to leap from the circle and do battle, but he stayed in place, waiting for a command from his master.

"How is it the horse stands so unafraid?" Leesha asked. "Even Messengers stake down their horses at night to keep them from bolting, but yours seems to *want* to fight."

"I've been training Twilight Dancer since he was foaled," the Warded Man said. "He's always been warded, so he's never learned to fear corelings. His sire was the biggest, most aggressive beast I could find, and his dam the same."

"But he seemed so gentle when we rode him," Leesha said.

"I've taught him to channel his aggressive urges," the Warded Man said, pride evident in his normally emotionless tone. "He returns kindness, but if he's threatened, or I am, he'll attack without hesitation. He once crushed the skull of a wild boar that would have gored me for sure."

Finished with the flame demons, the wood demons began to circle the wards, drawing closer and closer. The Warded Man strung his yew bow and took out his quiver of heavy-tipped arrows, but he ignored the creatures as they slashed at the barrier and were thrown back. When they finished their meal, he selected an unmarked arrow and took an etching tool from his warding kit, slowly inscribing the shaft with wards.

"If we weren't here . . ." Leesha asked.

"I would be out there," the Warded Man answered, not looking up at her. "Hunting."

Leesha nodded, and was quiet for a time, watching him. Rojer shifted uncomfortably at her obvious fascination.

"Have you seen my home?" she asked softly.

The Warded Man looked at her curiously, but made no reply.

"If you've come from the south, you must've come through the Hollow," Leesha said.

The Warded Man shook his head. "I give the hamlets a wide berth," he said. "The first person to see me runs off, and before long I'm met by a cluster of angry men with pitchforks."

Leesha wanted to protest, but she knew the people of Cutter's Hollow would act much as he described. "They're only afraid," she said lamely.

"I know," the Warded Man said. "And so I leave them in peace. There's more to the world than hamlets and cities, and if the price of one is losing the other . . ." He shrugged. "Let people hide in their homes, caged like chickens. Cowards deserve no better."

"Then why did you save us from the demons?" Rojer asked.

The Warded Man shrugged. "Because you're human and they're abominations," he said. "And because you struggled to survive, right up to the last minute."

"What else could we have done?" Rojer asked.

"You'd be amazed how many just lie down and wait for the end," the Warded Man said.

They made good time the fourth day out from Angiers. Neither the Warded Man nor his stallion seemed to know fatigue, Twilight Dancer easily paced his master's loping run.

When they finally made camp for the night, Leesha made a thin soup from the Warded Man's remaining stores, but it barely filled their bellies. "What are we going to do for food?" she asked him, as the last of it vanished down Rojer's throat.

The Warded Man shrugged. "I hadn't planned for company," he said as he sat back, carefully painting wards onto his fingernails.

"Two more days of riding is a long way to go without food," Rojer lamented.

"You want to cut the trip in half," the Warded Man said, blowing on a nail to dry it, "we could travel by night, as well. Twilight Dancer can outrun most corelings, and I can kill the rest."

"Too dangerous," Leesha said. "We'll do Cutter's Hollow no good if we all get killed. We'll just have to travel hungry."

"I'm not leaving the wards at night," Rojer agreed, rubbing his stomach regretfully.

The Warded Man pointed to a coreling stalking the camp. "We could eat that," he said.

"You can't be serious!" Rojer cried in disgust.

"Just the *thought* is sickening," Leesha agreed.

"It's not so bad, really," the man said.

"You've actually *eaten* demon?" Rojer asked.

"I do what I have to, to survive," the man replied.

"Well, I'm certainly not going to eat demon meat," Leesha said.

"Me neither," Rojer agreed.

"Very well," the Warded Man sighed, getting up and taking his bow, a quiver of arrows, and a long spear. He stripped off his robe, revealing his warded flesh, and moved to the edge of the circle. "I'll see what I can hunt up."

"You don't need to . . . !" Leesha called, but the man ignored her. A moment later, he had vanished into the night.

It was more than an hour before he returned, carrying a plump pair of rabbits by the ears. He handed the catch to Leesha, and returned to his seat, picking up the tiny warding brush.

"You make music?" he asked Rojer, who had just finished restringing his fiddle and was plucking at the strings, adjusting the tensions.

Rojer jumped at the comment. "Y-yes," he managed.

"Will you play something?" the Warded Man asked. "I can't remember the last time I heard music."

"I would," Rojer said sadly, "but the bandits kicked my bow into the woods."

The man nodded and sat in thought a moment. Then he stood suddenly, producing a large knife. Rojer shrank back, but the man just stepped back out of the circle. A wood demon hissed at him, but the Warded Man hissed right back, and the demon shied away.

He returned soon after with a supple length of wood, shearing the bark with his wicked blade. "How long was it?" he asked.

"E-eighteen inches," Rojer stuttered.

The Warded Man nodded, cutting the branch to the appropriate length and walking over to Twilight Dancer. The stallion did not react as he cut a length of hair from its tail. He notched the wood and tied the horsehair flat and thick on one side. He knelt next to Rojer, bending the branch. "Tell me when the tension is right," he said, and Rojer laid the fingers of his crippled hand on the hair. When he was satisfied, the Warded Man tied the other end and handed it to him.

Rojer beamed at the gift, treating it with resin before taking up his fiddle. He put the instrument to his chin and gave it a few strokes with the new bow. It wasn't ideal, but he grew more confident, pausing to tune once more before beginning to play.

His skillful fingers filled the air with a haunting melody that took Leesha's thoughts to Cutter's Hollow, wondering at its fate. Vika's letter was almost a week gone. What would she find when she arrived? Perhaps the flux had passed with no more loss, and this desperate ordeal had been for nothing.

Or perhaps they needed her more than ever.

The music affected the Warded Man as well, she noticed, for his hands stopped their careful work, and he stared off into the night. Shadows draped his face, obscuring the tattoos, and she saw in his sad countenance that he had been comely once. What pain had driven him to this existence, scarring himself and shunning his own kind for the company of corelings? She found herself aching to heal him, though he showed no hurt.

Suddenly, the man shook his head as if to clear it, startling Leesha from her reverie. He pointed off into the darkness. "Look," he whispered. "They're dancing."

Leesha looked out in amazement, for indeed, the corelings had ceased to test the wards, had ceased even to hiss and shriek. They circled the camp, swaying in time to the music. Flame demons leapt and twirled, sending ribbons of fire spiraling away from their knotted limbs, and wind demons looped and dove through the air. Wood demons had crept from the cover of the forest, but they ignored the flame demons, drawn to the melody.

The Warded Man looked at Rojer. "How are you doing that?" he asked, his voice awed.

Rojer smiled. "The corelings, they have an ear for music," he said. He rose to his feet, walking to the edge of the circle. The demons clustered there, watching him intently. He began to walk the circle's perimeter, and they followed, mesmerized. He stopped and swayed from side to side as he continued to play, and the corelings mirrored his movements almost exactly.

"I didn't believe you," Leesha apologized quietly. "You really *can* charm them."

"And that's not all," Rojer boasted. With a twist and a series of sharp strokes of the bow, he turned the melody sour; once pure notes ringing out discordant and tainted. Suddenly, the corelings were shrieking again, covering their ears with their talons and scrambling away from Rojer. They drew back further and further as the musical assault continued, vanishing into the shadows beyond the firelight.

"They haven't gone far," Rojer said. "As soon as I stop, they'll be back."

"What else can you do?" the Warded Man asked quietly.

Rojer smiled, as content to perform for an audience of two as he was for a cheering crowd. He softened his music again, the chaotic notes smoothly flowing back into the haunting melody. The corelings reappeared, drawn to the music once more.

"Watch this," Rojer instructed, and changed the sound again, the notes rising high and grating, causing even Leesha and the Warded Man to grit their teeth and lean away.

The reaction of the corelings was more pronounced. They grew enraged, shrieking and roaring as they threw themselves at the barrier with abandon. Again and again the wards flared and threw them back, but the demons did not relent, smashing themselves against the wardnet in an insane attempt to reach Rojer and silence him forever.

Two rock demons joined the throng, shoving past the others and hammering at the wards as yet more added to the press. The Warded Man rose silently behind Rojer and lifted his bow.

The string hummed, and one of the heavy, thick-headed arrows exploded into the chest of the nearest rock demon like a bolt of lightning, brightening the area for a moment. Again and again the Warded Man fired into the horde, his hands a blur. The warded bolts blasted the corelings back, and the few that rose again were quickly torn to pieces by their fellows.

Rojer and Leesha stood horrified at the slaughter. The Jongleur's bow slipped from the fiddle's strings, hanging forgotten in his limp hand as he watched the Warded Man work.

The demons were screaming still, but it was pain and fear now, their desire to attack the wards vanished with the music. Still the Warded Man fired, again and again until his arrows were all gone. He grabbed a spear, throwing it and striking a fleeing wood demon in the back.

There was chaos now, the few remaining corelings desperate to escape. The Warded Man stripped off his robe, ready to leap from the circle to kill demons with his bare hands.

"No, please!" Leesha cried, throwing herself at him. "They're running!"

"You would spare them?" the Warded Man roared, glaring at her, his face terrible with wrath. She fell back in fear, but she kept her eyes locked on his.

"Please," she begged. "Don't go out there."

Leesha feared he might strike her, but he only stared at her, his breath heaving. Finally, after what seemed an eternity, he calmed and took up his robe, covering his wards once more.

"Was that necessary?" she asked, breaking the silence.

"The circle wasn't designed to forbid so many corelings at once," the Warded Man said, his voice again a cold monotone. "I don't know that it would have held."

"You could have just asked me to stop playing," Rojer said.

"Yes," the Warded Man agreed, "I could have."

"Then why didn't you?" Leesha demanded.

The Warded Man didn't answer. He strode out of the circle and began cutting his arrows from the demon corpses.

Leesha was fast asleep later that night when the Warded Man approached Rojer. The Jongleur, staring out at the fallen demons, gave a startled jump when the man squatted down next to him.

"You have power over the corelings," he said.

Rojer shrugged. "So do you," he said. "More than I ever will."

"Can you teach me?" the Warded Man asked.

Rojer turned, meeting the man's gimlet eyes. "Why?" he asked. "You kill demons by the score. What's my trick compared to that?"

"I thought I knew my enemies," the Warded Man said. "But you've shown me otherwise."

"You think they may not be all bad, if they can enjoy music?" Rojer asked.

The Warded Man shook his head. "They are no patrons of art, Jongleur," he said. "The moment you ceased to play, they would have killed you without hesitation."

Rojer nodded, conceding the point. "Then why bother?" he asked. "Learning the fiddle is a lot of work to charm beasts you can just as easily kill."

The Warded Man's face hardened. "Will you teach me or not?" he asked.

"I will . . ." Rojer said, thinking it through, "but I want something in return."

"I have plenty of money," the Warded Man assured him.

Rojer waved his hand dismissively. "I can get money whenever I need it," he said. "What I want is more valuable."

The Warded Man said nothing.

"I want to travel with you," Rojer said.

The Warded Man shook his head. "Out of the question," he said.

"You don't learn the fiddle overnight," Rojer argued. "It'll take weeks to become even passable, and you'll need more skill than that to charm even the least discriminating coreling."

"And what do you get out of it?" the Warded Man asked.

"Material for stories that will fill the duke's amphitheater night after night," Rojer said.

"What about her?" the Warded Man asked, nodding back toward Leesha. Rojer looked at the Herb Gatherer, her breast gently rising and falling as she slept, and the Warded Man did not miss the significance of that gaze.

"She asked me to escort her home, nothing more," Rojer said at last.

"And if she asks you to stay?"

"She won't," Rojer said quietly.

"My road is no Marko Rover tale, boy," the Warded Man said. "I've no time to be slowed by one who hides at night."

"I have my fiddle now," Rojer said with more bravery than he felt. "I'm not afraid."

"You need more than courage," the Warded Man said. "In the wild, you kill or be killed, and I don't just mean demons."

Rojer straightened, swallowing the lump in his throat. "Everyone who tries to protect me ends up dead," he said. "It's time I learned to protect myself."

The Warded Man leaned back, considering the young Jongleur.

"Come with me," he said at last, rising.

"Out of the circle?" Rojer asked.

"If you can't do that, you're no use to me," the Warded Man said. When Rojer looked around doubtfully, he added, "Every coreling for miles heard what I did to their fellows. It's doubtful we'll see more tonight."

"What about Leesha?" Rojer asked, rising slowly.

"Twilight Dancer will protect her, if need be," the man said. "Come on." He moved out of the circle and vanished into the night.

Rojer swore, but he grabbed his fiddle and followed the man down the road.

Rojer clutched his fiddle case tightly as they moved through the trees. He had made to take it out at first, but the Warded Man had waved for him to put it away.

"You'll draw attention we don't want," he whispered.

"I thought you said we weren't likely to see any corelings tonight," Rojer hissed back, but the Warded Man ignored him, moving through the darkness as if it were broad day.

"Where are we going?" Rojer asked for what seemed the hundredth time.

They climbed a small rise, and the Warded Man lay flat, pointing downward.

"Look there," he told Rojer. Below, Rojer could see three very familiar men and a horse sleeping within the tight confines of an even more familiar portable circle.

"The bandits," Rojer breathed. A flood of emotions washed over him—fear, rage, and helplessness—and in his mind's eye, he relived the ordeal they had put him and Leesha through. The mute stirred in his sleep, and Rojer felt a stab of panic.

"I've been tracking them since I found you," the Warded Man said. "I spotted their fire while I was hunting tonight."

"Why did you bring me here?" Rojer asked.

"I thought you might like a chance to get your circle back," the Warded Man said.

Rojer looked back at him. "If we steal the circle while they're sleeping, the corelings will kill them before they know what's happening."

"The demons are thin," the Warded Man said. "They'll have better odds than you did."

"Even so, what makes you think I'd want to risk it?" Rojer asked.

"I watch," the man said, "and I listen. I know what they did to you . . . and to Leesha."

Rojer was quiet a long while. "There are three of them," he said at last.

"This is the wild," the Warded Man said. "If you want to live in safety, go back to the city." He spat the last word like a curse.

But Rojer knew there was no safety in the city, either. Unbidden, he saw Jaycob crumple to the ground, and heard Jasin's laughter. He could have sought justice after the attack, but he chose to flee, instead. He was forever fleeing, and letting others die in his stead. His hand searched for a talisman that was no longer there as he stared down at the fire.

"Was I wrong?" the Warded Man asked. "Shall we go back to our camp?"

Rojer swallowed. "As soon as I have what belongs to me," he decided.

CHAPTER 28

SECRETS
332 AR

LEESHA AWOKE TO A SOFT NICKERING. She opened her eyes to see Rojer brushing down the russet mare she had purchased in Angiers, and for a moment, she dared think the last two days a dream.

But then Twilight Dancer stepped into view, the giant stallion towering over the mare, and it all came rushing back.

"Rojer," she asked quietly, "where did my horse come from?"

Rojer opened his mouth to reply, but the Warded Man strode into the camp then, with two small rabbits and a handful of apples. "I saw your friends' fire last night," he explained, "and thought we would travel faster all ahorse."

Leesha was quiet a long time, digesting the news. A dozen emotions ran through her, many of them shameful and unsavory. Rojer and the Warded Man gave her time, and she was thankful for that. "Did you kill them?" she asked at last. A cold part of her wanted him to say yes, even though it went against everything she believed; everything Bruna had taught her.

The Warded Man looked her in the eye. "No," he said, and an immense relief flooded through her. "I scattered them long enough to steal the horse, but that was all."

Leesha nodded. "We'll send word of them to the duke's magistrate with the next Messenger to pass through the Hollow."

Her herb blanket was rolled crudely and strapped to the saddle. She pulled it off and examined it, relief washing over her as she found most of the bottles and pouches intact. They had smoked all her tampweed, but that was easy enough to replace.

After breakfast, Rojer rode the mare while Leesha sat behind the Warded Man on Twilight Dancer. They traveled swiftly, for there were clouds gathering, and threat of rain.

Leesha felt like she should have been afraid. The bandits were alive and ahead of them. She remembered the leering face of the black-bearded man and the raucous laughter of his companion. Worst of all, she remembered the terrible weight and dumb, violent lust of the mute.

She should have been afraid, but she wasn't. Even more than Bruna, the Warded Man made her feel safe. He did not tire. He did not fear. And she knew without a doubt that no harm could ever come to her while she was under his protection.

Protection. It was an odd feeling, needing protection, like something out of another life. She had been protecting herself for so long, she had forgotten what it was like. Her skills and wits were enough to keep her safe in civilized places, but those things meant little in the wild.

The Warded Man shifted, and she realized she had tightened her hands around his waist, pressing close to him with her head resting on his shoulder. She pulled away, so caught up in her embarrassment that she almost didn't see the hand, lying in the scrub at the side of the road.

When she did, she screamed.

The Warded Man pulled up, and Leesha practically fell off the horse, rushing to the spot. She brushed the weeds aside, gasping as she realized the hand wasn't attached to anything; bitten clean off.

"Leesha, what is it?" Rojer cried, as he and the Warded Man ran to her.

"Were they camped near here?" Leesha asked, holding up the appendage. The Warded Man nodded. "Take me there," Leesha ordered.

"Leesha, what good could . . ." Rojer began, but she ignored him, keeping her eyes locked on the Warded Man.

"Take. Me. There," she said. The Warded Man nodded, putting down a stake and tying the mare's reins to it.

"Guard," he said to Twilight Dancer, and the stallion nickered.

They found the camp soon after, awash in blood and half-eaten bodies. Leesha lifted her apron to cover her mouth against the stench. Rojer retched and ran from the clearing.

But Leesha was no stranger to blood. "Only two," she said, examining the remains with feelings too mixed for her to begin to sort.

The Warded Man nodded. "The mute is missing," he said. "The giant."

"Yes," Leesha said. "And the circle as well."

"The circle, as well," the Warded Man agreed after a moment.

The heavy clouds continued to gather as they made their way back to the horses. "There's a Messenger cave ten miles up the road," the Warded Man said. "If we press hard and skip lunch, we should make it there before the rain comes. We'll have to take refuge until the storm passes."

"The man who kills corelings with his bare hands is afraid of a little rain?" Leesha asked.

"If the cloud is thick enough, corelings might rise early," the Warded Man said.

"Since when are you afraid of corelings?" Leesha pressed.

"It's stupid and dangerous to fight in the rain," the Warded Man said. "Rain makes mud, and mud obscures wards and ruins footing."

They were barely settled in the cave before the storm struck. Drenching sheets of rain turned the road to mud and the sky went dark, save for the sharp strikes of lightning. The wind howled at them, punctuated by roaring thunder.

Much of the cave mouth was warded already, symbols of power etched deeply into the rock, and the Warded Man quickly secured the rest with a cache of wardstones left within.

As the Warded Man predicted, a few demons rose early in the false dark. He watched grimly as they crept out from the darkest parts of the wood, relishing their early release from the Core. The brief flashes of light outlined their sinuous forms as they frolicked in the wet.

They tried to break into the cave, but the wards held strong. Those that ventured too close regretted it, greeted with a jab from the scowling Warded Man's spear.

"Why are you so angry?" Leesha asked, drawing bowls and spoons from her bag as Rojer worked to light a small fire.

"Bad enough they come at night," the Warded Man spat. "They've no right to the day."

Leesha shook her head. "You'd be happier if you could accept what is," she advised.

"I don't want to be happy," he replied.

"Everyone wants to be happy," Leesha scoffed. "Where's the cookpot?"

"In my bag," Rojer said. "I'll get it."

"No need," Leesha said, rising. "Mind the fire. I'll fetch it."

"No!" Rojer cried, but even as he leapt to his feet, he saw he was too late. Leesha drew forth his portable circle with a gasp.

"But . . ." she stammered, "they took this!" She looked at Rojer, and saw his eyes flick to the Warded Man. She turned to him, but could read nothing in the shadows of his cowl.

"Is someone going to explain?" she demanded.

"We . . . got it back," Rojer said lamely.

"I know you got it back!" Leesha shouted, whipping the coil of rope and wooden plates to the cave floor. "How?"

"I took it when I took the horse," the Warded Man said suddenly. "I didn't want it on your conscience, so I kept it from you."

"You stole it?"

"*They* stole it," the Warded Man corrected. "I took it back."

Leesha looked at him for a long time. "You took it at night," she said quietly.

The Warded Man said nothing.

"Were they using it?" Leesha demanded through gritted teeth.

"The road is dangerous enough without such men," the Warded Man replied.

"You murdered them," Leesha said, surprised to find her eyes filling with tears. *Find the worst human being you can,* her father had said, *and you'll still find something worse by looking out the window at night.* No one deserved to be fed to a coreling. Not even them.

"How could you?" she asked.

"I murdered no one," the Warded Man said.

"As good as!"

The man shrugged. "They did the same to you."

"That makes it right?" Leesha cried. "Look at you! You don't even care! Two men dead at least, and you sleep no worse! You're a monster!" She sprang at him, trying to beat him with her fists, but he caught her wrists, and watched impassively as she struggled with him.

"Why do you care?" he asked.

"I'm an Herb Gatherer!" she screamed. "I've taken an oath! I've sworn to heal, but you"—she looked at him coldly—"all you're sworn to do is kill."

After a moment, the fight left her and she pulled away. "You mock what I am," she said, slumping down and staring at the cave floor for several minutes. Then she looked up at Rojer.

"You said 'we,' " she accused.

"What?" the Jongleur asked, trying to appear confused.

"Before," she clarified. "You said 'we got it back.' And the circle was in your bag. Did you go with him?"

"I . . ." Rojer stalled.

"Don't you lie to me, Rojer!" Leesha growled.

Rojer's eyes dropped to the floor. After a moment, he nodded.

"He was telling the truth before," Rojer admitted. "All he took was the horse. While they were distracted, I took the circle and your herbs."

"Why?" Leesha asked, her voice cracking slightly. The disappointment in her tone cut the young Jongleur like a knife.

"You know why," Rojer replied somberly.

"Why?" Leesha demanded again. "For me? For my honor? Tell me, Rojer. Tell me you killed in my name!"

"They had to pay," Rojer said tightly. "They had to pay for what they did. It was unforgivable."

Leesha laughed out loud, though there was no humor in the sound. "Don't you think I know that?" she shouted. "Do you think I saved myself for twenty-seven years to give my flower to a gang of thugs?"

Silence hung in the cave for a long moment. A peal of thunder cut the air.

"Saved yourself . . ." Rojer echoed.

"Yes, corespawn you!" Leesha shrieked, angry tears streaking her face. "I was a virgin! Does even that justify giving men to the corelings?"

"Giving?" the Warded Man echoed.

Leesha whirled on him. "Of course giving!" she shouted. "I'm sure your friends the demons were overjoyed at your little present. Nothing pleases them more than having humans to kill. With so few of us left, we're a rare treat!"

The Warded Man's eyes widened, reflecting the firelight. It was a more human expression than Leesha had ever seen on his face, and the sight made her momentarily forget her anger. He looked utterly terrified, and backed away from them, all the way to the cave mouth.

Just then, a coreling threw itself against the wardnet, filling the cave with a flash of silver light. The Warded Man whirled and screamed at the demon, a sound unlike anything Leesha had ever heard, but one she recognized all the same. It was a vocalization of what she had felt inside when she had been pinned, that terrible evening on the road.

The Warded Man snatched up one of his spears, hurling it out into the rain. There was an explosion of magic as it struck the demon, blasting it into the mud.

"Damn you!" the Warded Man roared, ripping off his robes and leaping out into the downpour. "I swore I would give you nothing! Nothing at all!" He pounced on a wood demon from behind, crushing it to him. The massive ward on his chest flared, and the coreling burst into flame, despite the pouring rain. He kicked away as the creature flailed about.

"Fight me!" the Warded Man demanded of the others, planting his feet in the mud. Corelings leapt to oblige, slashing and biting, but the man fought like a demon himself, and they were flung away like autumn leaves against the wind.

From the rear of the cave, Twilight Dancer whinnied and pulled at his hobble, trained to fight by his master's side. Rojer moved to calm the animal, looking to Leesha in confusion.

"He can't fight them all," Leesha said. "Not in the mud." Already, many of the man's wards were splattered with muck.

"He means to die," she said.

"What should we do?" Rojer asked.

"Your fiddle!" Leesha cried. "Drive them away!"

Rojer shook his head. "The wind and thunder would drown me out," he said.

"We can't just let him kill himself!" Leesha screamed at him.

"You're right," Rojer agreed. He strode over to the Warded Man's weapons, taking a light spear and the warded shield. Realizing what he meant to do, Leesha moved to stop him, but he stepped out of the cave before she could reach him, rushing to the Warded Man's side.

A flame demon spat fire at Rojer, but it fizzled in the rain and fell short. The coreling leapt at him, but he lifted the warded shield and the creature was deflected. His concentration in front, he didn't see the other flame demon behind him until it was too late. The coreling sprang, but the Warded Man snatched the three-foot-tall demon right out of the air, hurling it away, its flesh sizzling at his touch.

"Get inside!" the man ordered.

"Not without you!" Rojer shot back. His red hair was soaked and matted to his face, and he squinted in the wind and pelting rain, but he faced the Warded Man squarely, not backing down an inch.

Two wood demons leapt for them, but the Warded Man dropped to the mud, sweeping Rojer's legs from under him. The slashing claws missed as the Jongleur fell, and the Warded Man's fists drove the creatures back. Other corelings were gathering, though, attracted by the flashes of light and the sounds of battle. Too many to fight.

The Warded Man looked at Rojer, lying in the mud, and the madness left his eyes. He held out a hand, and the Jongleur took it. The two of them darted back into the cave.

"What were you thinking?" Leesha demanded, tying off the last of the bandages. "Both of you!"

Rojer and the Warded Man, bundled in blankets by the fire, said nothing as she berated them. After a time, she trailed off, preparing a hot broth with herbs and vegetables and handing it to them wordlessly.

"Thank you," Rojer said quietly, the first words he had spoken since returning to the cave.

"I'm still angry with you," Leesha said, not meeting his eyes. "You lied to me."

"I didn't," Rojer protested.

"You kept things from me," Leesha said. "It's no different."

Rojer looked at her for a time. "Why did you leave Cutter's Hollow?" he asked.

"What?" Leesha asked. "Don't change the subject."

"If these people mean so much to you that you're willing to risk anything, endure anything, to get home," Rojer pressed, "why did you leave?"

"My studies . . ." Leesha began.

Rojer shook his head. "I know something about running away from problems, Leesha," he said. "There's more to it than that."

. . "I don't see that it's any of your business," Leesha said.

"Then why am I waiting out a rainstorm in a cave surrounded by corelings in the middle of nowhere?" Rojer asked.

Leesha looked at him for long moments, then sighed, her will for the fight fading. "I suppose you'll be hearing about it soon enough," Leesha said. "The people of Cutter's Hollow have never been very good at keeping secrets."

She told them everything. She didn't mean to, but the cold and damp cave became a Tender's confessional of sorts, and once she began, the words overflowed; her mother, Gared, the rumors, her flight to Bruna, her life as an outcast. The Warded Man leaned forward and opened his mouth at the mention of Bruna's liquid demonfire, but he closed it again and sat back, choosing not to interrupt.

"So that's it," Leesha said. "I'd hoped to stay in Angiers, but it seems the Creator has another plan."

"You deserve better," the Warded Man said.

Leesha nodded, looking at him. "Why did you go out there?" she asked quietly, pointing her chin toward the cave mouth.

The Warded Man slumped, staring at his knees. "I broke a promise," he said.

"That's all?"

He looked up at her, and for once, she didn't see the tattoos lining his face, only his eyes, piercing her. "I swore I would never give them anything," he said. "Not even to save my own life. But instead, I've given them everything that made me human."

"You didn't give them anything," Rojer said. "I was the one that took the circle." Leesha's hands tightened on her bowl, but she said nothing.

The Warded Man shook his head. "I facilitated it," he said. "I knew how you felt. Giving them to you was the same as giving them to the corelings."

"They would have continued to prey on the road," Rojer said. "The world is better without them."

The Warded Man nodded. "But that's no excuse for giving them to demons," he said. "I could as easily have taken the circle—killed them even—face-to-face, in the light of day."

"So you went out there tonight out of guilt," Leesha said. "Why all the times before? Why this war on corelings?"

"If you haven't noticed," the Warded Man replied, "the corelings have been at war with us for centuries. Is it so wrong to take the fight to them?"

"You think yourself the Deliverer, then?" Leesha asked.

The Warded Man scowled. "Waiting for the Deliverer has left humanity crippled for three hundred years," he said. "He's a myth. He's not coming, and it's time people saw that and began standing up for themselves."

"Myths have power," Rojer said. "Don't be so quick to dismiss them."

"Since when are you a man of faith?" Leesha asked.

"I believe in hope," Rojer said. "I've been a Jongleur all my life, and if I've learned one thing in twenty-three years, it's that the stories people cry for, the ones that stay with them, are the ones that offer hope."

"Twenty," Leesha said suddenly.

"What?"

"You told me you were twenty."

"Did I?"

"You're not even that, are you?" she asked.

"I am!" Rojer insisted.

"I'm not stupid, Rojer," Leesha said. "I've not known you three months, and you've grown an inch in that time. No twenty-year-old does that. What are you? Sixteen?"

"Seventeen," Rojer snarled. He threw down his bowl, spilling the remaining broth. "Does that please you? You were right to tell Jizell you were nearly old enough to be my mother."

Leesha stared at him. She opened her mouth to say something sharp, but closed it again. "I'm sorry," she said instead.

"And you, Warded Man?" Rojer asked, turning to him. "Will you add 'too young' to your list of reasons why I shouldn't travel with you?"

"I became a Messenger at seventeen," the man replied, "and I was traveling much younger than that."

"And how old is the Warded Man?" Rojer asked.

"The Warded Man was born in the Krasian desert, four summers ago," he replied.

"And the man beneath the wards?" Leesha asked. "How old was he when he died?"

"It doesn't matter how many summers he had," the Warded Man said. "He was a stupid, naive child, with dreams too big for his own good."

"Is that why he had to die?" Leesha asked.

"He was killed. And yes."

"What was his name?" Leesha asked quietly.

The Warded Man was quiet a long time. "Arlen," he said finally. "His name was Arlen."

CHAPTER 29

IN THE
PREDAWN LIGHT
332 AR

WHEN THE WARDED MAN AWOKE, the storm had broken temporarily, but gray clouds hung heavy in the sky, promising more rain to come. He looked into the cave, his warded eyes easily piercing the dark, and made out the two horses and the sleeping Jongleur. Leesha, however, was missing.

It was early still; the false light before true sunrise. Most of the corelings had likely fled to the Core long since, but with the heavy cloud, one could never be sure. He rose to his feet, tearing away the bandages Leesha had tied the night before. The wounds were all healed.

The Herb Gatherer's path was easy to follow in the thick muck, and he found her not far off, kneeling on the ground picking herbs. Her skirts were hiked up far above her knees to keep them from the mud, and the sight of her smooth white thighs made him flush. She was beautiful in the predawn light.

"You shouldn't be out here," he said. "The sun's not yet risen. It's not safe."

Leesha looked at him, and smiled. "Are *you* in a position to lecture *me* on putting myself in danger?" she asked with a raised eyebrow. "Besides," she went on when he made no reply, "what demon could harm me with you here?"

The Warded Man shrugged, squatting beside her. "Tampweed?" he asked.

Leesha nodded, holding up the rough-leafed plant with thick, clustered buds. "Smoked from a pipe, it relaxes the muscles, inducing a feeling of euphoria. Combined with skyflower, I can use it to brew a sleeping potion strong enough to put down an angry lion."

"Would that work on a demon?" the Warded Man asked.

Leesha frowned. "Don't you ever think of anything else?" she asked.

The Warded Man looked hurt. "Don't presume to know me," he said. "I kill corelings, yes, and because of that, I have seen places no living man remembers. Shall I recite poetry I've translated from ancient Rusk? Paint for you the murals of Anoch Sun? Tell you of machines from the old world that could do the work of twenty men?"

Leesha laid a hand on his arm, and he fell silent. "I'm sorry," she said. "I was wrong to judge. I know something of the weight of guarding the knowledge of the old world."

"It's no hurt," the Warded Man said.

"That doesn't make it right," Leesha said. "To answer your question, I honestly don't know. Corelings eat and shit, so it reasons they can be drugged. My mentor said the Herb Gatherers of old took great tolls in the Demon War. I have some skyflower. I can brew the potion when we get to Cutter's Hollow, if you like."

The Warded Man nodded eagerly. "Can you brew me something else, as well?" he asked.

Leesha sighed. "I wondered when you would ask that," she said. "I won't make you liquid demonfire."

"Why not?" the Warded Man asked.

"Because men cannot be trusted with the secrets of fire," Leesha said, turning to face him. "If I give it to you, you will use it, even if it means setting half the world on fire."

The Warded Man looked at her, and made no reply.

"And what do you need it for, anyway?" she asked. "You already have powers beyond anything a few herbs and chemics can create."

"I'm just a man . . ." he began, but Leesha cut him off.

"Demonshit," she said. "Your wounds heal in minutes, and you can run as fast as a horse all day without breathing hard. You throw wood demons around as if they were children, and you see in the dark as if it were broad day. You're not 'just' anything."

The Warded Man smiled. "There's no hiding from your eyes," he said.

Something about the way he said it sent a thrill through Leesha. "Were you always this way?" she asked.

He shook his head. "It's the wards," he said. "Wards work by feedback. Do you know this word?"

Leesha nodded. "It's in the books of old-world science," she said.

The Warded Man grunted. "Corelings are creatures of magic," he said. "Defensive wards siphon off some of that magic, using it to form their barrier. The stronger the demon, the stronger the force that repels it. Offensive wards work the same way, weakening the corelings' armor even as it strengthens the blow. Inanimate objects cannot hold the charge long, and it dissipates. But somehow, every time I strike a demon, or one strikes me, I absorb a little of its strength."

"I felt the tingle that first night, when I touched your skin," Leesha said.

The Warded Man nodded. "When I warded my flesh, it wasn't only my appearance that became . . . inhuman."

Leesha shook her head, taking his face in her hands. "Our bodies are not what make us human," she whispered. "You can take your humanity back, if only you wish it." She leaned closer, and kissed him softly.

He stiffened at first, but the shock wore off, and suddenly he was kissing her back. She closed her eyes and opened her mouth to him, her hands caressing the smoothness of his shaved head. She could not feel the wards, only his warmth, and his scars.

We both have scars, she thought. *His are just laid bare to the world.*

She leaned backward, pulling him with her. "We'll get muddy," he warned.

"We're already muddy," she said, falling onto her back with him atop her.

Blood pounded in Leesha's ears as the Warded Man kissed her. She ran her hands over his hard muscles and opened her legs, grinding her hips into his.

Let this be my first time, she thought. *Those men are dead and gone, and he can erase their mark from me, as well. I do this because I choose it.*

But she was afraid. *Jizell was right,* she thought. *I never should have waited this long. I don't know what to do. Everyone thinks I know what to do and I don't and he's going to expect me to know because I'm an Herb Gatherer . . .*

Oh, Creator, what if I can't please him? she worried. *What if he tells someone?*

She forced the thought from her head. *He'll never tell. That's why it has to be him. It's meant to be him. He's just like me. An outsider. He's walked the same road.*

She fumbled with his robes, untying the loincloth he wore beneath and releasing him. He groaned as she took him in her hand and pulled.

He knows I was a virgin, she reminded herself, hiking her skirts. *He is hard and I am wet and what else is there to know?*

"What if I get you with child?" he whispered.

"I hope you do," she whispered back, taking him and pulling him inside her.

What else is there to know? she thought again, and her back arched in pleasure.

Shock hit the Warded Man as Leesha kissed him. It had been only moments since he admired her thighs, but he had never dreamed she might share the attraction. That any woman would.

He stiffened momentarily, paralyzed, but as always when he was in need, his body took over for him, wrapping her in a crushing embrace and returning the kiss hungrily.

How long since he had last been kissed? How long since that night he had walked Mery home and been told she could never be a Messenger's wife?

Leesha fumbled with his robes, and he knew that she meant to take things further than he had ever gone before. Fear gripped him, an unfamiliar feeling. He had no idea what to do; how to please a woman. Was she expecting him to have the experience she lacked? Was she counting that his skill in battle would translate here as well?

But perhaps it would, for even as his thoughts raced, his body continued of its own accord, acting on instincts ingrained into every living thing since the dawn of time. The same instincts that called him to fight.

But this wasn't some battle. This was something else.

Is she the one? the thought echoed in his head.

Why her, and not Renna? If he had been anyone other than

who he was, he would have been married almost fifteen years now, raising a host of children. Not for the first time, an image flashed in his mind of what Renna might look like now, in the full flower of her womanhood, his and his only.

Why her, and not Mery? Mery, whom he would have married, had she consented to be a Messenger's wife. He would have tied himself to Miln for love, just as Ragen had. He would have been better off if he had married Mery. He saw that now. Ragen was right. He had Elissa . . .

An image of Elissa flashed in his mind as he pulled the top of Leesha's dress down, exposing her soft breasts. The time he'd seen Elissa free her breast to nurse Marya, and wished just for a moment that he could suckle there rather than the child. He had felt ashamed afterward, but that image always remained fresh in his mind.

Was Leesha the one meant for him? Did such a thing exist? He would have scoffed at the notion an hour ago, but he looked at Leesha, so beautiful and so willing, so understanding of who he was. She would understand if he was clumsy, if he didn't know quite where to touch or how to stroke. A muddy bit of ground in the predawn light was no fit marriage bed, but at the moment it seemed better than the feathered mattress in Ragen's manse.

But doubt niggled at him.

It was one thing to risk himself in the night; he had nothing left to lose, no one left to mourn him. If he died, he would not fill so much as a single tear bottle. But could he take those risks, if Leesha was waiting for him in safe succor? Would he give up the fight; become like his father? Become so accustomed to hiding that he could not stand up for his own?

Children need their father, he heard Elissa say.

"What if I get you with child?" he whispered between kisses, not knowing what he wanted her to say.

"I hope you do," she whispered back.

She pulled at him, threatening to pull apart his entire world, but she was offering something more, and he grasped at it.

And then he was inside her, and he felt whole.

For a moment, there was nothing in the world but the pounding of blood and the slide of skin on skin; their bodies easily managing the task as soon as their minds let go. His robe was flung aside. Her dress was a crumple around her midsection. They squirmed and grunted in the mud without a thought to anything but one another.

Until the wood demon struck.

The coreling had stalked them quietly, drawn by their animal sounds. It knew dawn was close, the hated sun soon to rise, but the sight of so much naked flesh aroused its hunger, and it leapt, seeking to return to the Core with hot blood on its talons and fresh meat in its jaws.

The demon struck hard at the Warded Man's exposed back. The wards there flared, throwing the coreling back and slamming the lovers' heads together.

Agile and undeterred, the wood demon recovered quickly, coiling as it struck the ground and springing again. Leesha screamed, but the Warded Man twisted, grasping the leading talons in his hands. He pivoted, using the creature's own momentum to hurl it into the mud.

He did not hesitate, pulling away from Leesha and pressing the advantage. He was naked, but that meant nothing. He had been fighting naked since he first warded his flesh.

He spun a full circuit, driving his heel into the coreling's jaw. There was no flare of magic, his wards covered in mud, but with his enhanced strength, the demon might as well have been kicked by Twilight Dancer. It stumbled back, and the Warded Man roared and advanced, knowing full well the damage it could do if given a moment to recover.

The coreling was big for its breed, standing near to eight feet, and strength for strength, the Warded Man was overmatched. He punched and kicked and elbowed, but there was mud everywhere, and almost all his wards were broken. Barklike armor tore his skin, and his blows were to no lasting effect.

The coreling spun, whipping its tail into the Warded Man's stomach, blasting the breath from his body and throwing him down. Leesha screamed again, and the sound drew the demon's attention. With a shriek, it launched itself at her.

The Warded Man scrambled after the beast, grabbing its trailing ankle just before it could reach her. He pulled hard, tripping the demon, and they wrestled frantically in the mud. Finally, he managed to hook his leg under its armpit and around its throat, locking with his other leg as he squeezed. With both hands, he held one of its legs bent, preventing the demon from rising.

The coreling thrashed and clawed at him, but the Warded Man had leverage now, and the creature could not escape. They rolled about for long moments, locked together, before the sun finally crested the horizon and found a break in the clouds. The barklike skin began to smoke, and the demon thrashed harder. The Warded Man tightened his grip.

Just a few moments more . . .

But then something unexpected happened. The world around him seemed to grow misty; insubstantial. He felt a pull from deep below the ground, and he and the demon began to sink.

A path opened to his senses, and the Core called to him.

Horror and revulsion filled him as the coreling dragged him down. The demon was still solid in his grip, even if the rest of the world had become only a shadow. He looked up, and saw the precious sun fading away.

He grasped at the sight like a lifeline, releasing his leglock and pulling hard on the demon's leg, dragging it back up toward the light. The coreling struggled madly, but terror gave the Warded Man new strength, and with a soundless cry of determination, he hauled the creature back to the surface.

The sun was there to greet them, bright and blessed, and the Warded Man felt himself become solid again as the creature burst into flames. It clawed at the ground, but he held it fast.

When he finally released the charred husk, he was oozing blood everywhere. Leesha ran to him, but he pushed her away, still reeling in horror. What was he, that he could find a path down into the Core? Had he become a coreling himself? What kind of monster would a child of his tainted seed turn out to be?

"You're hurt," she objected, reaching for him again.

"I'll heal," he said, pulling away. The gentle, loving voice he had used just minutes before was gone now, back to the cold monotone of the Warded Man. Indeed, many of his smaller cuts and scrapes were already crusting over.

"But . . ." Leesha protested, "what about . . . ?"

"I made my choice a long time ago, and I chose the night," the Warded Man said. "For a moment I thought I could take it back, but . . ." He shook his head. "There's no going back now."

He picked up his robe, heading for the small cold stream nearby to wash his wounds.

"Corespawn you!" Leesha cried at his back. "You and your mad obsession!"

CHAPTER 30

PLAGUE

332 AR

ROJER WAS STILL ASLEEP when they returned. They changed their muddy clothes silently, backs to one another, and then Leesha shook Rojer awake while the Warded Man saddled the horses. They ate a cold breakfast in silence, and were on the road before the sun had risen far. Rojer rode behind Leesha on her mare, the Warded Man alone on his great stallion. The sky was heavy with cloud, promising more rain to come.

"Shouldn't we have passed a Messenger headed north by now?" Rojer asked.

"You're right," Leesha said. She looked up and down the road, worried.

The Warded Man shrugged. "We'll reach Cutter's Hollow by high sun," he said. "I'll see you there, and be on my way."

Leesha nodded. "I think that's best," she agreed.

"Just like that?" Rojer asked.

The Warded Man inclined his head. "You were expecting more, Jongleur?"

"After all we've been through? Night, yes!" Rojer cried.

"Sorry to disappoint," the Warded Man replied, "but I've business to attend."

"Creator forbid you go a night without killing something," Leesha muttered.

"But what about what we discussed?" Rojer pressed. "Me traveling with you?"

"Rojer!" Leesha cried.

"I've decided it's a bad idea," the Warded Man told him. He glanced at Leesha. "If your music can't kill demons, it's no use to me. I'm better off on my own."

"I couldn't agree more," Leesha put in. Rojer scowled at her, and her cheeks burned. He deserved better, she knew, but she could offer no comfort or explanation when it was taking all her strength to hold back tears.

She had known the Warded Man for what he was. As much as she'd hoped otherwise, she had known his heart might not stay open for long, that all they might have was a moment. But oh, she had wanted that moment! She had wanted to feel safe in his arms, and to feel him inside her. She stroked her belly absently. If he had seeded her and she had found herself with child, she would have cherished it, never questioning whom the father might be. But now . . . there were pomm leaves enough in her stores for what must be done.

They rode on in silence, the coldness between them palpable. Before long, they turned a bend and caught their first glimpse of Cutter's Hollow.

Even from a distance, they could see the village was a smoking ruin.

Rojer held on tightly as they bounced along the road. Leesha had kicked into a gallop upon seeing the smoke, and the Warded Man followed suit. Even in the damp, fires still burned hungrily in Cutter's Hollow, casting billows of greasy black smoke into the air. The town was devastated, and again Rojer found himself reliving the destruction of Riverbridge. Gasping for breath, he squeezed his secret pocket before remembering that his talisman was broken and lost. The horse jerked, and he snapped his hand back to Leesha's waist to keep from being thrown.

Survivors could be seen wandering about like ants in the distance. "Why aren't they fighting the fires?" Leesha asked, but Rojer merely held on, having no answer.

They pulled up as they reached the town, taking in the devastation numbly. "Some of these have been burning for days," the Warded Man noted, nodding toward the remains of once-cozy homes. Indeed, many of the buildings were charred ruins, barely smoking, and others still were cold ash. Smitt's tavern, the only building in town with two floors, had collapsed in on itself, some of the beams still ablaze, and other buildings were missing roofs or entire walls.

Leesha took in the smudged and tear-streaked faces as she rode deeper into town, recognizing every one. All were too occupied with their own grief to take notice of the small group as they passed. She bit her lip to keep from crying.

In the center of town, the townspeople had collected the dead. Leesha's heart clenched at the sight: at least a hundred bodies, without even blankets to cover them. Poor Niklas. Saira and her mother. Tender Michel. Steave. Children she had never met, and elders she had known all her life. Some were burned, and others cored, but most had not a mark on them. Fluxed.

Mairy knelt by the pile, weeping over a small bundle. Leesha felt her throat close up, but somehow managed to get down from her horse and approach, laying a hand on Mairy's shoulder.

"Leesha?" Mairy asked in disbelief. A moment later she surged to her feet, wrapping the Herb Gatherer in a tight hug, sobbing uncontrollably.

"It's Elga," Mairy cried, referring to her youngest, a girl not yet two. "She . . . she's gone!"

Leesha held her tightly, cooing soothing sounds as words failed her. Others were taking note of her, but kept a respectful distance while Mairy poured out her grief.

"Leesha," they whispered. "Leesha's come. Thank the Creator."

Finally, Mairy managed to collect herself, pulling back and lifting her smudged and filthy apron to daub at her tears.

"What's happened?" Leesha asked softly. Mairy looked at her, eyes wide, and tears filled them again. She trembled, unable to speak.

"Plague," said a familiar voice, and Leesha turned to see Jona approaching, leaning heavily on a cane. His Tender's robes had been cut away from one leg, the lower half splinted and wrapped tight in bandages stained with blood. Leesha embraced him, glancing meaningfully at the leg.

"Broken tibia," he said, waving his hand dismissively. "Vika's seen to it." His face grew dark. "It was one of the last things she did, before she succumbed."

Leesha's eye's widened. "Vika's dead?" she asked in shock.

Jona shook his head. "Not yet, at least, but the flux has got her, and the fever has her raving. It won't be long." He looked around. "It may not be long for any of us," he said in a low voice meant for Leesha alone. "I fear you've chosen an ill time for your homecoming, Leesha, but perhaps that too is the Creator's plan. Had you waited another day, there might not have been a home for you to come to."

Leesha's eyes hardened. "I don't want to hear any more nonsense like that!" she scolded. "Where is Vika?" She turned a circle, taking in the small crowd. "Creator, where is *everyone*?"

"The Holy House," Jona said. "The sick are all there. Those that have recovered, or been blessed not to fall prey at all, are out collecting the dead, or mourning them."

"Then that's where we're going," Leesha said, tucking herself under Jona's arm to support him as they walked. "Now tell me what's happened. Everything."

Jona nodded. His face was pale, his eyes hollow. He was damp with sweat, and had obviously lost a great deal of blood, suppressing his pain only with great concentration. Behind them, Rojer and the Warded Man followed silently, along with most of the other villagers who had seen Leesha's arrival.

"The plague started months ago," Jona began, "but Vika and Darsy said it was just a chill, and thought little of it. Some that caught it, the young and strong, mostly, recovered quickly, but others took to their beds for weeks, and some eventually passed. Still, it seemed a simple flux, until it began to strengthen. Healthy people began to take ill rapidly, reduced overnight to weakness and delirium.

"That was when the fires started," he said. "People collapsing in their homes with candles and lamps in hand, or too sick to see to their wards. With your father and most of the other Warders in sickbed, nets began to fail all over town, especially with all the smoke and ash in the air marring every ward in sight. We fought the fires as best we could, but more and more people fell to the sickness, and there weren't enough hands.

"Smitt collected the survivors in a few warded buildings as far from the fires as possible, hoping for safety in numbers, but that just spread the plague faster. Saira collapsed last night during the storm, knocking over an oil lamp and starting a fire that soon had the whole tavern ablaze. The people had to flee into the night . . ." He choked, and Leesha stroked his back, not needing to hear more. She could well imagine what had happened next.

The Holy House was the only building in Cutter's Hollow made wholly of stone, and had resisted the flaming ash in the air, standing in proud defiance of the ruins. Leesha passed through the great doors, and gasped in shock. The pews had been cleared, and almost every inch of floor covered in straw pallets with only the barest space between them. Perhaps two hundred people lay there groaning, many bathed in sweat and thrashing about as others, weak with sickness themselves, tried to restrain them. She saw Smitt passed out on a pallet, and Vika not far off. Two more of Mairy's children, and others, so many others. But there was no sign of her father.

A woman looked up at them as they entered. She was prematurely gray and looked haggard and drawn, but Leesha knew her blocky frame instantly.

"Thank the Creator," Darsy said, catching sight of her. Leesha let go of Jona, and moved quickly to speak with her. After several minutes, she returned to Jona.

"Does Bruna's hut still stand?" she asked.

Jona shrugged. "So far as I know," he said. "No one has been there since she passed. Almost two weeks now."

Leesha nodded. Bruna's hut was far from the village proper, shielded by rows of trees. It was doubtful the soot had broken its wards. "I'll need to go there and get supplies," she said, stepping back outside. It was beginning to rain again, the sky bleak and bereft of hope.

Rojer and the Warded Man were there, along with a cluster of villagers.

"It *is* you," Brianne said, rushing up to embrace Leesha. Evin stood not far back, holding a young girl in his arms with Callen, grown tall though he was not yet ten, next to him.

Leesha returned the embrace warmly. "Has anyone seen my father?" she asked.

"He's home, where you should be," came a voice, and Leesha turned to see her mother approach, Gared at her heel. Leesha did not know whether to feel relief or dread at the sight.

"You come to check on everyone but your own family?" Elona demanded.

"Mum, I only just . . ." Leesha began, but her mother cut her off.

"Only this and only that!" Elona barked. "Always a reason to turn your back on your blood when it suits you! Your poor father is finding death's succor, and I find you here . . . !"

"Who's with him?" Leesha interrupted.

"His apprentices," Elona said.

Leesha nodded. "Have them bring him here with the others," she said.

"I'll do no such thing!" Elona cried. "Take him from the comfort of a feathered bed for an infested straw pallet in a room rife with plague?" She grabbed Leesha's arm. "You'll come see him now! You're his daughter!"

"Don't you think I know that?" Leesha demanded, snatching her arm away. Tears ran down her cheeks, and she made no effort to brush them aside. "Do you think I thought of anything else as I dropped everything and left Angiers? But he's not the only person in town, Mother! I can't abandon everyone to tend one man, even if he is my father!"

"You're a fool if you think these people ent dead already," Elona said, drawing gasps from the crowd. She pointed to the stone walls of the Holy House. "Will those wards hold back the corelings tonight?" she asked, drawing everyone's attention to the stone, blackened by smoke and ash. Indeed, there was barely a ward visible.

She drew close to Leesha, her voice lowering. "Our house is far from the others," she whispered. "It may be the last warded home in all of Cutter's Hollow. It can't hold everyone, but it can save *us,* if you come home!"

Leesha slapped her. Full in the face. Elona was knocked into the mud, and sat there dumbfounded, pressing her hand to her reddening cheek. Gared looked ready to rush Leesha and carry her off, but she checked him with a cold glare.

"I'm not going to hide away and leave my friends to the corelings!" she shouted. "We'll find a way to ward the Holy House, and make our stand here. Together! And if demons should dare come and try to take my children, I have secrets of fire that will burn them from this world!"

My children, Leesha thought, in the sudden silence that followed. *Am I Bruna now, to think of them so?* She looked around, taking in the scared and sooty faces, not a one taking charge, and realized for the first time that as far as everyone was concerned, she *was* Bruna. She was Herb Gatherer for Cutter's Hollow now. Sometimes that meant bringing healing, and sometimes . . .

Sometimes it meant a dash of pepper in the eyes, or burning a wood demon in your yard.

The Warded Man came forward. People whispered at the

sight of him, a robed and hooded specter hardly noticed a moment before.

"Wood demons won't be all you face," he said. "Flame demons will delight in your fire, and wind demons soar above it. The razing of your town might even have called rock demons down from the hills. They will be waiting when the sun sets."

"We're all going to die!" Ande cried, and Leesha felt panic building in the crowd.

"What do you care?" she demanded of the Warded Man. "You've kept your promise and seen us here! Get on your corespawned scary horse and be on your way! Leave us to our fate!"

But the Warded Man shook his head. "I swore an oath to give the corelings nothing, and I won't break it again. I'll be damned to the Core myself before I give them Cutter's Hollow."

He turned to the crowd, and pulled back his hood. There were gasps of shock and fear, and, for a moment, the rising panic was arrested. The Warded Man seized on that moment. "When the corelings come to the Holy House tonight, I will stand and fight!" he declared. There was a collective gasp, and a flare of recognition in many of the villagers' eyes. Even here, they had heard the tales of the tattooed man who killed demons.

"Will any of you stand with me?" he asked.

The men looked at each other doubtfully. Women took their arms, imploring them with their eyes not to say anything foolish.

"What can we do, 'cept get cored?" Ande called. "Ent nothing that can kill a demon!"

"You're wrong," the Warded Man said, and strode over to Twilight Dancer, pulling free a wrapped bundle. "Even a rock demon can be killed," he said, unwrapping a long, curved object and throwing it into the mud in front of the villagers.

It was three feet long from its wide broken base to its sharp point, smooth and colored an ugly yellow-brown, like a rotten tooth. As the villagers stared openmouthed, a weak ray of sun broke from the overcast sky, striking it. Even in the mud, the length began to smoke, sizzling away the fresh droplets of drizzle that struck it.

In a moment, the rock demon's horn burst into flame.

"Every demon can be killed!" the Warded Man cried, pulling a warded spear from Twilight Dancer and throwing it to stick in the burning horn. There was a flash, and the horn exploded in a burst of sparks like a festival flamework.

"Merciful Creator," Jona said, drawing a ward in the air. Many of the villagers followed suit.

The Warded Man crossed his arms. "I can make weapons that bite the corelings," he said, "but they are worthless without arms to wield them, so I ask again, who will stand with me?"

There was a long moment of silence. Then, "I will." The Warded Man turned, looking surprised to see Rojer come and stand by his side.

"And I," Yon Gray said, stepping forward. He leaned heavily on his cane, but there was hard determination in his eyes. "More'n seventy years I've watched 'em come and take us, one by one. If tonight's t'be my last, then I'll spit in a coreling's eye afore the end."

The other Hollowers stood dumbfounded, but then Gared stepped forward.

"Gared, you idiot, what are you doing?" Elona demanded, grabbing his arm, but the giant cutter shrugged off her grip. He reached out tentatively and pulled the warded spear free from the dirt. He looked, looking hard at the wards running along its surface.

"My da was cored last night," he said in a low, angry tone. He clutched the weapon and looked up at the Warded Man, showing his teeth. "I aim t'take his due."

His words spurred others. One by one and in groups, some of them in fear, some in anger, and many more in despair, the people of Cutter's Hollow rose up to meet the coming night.

"Fools," Elona spat, and stormed off.

"You didn't need to do that," Leesha said, her arms wrapped around the Warded Man's waist as Twilight Dancer raced up the road to Bruna's hut.

"What good is a mad obsession, if it doesn't help people?" he replied.

"I was angry this morning," Leesha said. "I didn't mean that."

"You meant it," the Warded Man assured her. "And you weren't wrong. I've been so occupied with what I was fighting *against,* I'd forgotten what I was fighting *for.* All my life I've dreamed of nothing but killing demons, but what good is it to kill corelings out in the wild, and ignore the ones that hunt men every night?"

They pulled up at the hut, and the Warded Man leapt down

and held a hand out to her. Leesha smiled, and let him assist her dismount. "The house is still intact," she said. "Everything we need should be inside."

They went into the hut, and Leesha meant to head straight for Bruna's stores, but the familiarity of the place struck her hard. She realized she was never going to see Bruna again, never hear her cursing or scold her for spitting on the floor, never again tap her wisdom or laugh at her ribaldry. That part of her life was over.

But there was no time for tears, so Leesha shoved the feelings aside and strode to the pharmacy, picking jars and bottles and shoving some into her apron, handing others to the Warded Man, who packed them quickly and loaded them on Twilight Dancer.

"I don't see why you needed me for this," he said. "I should be warding weapons. We only have a few hours."

She handed him the last of the herbs, and when they were safely stowed, led him to the center of the room, pulling up the carpet, revealing a trapdoor. The Warded Man opened it for her, revealing wooden steps leading down into darkness.

"Should I fetch a candle?" he asked.

"Absolutely not!" Leesha barked.

The Warded Man shrugged. "I can see well enough," he said.

"Sorry, I didn't mean to snap," she said. She reached into the many pockets of her apron, producing two small stoppered vials. She poured the contents of one into the other and shook it, producing a soft glow. Holding the vial aloft, she led them down the musty steps into a dusty cellar. The walls were packed dirt, wards painted onto the support beams. The small space was filled with storage crates, shelves of bottles and jars, and large barrels.

Leesha went to a shelf and lifted a box of flamesticks. "Wood demons can be hurt by fire," she mused. "What about a strong dissolvent?"

"I don't know," the Warded Man said. Leesha tossed him the box and got down on her knees, rummaging through some bottles on a low shelf.

"We'll find out," she said, passing back a large glass bottle full of clear liquid. The stopper was glass as well, held tightly in place with a twisted net of thin wire.

"Grease and oil will steal their footing," Leesha muttered,

still rummaging. "And burn hot and bright, even in the rain . . ." She handed him a pair of cured clay jugs, sealed in wax.

More items followed. Thundersticks, normally used to blow free unruly tree stumps, and a box of Bruna's celebration flamework: festival crackers, flamewhistles, and toss bangs.

Finally, at the back of the cellar, she brought them to a large water barrel.

"Open it," Leesha told the Warded Man. "Gently."

He did so, finding four ceramic jugs bobbing softly in the water. He turned to Leesha and looked at her curiously.

"That," she said, "is liquid demonfire."

Twilight Dancer's swift, warded hooves had them down to Leesha's father's house in minutes. Again, Leesha was struck hard by nostalgia, and again, she shoved the sentiment aside. How many hours until sunset? Not enough. That was sure.

The children and the elderly had begun to arrive, gathering in the yard. Brianne and Mairy had already put them to work collecting tools. Mairy's eyes were hollow as she watched the children. It had not been easy to convince her to leave her two children at the Holy House, but at last reason prevailed. Their father was staying, and if things went badly, the other children would need their mother.

Elona stormed out of the house as they arrived.

"Is this your idea?" she demanded. "Turning my house into a barn?"

Leesha pushed right past, the Warded Man at her side. Elona had no choice but to fall in behind them as they entered the house. "Yes, Mother," she said. "It was my idea. We may not have space for everyone, but the children and elderly who have avoided the flux thus far should be safe here, whatever else happens."

"I won't have it!" Elona barked.

Leesha whirled on her. "You have no choice!" she shouted. "You were right that we have the only strong wards left in town, so you can either suffer here in a crowded house, or stand and fight with the others. But Creator help me, the young and the old are staying behind Father's wards tonight."

Elona glared at her. "You wouldn't speak to me so, if your father were well."

"If he were well, he would have invited them himself," Leesha said, not backing down an inch.

She turned her attention to the Warded Man. "The paper shop is through those doors," she told him, pointing. "You should have space to work, and my father's warding tools. The children are collecting every weapon in town, and will bring them to you."

The Warded Man nodded, and vanished into the shop without a word.

"Where in the world did you find that one?" Elona asked.

"He saved us from demons on the road," Leesha said, going to her father's room.

"I don't know if it will do any good," Elona warned, putting a hand on the door. "Midwife Darsy says it's in the Creator's hands now."

"Nonsense," Leesha said, entering the room and immediately going to her father's side. He was pale and damp with sweat, but she did not recoil. She placed a hand to his forehead, and then ran her sensitive fingers over his throat, wrists, and chest. While she worked, she asked her mother questions about his symptoms, how long they had been manifest, and what she and Midwife Darsy had tried so far.

Elona wrung her hands, but answered as best she could.

"Many of the others are worse," Leesha said. "Da is stronger than you give him credit for."

For once, Elona had no belittling retort.

"I'll brew a potion for him," Leesha said. "He'll need to be dosed regularly, at least every three hours." She took a parchment and began writing instructions in a swift hand.

"You're not staying with him?" Elona asked.

Leesha shook her head. "There's near to two hundred people in the Holy House that need me, Mum," she said, "many of them worse off than Da."

"They have Darsy to look after them," Elona argued.

"Darsy looks as if she hasn't slept since the flux started," Leesha said. "She's dead on her feet, and even at her best, I wouldn't trust her cures against this sickness. If you stay with Da and follow my instructions, he'll be more likely to see the dawn than most in Cutter's Hollow."

"Leesha?" her father moaned. "S'that you?"

Leesha rushed to his side, sitting on the edge of the bed and taking his hand. "Yes, Da," she said, her eyes watering, "it's me."

"You came," Erny whispered, his lips curling into a slow smile. His fingers squeezed Leesha's hand weakly. "I knew you would."

"Of course I came," Leesha said.

"But you have to go," Erny sighed. When Leesha gave no reply, he patted her hand. "Heard what you said. Go do what needs be done. Just seeing you has given me new strength."

Leesha half sobbed, but tried to mask it as a laugh. She kissed his forehead.

"Is it bad as all that?" Erny whispered.

"A lot of folk are going to die tonight," Leesha said.

Erny's hand tightened on hers, and he sat up a bit. "Then you see to it that it's no more than need be," he said. "I'm proud of you and I love you."

"I love you, Da," Leesha said, hugging him tightly. She wiped her eyes and left the room.

Rojer tumbled about the tiny aisle of the makeshift hospit as he pantomimed the daring rescue the Warded Man had performed a few nights earlier.

"But then," he went on, "standing between us and the camp, was the biggest rock demon I've ever seen." He leapt atop a table and reached his arms into the air, waving them to show they were still not high enough to do the creature justice.

"Fifteen feet tall, it was," Rojer said, "with teeth like spears and a horned tail that could smash a horse. Leesha and I stopped up short, but did the Warded Man hesitate? No! He walked on, calm as Seventhday morning, and looked the monster right in the eyes."

Rojer enjoyed the wide eyes surrounding him, and hesitated, letting the tense silence build before shouting *"Bam!"* and clapping his hands together. Everyone jumped. "Just like that," Rojer said, "the Warded Man's horse, black as night and seeming like a demon itself, slammed its horns through the demon's back."

"The horse had horns?" an old man asked, raising a gray eyebrow as thick and bushy as a squirrel tail. Propped up in his pallet, the stump of his right leg soaked his bandages in blood.

"Oh, yes," Rojer confirmed, sticking fingers up behind his ears and getting coughing laughs. "Great ones of shining bright metal, strapped on by its bridle and sharply pointed, etched with wards of power! The most magnificent beast you have ever seen, it is! Its hooves struck the beast like thunderbolts, and as it smote the demon to the ground, we ran for the circle, and were safe."

"What about the horse?" one child asked.

"The Warded Man gave a whistle"—Rojer put his fingers to his lips and emitted a shrill sound—"and his horse came galloping through the corelings, leaping over the wards and into the circle." He clapped his hands against his thighs in a galloping sound and leapt to illustrate the point.

The patients were riveted by his tale, taking their minds off their sickness and the impending night. More, Rojer knew he was giving them hope. Hope that Leesha could cure them. Hope that the Warded Man could protect them.

He wished he could give himself hope, as well.

Leesha had the children scrub out the big vats her father used to make paper slurry, using them to brew potions on a larger scale than she had ever attempted. Even Bruna's stores quickly ran out, and she passed word to Brianne, who had the children ranging far and wide for hogroot and other herbs.

Frequently, her eyes flicked to the sunlight filtering through the window, watching it crawl across the shop's floor. The day was waning.

Not far off, the Warded Man worked with similar speed, his hand moving with delicate precision as he painted wards onto axes, picks, hammers, spears, arrows, and slingstones. The children brought him anything that might possibly be used as a weapon, and collected the results as soon as the paint dried, piling them in carts outside.

Every so often, someone came running in to relay a message to Leesha or the Warded Man. They gave instructions quickly, sending the runner off and turning back to their work.

With only a pair of hours before sunset, they drove the carts back through the steady rain to the Holy House. The villagers stopped work at the sight of them, coming quickly to help Leesha unload her cures. A few approached the Warded Man to assist unloading his cart, but a look from him turned them away.

Leesha went to him, carrying a heavy stone jug. "Tampweed and skyflower," she said, handing it to him. "Mix it with the feed of three cows, and see that they eat it all." The Warded Man took the jug and nodded.

As she turned to go into the Holy House, he caught her arm. "Take this," he said, handing her one of his personal spears. It was five feet long, made from light ash wood. Wards of power were etched into the metal tip, sharpened to a wicked edge. The shaft, too, was carved with defensive wards, lacquered hard and smooth, the butt capped in warded steel.

Leesha looked at it dubiously, making no move to take it. "Just what do you expect me to do with that?" she asked. "I'm an Herb . . ."

"This is no time to recite the Gatherer's oath," the Warded Man said, shoving the weapon at her. "Your makeshift hospit is barely warded. If our line fails, that spear may be all that stands between the corelings and your charges. What will your oath demand then?"

Leesha scowled, but she took the weapon. She searched his eyes for something more, but his wards were back in place, and she could no longer see his heart. She wanted to throw down the spear and wrap him in her arms, but she could not bear to be rebuffed again.

"Well . . . good luck," she managed to say.

The Warded Man nodded. "And to you." He turned to attend his cart, and Leesha stared after him, wanting to scream.

The Warded Man's muscles unclenched as he moved away. It had taken all his will to turn his back on her, but they couldn't afford to confuse one another tonight.

Forcing Leesha from his mind, he turned his thoughts to the coming battle. The Krasian holy book, the Evejah, contained accounts of the conquests of Kaji, the first Deliverer. He had studied it closely when learning the Krasian tongue.

The war philosophy of Kaji was sacred in Krasia, and had seen its warriors through centuries of nightly battle with the corelings. There were four divine laws that governed battle: Be unified in purpose and leadership. Do battle at a time and place of your choosing. Adapt to what you cannot control, and prepare the rest. Attack in ways the enemy will not expect, finding and exploiting their weaknesses.

A Krasian warrior was taught from birth that the path to salvation lay in killing *alagai*. When Jardir called for them to leap from the safety of their wards, they did so without hesitation, fighting and dying secure in the knowledge that they were serving Everam and would be rewarded in the afterlife.

The Warded Man feared the Hollowers would lack the same unity of purpose, failing to commit themselves to the fight, but watching as they scurried to and fro, readying themselves, he thought he might perhaps be underestimating them. Even in Tibbet's Brook, everyone came and stood by their neighbors in hard times. It was what kept the hamlets alive and thriving, despite their lack of warded walls. If he could keep them occupied, keep them from despairing when the demons rose, perhaps they would fight as one.

If not, everyone in the Holy House would die this night.

The strength of Krasia's resistance was due as much to Kaji's second law, choosing terrain, as it was the warriors themselves. The Krasian Maze was carefully designed to give the *dal'Sharum* layers of protection, and to funnel the demons to places of advantage.

One side of the Holy House faced the woods, where wood demons held sway, and two more faced the wrecked streets and rubble of the town. Too many places for corelings to take cover or hide. But past the cobbles of the main entrance lay the town square. If they could funnel the demons there, they might have a chance.

They were unable to clean the greasy ash off the rough stone walls of the Holy House and ward it in the rain, so the windows and great doors had been boarded and nailed shut, hasty wards chalked onto the wood. Ingress was limited to a small side entrance, with wardstones laid about the doorway. The demons would have an easier time getting through the wall.

The very presence of humans out in the naked night would act as a magnet to demons, but nevertheless, the Warded Man had taken pains to funnel the corelings away from the building and flanks, so that the path of least resistance would drive them to attack from the far end of the square. At his direction, the villagers had placed obstacles around the other sides of the Holy House, and interspersed hastily made wardposts, signs he had painted with wards of confusion. Any demon charging past them to attack the walls of the building would forget its intent, and inevitably be drawn toward the commotion in the town square.

Beside the square on one side was a day pen for the Tender's livestock. It was small, but its new wardposts were strong. A few animals milled around the men erecting a rough shelter within.

The other side of the square had been dug with trenches quickly filling with mucky rainwater, to urge flame demons to take an easier path. Leesha's oil was a thick sludge atop the water.

The villagers had done well in enacting Kaji's third law, preparation. Steady rain had made the square slick, a thin film of mud forming on the hard packed dirt. The Warded Man's messenger circles were set about the battlefield as he had directed, points of ambush and retreat, and a deep pit had been dug and covered with a muddy tarp. Thick, viscous grease was being spread on the cobbles with brooms.

And the fourth law, attacking the enemy in a way they would not expect, would take care of itself.

The corelings would not expect them to attack at all.

"I did as you asked," a man said, approaching him as he pondered the terrain.

"Eh?" the Warded Man said.

"I'm Benn, sir," the man said. "Mairy's husband." The Warded Man just stared. "The glassblower," he clarified, and the Warded Man's eyes finally lit with recognition.

"Let's see, then," he said.

Benn produced a small glass flask. "It's thin, like you asked," he said. "Fragile."

The Warded Man nodded. "How many did you and your apprentices have time to make?" he asked.

"Three dozen," Benn said. "May I ask what they're for?"

The Warded Man shook his head. "You'll see soon enough," he said. "Bring them, and find me some rags."

Rojer approached him next. "I've seen Leesha's spear," he said. "I've come for mine."

The Warded Man shook his head. "You're not fighting," he said. "You're staying inside with the sick."

Rojer stared at him. "But you told Leesha . . ."

"To give you a spear is to rob you of your strength," the Warded Man cut him off. "Your music would be lost out in the din outside, but inside, it'll prove more potent than a dozen spears. If the corelings break through, I'm counting on you to hold them back until I arrive."

Rojer scowled, but he nodded, and headed into the Holy House.

Others were already waiting for his attention. The Warded Man listened to reports on their progress, assigning further tasks that were leapt to immediately. The villagers moved with hunched quickness, like hares ready to flee at any moment.

No sooner than he had sent them off, Stefny came storming up to him, a group of angry women at her back. "What's this about sending us up to Bruna's hut?" the woman demanded.

"The wards there are strong," the Warded Man said. "There is no room for you in the Holy House or Leesha's family home."

"We don't care about that," Stefny said. "We're going to fight."

The Warded Man looked at her. Stefny was a tiny woman, barely five feet, and thin as a reed. She was well into her fifties; her skin was thin and rough, like worn leather. Even the smallest wood demon would tower over her.

But the look in her eyes told him it didn't matter. She was going to fight no matter what he said. The Krasians might not allow women to fight, but that was their failing. He would not deny any who were willing to stand in the night. He took a spear off his cart and handed it to her. "We'll find you a place," he promised.

Expecting an argument, Stefny was taken aback, but she took the weapon, nodding once and moving away. The other women came in turn, and he handed a spear to each.

The men came at once, seeing the Warded Man handing out weapons. The cutters took their own axes back, looking at the freshly painted wards dubiously. No axe blow had ever penetrated a wood demon's armor.

"Won't need this," Gared said, handing back the Warded Man's spear. "I ent one for spinning a stick around, but I know how to swing my axe."

One of the cutters brought a girl to him, perhaps thirteen summers old. "My name's Flinn, sir," the cutter said. "My daughter Wonda hunts with me sometimes. I won't have her out in the naked night, but if ya let her have a bow behind the wards, you'll find her aim is true."

The Warded Man looked at the girl. Tall and homely, she had taken after her father in size and strength. He went to Twilight Dancer and pulled down his own yew bow and heavy arrows. "I won't need these tonight," he said to her, and pointed to a high window at the apex of the Holy House's roof. "See if you can pry loose enough boards to shoot from there," he advised.

Wonda took the bow and ran off. Her father bowed and backed away.

Tender Jona limped out to meet him next.

"You should be inside, and off that leg," the Warded Man said, never comfortable around Holy Men. "If you can't carry a load or dig a trench, you're only in the way out here."

Tender Jona nodded. "I only wanted to have a look at the defenses," he said.

"They should hold," the Warded Man said with more confidence than he felt.

"They will," Jona said. "The Creator would not leave those in His house without succor. That's why He sent you."

"I'm not the Deliverer, Tender," the Warded Man said, scowling. "No one sent me, and nothing about tonight is assured."

Jona smiled indulgently, the way an adult might at the ignorance of a child. "It's coincidence, then, that you showed up in our moment of need?" he asked. "It's not for me to say if you are the Deliverer or not, but you are here, just like every one of us, because the Creator *put* you here, and He has reason for everything He does."

"He had a reason for fluxing half your village?" the Warded Man asked.

"I don't pretend to see the path," Jona said calmly, "but I know it's there all the same. One day, we'll look back and wonder how we ever missed it."

Darsy was squatting wearily by Vika's side, trying to cool her feverish brow with a damp cloth, when Leesha entered the Holy House.

Leesha went straight to them, taking the cloth from Darsy. "Get some sleep," she said, seeing the deep weariness in the woman's eyes. "The sun will set soon, and we'll all need our strength then. Go. Rest while you still can."

Darsy shook her head. "I'll rest when I'm cored," she said. "Till then I'll work."

Leesha considered her a moment, then nodded. She reached into her apron and pulled out a dark, gummy substance wrapped in waxed paper. "Chew this," she said. "You'll feel cored tomorrow, but it will keep you alert through the night."

Darsy nodded, taking the gum and popping it into her mouth while Leesha bent to examine Vika. She took a skin from around her shoulder, pulling the stopper. "Help her sit up a bit," she said, and Darsy complied, lifting Vika so that Leesha could give her the potion. She coughed a bit out, but Darsy massaged her throat, helping her swallow until Leesha was satisfied.

Leesha rose to her feet and scanned the seemingly endless mass of prone bodies. She had triaged and dealt with the worst of the injured before heading out to Bruna's hut, but there were plenty of hurts still in need of mending, bones to set and wounds to sew, not to mention forcing her potions down dozens of unconscious throats.

Given time, she was confident she could drive the flux off. Perhaps a few had progressed too far, and would remain sickly or pass, but most of her children would recover.

If they made it through the night.

She called the volunteers together, distributing medicine and instructing them on what to expect and do when the wounded from outside began to come.

Rojer watched Leesha and the others work, feeling cowardly as he tuned his fiddle. Inside, he knew the Warded Man was right: that he should work to his strengths, as Arrick had always said. But that did not make hiding behind stone walls while others stood fast feel any braver.

Not long ago, the thought of putting down his fiddle to pick up a tool had been abhorrent, but he had grown tired of hiding while others died for him.

If he lived to tell it, he imagined "The Battle of Cutter's Hollow" would be a tale that outlived his children's children. But what of his own part? Playing the fiddle from hiding was a deed hardly worth a line, let alone a verse.

CHAPTER 31

THE BATTLE OF
CUTTER'S HOLLOW
332 AR

AT THE FOREFRONT OF THE SQUARE stood the cutters. Chopping trees and hauling lumber had left most of them thick of arm and broad of shoulder, but some, like Yon Gray, were well past their prime, and others, like Ren's son Linder, had not yet grown into their full strength. They stood clustered in one of the portable circles, gripping the wet hafts of their axes as the sky darkened.

Behind the cutters, the Hollow's three fattest cows had been staked in the center of the square. Having consumed Leesha's drugged meal, they slumbered deeply on their feet.

Behind the cows was the largest circle. Those within could not match the raw muscle of the cutters, but they had greater numbers. Nearly half of them were women, some as young as fifteen. They stood grimly alongside their husbands, fathers, brothers, and sons. Merrem, Dug the butcher's burly wife, held a warded cleaver, and looked well ready to use it.

Behind them lay the covered pit, and then the third circle, directly before the great doors of the Holy House, where Stefny and the others too old or frail to run about the muddy square stood fast with long spears.

Each one was armed with a warded weapon. Some, those with the shortest reach, also carried round bucklers made from barrel lids, painted with wards of forbiddance. The Warded Man had made only one of those, but the others had copied it well enough.

At the edge of the day pen's fence, behind the wardposts,

stood the artillery, children barely in their teens, armed with bows and slings. A few adults had been given one of the precious thundersticks, or one of Benn's thin flasks, stuffed with a soaked rag. Young children held lanterns, hooded against the rain, to light the weapons. Those who had refused to fight huddled with the animals under the shelter behind them, which shielded Bruna's festival flamework from the rain.

More than a few, like Ande, had gone back on their promise to fight, accepting the scorn of their fellows as they hid behind the wards. As the Warded Man rode through the square astride Twilight Dancer, he saw others looking toward the pen longingly, fear etched on their faces.

There were screams as the corelings rose, and many took a step backward, their resolve faltering. Terror threatened to defeat the Hollowers before the battle even began. A few tips from the Warded Man on where and how to strike were meager against the weight of a lifetime of fear.

The Warded Man noticed Benn shaking. One of his pant legs was soaked and clinging to his twitching thigh, and not from the rain. He dismounted and stood before the glassblower.

"Why are you out here, Benn?" he asked, raising his voice so others could hear.

"M-my d-daughters," Benn said, nodding back toward the Holy House. It looked as if the spear he held was going to vibrate right out of his hands.

The Warded Man nodded. Most of the Hollowers were there to protect their loved ones lying helpless in the Holy House. If not, they would all be in the pen. He gestured to the corelings materializing in the square. "You fear them?" he asked, louder still.

"Y-yes," Benn managed, tears mixing with the rain on his cheeks. A glance showed others nodding as well.

The Warded Man stripped off his robes. None of the people had seen him unclad before, and their eyes widened as they took in the wards tattooed over every inch of his body. "Watch," he told Benn, but the command was meant for all.

He stepped from the circle, striding up to a seven-foot-tall wood demon that was just beginning to solidify. He looked back, meeting the eyes of as many Hollowers as he could. Seeing them watching intently, he shouted, "This is what you fear!"

Turning sharply, the Warded Man struck hard, smashing the

flat of his hand against the coreling's jaw, knocking the demon down in a flash of magic just as it became fully solid. The coreling shrieked in pain, but it recovered quickly, coiling on its tail to spring. The villagers stood openmouthed, their eyes locked on the scene, sure the Warded Man would be killed.

The wood demon lunged, but the Warded Man kicked off a sandal and spun, kicking up inside the coreling's reach. His warded heel struck its armored chest with a thunderclap, and the demon was sent reeling again, its chest scorched and blackened.

A smaller wood demon launched itself at him as he stalked his prey, but the Warded Man caught its arm and twisted himself behind its back, jabbing his warded thumbs into its eyes. There was a smoking sizzle, and the coreling screamed, staggering away and clawing at its face.

As the blind coreling stumbled about, the Warded Man resumed his pursuit of the first demon, meeting its next attack head-on. He pivoted and turned the coreling's momentum against it, latching on as it stumbled past him and wrapping his warded arms around its head. He squeezed, ignoring the demon's futile attempts to dislodge him, and waited as the feedback built in intensity. Finally, with a burst of magic, the creature's skull collapsed, and they fell to the mud.

The other demons kept their distance as the Warded Man rose from the corpse, hissing and searching for a sign of weakness. The Warded Man roared at them, and those closest took a step back from him.

"It is not you that should fear them, Benn the glassblower!" the Warded Man called, his voice like a hurricane. "It is *they* that should fear *you*!"

None of the Hollowers made a sound, but many fell to their knees, drawing wards in the air before them. He walked back up to Benn, who was no longer shaking. "Remember that," he said, using his robes to wipe the mud from his wards, "the next time they clutch at your heart."

"Deliverer," Benn whispered, and others began to mumble the same.

The Warded Man shook his head sharply, rainwater flying free. "You are the Deliverer!" he shouted, poking Benn hard in the chest. "And you!" he cried, spinning to roughly haul a kneeling man to his feet. "All of you are Deliverers!" he bellowed, sweeping his arms over all who stood in the night. "If the corelings fear a Deliverer, let them quail at a hundred of them!" He shook his fist, and the Hollowers roared.

The spectacle kept the newly formed demons at bay for a moment, issuing low growls as they stalked back and forth. But their pacing soon slowed, and one by one they crouched, muscles bunching up as they tamped down.

The Warded Man looked to the left flank, his warded eyes piercing the gloom. Flame demons avoided the water-filled trench, but wood demons approached that way, heedless of the wet.

"Light it," he called, pointing to the trench with a thumb.

Benn struck a flamestick with his thumb, shielding the tiny blaze from the wind and rain as he touched it to the wick of a flamewhistle. As the wick sizzled and sparked, Benn uncoiled, flinging it toward the trench.

Halfway through its arc, the wick burned down and a jet of fire exploded from one end of the flamewhistle. The thick-wrapped paper tube spun rapidly in blazing pinwheel, emitting a high-pitched whine as it struck the oil sludge in the trench.

Wood demons shrieked as the water about their knees burst into flame. They fell back, beating the fire in terror, splashing oil and only spreading the flames.

Flame demons cried out in glee as they leapt into the fire, forgetting the water that lay beneath. The Warded Man smiled at their cries as the water boiled.

The flames filled the square with flickering light, and there were gasps from the cutters at the size of the host before them. Wind demons cut the sky, adroit even in the wind and rain. Lissome flame demons darted about, eyes and mouths glowing red, silhouetting the hulking rock demons that stalked the edges of the gathering. And wood demons. So many wood demons.

"S'like the trees of the forest have risen up 'gainst the axemen," Yon Gray said in awe, and many of the cutters nodded in horror.

"Ent met a tree yet I can't chop down," Gared growled, holding his axe at the ready. The boast filtered through the rank, and the other cutters stood taller.

The corelings soon found their will, leaping at the cutters, talons leading. The wards of their circle stopped them short, and the cutters drew back to swing.

"Hold!" the Warded Man cried. "Remember the plan!"

The men checked themselves, letting the demons hammer the wards in vain. The corelings flowed around the circle, looking for a weakness, and the cutters were soon lost from view in a sea of barklike skin.

It was a flame demon no larger than a cat that first spotted the cows. It shrieked, leaping onto the back of one of the animals, talons digging deep. The cow woke and bleated in pain as the tiny coreling tore out a piece of hide in its jaws.

The sound made the other corelings forget the cutters. They fell on the cows in an explosion of gore, tearing the animals to pieces. Blood sprayed high into the air, mixing with the rain before splashing down in the mud. Even a wind demon swooped down to snatch a chunk of meat before leaping back into the air.

In a twinkling, the animals were devoured, though none of the corelings seemed satisfied. They moved toward the next circle, slashing at the wards and drawing sparks of magic in the air.

"Hold!" the Warded Man called again, as the people around him tensed. He held his spear back, watching the demons intently. Waiting.

But then he saw it. A demon stumbled, losing its balance.

"Now!" he roared, and leapt from the circle, stabbing right through a demon's head.

The Hollowers screamed a primal cry and charged, falling upon the drugged corelings with abandon, hacking and stabbing. The demons shrieked, but thanks to Leesha's potion, their response was sluggish. As instructed, the Hollowers worked in small teams, stabbing demons from behind when they turned their attention toward another. Warded weapons flared, and this time it was demon ichor that arced into the air.

Merrem chopped a wood demon's arm clean off with her cleaver, and her husband Dug stabbed his butcher's knife deep into its armpit. The wind demon that had eaten the drugged meat came crashing down into the square, and Benn drove his spear into it, twisting hard as the warded head flared hot to pierce the coreling's hide.

Demon claws could not penetrate the ward on the wooden shields, and when the shieldbearers saw this, they gained confidence, striking harder still against the dazed corelings.

But not all the demons had been drugged. Those in the back

increased their press to get forward. The Warded Man waited until their advantage of surprise waned, then cried, "Artillery!"

The children in the pen gave a great cry, placing flasks in their slings and launching them at the horde of demons in front of the cutters' circle. The thin glass shattered easily against the bark-like armor of the wood demons, coating them in liquid that clung despite the rain. The demons roared, but could not penetrate the wardposts of the small pen.

While the corelings raged, the lanternbearers ran to and fro, touching the flames to rag-wrapped arrowheads dipped in pitch and the wicks of Bruna's flamework. They did not fire as one as they had been instructed, but it made little difference. With the first arrow, the liquid demonfire exploded across the back of a wood demon, and the creature screamed, thrashing into another and burning it as well. Festival crackers, toss bangs, and flame-whistles joined the volley of arrows, frightening some demons with light and sound, and igniting others. The night lit up as the demons burned.

One flamewhistle hit the shallow rut in front of the cutters' circle, which stretched the full width of the square. The spark lit the liquid demonfire within, and the fell brew burst into an intense fire, setting several more wood demons alight and cutting the rest off from their fellows.

But between the circles and away from the flamework, the battle raged fiercely. The drugged demons fell quickly, but their fellows were uncowed by the armed villagers. Teams were breaking up, and some of the Hollowers were taken by fear and stumbled back, giving the corelings an opening to pounce.

"Cutters!" the Warded Man cried as he spit a flame demon on his spear.

With their backs secure, Gared and the other cutters roared and leapt from their circle, pressing the demons attacking the Warded Man's group from behind. Even without magic, wood demon hide was as thick and gnarled as old bark, but cutters hacked through bark all day, and the wards on their axes drained away the magic that strengthened it further.

Gared was the first to feel the jolt as the wards tapped into the demons' magic, using the corelings' own power against them. The shock ran up the haft of his axe and made his arms tingle as a split second of ecstasy ran through him. He struck the demon's head clean off and howled, charging the next one in line.

Pressed from both sides, the demons were hit hard. Centuries of dominance had taught them that humans, when they fought at all, were not to be feared, and they were unprepared for the resistance. High in the window of the Holy House's choir loft, Wonda fired her bow with frightening accuracy, every warded arrowhead striking demon flesh like a bolt of lightning.

But the smell of blood was thick in the air, and the cries of pain could be heard for miles around. In the distance, corelings howled in answer to the sound. Reinforcements would soon come, and the humans had none.

It wasn't long before the demons recovered. Even without their impenetrable armor, few humans could ever hope to stand toe to toe with a wood demon. The smallest of the demons were closer to Gared in strength than to a normal man.

Merrem charged a flame demon the size of a large dog, her cleaver already blackened with demon ichor. She held her shield out defensively, her cleaver arm cocked back and ready.

The coreling shrieked and spat fire at her. She brought up her shield to block, but the ward painted there had no power over fire, and the wood exploded into flames. Merrem screamed as her arm ignited, dropping and rolling in the mud. The demon leapt at her, but her husband Dug was there to meet it. The heavy butcher gutted the flame demon like a hog, but screamed himself as its molten blood struck his leather apron, setting it alight.

A wood demon ducked down to all fours under Evin's wild axe swing, springing up when he was off guard and bearing him to the ground. He screamed as the jaws came for him, but there was a bark, and his wolfhounds crashed into the demon from the side, knocking it away. Evin recovered quickly, chopping down on the prone coreling, though not before it disemboweled one of the giant dogs. Evin cried in rage and hacked again before whirling to find another foe, his eyes wild.

Just then, the trench of demonfire burned out, and the wood demons trapped on the far side began to advance again.

"Thundersticks!" the Warded Man cried, as he trampled a rock demon under Twilight Dancer's hooves.

At the call, the eldest of his artillery took out some of the precious and volatile weapons. There were less than a dozen, for Bruna had been niggardly in their making, lest the powerful tools be abused.

Wicks flared, and the sticks were launched at the approaching demons. One villager dropped his rain-slick stick in the mud and bent quickly to snatch it up, but not quickly enough. The thunderstick went off in his hands, blowing him and his lamp-bearer to pieces in a blast of fire as the concussive force knocked several others in the pen to the ground, screaming in pain.

One of the thundersticks exploded between a pair of wood demons. Both were thrown down, twisted wrecks. One, its bark-like skin aflame, did not rise. The other, extinguished by the mud, twitched and put a talon under itself as it struggled to rise. Already, its fell magic was healing its wounds.

Another thunderstick sailed at a nine-foot-tall rock demon, which caught it in a talon and leaned in close, peering at the curious object as it went off.

But when the smoke had cleared, the demon stood unfazed, and continued on toward the villagers in the square. Wonda planted three arrows in it, but it shrieked and came on, its anger only doubled.

Gared met it before it reached the others, returning its shriek with a roar of his own. The burly cutter ducked under its first blow and planted his axe in its sternum, glorying in the rush of magic that ran up his arms. The demon collapsed at last, and Gared had to stand atop it to pull his weapon free of its thick armor.

A wind demon swooped in, its hooked talons nearly cutting Flinn in half. From the choir loft window, Wonda gave a cry and killed the coreling with an arrow to the back, but the damage was done, and her father collapsed.

A swipe from a wood demon took Ren's head clean off, launching it far from his body. His axe fell into the muck, even as his son Linder hacked the arm from the offending demon.

Near the pen on the right flank, Yon Gray was struck a glancing blow, but it was enough to drop the old man to the ground. The coreling stalked him as he clutched the mud, trying to rise, but Ande gave a choked cry and leapt from the warded pen, grabbing Ren's axe and burying it in the creature's back.

Others followed his lead, their fear forgotten, leaving the safety of the pen to take up the weapons of the fallen or to drag the wounded to safety. Keet stuffed a rag into the last of the demonfire flasks, lighting it and hurling it into the face of a wood demon to cover his sisters as they pulled a man into the pen. The demon burst into flames, and Keet cheered until a flame demon leapt atop the immolated coreling, shrieking in glee as it basked in the fire. Keet turned and ran, but it leapt onto his back and bore him down.

The Warded Man was everywhere in the battle, killing some demons with his spear, and others with only bare hands and feet. Twilight Dancer kept close to him, striking with hoof and horn. They burst in wherever the fighting was thickest, scattering the corelings and leaving them as prey for the others. He lost count of how many times he kept demons from landing a killing blow, letting their victims regain their feet and return to the fight.

In the chaos, a group of corelings stumbled through the center line and past the second circle, stepping onto the tarp and falling onto the warded spikes laid at the bottom of the pit. Most of them twitched wildly, impaled on the killing magic, but one of the demons avoided the spikes and clawed its way back out of the pit. A warded axe took its head before it could return to the fight or flee.

But the corelings kept coming, and once the pit was revealed, they flowed smoothly around it. There was a cry, and the Warded Man turned to see a harsh fight for the great doors of the Holy House. The corelings could smell the sick and weak within, and were in a frenzy to break through and begin the slaughter. Even the chalked wards were gone now, washed away by the ever-present rain.

The thick grease spread on the cobbles outside the doors slowed the corelings somewhat. More than one fell on its tail, or skidded into the wards of the third circle. But they flexed their claws, digging in to secure their footing, and continued on.

The women at the doors stabbed out from the safety of their circle with their long spears, and held their own for a moment, but Stefny's spearhead caught fast in the gnarled skin of one demon, and she was yanked outward, her trailing foot catching the rope of the portable circle. In an instant, the wards fell out of alignment, and the net collapsed.

The Warded Man moved with all the speed he could muster, taking the twelve-foot-wide pit in a single leap, but even he could not move fast enough to prevent the slaughter. Bodies were being flung about in bloody abandon when he came crashing in, attacking wildly.

When the melee was over, he stood panting with the few surviving women, Stefny, amazingly, among them. She was splattered with ichor, but seemed none the worse for wear, her eyes full of hard determination.

A great wood demon charged them, and they turned as one to stand firm, but the coreling crouched just out of reach and sprang, clearing them fully to reach the stone wall of the Holy House. Its claws found easy purchase between the piled stones, and it climbed out of reach before the Warded Man could catch its swinging tail.

"Look out!" the Warded Man called to Wonda, but the girl was too intent on aiming her bow, and did not hear until it was too late. The demon caught her in its claws and threw her back over its head as if she were nothing but a nuisance. The Warded Man ran hard and skidded across the grease and mud on his knees, catching her bloody and broken body before it struck the ground, but as he did, the demon pulled itself through the open window and into the Holy House.

The Warded Man ran for the side entrance, but then skidded to a halt as he turned the corner, his way barred by a dozen demons standing dazed by his wards of confusion. He roared, leaping into their midst, but he knew he would never make it inside in time.

The stone walls of the Holy House echoed with screams of pain, and the cries of the demons just outside the doors had everyone in the Holy House on edge. Inside, some wept openly, or rocked slowly back and forth, shaking with fear; some raved and thrashed.

Leesha fought to keep them calm, speaking soothing words to the most reasonable and drugging the least, keeping them from tearing their stitches, or hurting themselves in a feverish rage.

"I am fit to fight!" Smitt insisted, the big innkeeper dragging Rojer across the floor as the poor Jongleur tried in vain to restrain him.

"You're not well!" Leesha shouted, rushing over. "You'll be killed if you go out there!" As she went, she emptied a small bottle into a rag. Pressed to his face, the fumes would put him down quickly.

"My Stefny is out there!" Smitt cried. "My son and daughters!" He caught Leesha's arm as she reached out with the cloth, shoving her violently aside. She tumbled into Rojer, and the two of them went down in a tangle. He reached for the bar on the main doors.

"Smitt, no!" Leesha cried. "You'll let them in and get us all killed!"

But the fever-mad innkeeper was heedless of her warning, grabbing the bar in two hands and heaving.

Darsy grabbed his shoulder, spinning him around to catch her fist on his jaw. Smitt twisted around once more with the force of the blow, and collapsed to the ground.

"Sometimes the direct approach works better than herbs and needles," Darsy told Leesha, shaking the sting from her hand.

"I see why Bruna needed a stick," Leesha agreed, the two of them ducking under Smitt's arms to haul him back to his pallet. Beyond the doors, sounds of battle raged.

"Sounds like all the demons in the Core are trying to get in," Darsy muttered.

There was a crash above, and a scream from Wonda. The choir loft railing shattered, and beams of wood came crashing down, killing the one unfortunate man directly below and wounding another. A huge shape dropped into their midst, howling as it landed on another patient and tore out her throat before she even knew what struck her.

The wood demon rose to its full height, huge and terrible, and Leesha felt her heart stop. She and Darsy froze, Smitt a dead weight between them. The spear the Warded Man had given her leaned against a wall, far from reach, and even if she had it in her hands, she doubted it would do much to slow the giant coreling. The creature shrieked at them, and she felt her knees turn to water.

But then Rojer was there, interposing himself between them and the demon. The coreling hissed at him, and he swallowed hard. Every instinct told him to run and hide, but instead he tucked his fiddle under his chin, and brought bow to string, filling the Holy House with a mournful, haunting melody.

The coreling hissed at the Jongleur and bared its teeth, long and sharp as carving knives, but Rojer did not slow his playing, and the wood demon held its ground, cocking its head and staring at him curiously.

After a few moments, Rojer began to rock from side to side. The demon, its eyes locked on the fiddle, began to do the same.

Encouraged, Rojer took a single step to the left.

The demon mirrored him.

He stepped back to the right, and the coreling did the same.

Rojer went on, walking around the wood demon in a slow, wide arc. The mesmerized beast turned as he went, until it was facing away from the shocked and terrified patients.

By then, Leesha had set Smitt down and retrieved her spear. It seemed little more than a thorn, the demon's reach far longer, but she stepped forward nonetheless, knowing she would never get a better chance. She gritted her teeth and charged, burying the warded spear in the coreling's back with all her might.

There was a flash of power and a burst of ecstasy as the magic ran up her arms, and then Leesha was thrown back. She watched as the demon screamed and thrashed about, trying to dislodge the glowing spear still sticking from its back. Rojer dodged aside as it crashed into the great doors in its death throes, breaking open the portal even as it fell dead.

Demons howled with glee and charged the opening, but they were met by Rojer's music. Gone was the soothing, hypnotizing melody, replaced by sharp and jarring sounds that had the corelings clawing at their ears as they stumbled backward.

"Leesha!" The side door opened with a crash, and Leesha turned to see the Warded Man, awash in demon ichor and his own blood, burst into the room, looking about frantically. He saw the wood demon lying dead, and turned to meet her eyes. His relief was palpable.

She wanted to throw herself into his arms, but he turned and charged for the shattered doors. Rojer alone held the entrance, his music holding the demons back as surely as any wardnet. The Warded Man shoved the wood demon's corpse aside, pulling the spear free and throwing it back to Leesha. Then he was gone into the night.

Leesha looked out upon the carnage in the square, and her heart clenched. Dozens of her children lay dead and dying in the mud, even as the battle continued to rage.

"Darsy!" she cried, and when the woman rushed to her side, they ran out into the night, pulling wounded inside.

Wonda lay gasping on the ground when Leesha reached her, her clothes torn and bloody where the demon had clawed her. A wood demon charged them as she and Darsy bent to lift her, but Leesha pulled a vial from her apron and threw it, shattering the thin glass in its face. The demon shrieked as the dissolvent ate away its eyes, and the two Herb Gatherers hurried away with their charge.

They deposited the girl inside and Leesha shouted instructions to one of her assistants before running out again. Rojer stood at the entrance, the screeching of his fiddle forming a wall of sound that held the way clear, shielding Leesha and the others who began to drag the wounded inside.

The battle waxed and waned through the night, letting those villagers too tired to go on stagger back to their circles or into the Holy House to catch their breath or gulp down a swallow of water. There was an hour when not a demon could be seen, and another after that when a pack that must have come running from miles away fell upon them.

The rain stopped at some point, but no one could recall quite when, too preoccupied with attacking the enemy and helping the wounded. The cutters formed a wall at the great doors, and Rojer roamed the square, driving demons back with his fiddle as the wounded were collected.

By the time dawn's first light peeked over the horizon, the mud of the square had been churned into a foul stew of human blood and demon ichor, bodies and limbs scattered everywhere. Many jumped in fright as the sun struck the demon corpses, setting their flesh alight. Like bursts of liquid demonfire all over the square, the sun finished the battle, incinerating the few demons that still twitched.

The Warded Man looked out at the faces of the survivors, half his fighters at least, and was amazed at the strength and determination he saw. It seemed impossible that these were the same people who were so broken and terrified less than a day before. They might have lost many in the night, but the Hollowers were stronger than ever.

"Creator be praised," Tender Jona said, staggering out into the square on his crutch, drawing wards in the air as the demons burned in the morning light. He made his way to the Warded Man, and stood before him.

"This is thanks to you," he said.

The Warded Man shook his head. "No. You did this," he said. "All of you."

Jona nodded. "We did," he agreed. "But only because you came and showed us the way. Can you still doubt this?"

The Warded Man scowled. "For me to claim this victory as my own cheapens the sacrifice of all that died during the night," he said. "Keep your prophecies, Tender. These people do not need them."

Jona bowed deeply. "As you wish," he said, but the Warded Man sensed the matter was not closed.

CHAPTER 32

CUTTER'S NO MORE
332 AR

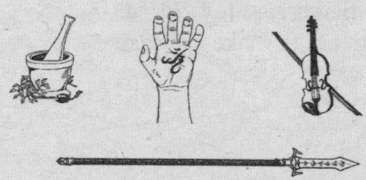

LEESHA WAVED AS ROJER and the Warded Man rode up the path. She set her brush back in its bowl on the porch as they dismounted.

"You learn quickly," the Warded Man said, coming up to study the wards she had painted on the rails. "These would hold a horde of corelings at bay."

"Quickly?" Rojer asked. "Night, that's undersaid. It's not been a month since she couldn't tell a wind ward from a flame."

"He's right," the Warded Man said. "I've seen five-year journeyman Warders whose lines weren't half so neat."

Leesha smiled. "I've always been a quick study," she said. "And you and my father are good teachers. I only wish I had bothered to learn sooner."

The Warded Man shrugged. "Would that we all could go back and make decisions based on what was to come."

"I think I'd have lived my whole life different," Rojer agreed.

Leesha laughed, ushering them inside the hut. "Supper's almost ready," she said, heading for the fire. "How did the village council meeting go?" she asked, stirring the steaming pot.

"Idiots," the Warded Man grumbled.

She laughed again. "That well?"

"The council voted to change the village name to Deliverer's Hollow," Rojer said.

"It's only a name," Leesha said, joining them at the table and pouring tea.

"It's not the name that bothers, it's the *notion,*" the Warded

Man said. "I've gotten the villagers to stop calling me Deliverer to my face, but I still hear it whispered behind my back."

"It will go easier for you if you just embrace it," Rojer said. "You can't stop a story like that. By now, every Jongleur north of the Krasian desert is telling it."

The Warded Man shook his head. "I won't lie and pretend to be something I'm not to make life easier. If I'd wanted an easy life . . ." He trailed off.

"What of the repairs?" Leesha asked, pulling him back to them as his eyes went distant.

Rojer smiled. "With the Hollowers back on their feet thanks to your cures, it seems a new house goes up every day," he said. "You'll be able to move back into the village proper soon."

Leesha shook her head. "This hut is all I have left of Bruna. This is my home now."

"This far from the village, you'll be outside the forbiddance," the Warded Man warned.

Leesha shrugged. "I understand why you laid out the new streets in the form of a warding," she said, "but there are benefits to being outside the forbiddance, as well."

"Oh?" the Warded Man asked, raising a warded brow.

"What benefit could there be to living on land that demons can set foot on?" Rojer asked.

Leesha sipped her tea. "My mum refuses to move, too," she said. "Says between your new wards and the cutters running about chopping every demon in sight, it's a needless bother."

The Warded Man frowned. "I know it seems like we have the demons cowed, but if the histories of the Demon Wars are anything to go by, they won't stay that way. They'll be back in force, and I want Cutter's Hollow to be ready."

"Deliverer's Hollow," Rojer corrected, smirking at the Warded Man's scowl.

"With you here, it will be," Leesha said, ignoring Rojer and sipping at her tea. She watched the Warded Man carefully over the rim of her cup.

When he hesitated, she set her cup down. "You're leaving," she said. "When?"

"When the Hollow is ready," the Warded Man said, not bothering to deny her conclusion. "I've wasted years, hoarding wards that can make the Free Cities that in more than name. I owe it to every city and hamlet in Thesa to see to it they have what they need to stand tall in the night."

Leesha nodded. "We want to help you," she said.

"You are," the Warded Man said. "With the Hollow in your hands, I know it will be safe while I'm away."

"You'll need more than that," Leesha said. "Someone to teach other Gatherers to make flamework and poisons, and to treat coreling wounds."

"You could write all that down," the Warded Man said.

Leesha snorted. "And give a man the secrets of fire? Not likely."

"I can't write fiddling lessons, in any event," Rojer said, "even if I had letters."

The Warded Man hesitated, then shook his head. "No," he said. "The two of you will only slow me down. I'll be weeks in the wilds, and you don't have the stomach for that."

"Don't have the stomach?" Leesha asked. "Rojer, close the shutters," she ordered.

Both men looked at her curiously.

"Do it," she ordered, and Rojer rose to comply, cutting off the sunlight and filling the hut with a dark gloom. Leesha was already shaking a vial of chemics, bathing herself in a phosphorescent glow.

"The trap," she said, and the Warded Man lifted the trapdoor down to the cellar where the demonfire had been kept. The scent of chemics was thick in the air that escaped.

Leesha led the way down into the darkness, her vial held high. She moved to sconces on the wall, adding chemics to glass jars, but the Warded Man's warded eyes, as comfortable in utter darkness as in clear day, had already widened before the light filled the room.

Heavy tables had been brought down into the cellar, and there, spread out before him, were half a dozen corelings in various states of dissection.

"Creator!" Rojer cried, gagging. He ran back up the stairs, and they could hear him gasping for air.

"Well, perhaps Rojer doesn't have the stomach yet," Leesha conceded with a grin. She looked at the Warded Man. "Did you know that wood demons have two? Stomachs, I mean. One stacked atop the other, like an hourglass." She took an instrument, peeling back layers of the dead demon's flesh to illustrate.

"Their hearts are off-center, down to the right," she added, "but there's a gap between their third and fourth ribs. Something a man looking to deliver a killing thrust should know."

The Warded Man looked on in amazement. When he looked back at Leesha, it was as if he were seeing her for the first time. "Where did you get these . . . ?"

"A word to the cutters you sent to patrol this end of the Hollow," Leesha said. "They were happy to oblige me with specimens. And there's more. These demons have no sex organs. They're all neuter."

The Warded Man looked at her in surprise. "How is that possible?" he asked.

"It's not that uncommon among insects," Leesha said. "There are drone castes for labor and defense, and sexed castes that control the hive."

"Hive?" the Warded Man asked. "You mean the Core?"

Leesha shrugged.

The Warded Man frowned. "There were paintings in the tombs of Anoch Sun; paintings of the First Demon War that depicted strange breeds of corelings I have never seen."

"Not surprising," Leesha said. "We know so little about them."

She reached out, taking his hands. "All my life, I've felt like I was waiting for something bigger than brewing chill cures and delivering children," she said. "This is my chance to make a difference to more than just a handful of people. You believe there's a war coming? Rojer and I can help you win it."

The Warded Man nodded, squeezing her hands in return. "You're right," he said. "The Hollow survived that first night as much because of you and Rojer as me. I'd be a fool not to accept your help now."

Leesha stepped forward, reaching into his hood. Her hand was cool on his face, and for a moment, he leaned into it. "This hut is big enough for two," she whispered.

His eyes widened, and she felt him go tense.

"Why does that terrify you more than facing down demons?" she asked. "Am I so repulsive?"

The Warded Man shook his head. "Of course not," he said.

"Then what?" she asked. "I won't keep you from your war."

The Warded Man was quiet for some time. "Two would soon become three," he said at last, letting go of her hands.

"Is that so terrible?" Leesha asked.

The Warded Man took a deep breath, moving away to another

table, avoiding her eyes. "That morning when I wrestled the demon . . ." he said.

"I remember," Leesha prompted, when he did not go on.

"The demon tried to escape back to the Core," he said.

"And tried to take you with it," Leesha said. "I saw you both go misty, and slip beneath the ground. I was terrified."

The Warded Man nodded. "No more than me," he said. "The path to the Core opened up to me, calling me, pulling me down."

"What does that have to do with us?" Leesha asked.

"Because it wasn't the demon, it was me," the Warded Man said. "*I* took control of the transition; dragged the demon back up to the sun. Even now, I can feel the pull of the Core. If I let myself, I could slip down into its infernal depths with the other corelings."

"The wards . . ." Leesha began.

"It's not the wards," he said, shaking his head. "I'm telling you it's *me*. I've absorbed too much of their magic over the years. I'm not even human anymore. Who knows what kind of monster would spring from my seed?"

Leesha went to him, taking his face in her hands as she had that morning they made love. "You're a good man," she said, her eyes welling with tears. "Whatever the magic has done to you, it hasn't changed that. Nothing else matters."

She leaned in to kiss him, but he had hardened his heart to her, and held her back.

"It matters to me," he said. "Until I know what I am, I can't be with you, or anyone."

"Then I'll discover what you are," Leesha said. "I swear it."

"Leesha," he said, "you can't . . ."

"Don't you tell me what I can't do!" she barked. "I've had enough of that from others to last a lifetime."

He held up his hands in submission. "I'm sorry," he said.

Leesha sniffed, and closed her hands over his. "Don't be sorry," she said. "This is a condition to diagnose and cure, like any other."

"I'm not sick," the Warded Man said.

She looked at him sadly. "I know that," she said, "but it seems you don't."

Out in the Krasian desert, there was a stirring on the horizon. Lines of men appeared, thousand upon thousand, swathed in loose black cloth drawn about their faces to ward off the stinging sand. The vanguard was composed of two mounted groups, the smaller riding light, quick horses, and the larger upon powerful humped beasts suited to desert crossings. They were followed by columns of footmen, and they, in turn, by a seemingly endless train of carts and supplies. Each warrior carried a spear etched with an intricate pattern of wards.

At their head rode a man dressed all in white, atop a sleek charger of the same color. He raised a hand, and the horde behind him halted and stood in silence to gaze upon the ruins of Anoch Sun.

Unlike the wood and iron spears of his warriors, this man carried an ancient weapon made of a bright, unknown metal. He was Ahmann asu Hoshkamin am'Jardir, but his people had not used that name in years.

They called him *Shar'Dama Ka,* the Deliverer.

End Book I

If you enjoyed *The Warded Man,*
be sure not to miss the riveting sequel:

THE DESERT SPEAR
by
Peter V. Brett

Just as humanity has begun to claw its way back from the brink of
extinction, a new breed of demon has risen from the Core, more powerful than any seen before. Its purpose: to crush the human resistance
before it can truly take hold. Now old allegiances must be tested and
new alliances formed if any are to survive the night . . .

Here's a special preview.

333 AR WINTER

IT WAS THE NIGHT before new moon, during the darkest hours
when even that bare sliver had set. In a small patch of true darkness beneath the thick boughs of a cluster of trees, an evil
essence seeped up from the Core.

The dark mist coalesced slowly into a pair of giant demons,
their rough brown skin knobbed and gnarled like tree bark.
Standing nine feet at the shoulder, their hooked claws dug at
the frozen scrub and pine of the forest floor as they sniffed at
the air. A low rumble sounded in their throats as black eyes
scanned their surroundings.

Satisfied, they moved apart and squatted on their haunches,
coiled and ready to spring. Behind them, the patch of true darkness deepened, corruption blackening the forest bed as another
pair of ethereal shapes materialized.

These were slender, barely five feet tall, with soft charcoal flesh
quite unlike the gnarled armor of their larger brethren. On the
ends of delicate fingers and toes, their claws seemed fragile—thin
and straight like a woman's manicured nail. Their sharp teeth
were short, only a single row set in a snoutless mouth.

Their heads were bloated, with huge, lidless eyes and high, conical craniums. The flesh over their skulls was knobbed and textured, pulsing around the vestigial nubs of horns.

For long moments, the two newcomers stared at each other, foreheads throbbing, as a vibration passed in the air between them.

One of the larger demons caught movement in the brush and reached out with frightening quickness to snatch a rat from its cover. The coreling brought the rodent up close, studying it curiously. As it did, the demon's snout became ratlike, nose and whiskers twitching as it grew a pair of long incisors. The coreling's tongue slithered out to test their sharpness.

One of the slender demons turned to regard it, forehead pulsing. With a flick of its claw, the mimic demon eviscerated the rat and cast it aside. At the command of the coreling princes, the two mimics changed shape, becoming enormous wind demons.

The mind demons hissed as they left the patch of true darkness and starlight struck them. Their breath fogged with the cold, but they gave no sign of discomfort, leaving clawed footprints in the snow. The mimics bent low, and the coreling princes walked up their wings to take perch on their backs as they leapt into the sky.

They passed over many drones as they winged north. Big and small, these all cowered until the coreling princes passed, only to follow the call left vibrating in their wake.

The mimics landed on a high rise, and the mind demons slid down to the ground, taking in the sight below. A vast army spread out on the plain, white tents dotting the land where the snow had been trampled to mud and frozen solid. Great humped beasts of burden stood hobbled in circles of power, covered in blankets against the cold. The wards around the camp were strong, and sentries, their faces wrapped in black cloth, patrolled its perimeter. Even from this distance, the mind demons could sense the power of their warded weapons.

Beyond the camp's wards, the bodies of dozens of drones littered the field, waiting for the day star to burn them away.

Flame drones were the first to reach the rise where the princes waited. Keeping a respectful distance, they began to dance in worship, shrieking their devotion.

Another throb, and the drones quieted. The night grew deathly silent even as a great demon host gathered, drawn to the call of the coreling princes. Wood and flame drones stood side by side, their racial hatred forgotten, as wind drones circled in the sky above.

Ignoring the congregation, the mind demons kept their eyes on the plain below, their craniums pulsing. After a moment, one glanced to its mimic, imparting its desires, and the creature's flesh melted and swelled, taking the form of a massive rock demon. Silently, the gathered drones followed it down the hill.

On the rise, the two princes and the remaining mimic waited. And watched.

When they were close to the camp, still under the cover of darkness, the mimic slowed and waved the flame drones ahead.

The smallest and weakest of corelings, flame drones glowed about the eyes and mouth from the fires within them. The sentries spotted them immediately but the drones were quick, and before the sentries could raise an alarm they were upon the wards, spitting fire.

The firespit fizzled where it struck the wards, but at the mind demons' bidding, the drones focused instead on the piled snow outside the perimeter, their breath instantly turning it to scalding steam. Safe behind the wards, the sentries were unharmed, but a hot, thick fog arose, stinging their eyes and tainting the air even through their veils.

One of the sentries ran off through the camp, ringing a loud bell. As he did, the others darted fearlessly beyond the wards to skewer the nearest flame demons on their warded spears. Magic sparked as the weapons punched through their sharp, overlapping scales.

Other drones attacked from the sides, but the sentries worked in unison, their warded shields covering one another as they fought. Shouts could be heard inside the camp as other warriors rushed to join in the battle.

But under cover of fog and dark, the mimic's host advanced. One moment the sentries' cries were of victory, and the next they were of shock as the demons emerged from the haze.

The mimic took the first human it encountered easily, sweeping the man's feet away with its heavy tail and snatching a flailing leg as he fell. The hapless warrior was lifted aloft by the limb, his spine cracked like a whip. Those unlucky warriors who faced the mimic next were beaten down by the body of their fallen comrade.

The other drones followed suit, with mixed success. The few sentries were quickly overwhelmed, but many drones were slow to take advantage, wasting precious time rending the dead bodies rather than preparing for the next wave of warriors.

More and more of the veiled men flowed out of the camp, falling quickly into ranks and killing with smooth, brutal efficiency. The wards on their weapons and shields flared repeatedly in the darkness.

Up on the rise, the mind demons watched the battle impassively, showing no concern for the drones falling to the enemy spears. There was a throb in the cranium of one as it sent a command to its mimic on the field.

Immediately, the mimic hurled the corpse into one of the wardposts around the camp, smashing it and creating a breach. Up on the rise, there was another throb, and the other corelings broke off from engaging the warriors and poured through the gap into the enemy camp.

Left off balance, the warriors turned back to see tents blazing as flame drones scurried about, and hear the screams of their women and children as the larger corelings broke through charred and scorched inner wards.

The warriors cried out and rushed to their loved ones, all semblance of order lost. In moments the tight, invincible units had fragmented into thousands of separate creatures, little more than prey.

It seemed as if the camp would be overrun and burned to the ground, but then a figure appeared from the central pavilion. He was clad in black, like the warriors, but his outer robe, headwrap, and veil were the purest white. At his brow was a circlet of gold, and in his hands was a great spear of shining metal. The coreling princes hissed at the sight.

There were cries at the man's approach. The mind demons sneered at the primitive grunts and yelps that passed for communication among men, but the meaning was clear. The others were drones. This one was their mind.

Under the domination of the newcomer, the warriors remembered their castes and returned to their previous cohesion. A unit broke off to seal the outer breach. Another two fought fire. One more ushered the defenseless to safety.

Thus freed, the remainder scoured the camp, and the drones could not long stand against them. In minutes the camp was as littered with coreling bodies as the field outside. The mimic, still disguised as a rock demon, was soon the only coreling left, too quick to be taken by spear but unable to break through the wall of shields without revealing its true self.

There was a throb from the rise, and the mimic vanished into a shadow, dematerializing and seeping out of the camp through a tiny gap in the wards. The enemy was still searching for it when the mimic returned to its place by its master's side.

The two slender corelings stood atop the rise for several minutes, silent vibrations passing between them. Then, as one, the coreling princes turned their eyes to the north, where the other human mind was said to be.

One of the mind demons turned to its mimic, kneeling back in the form of a gigantic wind demon, and walked up its extended wing. As it vanished into the night, the remaining mind demon turned back to regard the smoldering enemy camp.